Be sure to check out the sequel to *Darwin's Radio* . . .

Darwin's Children

*A decade has passed since the human race underwent
a sudden leap in evolution, and millions of genetically
enhanced children have been born across the globe.*
Darwin's Children *is the compelling story of
Stella Nova and other "new" humans as they fight to
survive in a world full of people who, threatened by
what they view as the extinction of their own kind,
will do anything to stop these special children
from growing up.*

Coming to bookstores in APRIL 2003

Books published by The Random House Publishing Group
are available at quantity discounts on bulk purchases for
premium, educational, fund-raising, and special sales
use. For details, please call 1-800-733-3000.

DARWIN'S RADIO

Greg Bear

BALLANTINE BOOKS • NEW YORK

A Ballantine Book
Published by The Random House Publishing Group
Copyright © 1999 by Greg Bear

All rights reserved under International and Pan-American Copyright Conventions. Published in the United States by The Random House Publishing Group, a division of Random House, Inc., New York, and simultaneously in Canada by Random House of Canada Limited, Toronto.

Ballantine and colophon are registered trademarks of Random House, Inc.

www.ballantinebooks.com

A copy of the Library of Congress Catalog Card Number is available upon request from the publisher.

ISBN 0-345-43524-9

Manufactured in the United States of America

First Hardcover Edition: September 1999
First Mass Market Edition: July 2000

10

PART ONE

HEROD'S WINTER

The Alps, near the Austrian Border with Italy
AUGUST

The flat afternoon sky spread over the black and gray mountains like a stage backdrop, the color of a dog's pale crazy eye.

His ankles aching and back burning from a misplaced loop of nylon rope, Mitch Rafelson followed Tilde's quick female form along the margin between the white firn and a dust of new snow on the field. Mingled with the ice boulders of the fall, crenels and spikes of old ice had been sculpted by summer heat into milky, flint-edged knives.

To Mitch's left, the mountains rose over the jumble of black boulders flanking the broken slope of the ice fall. On the right, in the full glare of the sun, the ice rose in blinding brilliance to the perfect catenary of the cirque.

Franco was about twenty yards to the south, hidden by the rim of Mitch's goggles. Mitch could hear him but not see him. Some kilometers behind, also out of sight now, was the brilliant orange, round fiberglass-and-aluminum bivouac where they had made their last rest stop. He did not know how many kilometers they were from the last hut, whose name he had forgotten; but the memory of bright sun and warm tea in the sitting room, the *Gaststube*, gave him some strength. When this ordeal was over, he would get another cup of strong tea and sit in the *Gaststube* and thank God he was warm and alive.

They were approaching the wall of rock and a bridge of snow lying over a chasm dug by meltwater. These now-frozen

3

streams formed during the spring and summer and eroded the edge of the glacier. Beyond the bridge, depending from a U-shaped depression in the wall, rose what looked like a gnome's upside-down castle, or a pipe organ carved from ice: a frozen waterfall spread out in many thick columns. Chunks of dislodged ice and drifts of snow gathered around the dirty white of the base; sun burnished the cream and white at the top.

Franco came into view as if out of a fog and joined up with Tilde. So far they had been on relatively level glacier. Now it seemed that Tilde and Franco were going to scale the pipe organ.

Mitch stopped for a moment and reached behind to pull out his ice ax. He pushed up his goggles, crouched, then fell back on his butt with a grunt to check his crampons. Ice balls between the spikes yielded to his knife.

Tilde walked back a few yards to speak to him. He looked up at her, his thick dark eyebrows forming a bridge over a pushed-up nose, round green eyes blinking at the cold.

"This saves us an hour," Tilde said, pointing at the pipe organ. "It's late. You've slowed us down." Her English came precise from thin lips, with a seductive Austrian accent. She had a slight but well-proportioned figure, white blond hair tucked under a dark blue Polartec cap, an elfin face with clear gray eyes. Attractive, but not Mitch's type; still, they had been lovers of the moment before Franco arrived.

"I told you I haven't climbed in eight years," Mitch said. Franco was showing him up handily. The Italian leaned on his ax near the pipe organ.

Tilde weighed and measured everything, took only the best, discarded the second best, yet never cut ties in case her past connections should prove useful. Franco had a square jaw and white teeth and a square head with thick black hair shaved at the sides, an eagle nose, Mediterranean olive skin, broad shoulders and arms knotted with muscles, fine hands, very strong. He was not too smart for Tilde, but no dummy, either. Mitch could imagine Tilde pulled from her thick Austrian forest by the prospect of bedding Franco, light against dark, like layers in a torte. He felt curiously detached from this image. Tilde made love with a mechanical rigor that had deceived Mitch for a time, until he realized she was merely going through the moves, one after the other, as a kind of intellectual exercise. She ate the same way. Nothing moved her deeply, yet she had real wit at times, and a lovely smile that drew lines on the corners of those thin, precise lips.

"We must go down before sunset," Tilde said. "I don't know what the weather will do. It's two hours to the cave. Not very far, but a hard climb. If we're lucky, you'll have an hour to look at what we've found."

"I'll do my best," Mitch said. "How far are we from the tourist trails? I haven't seen any red paint in hours."

Tilde pulled away her goggles to wipe them, gave him a flash smile with no warmth. "No tourists up here. Most good climbers stay away, too. But I know my way."

"Snow goddess," Mitch said.

"What do you expect?" she said, taking it as a compliment. "I've climbed here since I was a girl."

"You're still a girl," Mitch said. "Twenty-five, twenty-six?"

She had never revealed her age to Mitch. Now she appraised him as if he were a gemstone she might reconsider purchasing. "I am thirty-two. Franco is forty but he's faster than you."

"To hell with Franco," Mitch said without anger.

Tilde curled her lip in amusement. "We are all weird today," she said, turning away. "Even Franco feels it. But another Iceman . . . what would that be worth?"

The very thought shortened Mitch's breath, and he did not need that now. His excitement curled back on itself, mixing with his exhaustion. "I don't know," he said.

They had opened their mercenary little hearts to him back in Salzburg. They were ambitious but not stupid; Tilde was absolutely certain that their find was not just another climber's body. She should know. At fourteen, she had helped carry out two bodies spit loose from the tongues of glaciers. One had been over a hundred years old.

Mitch wondered what would happen if they had found a true Iceman. Tilde, he was sure, would in the long run not know how to handle fame and success. Franco was stolid enough to make do, but Tilde was in her own way fragile. Like a diamond, she could cut steel, but strike her from the wrong angle and she would come to pieces.

Franco might survive fame, but would he survive Tilde? Mitch, despite everything, liked Franco.

"It's another three kilometers," Tilde told him. "Let's go."

Together, she and Franco showed him how to climb the frozen waterfall. "This flows only during midsummer," Franco said. "It is ice for a month now. Understand how it freezes. It is strong down here." He struck the pale gray ice of the pipe organ's massive base with his ax. The ice tinked, spun off a few chips. "But it is verglas, lots of bubbles, higher up—mushy. Big chunks fall if you hit it wrong. Hurt somebody. Tilde could cut some steps there, not you. You climb between Tilde and me."

Tilde would go first, an honest acknowledgment by Franco that she was the better climber. Franco slung the ropes and Mitch showed them he remembered the loops and knots from climbing in the Cascades, in Washington state. Tilde made a face and retied the loop Alpine style around his waist and shoulders. "You can front most of the way. Remember, I will chisel steps if you need them," Tilde said. "I don't want you sending ice down on Franco."

She took the lead.

Halfway up the pillar, digging in with the front points of his crampons, Mitch passed a threshold and his exhaustion seemed to leak away in spurts through his feet, leaving him nauseated for a moment. Then his body felt clean, as if flushed with fresh water, and his breath came easy. He followed Tilde, chunking his crampons into the ice and leaning in very close, grabbing at whatever holds were available. He used his ax sparingly. The air was actually warmer near the ice.

It took them fifteen minutes to climb past the midpoint, onto the cream-colored ice. The sun came from behind low gray clouds and lit up the frozen waterfall at a sharp angle, pinning him on a wall of translucent gold.

He waited for Tilde to tell them she was over the top and secure. Franco gave his laconic reply. Mitch wedged his way between two columns. The ice was indeed unpredictable here. He dug in with side points, sending a cloud of chips down on Franco. Franco cursed, but not once did Mitch break free and simply hang, and that was a blessing.

He fronted and crawled up the bumpy, rounded lip of the waterfall. His gloves slipped alarmingly on runnels of ice. He flailed with his boots, caught a ridge of rock with his right boot, dug in, found purchase on more rock, waited for a moment to catch his breath, and humped up beside Tilde like a walrus.

Dusty gray boulders on each side defined the bed of the frozen creek. He looked up the narrow rocky valley, half in shadow, where a small glacier had once flowed down from the east, carving its characteristic U-shaped notch. There had not been much snow for the last few years and the glacier had flowed on, vanishing from the notch, which now lay several dozen yards above the main body of the glacier.

Mitch rolled on his stomach and helped Franco over the top. Tilde stood to one side, perched on the edge as if she knew no fear, perfectly balanced, slender, gorgeous.

She frowned down on Mitch. "We are getting later," she said. "What can you learn in half an hour?"

Mitch shrugged.

"We must start back no later than sunset," Franco said to Tilde, then grinned at Mitch. "Not so tough son of a bitch ice, no?"

"Not bad," Mitch said.

"He learns okay," Franco said to Tilde, who lifted her eyes. "You climb ice before?"

"Not like that," Mitch said.

They walked over the frozen creek for a few dozen yards. "Two more climbs," Tilde said. "Franco, you lead."

Mitch looked up through crystalline air over the rim of the notch at the sawtooth horns of higher mountains. He still could not tell where he was. Franco and Tilde preferred him ignorant. They had come at least twenty kilometers since their stay in the big stone *Gaststube*, with the tea.

Turning, he spotted the orange bivouac, about four kilometers away and hundreds of meters below. It sat just behind a saddle, now in shadow.

The snow seemed very thin. The mountains had just passed through the warmest summer in modern Alpine history, with increased glacier melt, short-term floods in the valleys from heavy rain, and only light snow from past seasons. Global warming was a media cliché now; from where he sat, to his inexpert eye, it seemed all too real. The Alps might be naked in a few decades.

The relative heat and dryness had opened up a route to the old cave, allowing Franco and Tilde to discover a secret tragedy.

Franco announced he was secure, and Mitch inched his way up the last rock face, feeling the gneiss chip and skitter beneath his boots. The stone here was flaky, powdery soft in places; snow had lain over this area for a long time, easily thousands of years.

Franco lent him a hand and together they belayed the rope as Tilde scrambled up behind. She stood on the rim, shielded her eyes against the direct sun, now barely a handspan above the ragged horizon. "Do you know where you are?" she asked Mitch.

Mitch shook his head. "I've never been this high."

"A valley boy," Franco said with a grin.

Mitch squinted.

They stared over a rounded and slick field of ice, the thin finger of a glacier that had once flowed nearly seven miles in several spectacular cascades. Now, along this branch, the flow was lagging. Little new snow fed the glacier's head, higher up. The sun-blazed rock wall above the icy rip of the bergschrund rose several thousand feet straight up, the peak higher than Mitch cared to look.

"There," Tilde said, and pointed to the opposite rocks below an arête. With some effort, Mitch made out a tiny red dot against the shadowed black and gray: a cloth banner Franco had planted on their last trip. They set off over the ice.

The cave, a natural crevice, had a small opening, three feet in diameter, artificially concealed by a low wall of head-size boulders. Tilde took out her digital camera and photographed the opening from several angles, backing up and walking around while Franco pulled down the wall and Mitch surveyed the entrance.

"How far back?" Mitch asked when Tilde rejoined them.

"Ten meters," Franco said. "Very cold back there, better than a freezer."

"But not for long," Tilde said. "I think this is the first year this area has been so open. Next summer, it could get above freezing. A warm wind could get back in there." She made a face and pinched her nose.

Mitch unslung his pack and rummaged for the electric torches, the box of hobby knives, vinyl gloves, all he could find in the stores down in the town. He dropped these into a small plastic bag, sealed the bag, slipped it into his coat pocket, and looked between Franco and Tilde.

"Well?" he said.

"Go," Tilde said, making a pushing motion with her hands. She smiled generously.

He stooped, got on his hands and knees, and entered the cave first. Franco came a few seconds later, and Tilde just behind him.

Mitch held the strap of the small torch in his teeth, pushing and squeezing forward six or eight inches at a time. Ice and fine powdered snow formed a thin blanket on the floor of the cave. The walls were smooth and rose to a tight wedge near the ceiling. He would not be able to even crouch here. Franco called forward, "It will get wider."

"A cozy little hole," Tilde said, her voice hollow.

The air smelled neutral, empty. Cold, well below zero. The rock sucked away his heat even through the insulated jacket and snow pants. He passed over a vein of ice, milky against the black rock, and scraped it with his fingers. Solid. The snow and ice must have packed in at least this far when the cave was covered. Just beyond the ice vein, the cave began to slant upward, and he felt a faint puff of air from another wedge in the rock recently cleared of ice.

Mitch felt a little queasy, not at the thought of what he was about to see, but at the unorthodox and even criminal character of this investigation. The slightest wrong move, any breath of this getting out, news of his not going through the proper channels and making sure everything was legitimate . . .

Mitch had gotten in trouble with institutions before. He had lost his job at the Hayer Museum in Seattle less than six months before, but that had been a political thing, ridiculous and unfair.

Until now, he had never slighted Dame Science herself.

He had argued with Franco and Tilde back in the hotel in Salzburg for hours, but they had refused to budge. If he had not decided to go with them, they would have taken somebody else—Tilde had suggested perhaps an unemployed medical student she had once dated. Tilde had a wide selection of ex-boyfriends, it seemed, all of them much less qualified and far less scrupulous than Mitch.

Whatever Tilde's motives or moral character, Mitch was not the type to turn her down, then turn them in; everybody has his limits, his boundary in the social wilderness. Mitch's boundary began at the prospect of getting ex-girlfriends in trouble with the Austrian police.

Franco plucked a crampon on the sole of Mitch's boot. "Problem?" he asked.

"No problem," Mitch replied, and grunted forward another six inches.

A sudden oblong of light formed in one eye, like a large out-of-focus moon. His body seemed to balloon in size. He swallowed hard. "Shit," he muttered, hoping that didn't mean what he thought it meant. The oblong faded. His body returned to normal.

Here, the cave constricted to a narrow throat, less than a foot high and twenty-one or twenty-two inches wide. Angling his head sideways, he grabbed hold of a crack just beyond the throat and shinnied through. His coat caught and he heard a tearing sound as he strained to unhook and slip past.

"That's the bad part," Franco said. "I can barely make it."

"Why did you go this far?" Mitch asked, gathering his courage in the broader but still dark and cramped space beyond.

"Because it was here, no?" Tilde said, voice like the call of a distant bird. "I dared Franco. He dared me." She laughed and the tinkling echoed in the gloom beyond. Mitch's neck hair rose. The new Iceman was laughing with them, perhaps at them. He was dead already. He had nothing to worry about, plenty to be amused about, that so many people would make themselves miserable to see his mortal remains.

"How long since you last came here?" Mitch asked. He wondered why he hadn't asked before. Perhaps until now he hadn't really believed. They had come this far, no sign of pulling a joke on him, something he doubted Tilde was constitutionally capable of anyway.

"A week, eight days," Franco said. The passage was wide enough that Franco could push himself up beside Mitch's legs, and Mitch could shine the torch back into his face. Franco gave him a toothy Mediterranean smile.

Mitch looked forward. He could see something ahead, dark, like a small pile of ashes.

"We are close?" Tilde asked. "Mitch, first it is just a foot."

Mitch tried to parse this sentence. Tilde spoke pure metric. A "foot," he realized, was not distance, it was an appendage. "I don't see it yet."

"There are ashes first," Franco said. "That may be it." He

pointed to the small black pile. Mitch could feel the air falling slowly just in front of him, flowing along his sides, leaving the rear of the cave undisturbed.

He moved forward with reverent slowness, inspecting everything. Any slightest bit of evidence that might have survived an earlier entry—chips of stone, pieces of twig or wood, markings on the walls . . .

Nothing. He got on his hands and knees with a great sense of relief and crawled forward. Franco became impatient.

"It is right ahead," Franco said, tapping his crampon again.

"Damn it, I'm taking this real slow, not to miss anything, you know?" Mitch said. He restrained an urge to kick out like a mule.

"All right," Franco said amiably.

Mitch could see around the curve. The floor flattened slightly. He smelled something grassy, salty, like fresh fish. His neck hair rose again, and a mist formed over his eyes. Ancient sympathies.

"I see it," he said. A foot pushed out beyond a ledge, curled up on itself—small, really, like a child's, very wrinkled and dark brown, almost black. The cave opened up at that point and there were scraps of dried and blackened fiber spread on the floor—grass, perhaps. Reeds. Ötzi, the original Iceman, had worn a reed cape over his head.

"My God," Mitch said. Another white oblong in his eye, slowly fading, and a whisper of pain in his temple.

"It's bigger up there," Tilde called. "We can all fit and not disturb them."

"Them?" Mitch asked, shining his light back between his legs.

Franco smiled, framed by Mitch's knees. "The real surprise," Franco said. "There are two."

2

Republic of Georgia

Kaye curled up in the passenger seat of the whining little Fiat as Lado guided it along the alarming twists and turns of the Georgian Military Road. Though sunburned and exhausted, she could not sleep. Her long legs twitched with every curve. At a piggish squeal of the nearly bald tires, she pushed her hands back through short-cut brown hair and yawned deliberately.

Lado sensed the silence had gone on too long. He glanced at Kaye with soft brown eyes in a finely wrinkled sun-browned face, lifted his cigarette over the steering wheel, and jutted out his chin. "In shit is our salvation, yes?" he asked.

Kaye smiled despite herself. "Please don't try to cheer me up," she said.

Lado ignored that. "Good on us. Georgia has something to offer the world. We have great sewage." He rolled his *r*s elegantly, and "sewage" came out *see-yu-edge*.

"Sewage," she murmured. "Seee-yu-age."

"I say it right?" Lado asked.

"Perfectly," Kaye said.

Lado Jakeli was chief scientist at the Eliava Institute in Tbilisi, where they extracted bacteriophages—viruses that attack only bacteria—from local city and hospital sewage and farm waste, and from specimens gathered around the world. Now, the West, including Kaye, had come hat in hand to learn more from the Georgians about the curative properties of phages.

She had hit it off with the Eliava staff. After a week of conferences and lab tours, some of the younger scientists had invited her to accompany them to the rolling hills and brilliant green sheep fields at the base of Mount Kazbeg.

Things had changed so quickly. Just this morning, Lado had driven all the way from Tbilisi to their base camp near the old and solitary Gergeti Orthodox church. In an envelope he had carried a fax from UN Peacekeeping headquarters in Tbilisi, the capital.

Lado had downed a pot of coffee at the camp, then, ever the gentleman, and her sponsor besides, had offered to take her to Gordi, a small town seventy-five miles southwest of Kazbeg.

Kaye had had no choice. Unexpectedly, and at the worst possible time, her past had caught up with her.

The UN team had gone through entry records to find non-Georgian medical experts with a certain expertise. Hers was the only name that had come up: Kaye Lang, thirty-four, partner with her husband, Saul Madsen, in EcoBacter Research. In the early nineties, she had studied forensic medicine at the State University of New York with an eye to going into criminal investigation. She had changed her perspective within a year, switching to microbiology, with emphasis on genetic engineering; but she was the only foreigner in Georgia with even the slightest degree of the training the UN needed.

Lado was driving her through some of the most beautiful countryside she had ever seen. In the shadows of the central Caucasus they had passed terraced mountain fields, small stone farmhouses, stone silos and churches, small towns with wood and stone buildings, houses with friendly and beautifully carved porches opening onto narrow brick or cobble or dirt roads, towns dotted loosely on broad rumpled blankets of sheep- and goat-grazed meadow and thick forest.

Here, even the seemingly empty expanses had been swarmed over and fought for across the centuries, like every place she had seen in Western and now Eastern Europe. Sometimes she felt suffocated by the sheer closeness of her fellow humans, by the gap-toothed smiles of old men and women standing by the side of the road watching traffic come and go from new and unfamiliar worlds. Wrinkled friendly faces, gnarled hands waving at the little car.

All the young people were in the cities, leaving the old to tend the countryside, except in the mountain resorts. Georgia was planning to turn itself into a nation of resorts. Her economy was growing in double digits each year; her currency, the lari, was strengthening as well, and had long since replaced rubles; soon it would replace Western dollars. They were opening oil pipelines from the Caspian to the Black Sea; and in the land where wine got its name, it was becoming a major export.

In the next few years, Georgia would export a new and very different wine: solutions of phages to heal a world losing the war against bacterial diseases.

The Fiat swung into the inside lane as they rounded a blind curve. Kaye swallowed hard but said nothing. Lado had been very solicitous toward her at the institute. At times in the past week, Kaye had caught him looking at her with an expression of gnarled, old world speculation, eyes drawn to wrinkled slits, like a satyr carved out of olive wood and stained brown. He had a reputation among the women who worked at Eliava, that he could not be trusted all the time, particularly with the young ones. But he had always treated Kaye with the utmost civility, even, as now, with concern. He did not want her to be sad, yet he could not think of any reason she should be cheerful.

Despite its beauty, Georgia had many blemishes: civil war, assassinations, and now, mass graves.

They lurched into a wall of rain. The windshield wipers flapped black tails and cleaned about a third of Lado's view. "Good on Ioseb Stalin, he left us sewage," he mused. "Good son of Georgia. Our most famous export, better than wine." Lado grinned falsely at her. He seemed both ashamed and defensive. Kaye could not help but draw him out.

"He killed millions," she murmured. "He killed Dr. Eliava."

Lado stared grimly through the streaks to see what lay beyond the short hood. He geared down and braked, then careened around a ditch big enough to hide a cow. Kaye made a small squeak and grabbed the side of her seat. There were no guardrails on this stretch, and below the highway yawned a steep drop of at least three hundred meters to a glacial melt river. "It was Beria declared Dr. Eliava a People's Enemy," Lado said matter-of-factly, as if relating old family history. "Beria was head of Georgian KGB then, local child-abusing sonabitch, not mad wolf of all Russia."

"He was Stalin's man," Kaye said, trying to keep her mind off the road. She could not understand any pride the Georgians took in Stalin.

"They were all Stalin's men, or they died," Lado said. He shrugged. "There was a big stink here when Khruschev said Stalin was bad. What do we know? He screwed us so many ways for so many years we thought he must be a husband."

This Kaye found amusing. Lado took encouragement from her grin.

"Some still want to return to prosperity under Communism. Or we have prosperity in shit." He rubbed his nose. "I'll take the shit."

They descended in the next hour into less fearsome foothills and plateaus. Road signs in curling Georgian script showed the rusted pocks of dozens of bullet holes. "Half an hour, no more," Lado said.

The thick rain made the border between day and night difficult to judge. Lado switched on the Fiat's dim little headlights as they approached a crossroads and the turnoff to the small town of Gordi.

Two armored personnel carriers flanked the highway just before the crossroads. Five Russian peacekeepers dressed in slickers and rounded piss-bucket helmets wearily flagged them down.

Lado braked the Fiat to a stop, canted slightly on the

shoulder. Kaye could see another ditch just yards ahead, right in the crotch of the crossroads. They would have to drive on the shoulder to go around it.

Lado rolled down his window. A Russian soldier of nineteen or twenty, with rosy choirboy cheeks, peered in. His helmet dribbled rain on Lado's sleeve. Lado spoke to him in Russian.

"American?" the young Russian asked Kaye. She showed him her passport, her E.U. and C.I.S. business licenses, and the fax requesting—practically ordering—her presence in Gordi. The soldier took the fax and frowned as he tried to read it, getting it thoroughly wet. He stepped back to consult with an officer squatting in the rear hatch of the nearest carrier.

"They do not want to be here," Lado muttered to Kaye. "And we do not want them. But we asked for help . . . Who do we blame?"

The rain stopped. Kaye stared into the misting gloom ahead. She heard crickets and birdsong above the engine whine.

"Go down, go left," the soldier told Lado, proud of his English. He smiled for Kaye's benefit and waved them on to another soldier standing like a fence post in the gray gloom beside the ditch. Lado engaged the clutch and the little car bucked around the ditch, past the third peacekeeper and onto the side road.

Lado opened the window all the way. Cool moist evening air swirled through the car and lifted the short hair over Kaye's neck. The roadsides were covered with tight-packed birch. Briefly the air smelled foul. They were near people. Then Kaye thought maybe it was not the town's sewage that smelled so. Her nose wrinkled and her stomach knotted. But that was not likely. Their destination was a mile or so outside the town, and Gordi was still at least two miles off the highway.

Lado came to a stream and slowly forded the quick-rushing shallow water. The wheels sank to their hubcaps, but the car emerged safely and continued on for another hundred meters. Stars peeked through swift-gliding clouds. Mountains drew jagged dark blanks against the sky. The forest came up and fell back and then they saw Gordi, stone buildings, some newer two-story square wooden houses with tiny windows, a single concrete municipal cube without decoration, roads of rutted asphalt and old cobbles. No lights. Black sightless windows. The electricity was out again.

"I don't know this town," Lado muttered. He slammed on the brakes, jolting Kaye from a reverie. The car idled noisily in the small town square, surrounded by two-story buildings. Kaye could make out a faded Intourist sign over an inn named the Rustaveli Tiger.

Lado switched on the tiny overhead light and pulled out the faxed map. He flung the map aside in disgust and heaved open the Fiat's door. The hinges made a loud metal groan. He leaned out and yelled in Georgian, "Where is the grave?"

Darkness was its own excuse.

"Beautiful," Lado said. He slammed the door twice to make it catch. Kaye pressed her lips together firmly as the car lurched forward. They descended with a high-pitched gnash of gears through a small street of shops, dark and shuttered with corrugated steel, and out the back side of the village, past two abandoned shacks, heaps of gravel, and scattered bales of straw.

After a few minutes, they spotted lights and the glow of torches and a single small campfire, then heard the racketing burr of a portable generator and voices loud in the hollow of the night.

The grave was closer than the map had showed, less than a mile from the town. She wondered if the villagers had heard the screams, or indeed if there had been any screams.

The fun was over.

The UN team wore gas masks equipped with industrial aerosol filters. Nervous Georgian Republic Security soldiers had to resort to bandannas tied around their faces. They looked sinister, comically so under other circumstances. Their officers wore white cloth surgical masks.

The head of the *sakrebulo*, the local council, a short big-fisted man with a tall shock of wiry black hair and a prominent nose, stood with a doggishly unhappy face beside the security officers.

The UN team leader, a U.S. Army colonel from South Carolina named Nicholas Beck, made quick introductions and passed Kaye one of the UN masks. She felt self-conscious but put it on. Beck's aide, a black female corporal named Hunter, passed her a pair of white latex surgical gloves. They gave familiar slaps against her wrists as she tugged them on.

Beck and Hunter led Kaye and Lado away from the campfire and the white Jeeps, down a small path through ragged forest and scrub to the graves.

"The council chief out there has his enemies. Some locals from the opposition dug the trenches and then called UN headquarters in Tbilisi," Beck told her. "I don't think the Republic Security folks want us here. We can't get any cooperation in Tbilisi. On short notice, you were the only one we could find with any expertise."

Three parallel trenches had been reopened and marked by electric lights on tall poles, staked into the sandy soil and powered by a portable generator. Between the stakes lengths of red and yellow plastic tape hung lifeless in the still air.

Kaye walked around the first trench and lifted her mask. Wrinkling her nose in anticipation, she sniffed. There was no distinct smell other than dirt and mud.

"They're more than two years old," she said. She gave Beck the mask. Lado stopped about ten paces behind them, reluctant to go near the graves.

"We need to be sure of that," Beck said.

Kaye walked to the second trench, stooped, and played the beam of her flashlight over the heaps of fabric and dark bones and dry dirt. The soil was sandy and dry, possibly part of the bed of an old melt stream from the mountains. The bodies were almost unrecognizable, pale brown bone encrusted with dirt, wrinkled brown and black flesh. Clothing had faded to the color of the soil, but these patches and shreds were not army uniforms: they were dresses, pants, coats. Woolens and cottons had not completely decayed. Kaye looked for brighter synthetics; they could establish a maximum age for the grave. She could not immediately see any.

She moved the beam up to the walls of the trench. The thickest roots visible, cut through by spades, were about half an inch in diameter. The nearest trees stood like tall thin ghosts ten yards away.

A middle-aged Republic Security officer with the formidable name of Vakhtang Chikurishvili, handsome in a burly way, with heavy shoulders and a thick, often-broken nose, stepped forward. He was not wearing a mask. He held up something dark. It took Kaye a few seconds to recognize it as a boot. Chikurishvili addressed Lado in consonant-laden Georgian.

"He says the shoes are old," Lado translated. "He says these people died fifty years ago. Maybe more."

Chikurishvili angrily swung his arm around and shot a quick stream of mixed Georgian and Russian at Lado and Beck.

Lado translated. "He says the Georgians who dug this up are stupid. This is not for the UN. This was from long before the civil war. He says these are not Ossetians."

"Who mentioned Ossetians?" Beck asked dryly.

Kaye examined the boot. It had a thick leather sole and leather uppers, and its hanging strings were rotted and encrusted with powdery clods. The leather was hard as a rock. She peered into the interior. Dirt, but no socks or tissue—the boot had not been pulled from a decayed foot. Chikurishvili met her querulous look defiantly, then whipped out a match and lit up a cigarette.

Staged, Kaye thought. She remembered the classes she had taken in the Bronx, classes that had eventually driven her from criminal medicine. The field visits to real homicide scenes. The putrescence protection masks.

Beck spoke to the officer soothingly in broken Georgian

and better Russian. Lado gently retranslated his attempts. Beck then took Kaye's elbow and moved her to a long canvas canopy that had been erected a few yards from the trenches.

Under the canopy, two battered folding card tables supported pieces of bodies. *Completely amateur,* Kaye thought. Perhaps the enemies of the head of the *sakrebulo* had laid out the bodies and taken pictures to prove their point.

She circled the table: two torsos and a skull. There was a fair amount of mummified flesh left on the torsos and some unfamiliar ligaments like dark dry straps on the skull, around the forehead, eyes, and cheeks. She looked for signs of insect casings and found dead blowfly larvae on one withered throat, but not many. The bodies had been buried within a few hours of death. She surmised they had not been buried in the dead of winter, when blowflies were not about. Of course, winters at this altitude were mild in Georgia.

She picked up a small pocket knife lying next to the closest torso and lifted a shred of fabric, what had once been white cotton, then pried up a stiff, concave flap of skin over the abdomen. There were bullet entry holes in the fabric and skin overlying the pelvis. "God," she said.

Within the pelvis, cradled in dirt and stiff wraps of dried tissue, lay a smaller body, curled, little more than a heap of tiny bones, its skull collapsed.

"Colonel." She showed Beck. His face turned stony.

The bodies could conceivably have been fifty years old, but if so, they were in remarkably good condition. Some wool and cotton remained. Everything was very dry. Drainage swept around this area now. The trenches were deep. But the roots—

Chikurishvili spoke again. His tone seemed more cooperative, even guilty. There was a lot of guilt to go around over the centuries.

"He says they are both female," Lado whispered to Kaye.

"I see that," she muttered.

She walked around the table to examine the second torso. This one had no skin over the abdomen. She scraped the dirt aside, making the torso rock with a sound like a dried gourd. Another small skull lay within the pelvis, a fetus about six months along, same as the other. The torso's limbs were missing; Kaye could not tell if the legs had been held together in the grave. Neither of the fetuses had been expelled by pressure of abdominal gases.

"Both pregnant," she said. Lado translated this into Georgian.

Beck said in a low voice, "We count about sixty individuals. The women seem to have been shot. It looks as if the men were shot or clubbed to death."

Chikurishvili pointed to Beck, and then back to the camp, and shouted, his face ruddy in the backwash of flashlight glow. "Jugashvili, Stalin." The officer said the graves had been dug a few years before the great People's War, during the purges. The late 1930s. That would make them almost seventy years old, ancient news, nothing for the UN to become involved in.

Lado said, "He wants the UN and the Russians out of here. He says this is an internal matter, not for peacekeepers."

Beck spoke again, less soothingly, to the Georgian officer. Lado decided he did not want to be in the middle of this exchange and walked around to where Kaye was leaning over the second torso. "Nasty business," he said.

"Too long," Kaye spoke softly.

"What?" Lado asked.

"Seventy years is much too long," she said. "Tell me what they're arguing about." She prodded the unfamiliar straps of tissue around the eye sockets with the pocket knife. They seemed to form a kind of mask. Had they been hooded before being executed? She did not think so. The attachments were dark and stringy and persistent.

"The UN man is saying there is no limit on war crimes," Lado told her. "No statue—what is it—statute of limitations."

"He's right," Kaye said. She rolled the skull over gently. The occiput had been fractured laterally and pushed in to a depth of three centimeters.

She returned her attention to the tiny skeleton cradled within the pelvis of the second torso. She had taken some courses in embryology in her second year in med school. The fetus's bone structure seemed a little odd, but she did not want to damage the skull by pulling it loose from the caked soil and dried tissue. She had intruded enough already.

Kaye felt queasy, sickened not by the shriveled and dried remains, but by what her imagination was already reconstructing. She straightened and waved to get Beck's attention.

"These women were shot in the stomach," she said. *Kill all the firstborn children. Furious monsters.* "Murdered." She clamped her teeth.

"How long ago?"

"He may be right about the age of the boot, if it came from here, but this grave isn't that old. The roots around the edge of the trenches are too small. My guess is the victims died as recently as two or three years ago. The dirt here looks dry, but the soil is probably acid, and that would dissolve any bones over a few years old. Then there's the fabric; it looks like wool and cotton, and that means the grave is just a few years old. If it's synthetic, it could be older, but that gives us a date after Stalin, too."

Beck approached her and lifted his mask. "Can you help us until the others get here?" he asked in a whisper.

"How long?" Kaye asked.

"Four, five days," Beck said. Several paces distant, Chikurishvili shifted his gaze between them, jaw clenched, resentful, as if cops had interrupted a domestic quarrel.

Kaye caught herself holding her breath. She turned away, stepped back, sucked in some air, then asked, "You're going to start a war crimes investigation?"

"The Russians think we should," Beck said. "They're hot to discredit the new Communists back home. A few old atrocities could supply them with fresh ammunition. If you could give us a best guess—two years, five, thirty, whatever?"

"Less than ten. Probably less than five. I'm very rusty," she said. "I can only do a few things. Take samples, some tissue specimens. Not a full autopsy, of course."

"You're a thousand times better than letting the locals muck around," Beck said. "I don't trust any of them. I'm not sure the Russians can be trusted, either. They all have axes to grind, one way or the other."

Lado kept a stiff face and did not comment, nor did he translate for Chikurishvili.

Kaye felt what she had known would come, had dreaded: the old dark mood creeping over her.

She had thought that by traveling and being away from Saul, she might shake the bad times, the bad feelings. She had felt liberated watching the doctors and technicians working at the Eliava Institute, doing so much good with so few resources, literally pulling health out of sewage. The grand and beautiful side of the Republic of Georgia. Now . . . Flip the coin. Papa Ioseb Stalin or ethnic cleansers, Georgians trying to move out Armenians and Ossetians, Abkhazis trying to move out Georgians, Russians sending in troops, Chechens becoming involved. Dirty little wars between ancient neighbors with ancient grievances.

This was not going to be good for her, but she could not refuse.

Lado wrinkled his face and stared up at Beck. "They were going to be mothers?"

"Most of them," Beck said. "And maybe some were going to be fathers."

3

The Alps

The end of the cave was very cramped. Tilde lay under a low shelf of rock, knees drawn up, and watched Mitch as he knelt before the ones they had come here to see. Franco squatted behind Mitch.

Mitch's mouth hung half open, like a surprised little boy's. He could not speak for a time. The end of the cave was utterly still and quiet. Only the beam of light moved as he played the torch up and down the two forms.

"We touched nothing," Franco said.

The blackened ashes, ancient fragments of wood, grass, and reed, looked as if a breath would scatter them but still formed the remains of a fire. The skin of the bodies had fared much better. Mitch had never seen more startling examples of deep-freeze mummification. The tissues were hard and dry, the moisture sucked from them by the dry deep cold air. Near the heads, where they lay facing each other, the skin and muscle had hardly shrunk at all before being fixed. The features were almost natural, though the eyelids had withdrawn and the eyes beneath were shrunken, dark, unutterably sleepy. The bodies as well were full; only near the legs did the flesh seem to shrivel and darken, perhaps because of the intermittent breeze from farther up the shaft. The feet were wizened, black as little dried mushrooms.

Mitch could not believe what he was seeing. Perhaps there was nothing so extraordinary about their pose—lying on their sides, a man and a woman facing each other in death,

25

freezing finally as the ashes of their last fire cooled. Nothing unexpected about the hands of the man reaching toward the face of the woman, the woman's arms low in front of her as if she had clasped her stomach. Nothing extraordinary about the animal skin beneath them, or another skin rumpled beside the male, as if it had been tossed aside.

In the end, with the fire out, freezing to death, the man had felt too warm and had thrown off his covering.

Mitch looked down at the woman's curled fingers and swallowed a rising lump of emotion he could not easily define or explain.

"How old?" Tilde asked, interrupting his focus. Her voice sounded crisp and clear and rational, like the ring of a struck knife.

Mitch jerked. "Very old," he said quietly.

"Yes, but like the Iceman?"

"Not like the Iceman," Mitch said. His voice almost broke.

The female had been injured. A hole had been punched in her side, at hip level. Blood stains surrounded the hole and he thought he could make out stains on the rock beneath her. Perhaps it had been the cause of her death.

There were no weapons in the cave.

He rubbed his eyes to force aside the little jagged white moon that threatened to distract him, then looked at the faces again, short broad noses pointing up at an angle. The woman's jaw hung slack, the man's was closed. The woman had died gasping for air. Mitch could not know this for sure, but he did not question the observation. It fit.

Only now did he carefully maneuver around the figures, crouched low, moving so slowly, keeping his bent knees an inch above the man's hip.

"They look old," Franco said, just to make a sound in the cave. His eyes glittered. Mitch glanced at him, then down at the male's profile.

Thick brow ridge, broad flattened nose, no chin. Powerful shoulders, narrowing to a comparatively slender waist. Thick arms. The faces were smooth, almost hairless. All the skin below the neck, however, was covered with a fine dark downy fur, visible only on close examination. Around their temples, the short-trimmed hair seemed to have been shaved in patterns, expertly barbered.

So much for shaggy museum reconstructions.

Mitch bent closer, the cold air heavy in his nostrils, and propped his hand against the top of the cave. Something like a mask lay between the bodies, actually two masks, one beside and bunched under the man, the other beneath the woman. The edges of the masks appeared torn. Each had eye holes, nostrils, the appearance of an upper lip, all lightly covered with fine hair, and below that, an even hairier flap that might have once wrapped around the neck and lower jaw. They might have been lifted from the faces, flayed away, yet there was no skin missing from the heads.

The mask nearest the woman seemed attached to her forehead and temple by thin fibers like the beard of a mussel.

Mitch realized he was focusing on little mysteries to get past one big impossibility.

"How old are they?" Tilde asked again. "Can you tell yet?"

"I don't think there have been people like this for tens of thousands of years," Mitch said.

Tilde seemed to miss this statement of deep time. "They are European, like the Iceman?"

"I don't know," Mitch said, but shook his head and held up his hand. He did not want to talk; he wanted to think. This was an extremely dangerous place, professionally, mentally, from any angle of approach. Dangerous and dreamlike and impossible.

"Tell me, Mitch," Tilde pleaded with surprising gentleness. "Tell me what you see." She reached out to stroke his knee. Franco observed this caress with maturity.

Mitch began, "They are male and female, each about a hundred and sixty centimeters in height."

"Short people," Franco said, but Mitch talked right over him.

"They appear to be genus *Homo*, species *sapiens*. Not like us, though. They might have suffered from some kind of dwarfism, distortion of the features . . ." He stopped himself and looked again at the heads, saw no signs of dwarfism, though the masks bothered him.

The classic features. "They're not dwarfs," he said. "They're Neandertals."

Tilde coughed. The dry air parched their throats. "Pardon?"

"Cavemen?" Franco said.

"Neandertals," Mitch said again, as much to convince himself as to correct Franco.

"That is bullshit," Tilde said, her voice crackling with anger. "We are not children."

"No bullshit. You have found two well-preserved Neandertals, a man and a woman. The first Neandertal mummies . . . anywhere. Ever."

Tilde and Franco thought about that for a few seconds. Outside, wind hooted past the cave entrance.

"How old?" Franco asked.

"Everyone thinks the Neandertals died out between a hundred thousand and forty thousand years ago," Mitch said. "Maybe everyone is wrong. But I doubt they could have stayed in this cave, in this state of preservation, for forty thousand years."

"Maybe they were the last," Franco said, and crossed himself reverently.

"Incredible," Tilde said, her face flushed. "How much would they be worth?"

Mitch's leg cramped and he moved back to squat beside Franco. He rubbed his eyes with a gloved knuckle. So cold. He was shivering. The moon of light blurred and shifted. "They're not worth anything," he said.

"Don't joke," Tilde said. "They are rare—nothing like them, right?"

"Even if we—if you, I mean—could get them out of this cave safely, intact, and down the mountain, where would you sell them?"

"There are people who collect such things," Franco said. "People with lots of money. We have talked to some about an Iceman already. Surely an Iceman and woman—"

"Maybe I should be more blunt," Mitch said. "If these aren't handled in a proper scientific fashion, I will go to the authorities in Switzerland, Italy, wherever the hell we are. I will tell them."

Another silence. Mitch could almost hear Tilde's thoughts, like a little Austrian clockwork.

Franco slapped the floor of the cave with his gloved hand and glared at Mitch. "Why fuck us up?"

"Because these people don't belong to you," Mitch said. "They don't belong to anybody."

"They are dead!" Franco shouted. "They do not belong to themselves, do they, anymore?"

Tilde's lips formed a straight, grim line. "Mitch is right. We are not going to sell them."

A little scared now, Mitch's next words rushed out. "I don't know what else you might plan to do with them, but I don't think you're going to control them, or sell the rights, make Caveman Barbie dolls or whatever." He took a deep breath.

"No, again, I say Mitch is right," Tilde stated slowly. Franco regarded her with a speculative squint. "This is very huge. We will be good citizens. They are everybody's ancestors. Mama and Papa to the world."

Mitch could definitely feel the headache creeping up. The earlier oblong of light had been a familiar warning: oncoming head-crushing train. Climbing back down the mountain would be difficult or even impossible if he was going to fall under the spell of a migraine, a real brain-splitter. He hadn't brought any medicine. "Are you planning to kill me up here?" he asked Tilde.

Franco shot a glance at him, then rolled to look at Tilde, waiting for an answer.

Tilde grinned and tapped her chin. "I am thinking," she

said. "What rogues we would be. Famous stories. Pirates of the prehistoric. Yo ho ho and a bottle of Schnapps."

"What we need to do," Mitch said, assuming that she had answered in the negative, "is to take a tissue sample from each body, with minimal intrusion. Then—"

He reached for the torch and shone the light beyond the close, sleepy-eyed heads of the male and female to the far recesses, about three yards farther back in the cave. Something small lay there, bundled in fur.

"What's that?" he and Franco asked simultaneously.

Mitch considered. He could hunker and sidle his way around the female without disturbing anything except the dust. On the other hand, it would be best to leave everything completely untouched, to retreat from the cave now and bring back the real experts. The tissue samples would be enough evidence, he thought. Enough was known about Neandertal DNA from bone studies. A confirmation could be made and the cave could be kept sealed until—

He pressed his temples and closed his eyes.

Tilde tapped his shoulder and gently pushed him out of the way. "I am smaller," she said. She crawled beside the female toward the rear of the cave.

Mitch watched and said nothing. This was what it felt like to truly sin—the sin of overwhelming curiosity. He would never forgive himself, but, he rationalized, how could he stop her without harming the bodies? Besides, she was being careful.

Tilde squeezed so low her face was on the floor beside the bundle. She gripped one end of the fur with two fingers and slowly turned it around. Mitch's throat seized with anguish. "Shine a light," she demanded. Mitch did so.

Franco aimed his torch as well.

"It's a doll," Tilde said.

From the top of the bundle peered a small face, like a dark and wrinkled apple, with two tiny sunken black eyes.

"No," Mitch said. "It's a baby."

Tilde pushed back a few inches and made a small surprised *hmm!*

Mitch's headache rolled over him like thunder.

Franco held Mitch's arm near the cave entrance. Tilde was still inside. Mitch's migraine had progressed to a real Force 9, with visuals and all, and it was an effort to keep from curling up and screaming. He had already experienced dry heaves, by the side of the cave, and he was now shivering violently.

He knew with absolute certainty that he was going to die up here, on the threshold of the most extraordinary anthropological discovery of all time, leaving it in the hands of Tilde and Franco, who were little better than thieves.

"What is she doing in there?" Mitch moaned, head bowed. Even the twilight seemed too bright. It was getting dark quickly, however.

"Not your worry," Franco said, and gripped his arm more tightly.

Mitch pulled back and felt blindly in his pocket for the vials containing the samples. He had managed to take two small plugs from the upper thighs of the man and the woman before the pain had peaked; now, he could hardly see straight.

Forcing his eyes open, he looked out upon a heavenly sapphire blueness precisely painting the mountain, the ice, the snow, overlain by flashes in the corners of his eyes like tiny bolts of lightning.

Tilde emerged from the cave, camera in one hand, pack in the other. "We have enough to prove everything," she said. She spoke Italian to Franco, rapidly and in a low voice. Mitch did not understand, nor did he care to.

He simply wanted to get down the mountain and climb into a warm bed and sleep, to wait for the extraordinary pain, all too familiar but ever fresh and new, to subside.

Dying was another option, not without its attractions.

Franco roped him up deftly. "Come, old friend," the Italian said with a kindly jerk on the rope. Mitch lurched forward, clenching his fists by his sides to keep from pounding his head. "The ax," Tilde said, and Franco slipped Mitch's ice ax out of his belt, where it tangled with his legs, and into his pack. "You are in bad shape," Franco said. Mitch clenched his eyes shut; the twilight was filled with lightning, and the thunder was pain, a silent crushing of his head with every step. Tilde took the lead and Franco followed close behind. "Different way," Tilde said. "It's icing badly and the bridge is rotten."

Mitch opened his eyes. The arête was a rusty knife edge of carbon shadow against the purest ultramarine sky, fading to starry black. Each breath was colder and harder to take. He sweated profusely.

He plodded automatically, tried to descend a rock slope dotted with patches of crunchy snow, slipped and caught on the rope, dragging Franco a couple of yards down the slope. The Italian did not protest, instead rearranged the rope around Mitch and soothed him like a child. "Okay, old friend. This is better. This is better. Watch the step." "I can't stand it much more, Franco," Mitch whispered. "I haven't had a migraine for over two years. I didn't even bring pills." "Never mind. Just watch your feet and do what I say." Franco shouted ahead to Tilde. Mitch felt her near and squinted up at her. Her face was framed with clouds and his own lights and sparks. "Snow coming," she said. "We have to hurry." They spoke in Italian and German and Mitch thought they were talking about leaving him here on the ice. "I can go," he said. "I can walk." So they began walking again on the glacier slope, accompanied by the sound of the ice fall as the slow ancient river flowed on, splitting and booming, rattling and cracking on its descent. Somewhere giant hands seemed to applaud. The wind picked up and Mitch turned away from it. Franco turned him around again and pushed less gently. "No time for stupidity, old friend. Walk." "I'm trying." "Just walk." The wind became a fist pressed against his face. He leaned into it. Ice crystals stung his cheeks and he tried to pull up his hood and his fingers were like sausages in his gloves. "He can't do this," Tilde said, and Mitch saw her walk around him, wrapped in swirling snow. The snow straightened suddenly and they all jerked as the wind grabbed them. Franco's torch illuminated millions of flakes whipping past in horizontal streaks. They discussed building a snow cave, but the ice was too hard, it would take too long to dig out. "Go! Just head down!" Franco shouted at Tilde, and she mutely complied. Mitch did not know where they were going, did not much care. Franco cursed steadily in Italian but the wind drowned him out, and Mitch, as he dragged forward, pulling up and putting down his boots, digging in his crampons, trying to stay upright, Mitch knew that Franco was there only by his pressure on the ropes. "The gods are angry!" Tilde yelled, a cry half triumphant, half jesting, with high excitement and even exaltation. Franco must have fallen, because Mitch found himself being tugged hard from the rear. He had somehow come to be holding his ax and as he went over, he fell on his stomach and had the clarity of will to dig the ax into the ice and stop his descent. Franco seemed to dangle for a moment, a few yards down the slope. Mitch looked in that direction. The lights were gone from his vision. Somehow he was freezing, really freezing, and that was allaying the pain of his migraine. Franco was not visible in the straight parallel bands of snow. The wind whistled and then shrieked and Mitch pulled his face close to the ice. His ax slipped from its hole and he slid two or three yards. With the pain fading, he wondered how he might get out of this alive. He dug his crampons into the ice and pulled himself back up the slope, by main force dragging Franco with him. Tilde helped Franco get to his feet. His nose was bloody and he seemed stunned. He must have hit his head on the ice. Tilde glanced at Mitch. She smiled and touched his shoulder. So friendly. Nobody said anything. Sharing the pain and the creeping evil warmth made them very close. Franco made a sobbing, sucking sound, licked at his bloody lip, pulled their ropes closer. They were so exposed. The fall cracked above the shrieking wind, boomed, snapped, made a sound like a tractor on a gravel road. Mitch felt the ice beneath him shudder. They were too close to the fall and it was really active, making a lot of noise. He pulled on the ropes to Tilde and they came back loose, cut. He pulled on the ropes behind him. Franco stumped out of the wind and snow, his face covered with blood, his eyes glaring behind his goggles. Franco knelt beside Mitch and then leaned over on his gloved hands, rolled to one side. Mitch grabbed his shoulder but Franco refused to budge. Mitch got up and faced downslope. The wind blew from up the slope and he keeled forward. He tried it again, leaning backward awkwardly, and fell. Crawling was the only option. He dragged Franco behind him, but that was impossible after a few feet. He crawled back to Franco and began to push him. The ice was rough, not slick, and did not help. Mitch did not know what to do. They had to get out of the wind, but he could not see well enough where they were to choose any particular direction. He was glad Tilde had abandoned them. She could get away now and maybe someone would make babies with her, neither of them of course; they were now out of the old evolutionary loop. All responsibility shed. He felt sorry that Franco was so banged up. "Hey, old friend," he shouted into the man's ear. "Wake up and give me some help or we're going to die." Franco did not respond. It was possible he was dead already, but Mitch did not think a simple fall could kill someone. Mitch found the torch around Franco's wrist, removed it, switched it on, peered into Franco's eyes as he tried to open them with his gloved fingers, not easy, but the pupils were small and uneven. Yup. He had pranged himself hard on the ice, causing concussion and flattening his nose. That was where all the new blood was coming from. The blood and snow made a red messy slush on Franco's face. Mitch gave up talking to him. He thought about cutting himself loose, but couldn't bring himself to do that. Franco had treated him well. Rivals united on the ice by death. Mitch doubted any woman would really feel a romantic pang, hearing about this. In his experience, women did not much care about such things. Dying, yes, but not the camaraderie of men. So confusing now and warming rapidly. His coat was very warm, as was his snow pants. Topping it off was that he had to pee. Death with dignity was apparently out of the question. Franco groaned. No, it wasn't Franco. The ice beneath them vibrated, then jumped, and they tumbled and slid to one side. Mitch caught sight of the torch beam illuminating a big block of ice rising, or they were falling. Yes, indeed, and he closed his eyes in anticipation. But he did not hit his head, though all the breath was slammed out of him. They landed in snow and the wind stopped. Clumped snow fell on them, and a couple of heavy chunks of ice pinned Mitch's leg. It got quiet and still. Mitch tried to lift his leg but soft warmth resisted and the other leg was stiff. It was decided.

In no time at all, he opened his eyes wide to the sky-spanning glare of a blinding blue sun.

4

Gordi

Lado, shaking his head in sad embarrassment, left Kaye in Beck's care to return to Tbilisi. He could not be away from the Eliava Institute for long.

The UN took over the small Rustaveli Tiger in Gordi, renting all of the rooms. The Russians pitched more tents and slept between the village and the graves.

Under the pained but smiling attention of the innkeeper, a stout black-haired woman named Lika, the UN peacekeepers ate a late supper of bread and tripe soup, served with big glasses of vodka. Everyone retired to bed shortly after, except for Kaye and Beck.

Beck pulled a chair up to the wooden table and placed a

glass of white wine in front of her. She had not touched the vodka.

"This is Manavi. Best they have here—for us, at any rate." Beck sat and directed a belch into his fist. "Excuse me. What do you know about Georgian history?"

"Not a lot," Kaye said. "Recent politics. Science."

Beck nodded and folded his arms. "Our dead mothers," he said, "could conceivably have been murdered during the troubles—the civil war. But I don't know of any actions in or around Gordi." He made a dubious face. "They *could* be victims from the 1930s, the '40s, or the 1950s. But you say no. Good point about the roots." He rubbed his nose and then scratched his chin. "For such a beautiful country, there's a fair amount of grim history."

Beck reminded Kaye of Saul. Most men his age somehow reminded Kaye of Saul, twelve years her senior, back on Long Island, far away in more than just distance. Saul the brilliant, Saul the weak, Saul whose mind creaked more every month. She sat up and stretched her arms, scraping the legs of her chair against the tile floor.

"I'm more interested in her future," Kaye said. "Half the pharmaceutical and medical companies in the United States are making pilgrimages here. Georgia's expertise could save millions."

"Helpful viruses."

"Right," Kaye said. "Phages."

"Attack only bacteria."

Kaye nodded.

"I read that Georgian troops carried little vials filled with phages during the troubles," Beck said. "They swallowed them if they were going into battle, or sprayed them on wounds or burns before they could get to hospital."

Kaye nodded. "They've been using phage therapy since the twenties, when Felix d'Hérelle came here to work with George Eliava. D'Hérelle was sloppy; the results were mixed back then, and soon enough we had sulfa and then penicillin. We've pretty much ignored phages until now. So we end up with deadly bacteria resistant to all known antibiotics. But not to phages."

Through the window of the small lobby, over the roofs of the low houses across the street, she could see the mountains gleaming in the moonlight. She wanted to go to sleep but knew she would lie awake in the small hard bed for hours.

"Here's to the prettier future," Beck said. He lifted his glass and drained it. Kaye took a sip. The wine's sweetness and acidity made a lovely balance, like tart apricots.

"Dr. Jakeli told me you were climbing Kazbeg," Beck said. "Taller than Mont Blanc. I'm from Kansas. No mountains at all. Hardly any rocks." He smiled down at the table, as if embarrassed to meet her gaze. "I love mountains. I apologize for dragging you away from your business . . . and your pleasure."

"I wasn't climbing," she said. "Just hiking."

"I'll try to have you out of here in a few days," Beck said. "Geneva has records of missing persons and possible massacres. If there's a match and we can date it to the thirties, we'll hand it over to the Georgians and the Russians." Beck wanted the graves to be old, and she could hardly blame him.

"What if it's recent?" Kaye asked.

"We'll bring in a full investigation team from Vienna."

Kaye gave him a clear, no-nonsense look. "It's recent," she said.

Beck finished off his glass, stood, and clutched the back of his chair with his hands. "I agree," he said with a sigh. "What made you give up on criminology? If I'm not intruding . . ."

"I learned too much about people," Kaye said. *Cruel, rotten, dirty, desperately stupid people.* She told Beck about the Brooklyn homicide lieutenant who had taught her class. He had been a devout Christian. Showing them pictures of a particularly horrendous crime scene, with two dead men, three dead women, and a dead child, he had told the students, "The souls of these victims are no longer in their bodies. Don't sympathize with them. Sympathize with the ones left behind. Get over it. Get to work. And remember: you work for God."

"His beliefs kept him sane," Kaye said.

"And you? Why did you change your major?"

"I didn't believe," Kaye said.

Beck nodded, flexed his hands on the back of the chair. "No armor. Well, do your best. You're all we've got for the time being." He said good night and walked to the narrow stairs, climbing with a fast, light tread.

Kaye sat at the table for several minutes, then stepped through the inn's front door. She stood on the granite flagstone step beside the narrow cobbled street and inhaled the night air, with its faint odor of town sewage. Over the rooftop of the house opposite the inn she could see the snow-capped crest of a mountain, so clear she could almost reach out and touch it.

In the morning, she came awake wrapped in warm sheets and a blanket that hadn't been laundered in some time. She stared at a few stray hairs, not her own, trapped in the thick gray wool near her face. The small wooden bed with carved and red-painted posts occupied a plaster-walled room about eight feet wide and ten feet long, with a single window behind the bed, a single wooden chair, and a plain oak table bearing a washstand. Tbilisi had modern hotels, but Gordi was away from the new tourist trails, too far off the Military Road.

She slipped out of bed, splashed water on her face, and pulled on her denims and blouse and coat. She was reaching for the iron latch when she heard a heavy knock. Beck called her name. She opened the door and blinked at him owlishly.

"They're running us out of town," he said, his face hard. "They want all of us back in Tbilisi by tomorrow."

"Why?"

"We're not wanted. Regular army soldiers are here to escort us. I've told them you're a civilian advisor and not a member of the team. They don't care."

"Jesus," Kaye said. "Why the turnaround?"

Beck made a disgusted face. "The *sakrebulo*, the council, I presume. Nervous about their nice little community. Or maybe it comes from higher up."

"Doesn't sound like the new Georgia," Kaye said. She was concerned about how this might affect her work with the institute.

"I'm surprised, too," Beck said. "We've stepped on somebody's toes. Please pack your case and join us downstairs."

He turned to go, but Kaye took his arm. "Are the phones working?"

"I don't know," he said. "You're welcome to use one of our satellite phones."

"Thanks. And—Dr. Jakeli is back in Tbilisi by now. I'd hate to make him drive out here again."

"We'll take you to Tbilisi," Beck said. "If that's where you want to go."

Kaye said, "That'll be fine."

The white UN Cherokees gleamed in the bright sun outside the inn. Kaye peered at them through the window panes of the lobby and waited for the innkeeper to bring out an antiquated black dial phone and plug it into the jack by the front desk. She picked up the receiver, listened to it, then handed it to Kaye: dead. In a few more years, Georgia would catch up with the twenty-first century. For now, there were less than a hundred lines to the outside world, and with all calls routed through Tbilisi, service was sporadic.

The innkeeper smiled nervously. She had been nervous since they arrived.

Kaye carried her bag outside. The UN team had assembled, six men and three women. Kaye stood beside a Canadian woman named Doyle, while Hunter brought out the satellite phone.

First Kaye made a call to Tbilisi to speak with Tamara Mirianishvili, her main contact at the institute. After several tries, the call went through. Tamara sympathized and wondered what the fuss was about, then said Kaye was welcome to come back and stay a few more days. "It is shameful, to push your nose into this. We'll have fun, make you cheerful again," Tamara said.

"Have there been any calls from Saul?" Kaye asked.

"Twice he calls," Tamara said. "He says ask more about biofilms. How do phages work in biofilms, when the bacteria get all socialized."

"And are you going to tell us?" Kaye asked in jest.

Tamara gave her a tinkling, sunny laugh. "Must we tell you all our secrets? We have no contracts yet, Kaye dear!"

"Saul's right. It could be a big issue," Kaye said. Even at the worst of times, Saul was on track with their science and their business.

"Come back, and I'll show you some of our biofilm research, special, just because you are nice," Tamara said.

"Wonderful."

Kaye thanked Tamara and handed the phone back to the corporal.

A Georgian staff car, an old black Volga, arrived with several army officers, who exited on the left side. Major Chikurishvili of the security forces stepped out from the right, his face stormier than ever. He looked like he might explode in a cloud of blood and spit.

A young army officer—Kaye had no idea what rank—approached Beck and spoke to him in broken Russian. When they were finished, Beck waved his hand and the UN team climbed into their Jeeps. Kaye rode in the Jeep with Beck.

As they drove west out of Gordi, a few of the townspeople gathered to watch them leave. A little girl stood beside a plastered stone wall and waved: brown-haired, tawny, gray-eyed, strong and lovely. A perfectly normal and delightful little girl.

There was little conversation as Hunter drove them south along the highway, leading the small caravan. Beck stared thoughtfully ahead. The stiff-sprung Jeep bounced over bumps and dropped into ruts and swerved around potholes.

Riding in the right rear seat, Kaye thought she might be getting carsick. The radio played pop tunes from Alania and pretty good blues from Azerbaijan and then an incomprehensible talk show that Beck occasionally found amusing. He glanced back at Kaye and she tried to smile bravely.

After a few hours she dozed off and dreamed of bacterial buildups inside the bodies within the trench graves. Biofilms, what most people thought of as slime: little industrious bacterial cities reducing these corpses, these once-living giant evolutionary offspring, back to their native materials. Lovely polysaccharide architectures being laid down within the interior channels, the gut and lungs, the heart and arteries and eyes and brain, the bacteria giving up their wild ways and becoming citified, recycling all; great garbage dump cities of bacteria, cheerfully ignorant of philosophy and history and the character of the dead hulks they now reclaimed.

Bacteria made us. They take us back in the end. Welcome home.

She woke up in a sweat. The air was getting warmer as they descended into a long, deep valley. How nice it would be to know nothing about all the inner workings. Animal innocence; the unexamined life is the sweetest. But things go wrong and prompt introspection and examination. The root of all awareness.

"Dreaming?" Beck asked her as they pulled over near a small filling station and garage clapped together from sheets of corrugated metal.

"Nightmares," Kaye said. "Too much into my work, I guess."

5

Innsbruck, Austria

Mitch saw the blue sun swing around and darken and he assumed it was night, but the air was dim green and not at all cold. He felt a prick of pain in his upper thigh, a general sense of unease in his stomach.

He wasn't on the mountain. He tried to blink the gunk from his eyes and reached up to rub his face. A hand stopped him and a soft female voice told him in German to be a good boy. As she wiped his forehead with a cold damp cloth, the woman said, in English, that he was a little chapped and his nose and fingers were frostbitten and that he had a broken leg. A few minutes later he went to sleep again.

No time at all after that, he awoke and managed to sit up in a crisp, firm hospital bed. He was in a room with four other patients, two beside him and two across from him, all male, all less than forty years old. Two had broken legs in movie-comedy slings. The other two had broken arms. Mitch's own leg was in a cast but not in a sling.

All the men were blue-eyed, wiry, handsome in an aquiline way, with thin necks and long jaws. They watched him attentively.

Mitch saw the room clearly now: painted concrete walls, white enameled bed frames, a portable lamp on a chromed stand that he had mistaken for a blue sun, mottled brown tile floor, the dusty smell of steam heat and antiseptic, a general odor of peppermint.

On Mitch's right, a heavily snow-burned young man, skin

peeling from his baby-pink cheeks, leaned over to say, "You are the lucky American, are you not?" The pulley and weights on his elevated leg creaked.

"I'm American," Mitch croaked. "I must be lucky because I'm not dead."

The men exchanged solemn glances. Mitch could see he had been a topic of conversation for some time.

"We all agree, it is best for fellow mountaineers to inform you."

Before Mitch could protest that he was not really a mountaineer, the snow-burned young man told him that his companions were dead. "The Italian you were found with, in the serac, he is broken-neck. And the woman is found much lower down, buried in ice." Then, his eyes sharply inquisitive—eyes the color of the wild-dog sky Mitch had first seen over the arête—the young man asked, "The newspapers say, the TV say. Where did she get the little corpse baby?"

Mitch coughed. He saw a pitcher of water on a tray by his bed and poured a glass. The mountaineers watched him like athletic elves trussed up in their beds.

Mitch returned their gazes. He tried to hide his dismay. It did him no good to judge Tilde now; no good at all.

The inspector from Innsbruck arrived at noon and sat beside his bed with an attending local police officer to ask questions. The officer spoke better English and translated for him. Their questions were routine, the inspector said, all part of the accident report. Mitch told them he did not know who the woman was, and the inspector responded, after a decent pause, that they had all been seen together in Salzburg. "You and Franco Maricelli and Mathilda Berger."

"That was Franco's girlfriend," he said, feeling sick, trying not to show it. The inspector sighed and pursed his lips disapprovingly, as if this was all very trivial and only a little irritating.

"She was carrying the mummy of an infant. Perhaps a very old mummy. You have no idea where she got it?"

He hoped the police had not gone through his effects and found the vials and recognized their contents. Perhaps he had lost the pack on the glacier. "It's too bizarre for words," he said.

The inspector shrugged. "I am not an expert on bodies in the ice. Mitchell, I give you some fatherly advice. I am old enough?"

Mitch admitted the inspector might be old enough. The mountaineers did not even attempt to hide their interest in the proceedings.

"We have spoken to your former employers, the Hayer Museum, in Seattle."

Mitch blinked slowly.

"They tell us you were involved in the theft of antiquities from the federal government, the skeletal remains of an Indian, called Pasco man, very old. Ten thousand years, found on the banks of the Columbia River. You refused to hand over these remains to the Army Corpse of Engineers."

"Corps," Mitch said softly.

"So they arrest you under an antiquities act, and the museum fires you because there is so much publicity."

"The Indians claimed the bones belonged to an ancestor," Mitch said, his face flushing with anger at the memory. "They wanted to bury them again."

The inspector read from his notes. "You were denied access to your collections in the museum, and the bones were confiscated from your house. With many photographs and more publicity."

"It was legal bullshit! The Army Corps of Engineers had no right to those bones. They were scientifically invaluable—"

"Like this mummified baby from the ice, perhaps?" the inspector asked.

Mitch closed his eyes and looked away. He could see it all very clearly now. *Stupid is not the word. This is fate, pure and simple.*

"You are going to throw up?" the inspector asked, backing away.

Mitch shook his head.

"Already it is known—you were seen with the woman in the Braunschweiger *Hütte*, not ten kilometers from where you were found. A striking woman, beautiful and blond, observers say."

The mountaineers nodded at this, as if they had been there.

"It is best you tell us everything and we hear it first. I will tell the police in Italy, and the police here in Austria will interview you and maybe it will all be nothing."

"They were acquaintances," he said. "She was—used to be—my girlfriend. I mean, we were lovers."

"Yes. Why did she return to you?"

"They had found something. She thought I might be able to tell them what they had found."

"Yes?"

Mitchell realized he had no choice. He drank another glass of water, then told the inspector most of what had happened, as precisely and clearly as he could. Since they had not mentioned the vials, he did not mention them, either. The officer took notes and recorded his confession on a small tape machine.

When he was finished, the inspector said, "Someone is sure to want to know where this cave is."

"Tilde—Mathilda had a camera," Mitch said wearily. "She took pictures."

"We found no camera. It might go much easier if you know where the cave is. Such a find . . . very exciting."

"They have the baby already," Mitch said. "That should be exciting enough. A Neandertal infant."

The inspector made a doubtful face. "Nobody says anything about Neandertal. So maybe this is a delusion or joke?"

Mitch was long past losing everything he cared about—his career, his standing as a paleontologist. Once more he had screwed things up royally. "Maybe it was the headache.

I'm just groggy. Of course, I'll help them find the cave," he said.

"Then there is no crime, merely tragedy." The inspector rose to leave, and the officer tipped his cap good-bye.

After they were gone, the mountaineer with the peeling cheeks told him, "You are not going home soon."

"The mountains want you back," said the least snow-burned of the four, across the room from Mitch, and nodded sagely, as if that explained everything.

"Screw you," Mitch muttered. He rolled over in the crisp white bed.

Eliava Institute, Tbilisi

Lado and Tamara and Zamphyra and seven other scientists and students gathered around the two wooden tables on the south end of the main laboratory building. They all lifted their beakers of brandy in toast to Kaye. Candles flickered around the room, reflecting the golden sparkles within the amber-filled glassware. The meal was only halfway finished, and this was the eighth round Lado had led this evening, as *tamada*, toastmaster, for the occasion. "For darling Kaye," Lado said, "who values our work . . . and promises to make us rich!"

Rabbits, mice, and chickens watched with sleepy eyes from their cages behind the table. Long black benches covered with glassware and racks and incubators and computers hooked to sequencers and analyzers retreated into the gloom at the unlighted end of the lab.

"To Kaye," Tamara added, "who has seen more of what Sakartvelo, of Georgia, has to offer . . . than we might wish. A brave and understanding woman."

"What are you, toastmistress?" Lado demanded in irritation. "Why remind us of unpleasant things?"

"What are you, talking of riches, of *money*, at a time like this?" Tamara snapped back.

"I am *tamada*!" Lado roared, standing beside the oak folding table and waving his sloshing glass at the students and scientists. Above slow smiles, none of them said a word in disagreement.

"All right," Tamara conceded. "Your wish is our command."

"They have no respect!" Lado complained to Kaye. "Will prosperity destroy tradition?"

The benches made crowded Vs in Kaye's narrowing perspective. The equipment was hooked into a generator that chugged softly out in the yard beside the building. Saul had supplied two sequencers and a computer; the generator had been supplied by Aventis, a huge multinational.

City power from Tbilisi had been shut off since late that afternoon. They had cooked the farewell dinner over Bunsen burners and in a gas oven.

"Go ahead, toastmaster," Zamphyra said in affectionate resignation. She waved her fingers at Lado.

"I will." Lado put down his glass and smoothed his suit. His dark wrinkled face, red as a beet with mountain sunburn, gleamed in the candlelight like rich wood. He reminded Kaye of a toy troll she had loved as a child. From a box concealed under the table he brought out a small crystal glass, intricately cut and beveled. He took a beautiful silver-chased ibex horn and walked to a large amphora propped in a wooden crate in the near corner, behind the table. The amphora, recently pulled from the earth of his own small vineyard outside Tbilisi, was filled with some immense quantity of wine. He lifted a ladle from the amphora's mouth and poured it slowly into the horn, then again, and again, seven times, until the horn was full. He swirled the wine gently to let it breathe. Red liquid sloshed over his wrist.

Finally, he filled the glass to the brim from the horn, and handed it to Kaye. "If you were a man," he said, "I would ask you to drink the entire horn, and give us a toast."

"Lado!" Tamara howled, slapping his arm. He almost dropped the horn, and turned on her in mock surprise.

"What?" he demanded. "Is the glass not beautiful?"

Zamphyra rose to her feet beside the table to waggle a finger at him. Lado grinned more broadly, transformed from a troll into a carmine satyr. He turned slowly toward Kaye.

"What can I do, dear Kaye?" Lado said with a flourish. More wine dripped from the tip of the horn. "They demand that you must drink *all* of this."

Kaye had already had her fill of alcohol and did not trust herself to stand. She felt deliciously warm and safe, among friends, surrounded by an ancient darkness thick with amber and golden stars.

She had almost forgotten the graves and Saul and the difficulties awaiting her in New York.

She held out her hands, and Lado danced forward with surprising grace, belying his clumsiness of a few moments before. Not spilling a drop, he deposited the ibex horn into her hands.

"Now, you," he said.

Kaye knew what was expected. She rose solemnly. Lado had delivered many toasts that evening that had rambled poetically and with no end of invention for long minutes. She doubted she could equal his eloquence, but she would do her best, and she had many things to say, things that had buzzed in her head for the two days since she had come down from Kazbeg.

"There is no land on Earth like the home of wine," she began, and lifted the horn high. All smiled and raised their beakers. "No land that offers more beauty and more promise to the sick of heart or the sick of body. You have distilled the nectars of new wines to banish the rot and disease the flesh is heir to. You have preserved the tradition and knowledge of seventy years, saving it for the twenty-first century. You are the mages and alchemists of the microscopic age, and now you join the explorers of the West, with an immense treasure to share."

Tamara translated in a loud whisper for the students and scientists who crowded around the table.

"I am honored to be treated as a friend, and as a colleague. You have shared with me this treasure, and the treasure of Sakartvelo—the mountains, the hospitality, the history, and by no means last or least, the wine."

She lifted the horn with one hand, and said, *"Gaumarjos phage!"* She pronounced it the Georgian way, *phah-gay.* *"Gaumarjos Sakartvelos!"*

Then she began to drink. She could not savor Lado's earth-hidden, soil-aged wine the way it deserved, and her eyes watered, but she did not want to stop, either to show her weakness or to end this moment. She swallowed gulp after gulp. Fire moved from her stomach into her arms and legs, and drowsiness threatened to steal her away. But she kept her eyes open and continued to the very bottom of the horn, then upended it, held it out, and lifted it.

"To the kingdom of the small, and all the labors they do for us! All the glories, the necessities, for which we must forgive the . . . the pain . . ." Her tongue became stiff and her words stumbled. She leaned on the folding table with one hand, and Tamara quietly and unobtrusively brought down her own hand to keep the table from upsetting. "All the things to which we . . . all we have inherited. To bacteria, our worthy opponents, the little mothers of the world!"

Lado and Tamara led the cheers. Zamphyra helped Kaye descend, it seemed from a great height, into her wooden folding chair.

"Wonderful, Kaye," Zamphyra murmured into her ear. "You come back to Tbilisi any time. You have a home, safe away from your own home."

Kaye smiled and wiped her eyes, for in her sodden sentiment and relief from the strain of the past days, she was weeping.

The next morning, Kaye felt somber and fuzzy, but experienced no other ill effects from the farewell party. In the two hours before Lado took her to the airport, she walked through the hallways in two of the three laboratory buildings, now almost empty. The staff and most of the graduate student assistants were attending a special meeting in Eliava Hall to discuss the various offers made by American and British and French companies. It was an important and heady moment for the institute; in the next two months, they would probably make their decisions on when and with whom to form alliances. But they could not tell her now. The announcement would come later.

The institute still showed decades of neglect. In most of the labs, the shiny, thick, white or pale green enamel had peeled to show cracked plaster. Plumbing dated from the 1960s, at the latest; much of it was from the twenties and thirties. The brilliant white plastic and stainless steel of new equipment only made more obvious the Bakelite and black enamel or the brass and wood of antique microscopes and other instruments. There were two electron microscopes enshrined in one building—great hulking brutes on massive vibration isolation platforms.

Saul had promised them three new top-of-the-line scanning tunneling microscopes by the end of the year—if EcoBacter was chosen as one of their partners. Aventis or Bristol-Myers Squibb could no doubt do better than that.

Kaye walked between the lab benches, peering through the glass doors of incubators at stacks of petri dishes within, their bottoms filled with a film of agar swept and clouded by bacterial colonies, sometimes marked by clear circular regions, called plaques, where phages had killed all the bacteria. Day after day, year after year, the researchers in the institute analyzed and cataloged naturally occurring bacteria and their phages. For every strain of bacteria there was at least one and often hundreds of specific phages, and as the bacteria mutated to throw off these unwanted intruders, the phages mutated to match them, a never-ending chase. The Eliava Institute kept one of the largest libraries of phages in the world, and they could respond to bacterial samples by producing phages within days.

On the wall over the new lab equipment, posters showed the bizarre spaceshiplike geometric head and tail structures of the ubiquitous T-even phages—T2, T4, and T6, so designated in the 1920s—hovering over the comparatively huge surfaces of *Escherichia coli* bacteria. Old photographs, old conceptions—that phages simply preyed upon bacteria, hijacking their DNA merely to produce new phages. Many phages did in fact do just that, keeping bacterial populations in check. Others, known as lysogenic phages, became genetic stowaways, hiding within the bacteria and inserting their genetic messages into the host DNA. Retroviruses did something very similar in larger plants and animals.

Lysogenic phages suppressed their own expression and assembly and were perpetuated within the bacterial DNA, carried down through the generations. They would jump ship when their host showed clear signs of stress, creating hundreds or even thousands of phage offspring per cell, bursting from the host to escape.

Lysogenic phages were almost useless in phage therapy. They were far more than mere predators. Often these viral invaders gave their hosts resistance to other phages. Sometimes they carried genes from one cell to the next, genes that could transform the cell. Lysogenic phages had been known to take relatively harmless bacteria—benign strains of *Vibrio*, for example—and transform them into virulent *Vibrio cholerae*. Outbreaks of deadly strains of *E. coli* in beef had been attributed to transfers of toxin-producing genes by phages. The institute worked hard to identify and eliminate these phages from their preparations.

Kaye, however, was fascinated by them. She had spent much of her career studying lysogenic phages in bacteria and retroviruses in apes and humans. Hollowed-out retroviruses were commonly used in gene therapy and genetic research as delivery systems for corrective genes, but Kaye's interest was less practical.

Many metazoans—nonbacterial life-forms—carried the dormant remains of ancient retroviruses in their genes. As much as one third of the human genome, our complete genetic record, was made up of these so-called endogenous retroviruses.

She had written three papers about human endogenous retrovirus, or HERV, suggesting they might contribute to novelty in the genome—and much more. Saul agreed with her. "Everyone knows they carry little secrets," he had once told her, when they were courting. Their courtship had been odd and lovely. Saul himself was odd and sometimes quite lovely and kind; she just never knew when those times would be.

Kaye paused for a moment by a metal lab stool and rested her hand on its Masonite seat. Saul had always been interested in the bigger picture; she, on the other hand, had been content with smaller successes, tidier chunks of knowledge. So much hunger had led to many disappointments. He had quietly watched his younger wife achieve so much more. She knew it hurt him. Not to have immense success, not to be a genius, was for Saul a major failing.

Kaye lifted her head and inhaled the air: bleach, steam heat, a waft of fresh paint and carpentry from the adjacent library. She liked this old lab with its antiques and humility and decades-old story of hardship and success. The days she had spent here, and on the mountain, had been among the most pleasant of her recent life. Tamara and Zamphyra and Lado had not only made her feel welcome, they had seemed to open up instantly and generously to become family to a wandering foreign woman.

Saul might have a very big success here. A double success, perhaps. What he needed to feel important and useful.

She turned and through the open doorway saw Tengiz, the stooped old lab caretaker, talking to a short, plump young

man in gray slacks and a sweatshirt. They stood in the corridor between the lab and the library. The young man looked
at her and smiled. Tengiz smiled as well, nodded vigorously,
and pointed to Kaye. The man sauntered into the lab as if he
owned it.

"Are you Kaye Lang?" he asked in American English with
a distinct Southern drawl. He was shorter than her by several
inches, about her age or a little older, with a thin black beard
and curly black hair. His eyes, also black, were small and
intelligent.

"Yes," she said.

"Pleasure to meet you. My name is Christopher Dicken.
I'm from the Epidemic Intelligence Service of the National
Center for Infectious Diseases in Atlanta—another Georgia,
a long way from here."

Kaye smiled and shook his hand. "I didn't know you were
going to be here," she said. "What's the NCID, the CDC—"

"You went out to a site near Gordi, two days ago," Dicken
interrupted her.

"They chased us away," Kaye said.

"I know. I spoke with Colonel Beck yesterday."

"Why would you be interested?"

"Could be for no good reason." He thinned his lips and
lifted his eyebrows, then smiled again, shrugging this off.
"Beck says the UN and all Russian peacekeepers have pulled
out of the area and returned to Tbilisi, at the vigorous request
of the parliament and President Shevardnadze. Odd, don't
you think?"

"Embarrassing for business," Kaye murmured. Tengiz listened from the hall. She frowned at him, more in puzzlement
than in warning. He wandered away.

"Yeah," Dicken said. "Old troubles. How old, would you
say?"

"What—the grave?"

Dicken nodded.

"Five years. Maybe less."

"The women were pregnant."

"Yesss . . ." She dragged her answer out, trying to riddle why this would interest a man from the Centers for Disease Control. "The two I saw."

"No chance of a misidentification? Full-term infants impacted in the grave?"

"None," she said. "They were about six or seven months along."

"Thanks." Dicken held out his hand again and shook hers politely. He turned to leave. Tengiz was crossing the hall outside the door and hustled aside as Dicken passed through. The EIS investigator glanced back at Kaye and tossed a quick salute.

Tengiz leaned his head to one side and grinned toothlessly. He looked guilty as hell.

Kaye sprinted for the door and caught up with Dicken in the courtyard. He was climbing into a small rental Nissan.

"Excuse me!" she called out.

"Sorry. Gotta go." Dicken slammed the door and turned on the engine.

"Christ, you sure know how to arouse suspicions!" Kaye said loudly enough for him to hear through the closed window.

Dicken rolled the window down and grimaced amiably. "Suspicions about what?"

"What in hell are you doing here?"

"Rumors," he said, looking over his shoulder to see if the way was clear. "That's all I can say."

He spun the car around in the gravel and drove off, maneuvering between the main building and the second lab. Kaye folded her arms and frowned after him.

Lado called from the main building, poking out of a window. "Kaye! We are done. You are ready?"

"Yes!" Kaye answered, walking toward the window. "Did you see him?"

"Who?" Lado asked, face blank.

"A man from the Centers for Disease Control. He said his name was Dicken."

"I saw no one. They have an office on Abasheli Street. You could call."

She shook her head. There wasn't time, and it was none of her business anyway. "Never mind," she said.

Lado was unusually somber as he drove her to the airport.

"Is it good news, or bad?" she asked.

"I am not allowed to say," he replied. "We should, as you say, keep our options open? We are like babes in the woods."

Kaye nodded and stared straight ahead as they entered the parking area. Lado helped her take her bags to the new international terminal, past lines of taxis with sharp-eyed drivers waiting impatiently. The check-in desk at British Mediterranean Airlines had a short line. Already Kaye felt she was in the middle zone between worlds, closer to New York than to Lado's Georgia or the Gergeti church or Mount Kazbeg.

As she reached the front of the line and pulled out her passport and tickets, Lado stood with arms folded, squinting at the watery sunlight through the terminal windows.

The clerk, a young blond woman with ghostly pale skin, slowly worked through the tickets and papers. She finally looked up to say, "No off going. No taking."

"Beg pardon?"

The woman lifted her eyes to the ceiling as if this would give her strength or cleverness and tried again. "No Baku. No Heathrow. No JFK. No Vienna."

"What, they're gone?" Kaye asked in exasperation. She looked helplessly at Lado, who stepped over the vinyl-covered ropes and addressed the woman in stern and reproving tones, then pointed to Kaye and lifted his bushy brows, as if to say, *Very Important Person!*

The pale young woman's cheeks acquired some color. With infinite patience, she looked at Kaye and began speaking, in rapid Georgian, something about the weather, hail moving in, unusual storm. Lado translated in spaced single words: hail, unusual, soon.

"When can I get out?" she asked the woman.

Lado listened to the clerk's explanation with a stern expression, then lifted his shoulders and turned his face toward Kaye. "Next week, next flight. Or flight to Vienna, Tuesday. Day after tomorrow."

Kaye decided to rebook through Vienna. There were now four people in line behind Kaye, and they were showing signs of both amusement and impatience. By their dress and language, they were probably not going to New York or London.

Lado walked with her up the stairs and sat across from her in the echoing waiting area. She needed to think, to sort out her plans. A few old women sold Western cigarettes and perfume and Japanese watches from small booths around the perimeter. Nearby, two young men slept on opposite benches, snoring in tandem. The walls were covered with posters in Russian, the lovely curling Georgian script, and in German and French. Castles, tea plantations, bottles of wine, the suddenly small and distant mountains whose pure colors survived even the fluorescent lights.

"I know, you need to call your husband, he will miss you," Lado said. "We can return to the institute—you are welcome, always!"

"No, thank you," Kaye said, suddenly feeling a little sick. Premonition had nothing to do with it: she could read Lado like a book. What had they done wrong? Had a larger firm made an even sweeter offer?

What would Saul do when he found out? All their planning had been based on his optimism about being able to convert friendship and charity into a solid business relationship . . .

They were so close.

"There is the Metechi Palace," Lado said. "Best hotel in Tbilisi . . . best in Georgia. I take you to the Metechi! You can be a real tourist, like in the guide books! Maybe you have time to take a hot spring bath . . . relax before you go home."

Kaye nodded and smiled but it was obvious her heart was not in it. Suddenly, impetuously, Lado leaned forward and clutched her hand in his dry, cracked fingers, roughened by so many washings and immersions. He pounded his hand and hers lightly on her knee. "It is no end! It is a beginning! We must all be strong and resourceful!"

This brought tears to Kaye's eyes. She looked at the posters again—Elbrus and Kazbeg draped with clouds, the Gergeti church, vineyards and high tilled fields.

Lado threw his hands up in the air, swore eloquently in Georgian, and leaped to his feet. "I tell them it is not best!" he insisted. "I tell the bureaucrats in the government, we have worked with you, with Saul, for three years, and it is not to be overturned in one night! Who needs an exclusive, no? I will take you to Metechi."

Kaye smiled her thanks and Lado sat down again, bending over, shaking his head glumly and folding his hands. "It is an outrage," he said, "what we have to do in today's world."

The young men continued snoring.

7

New York

Christopher Dicken arrived at JFK, by coincidence, on the same evening as Kaye Lang, and saw her waiting to go through customs. She was transferring her luggage to a cart and did not notice him.

She looked dragged out, wan. Dicken had been in the air himself for thirty-six hours, returning from Turkey with two locked metal cases and a duffel bag. He certainly did not want to run into Lang under the present circumstances.

Dicken was not sure why he had gone to see Lang at Eliava. Perhaps because they had separately experienced the same horror outside Gordi. Perhaps to discover if she knew what was happening in the United States, the reason he had been recalled; perhaps just to meet the attractive and intelligent woman whose picture he had seen on the EcoBacter web site.

He showed his CDC identification and NCID import pass to a customs supervisor, filled out the requisite five forms, and slouched through a side door into an empty hall. Coffee nerves gave everything an extra sour edge. He had not slept a wink on the entire flight and had slugged back five cups in the hour before landing. He had wanted time to research and think and be prepared for the meeting with Mark Augustine, the director of the Centers for Disease Control and Prevention.

Augustine was in Manhattan now, giving a talk at a conference on new AIDS treatments.

Dicken carried the cases to the parking garage. He had lost all track of time on the plane and in the airport; he was a little surprised to discover dusk falling over New York.

He made his way through a labyrinth of stairs and elevators and drove his government Dodge out of long-term parking and faced the bleak gray skies above Jamaica Bay. Traffic on the Van Wyck Expressway was dense. With a solicitous hand, he steadied the sealed cases on the passenger seat. The first case held dry ice to preserve a few vials of blood and urine from a patient in Turkey, and tissue samples from her rejected fetus. The second contained two sealed plastic pouches of mummified epidermal and muscle tissue, courtesy of the officer in charge of the United Nations extended peacekeeping mission in the Republic of Georgia, Colonel Nicholas Beck.

The tissue from the graves near Gordi was a long shot, but there was a pattern emerging in Dicken's mind—a very intriguing and disturbing pattern. He had spent three years tracking down the viral equivalent of a boojum: a sexually transmitted disease that struck only pregnant women and invariably caused miscarriages. It was a potential bombshell, just what Augustine had tasked Dicken to find: something so horrible, so provocative, that funding for the CDC would be guaranteed to rise.

During those years, Dicken had gone time and again to Ukraine, Georgia, and Turkey, hoping to gather samples and put together an epidemiological map. Time and again, public health officials in each of the three nations had stonewalled him. They had their reasons. Dicken had heard of no fewer than three and as many as seven mass graves containing the bodies of men and women who had supposedly been killed to prevent the spread of this disease. Getting samples from local hospitals had proven extremely difficult, even when the countries had made formal agreements with the CDC and the World Health Organization. He had been allowed to visit only the grave in Gordi, and that one because it was under UN investigation. He had taken his samples from the victims an hour after Kaye Lang had left.

Dicken had never before dealt with a conspiracy to hide the existence of a disease.

All his work could have been important, just what Augustine needed, but it was about to be overshadowed, if not blown wide open. While Dicken had been in Europe, the quarry had broken cover on the CDC's home turf. A young researcher at UCLA Medical Center, looking for a common element in seven rejected fetuses, had found an unknown virus. He had shipped the samples to CDC-funded epidemiologists in San Francisco. The researchers had copied and sequenced the virus's genetic material. They had reported their findings immediately to Mark Augustine.

Augustine had called Dicken home.

Rumors were spreading already about the discovery of the first infectious human endogenous retrovirus, or HERV. As well, there were a few scattered news stories about a virus that caused miscarriages. So far, no one outside the CDC had yet put the two together. On the plane from London, Dicken had spent an expensive half hour on the Internet, visiting key professional sites and news groups, finding nowhere a detailed description of the discovery, but everywhere a slam-dunk predictable curiosity. No wonder. Someone could end up getting a Nobel—and Dicken was ready to lay odds that that someone would be Kaye Lang.

As a professional virus hunter, Dicken had long had a fascination with HERV, the genetic fossils of ancient diseases. Lang had first come to Dicken's attention two years ago when she published three papers describing sites in the human genome, on chromosomes 14 and 17, where parts of potentially complete and infectious HERV could be found. Her most detailed paper had appeared in *Virology*: "A Model for Expression, Assembly, and Lateral Transmission of Chromosomally Scattered *env*, *pol*, and *gag* Genes: Viable Ancient Retroviral Elements in Humans and Simians."

The nature of the outbreak and its possible extent was a closely guarded secret for the time being, but a few insiders at the CDC knew this much: The retroviruses found in the fetuses were genetically identical with HERV that had been part of the human genome since the evolutionary branching of Old World and New World monkeys. Every human on Earth carried them, but they were no longer simply genetic garbage or abandoned fragments. Something had stimulated scattered segments of HERV to express, then assemble the proteins and RNA they encoded into a particle capable of leaving the body and infecting another individual.

All seven of the rejected fetuses had been severely malformed.

These particles were causing disease, probably the very disease that Dicken had been tracking for the past three years. The disease had already received an in-house name at the CDC: Herod's flu.

With the mix of brilliance and luck that characterized most great scientific careers, Lang had precisely pegged the locations of the genes that were apparently causing Herod's flu. But she did not yet have a clue what had happened; he could tell that in her eyes in Tbilisi.

Something more besides had drawn Dicken to Kaye Lang's work. With her husband, she had written papers on the evolutionary significance of transposable genetic elements, so-called jumping genes: transposons, retrotransposons, and even HERV. Transposable elements could change when, where, and how often genes expressed, causing mutations, ultimately altering the physical nature of an organism.

Transposable elements, retrogenes, had very likely once been the precursors of viruses; some had mutated and learned how to exit the cell, wrapped in protective capsids and envelopes, the genetic equivalents of space suits. A few had later returned as retroviruses, like prodigal sons; some of those, over the millennia, had infected germ-line cells—eggs or sperm or their precursors—and somehow lost their potency. These had become HERV.

In his travels, Dicken had heard from reliable sources in Ukraine of women bearing subtly and not-so-subtly different children, of children immaculately conceived, of entire villages being razed and sterilized . . . In the wake of a plague of miscarriages.

All rumors, but to Dicken evocative, even compelling. In his hunting, he relied on well-honed instincts. The stories resonated with something he had been thinking about for over a year.

Perhaps there had been a conspiracy of mutagens. Perhaps Chernobyl or some other Soviet-era radiation disaster had triggered the release of the endogenous retrovirus that caused Herod's flu. So far, he had mentioned this theory to no one, however.

In the Midtown Tunnel, a big panel truck decorated with happy dancing cows swerved and nearly hit him. He stood on the Dodge's brakes. Squealing tires and a miss of mere inches brought sweat to his brow and unleashed all his anger and frustration. "Fuck you!" he shouted at the unseen driver. "Next time I'll carry Ebola!"

He was feeling less than charitable. The CDC would have to go public, perhaps in a few weeks. By that time, if the charts were accurate, there would be well over five thousand cases of Herod's flu in the United States alone.

And Christopher Dicken would be credited with little more than a good soldier's footwork.

8

Long Island, New York

The green and white house stood on top of a low hill, medium in size but stately, 1940s Colonial, surrounded by old oaks and poplars, as well as rhododendrons she had planted three years ago.

Kaye had called from the airport and picked up a message from Saul. He was at a client lab in Philadelphia and would be back later in the evening. It was seven now and the twilight sky over Long Island was glorious. Fluffy clouds broke free from a dissipating mass of ominous gray. Starlings made the oaks noisy as a nursery.

She unlocked the door, pushed her bags through, and keyed in her code to deactivate the alarm. The house smelled musty. She put down her bags as one of their two cats, an orange tabby named Crickson, sallied into the hallway from the living room, claws ticking faintly on the warm teak floor. Kaye picked him up and skritched him under the neck and he purred and mewed like a sick calf. The other cat, Temin, was nowhere in sight. She guessed he was outside, hunting.

The living room made her heart sag. Dirty clothes had been scattered everywhere. Microwave cardboard dishes lay scattered on the coffee table and oriental rug before the couch. Books and newspapers and yellow pages torn from an old phone book sprawled over the dining table. The musty smell came from the kitchen: rotten vegetables, stale coffee grounds, plastic food wrappers.

Saul had had a bad time of it. As usual, she had returned just in time to clean up.

Kaye opened the front door and all the windows.

She fried herself a small steak and made a green salad with bottled dressing. As she opened a bottle of pinot noir, Kaye noticed an envelope on the white tile counter near the espresso maker. She set the wine out to breathe, then tore open the envelope. Inside was a flowery greeting card with a scrawled note from Saul.

> *Kaye,*
> *Sweetest Kaye, love love love I am so sorry. I missed you and this time it shows, all over the house. Don't clean up. I'll have Caddy do it tomorrow and pay her extra. Just relax. The bedroom is spotless. I made sure of that.*
> *Crazy old Saul*

Kaye folded the note with an unmollified sniff and stared at the counter and cabinets. Her eye fell on a neat stack of old journals and magazines, out of place on the butcher block table. She lifted the magazines. Underneath, she found a dozen or so printouts, and another note. She turned off the heat on the stove and put a lid over the pan to keep the steak warm, then picked up the pile and read the first sheet.

> *Kaye . . .*
> *You peeked! This stack by way of apology. Very exciting. Got it off Virion and asked Ferris and Farrakhan Mkebe at UCI what they know. They wouldn't tell me everything, but I think It's here, just like we predicted. They call it SHERVA—Scattered Human Endogenous Retrovirus*

Activation. There's very little useful on the web sites, but here's the discussion.

Love and admiration, Saul

Kaye did not know quite why, but this made her cry. Through a film of tears, she flipped through the papers, then put them on the tray beside her steak and salad. She was tired and overwrought. She carried the tray into the den to eat and watch television.

Saul had made a small fortune patenting a special variety of transgenic mouse six years ago; he had met and married Kaye the year after that, and immediately he had put most of his fortune into EcoBacter. Kaye's parents had contributed a substantial amount as well, just before their deaths in an auto accident. Thirty workers and five staff filled the rectangular gray and blue building in a Long Island industrial park, cheek-by-jowl with half a dozen other biotech companies. The park was four miles from their house.

She wasn't due at EcoBacter until noon tomorrow. She hoped that something would delay Saul and she would have more time by herself, to think and prepare, but this wish made her choke up again. She tossed her head in disgust at her rampant emotions and drank her wine through dripping, salty lips.

All she really wanted was for Saul to be healthy, to get better. She wanted her husband back, the man who had changed her perspective on life, her inspiration and partner and stable center in a rapidly spinning world.

As she chewed small bites of steak, she read the messages from the Virion discussion group. There were over a hundred, several from scientists, most from dilettantes and students, rehashing and speculating upon the spotty news.

She sprinkled A-1 sauce over the last of the meat and took a deep breath.

This could be important stuff. Saul had a right to be excited. There were so few specifics, however, and not a clue as to where the work had been done, or where it was going to be published, or who had leaked the news.

She took her tray into the kitchen just as the phone rang. With a little pirouette in her stocking feet, she balanced the tray on one hand and answered.

"Welcome home!" Saul said. His deep voice still sent a small thrill. "Dear far-traveling Kaye!" He became contrite. "I wanted to apologize for the mess. Caddy couldn't come in yesterday." Caddy was their housekeeper.

"It's good to be back," she said. "Working?"

"I'm stuck here. Can't get away."

"I've missed you."

"Don't clean up the house."

"I haven't. Not much."

"Did you read the printouts?"

"Yes. They were hidden on the counter."

"I wanted you to read them in the morning with coffee, when you're at your sharpest. I should have more solid news by then. I'll be back by eleven tomorrow. Don't go to the lab right away."

"I'll wait for you," she said.

"You sound beat. Long flight?"

"Bad air," she said. "I got a nosebleed."

"Poor *Mädchen*," he said. "Don't worry. I'm fine now that you're here. Did Lado . . . ?" He let the sentence trail off.

"Not a clue," Kaye lied. "I did my best."

"I know. Sleep snug and I'll make it up to you. There's going to be stunning news."

"You've heard more. Tell me," Kaye said.

"Not yet. Anticipation is its own joy."

Kaye hated games. "Saul—"

"I am adamant. Besides, I haven't got all the confirmation I need. I love you. I miss you." He made a kiss-sound good night, and after multiple good-byes, they broke the connection simultaneously, an old habit. Saul was sensitive about being last on the line.

Kaye looked around the kitchen, wrapped a dishrag around

her hand, and began to clean up. She did not want to wait for Caddy. After straightening to her satisfaction, she showered, washed her hair and wrapped it in a towel, put on her favorite rayon pajamas, and built a fire in the upstairs bedroom fireplace. Then she squatted in a lotus on the end of the bed, letting the bright flames and the soft smoothness of the rayon reassure her. Outside, the wind rose and she saw a single flash behind the lace curtains. The weather was turning rough.

Kaye climbed into bed and pulled the down comforter up under her neck. "At least I'm not feeling sorry for myself anymore," she said in a bold voice. Crickson joined her, parading his fluffy orange tail across the bed. Temin leaped up as well, more dignified, though a little damp. He condescended to be rubbed down with her towel.

For the first time since Mount Kazbeg, she felt safe and balanced. *Poor little girl,* she accused. *Waiting for her husband to return. Waiting for her real husband to return.*

New York City

Mark Augustine stood before the window of his small hotel room, holding a late night bourbon and water on the rocks, and listened to Dicken's report.

Augustine was a compact and efficient man with smiling brown eyes, a firmly rooted head of concentrated gray hair, a small but jutting nose, and expressive lips. His skin was permanently sun-browned from years spent in equatorial Africa, and from his years in Atlanta, his voice was soft and melodious. He was a tough and resourceful man, adept at politicking, as befitted a director, and it was said by many at the CDC that he was being groomed to be the next surgeon general.

When Dicken finished, Augustine put down his drink. "Ver-r-r-ry inter-esting," he said in an Artie Johnson voice. "Amazing work, Christopher."

Christopher smiled but waited for the long assessment.

"It fits with most of what we know. I've spoken with the SG," Augustine continued. "She thinks we're going to have to go public in small steps, and soon. I agree. First, we'll let the scientists have their fun, cloak it in a little romance. You know, tiny invaders from inside our own bodies, gee, isn't it fascinating, we don't know what they can do. That sort of thing. Doel and Davison in California can outline their discovery and do that for us. They've been working hard enough. They certainly deserve some glory." Augustine again lifted the glass of whiskey and twirled the ice and water with a quiet tinkle. "Did Dr. Mahy say when they can get your samples analyzed?"

"No," Dicken said.

Augustine smiled sympathetically. "You would rather have followed them to Atlanta."

"I'd rather have flown them there myself and done the work," Dicken said.

"I'm going to Washington Thursday," Augustine said. "I'm backing up the surgeon general before Congress. NIH could be there. We aren't bringing in the secretary of HHS yet. I want you with me. I'll tell Francis and Jon to put out their press release tomorrow morning. It's been ready for a week."

Dicken admired this with a private, slightly ironic smile. HHS—Health and Human Services—was the huge branch of government that oversaw the NIH, the National Institutes of Health, and the CDC, the Centers for Disease Control and Prevention in Atlanta, Georgia. "A well-oiled machine," he said.

Augustine took this as a compliment. "We've still got our

heads shoved up our asses. We've riled Congress with our stance on tobacco and firearms. The bastards in Washington have decided we're a big fat target. They cut our funding by a third to help pay for a new tax cut. Now a big one comes and it's not out of Africa or the rain forest. It has nothing to do with our little rape of Mother Nature. It's a fluke, and it comes from inside our own blessed little bodies." Augustine's smile turned wolfish. "It makes my hair prickle, Christopher. This is a *godsend*. We have to present this with timing, with *drama*. If we don't do this right, there's a real danger no one in Washington will pay attention until we lose an entire generation of babies."

Dicken wondered how he could contribute to this runaway train. There had to be some way he could promote his field-work, all those years tracking boojums. "I've been thinking about a mutation angle," he said, his mouth dry. He laid out the stories of mutated babies he had heard in Ukraine and outlined some of his theory of radiation-induced release of HERV.

Augustine narrowed his eyelids and shook his head. "We know about birth defects from Chernobyl. No news in that," he murmured. "But there's no radiation *here*. It doesn't gel, Christopher." He opened the room's window and the noise of traffic ten floors below grew. Breeze puffed the inner white curtains.

Dicken persisted, trying to salvage his argument, at the same time aware that his evidence was woefully inadequate. "There's a strong possibility that Herod's does more than cause miscarriages. It seems to pop up in comparatively isolated populations. It's been active at least since the 1960s. The political response has often been extreme. Nobody would wipe out a village or kill dozens of mothers and fathers and their unborn children, just because of a local run of miscarriages."

Augustine shrugged. "Much too vague," he said, staring down at the street below.

"Enough for an investigation," Dicken suggested.

Augustine frowned. "We're talking empty wombs, Christopher," he said calmly. "We have to play from a big scary idea, not rumors and science fiction."

10

Long Island, New York

Kaye heard footsteps up the stairs, sat up in bed and pulled her hair from her eyes in time to see Saul. He stalked on tiptoes into the bedroom, along the carpet runner, carrying a small package wrapped in red foil and tied with a ribbon, and a bouquet of roses and baby's breath.

"Damn," he said, seeing she was awake. He held the roses to one side with a flourish and bent over the bed to kiss her. His lips opened and were so slightly moist without being aggressive. That was his signal that her needs came first but he was interested, very. "Welcome home. I have missed you, *Mädchen*."

"Thank you. It's good to be here."

Saul sat on the side of the bed, staring at the roses. "I am in a good mood. My lady is home." He smiled broadly and lay beside her, swinging his legs up and resting his stocking feet on the bed. Kaye could smell the roses, intense and sweet, almost too much this early in the morning. He presented her with the gift. "For my brilliant friend."

Kaye sat up as Saul plumped her pillow into a backrest. Seeing Saul in fine form had its old effect on her: hope and joy at being home and a little closer to something centered. She hugged him awkwardly around the shoulders, nuzzling his neck.

"Ah," he said. "Now open the box."

She raised her eyebrows, pursed her lips, and pulled on the ribbon. "What have I done to deserve this?" she said.

"You have never really understood how valuable and wonderful you are," Saul said. "Maybe it's just that I love you. Maybe it's a special occasion just that you're back. Or . . . maybe we're celebrating something else."

"What?"

"Open it."

She realized with growing intensity that she had been away for weeks. She pulled off the red foil and kissed his hand slowly, eyes fixed on his face. Then she looked down at the box.

Inside was a large medallion bearing the familiar bust of a famous munitions manufacturer. It was a Nobel prize—made of chocolate.

Kaye laughed out loud. "Where . . . did you get *this*?"

"Stan loaned me his and I made a cast," Saul said.

"And you're not going to tell me what's going on?" Kaye asked, fingering his thigh.

"Not for a little while," Saul said. He put the roses down and removed his sweater and she began unbuttoning his shirt.

The curtains were still drawn and the room had not yet received its ration of morning sun. They lay on the bed with sheets and blankets and comforter rucked all around them. Kaye saw mountains in the rumples and stalked her fingers over a flowered peak. Saul arched his back with little cartilaginous pops and swallowed a few great gulps of air. "I'm out of shape," he said. "I'm becoming a desk jockey. I need to bench-press a few more test benches."

Kaye held out her thumb and forefinger and spaced them an inch apart, then raised and lowered them rhythmically. "Test tube exercises," she said.

"Right brain, left brain," Saul rejoined, grabbing his temples and shifting his head from side to side. "You've got three weeks' worth of Internet jokes to catch up on."

"Poor me," Kaye said.

"Breakfast!" Saul shouted, and swung his legs out of bed. "Downstairs, fresh, waiting to be reheated."

Kaye followed him in her dressing gown. *Saul is back,* she tried to convince herself. *My good Saul is back.*

He had stopped by the local grocery to pick up ham-and-cheese stuffed croissants. He arranged their plates between cups of coffee and orange juice on the little table on the back porch. The sun was bright, the air was clean after the squall and warming nicely. It was going to be a lovely day.

For Kaye, with every hour of good Saul, the lure of the mountains faded like a girlish hope. She did not need to get away. Saul chattered about what had been happening at EcoBacter, about his trip to California and Utah and then Philadelphia to confer with their client and partner labs. "We have four more preclinical tests mandated by our caseworker at the FDA," he said sardonically. "But at least we've shown them we can put antagonistic bacteria together in resource competition and force them to make chemical weapons. We've demonstrated we can isolate the bacteriocins, purify them, produce them in neutralized form in bulk—then activate them. Safe in rats, safe in hamsters and vervets, effective against resistant strains of three nasty pathogens. We're so far ahead of Merck and Aventis they can't even spit at our butts."

Bacteriocins were chemicals produced by bacteria that could kill other bacteria. They were a promising new weapon in a rapidly weakening arsenal of antibiotics.

Kaye listened happily. He had not yet told her the news he had promised; he was building to that moment in his own way, taking his own sweet time. Kaye knew the drill and did not give him the satisfaction of appearing eager.

"If that wasn't enough," he continued, his eyes bright, "Mkebe says we're close to finding a way to gum up the whole command and control and communication network in *Staphylococcus aureus*. We'll attack the little buggers from three different directions at once. Boom!" He pulled back his eloquent hands and wrapped his arms around himself like a satisfied little boy. Then his mood changed.

"Now," Saul said, and his face went suddenly blank. "Give it to me straight about Lado and Eliava."

Kaye stared at him for a moment with an intensity that almost crossed her eyes. Then she glanced down and said, "I think they've decided to go with someone else."

"Mr. Bristol-Myers Squibb," Saul said, and lifted a rolling and waving hand in dismissal. "Fossil corporate architecture versus young new blood. They are *so* wrong." He gazed across the yard at the sound, squinted at a few sailboats dodging small whitecaps in the light morning breezes. Then he finished his orange juice and smacked his lips dramatically. He fairly wriggled in the chair, leaned forward, fixed her with his deep gray eyes, and clasped her hands in his.

This is it, Kaye thought.

"They *will* regret it. In the next few months we are going to be so busy. The CDC just broke the news this morning. They have confirmed the existence of the first viable human endogenous retrovirus. They've shown that it can be transmitted laterally between individuals. They call it Scattered Human Endogenous RetroVirus Activation, SHERVA. They dropped the *R* for dramatic effect. That makes it SHEVA. Good name for a virus, don't you think?"

Kaye searched his face. "No joke?" she asked, voice unsteady. "It's confirmed?"

Saul grinned and held up his arms like Moses. "Absolutely. Science marches on to the promised land."

"What is it? How big is it?"

"It's a retrovirus, a true monster, eighty-two kilobases, thirty genes. Its *gag* and *pol* components are on chromosome 14, and its *env* is on chromosome 17. The CDC says it may be a mild pathogen, and humans show little or no resistance, so its been buried for a very long time."

He placed his hand over hers and squeezed it gently. "You predicted it, Kaye. You described the genes. Your prime candidate, a broken HERV-DL3, is the one they're targeting, and *they are using your name*. They've cited your papers."

"Wow," Kaye said, her face going pale. She leaned over her plate, the blood pounding in her head.

"Are you all right?"

"I'm fine," she said, feeling dizzy.

"Let's enjoy our privacy while we can," Saul said triumphantly. "Every science reporter is going to be calling. I give them about two minutes to go through their Rolodexes and search MedLine. You'll be on TV, CNN, *Good Morning America*."

Kaye simply could not wrap belief around this turn of events. "What kind of illness does it cause?" she managed to ask.

"Nobody seems clear on that."

Kaye's mind buzzed with possibilities. If she called Lado at the institute, told Tamara and Zamphyra—they might change their minds, go with EcoBacter. Saul would stay good Saul, happy and productive.

"My God, we're hot shit," Kaye said, still feeling a little woozy. She lifted her fingers, *la di da*.

"You're the one who's hot, my dear. It's your work, and it ain't shit."

The phone rang in the kitchen.

"That'll be the Swedish Academy," Saul said, nodding sagely. He held up the medallion and Kaye took a bite out of it.

"Bull!" she said happily, and went to answer.

11

Innsbruck, Austria

The hospital gave Mitch a private room as a show of respect
for his newfound notoriety. He was just as glad to get away
from the mountaineers—but it hardly mattered how he felt or
what he thought.

An almost total emotional numbness had stolen over him
in the past two days. Seeing his picture on the television
news, on the BBC and Sky World, and in the local papers,
proved what he knew already; it was over. He was finished.

According to the Zürich press, he was the "Sole Survivor of
Body-Snatching Mountain Expedition." In Munich, he was
"Kidnapper of Ancient Ice Baby." In Innsbruck, he was called
simply "Scientist/Thief." All reported his preposterous story
of Neandertal mummies, helpfully relayed by the police in
Innsbruck. All told of his stealing "American Indian Bones"
in the "Northwest United States."

He was widely described as an American crackpot, down
on his luck, desperate to get publicity.

The Ice Baby had been transferred to the University of
Innsbruck, where it was being studied by a team headed by
Herr Doktor Professor Emiliano Luria. Luria himself was
coming later in the afternoon to speak with Mitch about
the find.

So long as Mitch had information they needed, he was still in
the loop—he was still a kind of scientist, investigator, anthropologist. He was more than just a thief. When his usefulness
was over, then would come the deeper, darker vacuum.

74

He stared blankly at the wall as an elderly woman volunteer pushed a wheeled cart into his room to deliver his lunch. She was a cheerful, dwarfish woman about five feet tall, in her seventies, with a wizened apple face, and she spoke in rapid German with a soft Viennese accent. Mitch couldn't understand much of what she said.

The elderly volunteer unfolded his napkin and tucked it into his gown. She pressed her lips together and leaned back to examine him. "Eat," she advised. She frowned and added, "One damned *young* American, *nein*? I do not care who you are. Eat or sickness comes."

Mitch picked up the plastic fork, saluted her with it, and began to pick at the chicken and mashed potatoes on the plate. As the old woman left, she switched on the television mounted on the wall opposite his bed. "Too damned quiet," she said, and waved her hand back and forth in his direction, delivering a chiding, long-distance slap to his face. Then she pushed the cart through the door.

The television was tuned to Sky News. First came a report on the final and years-delayed destruction of a large military satellite. Spectacular video from Sakhalin Island traced the object's last flaming moments. Mitch stared at the telephoto images of the veering, sparkling fireball. *Outdated, useless, down in flames.*

He picked up the remote and was about to shut off the television once more when an inset of an attractive young woman with short dark hair, long bangs, large eyes, illustrated a story about an important biological discovery in the United States.

"A human provirus, lurking like a stowaway in our DNA for millions of years, has been associated with a new strain of flu that strikes only women," the announcer began. "Molecular biologist Dr. Kaye Lang of Long Island, New York, has been credited with predicting this incredible invader from humanity's past. Michael Hertz is on Long Island now."

Hertz was formally sincere and respectful as he spoke with the young woman outside a large, fashionable green and white house. Lang seemed suspicious of the camera.

"We've heard from the Centers for Disease Control, and now from the National Institutes of Health, that this new variety of flu has been positively identified in San Francisco and Chicago, and there's been a pending identification in Los Angeles. Do you think this could be the flu epidemic the world has dreaded since 1918?"

Lang stared nervously at the camera. "First of all, it's not really a flu. It's not like any influenza virus, and for that matter, doesn't resemble any virus associated with colds or flu . . . It isn't like any of them. For one thing, it seems to cause symptoms only in women."

"Could you describe this new, or rather very *old*, virus for us?" Hertz asked.

"It's large, about eighty kilobases, that is—"

"More specifically, what kind of symptoms does it cause?"

"It's a retrovirus, a virus that reproduces by transcribing its RNA genetic material into DNA and then inserting it into the DNA of a host cell. Like HIV. It seems quite specific to humans—"

The reporter's eyebrows shot up. "Is it as dangerous as the AIDS virus?"

"I've heard nothing that tells me it's dangerous. It's been carried in our own DNA for millions of years; in that way, at least, it's not at all like the HIV retrovirus."

"How can our women viewers know if they've caught this flu?"

"The symptoms have been described by the CDC, and I don't know anything more than what they've announced. Slight fever, sore throat, coughing."

"That could describe a hundred different viruses."

"Right," Lang said, and smiled. Mitch studied her face, her smile, with a sharp pang. "My advice is, stay tuned."

"Then what is so significant about this virus, if it doesn't kill, and its symptoms are so slight?"

"It's the first HERV—human endogenous retrovirus—to become active, the first to escape from human chromosomes and be laterally transmitted."

"What does that mean, *laterally transmitted*?"

"That means it's infectious. It can pass from one human to another. For millions of years, it's been transmitted vertically—passed from parents to children through their genes."

"Do other old viruses exist in our cells?"

"The latest estimate is that as much of one third of our genome could consist of endogenous retroviruses. They sometimes form particles within the cells, as if they were trying to break out again, but none of these particles have been efficient—until now."

"Is it safe to say that these remnant viruses were long ago broken or dumbed down?"

"It's complicated, but you could say that."

"How did they get into our genes?"

"At some point in our past, a retrovirus infected germ-line cells, sex cells such as egg or sperm. We don't know what symptoms the disease might have caused at that time. Somehow, over time, the provirus, the viral blueprint buried in our DNA, was broken or mutated or just plain shut down. Supposedly these sequences of retroviral DNA are now just scraps. But three years ago, I proposed that provirus fragments on different human chromosomes could express all the parts of an active retrovirus. All the necessary proteins and RNA floating inside the cell could put together a complete and infectious particle."

"And so it has turned out. Speculative science bravely marching ahead of the real thing . . ."

Mitch hardly heard what the reporter said, focusing instead on Lang's eyes: large, still wary, but not missing a thing. Very bold. A survivor's eyes.

He switched the TV off and rolled over on the bed to nap, to forget. His leg ached inside the long cast.

Kaye Lang was close to grabbing the brass ring, winning a big round in the science game. Mitch, on the other hand, had been handed a solid gold ring . . . And he had fumbled it badly, dropped it on the ice, lost it forever.

* * *

An hour later, he awakened to an authoritative knock on the door. "Come in," he said, and cleared his throat.

A male nurse in starched green accompanied three men and a woman, all in late maturity, all dressed conservatively. They entered and glanced around the room as if to take note of possible escape routes. The shortest of the three men stepped forward and introduced himself. He held out his hand.

"I am Emiliano Luria, of the Institute for Human Studies," he said. "These are my colleagues at the University of Innsbruck, *Herr Professor* Friedrich Brock . . ."

Names that Mitch almost immediately forgot. The nurse brought two more chairs in from the hallway, and then stood by the door at parade rest, folding his arms and lifting his nose like a palace guard.

Luria spun his chair around, back to front, and sat. His thick round eyeglasses gleamed in the gray light through the curtained windows. He fixed his gaze on Mitch, made a small *um* sound, then glared at the nurse. "We will be fine, alone," he said. "Please go. No stories sold to the newspapers, and no big damned goose chases for bodies on the glaciers!"

The nurse nodded amiably and left the room.

Luria then asked the woman, thin and middle-aged, with a stern, strong face and abundant gray hair tied in a bun, to make sure the nurse was not listening. She stood by the door and peered out.

"Inspector Haas in Vienna assures me they have no further interest in this matter," Luria said to Mitch after these formalities were observed. "This is between you and us, and I will work with the Italians and the Swiss, if we must cross any borders." He pulled a large folding map from his pocket, and Dr. Block or Brock or whatever his name was held out a box containing a number of picture books on the Alps.

"Now, young man," Luria said, his eyes swimming behind their thick lenses. "Help us repair this damage you have done to the fabric of science. These mountains, where you were found, are not unfamiliar to us. Just one range over is where the *real* Iceman was found. There has been a lot of traffic through these mountains for thousands of years, a trade route perhaps, or paths followed by hunters."

"I don't think they were on any trade route," Mitch said. "I think they were running away."

Luria looked at his notes. The woman edged closer to the bed. "Two adults, in very good condition but for the female, with a wound of some sort in the abdomen."

"A spear thrust," Mitch said. The room fell silent for a moment.

"I have made some phone calls and talked to people who know you. I am told your father is coming here to take you from the hospital, and I have spoken with your mother—"

"Please get to the point, Professor," Mitch said.

Luria raised his eyebrows and shuffled his papers. "I am told you were a very fine scientist, conscientious, an expert at arranging and carrying out meticulous digs. You found the skeleton known as Pasco man. When Native Americans protested and claimed Pasco man as one of their ancestors, you removed the bones from their site."

"To protect them. They had washed out of a bank and were on the shore of the river. The Indians wanted to put them back in the ground. The bones were too important to science. I couldn't let that happen."

Luria leaned forward. "I believe Pasco man died from an infected spear wound in his thigh, did he not?"

"He may have," Mitch said.

"You have a nose for ancient tragedies," Luria said, scratching his ear with a finger.

"Life was pretty hard back then."

Luria nodded agreement. "Here in Europe, when we find a skeleton, there are no such problems." He smiled at his colleagues. "We have no respect for our dead—dig them up, put them on display, charge tourists to see them. So this for us is not necessarily a big black mark, though it seems to have ended your relationship with your institution."

"Political correctness," Mitch said, trying to keep the acid out of his tone.

"Possibly. I am willing to listen to a man with your experience—but, Doctor Rafelson, to our chagrin, you have described a rather gross unlikelihood." Luria pointed his pen at Mitch. "What part of your story is lie, and what part truth?"

"Why should I lie?" Mitch asked. "My life is already shot to hell."

"Perhaps to keep a hand in the science? Not to be separated so quickly from Dame Anthropology?"

Mitch smiled ruefully. "Maybe I'd do that," he said. "But I wouldn't make up a story *this* crazy. The man and woman in the cave had distinct Neandertal characteristics."

"On what criteria do you base your identification?" Brock asked, entering the conversation for the first time.

"Dr. Brock is an expert on Neandertals," Luria said respectfully.

Mitch described the bodies slowly and carefully. He could close his eyes and see them as if they floated just over the bed.

"You are aware that different researchers use different criteria for describing so-called Neandertals," Brock said. "Early, late, middle, from different regions, gracile or robust, perhaps different racial groups within the subspecies. Sometimes the distinctions are such that an observer might be misled."

"These were not *Homo sapiens sapiens*." Mitch poured himself a glass of water, offered to pour more glasses. Luria and the woman accepted. Brock shook his head.

"Well, if they *are* found, we can resolve this matter easily enough. I am curious as to your timeline on human evolution—"

"I'm not dogmatic," Mitch said.

Luria waggled his head—*comme ci, comme ça*—and turned some pages of notes under. "Clara, please hand me the biggest book there. I've marked some photographs and charts, where you might have been before you were found. Do any of these look familiar?"

Mitch took the book and propped it open awkwardly on his lap. The pictures were bright, clear, beautiful. Most had been shot in full daylight with blue skies. He looked at the marked pages and shook his head. "I don't see a frozen waterfall."

"No guide knows of a frozen waterfall anywhere near the serac, or indeed along the main mass of the glacier. Perhaps you can give us some other clue . . ."

Mitch shook his head. "I would if I could, Professor."

Luria folded his papers decisively. "I think you are a sincere young man, perhaps even a good scientist. I will tell you one thing, if you do not go talking to papers or TV. Agreed?"

"I have no reason to talk to them."

"The baby was born dead or severely injured. The back of her head is broken, perhaps by the thrust of a fire-hardened pointed stick."

Her. The infant had been a girl. For some reason, this shook Mitch deeply. He took another sip of water. All the emotion of his present position, the death of Tilde and Franco . . . The sadness of this ancient story. His eyes watered, threatened to spill over. "Sorry," he said, and dabbed away the moisture with the sleeve of his gown.

Luria observed sympathetically. "This lends your story some credibility, no? But . . ." The professor lifted his hand and pointed at the ceiling, jabbing slightly, and concluding, "Still hard to believe."

"The infant most definitely isn't *Homo sapiens neandertalensis,*" Brock said. "She has interesting features, but she is modern in all particulars. Not, however, particularly European. More Anatolian, even Turkic, but that is just a guess for now. And I know of no specimens of that sort so recent. It would be incredible."

"I must have dreamed it," Mitch said, looking away.

Luria shrugged. "When you are well, would you be willing to walk the glacier with us, look for the cave again in person?"

Mitch did not hesitate. "Of course," he said.

"I will try to arrange it. But for now—" Luria glanced down at Mitch's leg.

"At least four months," he said.

"Not a good time to be climbing, four months from now. In the late spring, then, next year." Luria stood, and the woman, Clara, took his glass and hers and set them on Mitch's tray.

"Thank you," Brock said. "I hope you are right, Dr. Rafelson. It would be a marvelous find."

They bowed slightly, formally, as they left.

12

The Centers for Disease Control and Prevention, Atlanta
SEPTEMBER

Virgin females don't get our flu," Dicken said, looking up from the papers and graphs on his desk. "Is that what you're telling me?" He raised his black eyebrows until his broad forehead was a dubious washboard of wrinkles.

Jane Salter reached forward to plump the documents again, nervous, laying them with a solicitous finality on his desk. The concrete walls of his subbasement office enlivened the rustling sound.

Many of the offices in the lower floors of Building 1 of the Centers for Disease Control and Prevention had been converted from animal labs and holding cells. Concrete dikes jutted up near the walls. Dicken sometimes imagined he could still smell the disinfectant and monkey shit.

"That's the biggest surprise that I can pull out of the data," Salter confirmed. She was one of the best statisticians they had, a whiz with the variety of desktop computers tha ..id most of their tracking, modeling, and record-keeping. "Men sometimes get it, or test positive for it, but are asymptomatic. They become vectors for females, but probably not for other males. And . . ." She finger-tapped a drum roll on the desktop. "We can't get anyone to infect themselves."

"So SHEVA is a specialist," Dicken said, shaking his head. "How the hell do we know that?"

"Look at the footnote, Christopher, and the wording. 'Women in domestic partnering situations, or those who have had extensive sexual experience.' "

"How many cases so far—five thousand?"

"Six thousand two hundred women, and only about sixty or seventy men, all partners of infected women. Only constant reexposure transmits the retrovirus."

"That's not so crazy," Dicken said. "It's not unlike HIV, then."

"Right," Salter said, mouth twitching. "God has it in for females. Infection begins with the mucosa of nasal passages and bronchia, proceeds to the mild inflammation of alveoli, enters the bloodstream—mild inflammation of ovaries . . . and then it's gone. Aching and some coughing, a sore tummy. And if the woman gets pregnant, there's a very good chance she'll miscarry."

"Mark should be able to sell that," Dicken said. "But let's make his case stronger. He needs to scare a more reliable group of voters than young women. What about the geriatric set?" He looked at her hopefully.

"Older women don't get it," she said. "Nobody younger than fourteen or older than sixty. Look at the spread." She leaned over and pointed to a pie chart. "Mean age of thirty-one."

"It's too crazy. Mark wants me to make sense of this and strengthen the surgeon general's case by four o'clock this afternoon."

"Another briefing?" Salter asked.

"Before the chief of staff and the science advisor. This is

good, this is scary, but I know Mark. Look through the files again—maybe we can come up with a few thousand geriatric deaths in Zaire."

"Are you asking me to cook the books?"

Dicken grinned wickedly.

"Then screw you, sir," Salter said mildly, head cocked. "We haven't got any more statistics out of Georgia. Maybe you could call up Tbilisi," she suggested. "Or Istanbul."

"They're tight as clams," Dicken said. "I was never able to shake much out of them, and they refuse to admit they have any cases now." He glanced up at Salter.

Her nose wrinkled.

"Please, just one elderly passenger out of Tbilisi melting on an airplane," Dicken suggested.

Salter let loose an explosion of laughter. She took off her glasses and wiped them, then replaced them. "It's not funny. The charts are looking serious."

"Mark wants to let the drama build. He's playing this one like a marlin on a line."

"I'm not very savvy about politics."

"I pretend not to be," Dicken said. "But the longer I hang around here, the more savvy I get."

Salter glanced around the small room as if it might close in on her. "Are we done, Christopher?"

Dicken grinned. "Claustrophobia acting up?"

"It's this room," Salter said. "Don't you hear them?" She leaned over the desk with a spooky expression. Dicken could not always tell whether Jane Salter was joking or serious. "The *screaming* of the monkeys?"

"Yeah," Dicken said with a straight face. "I try to stay in the field as long as possible."

In the director's office in Building 4, Augustine looked at the statistics quickly, flipped through the twenty pages of numbers and computer-generated charts, and flung them down on the desk. "All very reassuring," he said. "At this rate we'll be out of business by the end of the year. We don't even know if

SHEVA causes miscarriages in *every* pregnant woman, or whether it's just a mild teratogen. Christ. I thought this was the one, Christopher."

"It's good. It's scary, and it's public."

"You underestimate how much the Republicans hate the CDC," Augustine said. "The National Rifle Association hates us. Big tobacco hates us because we're right in their backyard. Did you see that damned billboard just down the highway? By the airport? 'Finally, a Butt Worth Kissing.' What was it—Camels? Marlboros?"

Dicken laughed and shook his head.

"The surgeon general is going right into the bear's den. She's not very happy with me, Christopher."

"There's always the results I brought back from Turkey," Dicken said.

Augustine held up his hands and rocked back in his chair, fingers gripping the edge of the desk. "One hospital. Five miscarriages."

"Five out of five pregnancies, sir."

Augustine leaned forward. "You went to Turkey because your contact said they had a virus that might abort babies. But why Georgia?"

"There was an outbreak of miscarriages in Tbilisi five years ago. I couldn't get any information in Tbilisi, nothing official. A mortician and I did a little drinking together— unofficially. He told me there had been an outbreak of miscarriages in Gordi about the same time."

Augustine had not heard this part before. Dicken had not put it in his report. "Go on," he said, only half-interested.

"There was some sort of trouble, he wouldn't come right out and say what. So—I drove to Gordi, and there was a police cordon around the town. I did some asking around in a few local road stops and heard about a UN investigation, Russian involvement. I called the UN. They told me that they were asking an American woman to help them."

"That was—"

"Kaye Lang."

"Goodness," Augustine said, and pressed his lips into a thin smile. "Woman of the hour. You knew about her work on HERV?"

"Of course."

"So . . . you thought somebody in the UN was on to something and needed her advice."

"The thought crossed my mind, sir. But they called on her because she knew forensic pathology."

"So, what were *you* thinking about?"

"Mutations. Induced birth defects. Teratogenic viruses, maybe. And I was wondering why governments wanted parents dead."

"So there we are again," Augustine said. "Back to wild-eyed speculation."

Dicken made a face. "You know me better than that, Mark."

"Sometimes I haven't the slightest idea how you get such good results."

"I hadn't finished my work. You called me back and said we had something solid."

"God knows I've been wrong before," Augustine said.

"I don't think you're wrong. This is probably just the beginning. We'll have more to go on soon."

"Is that what your instincts tell you?"

Dicken nodded.

Mark drew his brows together and folded his hands tightly on the top of the desk. "Do you remember what happened in 1963?"

"I was just a baby then, sir. But I've heard. Malaria."

"I was seven years old myself. Congress pulled the plug on all funding for the elimination of insect-borne illnesses, including malaria. The stupidest move in the history of epidemiology. Millions of deaths worldwide, new strains of resistant disease . . . a disaster."

"DDT wouldn't have worked much longer anyway, sir."

"Who can say?" Augustine peaked two fingers. "Humans think like children, leaping from passion to passion. Suddenly world health just isn't hot. Maybe we overstated our case. We're backing down from the death of the rain forests, and global warming is still just a simmer, not a boil. There haven't been any devastating worldwide plagues, and Joe Sixpack never signed on to the whole Third World guilt trip. People are getting bored with apocalypse. If we don't have a politically defensible crisis soon, on our home turf, we are going to get creamed in Congress, Christopher, and it could be 1963 all over again."

"I understand, sir."

Augustine sighed through his nose and lifted his eyes to the ranks of fluorescent lights in the ceiling. "The SG thinks our apple is still too green to put on the president's desk, so she's having a convenient megrim. She's postponed this after-noon's meeting until next week."

Dicken suppressed a smile. The thought of the surgeon general faking a headache was precious.

Augustine fixed his gaze on Dicken. "All right, you smell something, go get it. Check miscarriage records in U.S. hos-pitals for the last year. Threaten Turkey and Georgia with ex-posure to the World Health Organization. Say we'll accuse them of breaking all our cooperation treaties. I'll back you. Find out who's been to the Near East and Europe and come down with SHEVA and maybe miscarried a baby or two. We have a week, and if it's not you and a more deadly SHEVA, then I'm going to have to go with an unknown spirochete caught by some shepherds in Afghanistan . . . consorting with sheep." Augustine mocked a hangdog expression. "Save me, Christopher."

13

Cambridge, Massachusetts

Kaye was exhausted, felt like a queen, had been treated for the past week with the respect and friendly adoration of colleagues saluting one who has after some adversity been recognized as having seen farther into the truth. She had not suffered the kind of criticism and injustice others in biology had experienced in the last one hundred and fifty years—certainly nothing like what her hero, Charles Darwin, had had to face. Not even what Lynn Margulis had encountered with the theory of symbiotic evolution of eucaryotic cells. But there had been enough—

Skeptical and angry letters in the journals from old-guard geneticists convinced she was chasing after a wild hair; comments at conferences from faintly superior, smiling men and women convinced they were closer to a big discovery . . . Farther up the ladder of success, closer to the brass ring of Knowledge and Acknowledgment.

That was fine by Kaye. That was science, all too human and better for it. But then there had been Saul's personal dustup with the editor of *Cell*, stalling any chance she had of publishing there. She had gone to *Virology* instead, a good journal, but a step down the ladder. She had never made it as far as *Science* or *Nature*. She had climbed a good distance, and then stalled out.

Now, it seemed, dozens of labs and research centers were eager to have her see the results of the work they had done to confirm her speculations. For the sake of her own peace of mind, she chose to accept invitations from those faculties, centers, and labs that had shown her some encouragement in the past few years—and in particular, the Carl Rose Center for Domain Research, based in Cambridge, Massachusetts.

The Rose Center stood on a hundred acres of pines planted in the 1950s, a thick forest surrounding a cubical lab building, the cube sitting not flat on the earth but elevated on one edge. Two floors of labs lay underground, directly beneath and to the east of the elevated cube. Funded in large part by an endowment from the enormously wealthy Van Buskirk family of Boston, the Rose Center had been doing molecular biology for thirty years.

Three scientists at Rose had been given grants by the Human Genome Project—the massive, heavily funded, multilateral effort to sequence and understand the sum total of human genetics—to analyze archaic gene fragments found in the so-called junk regions of human genes known as introns. The senior scientist managing this grant was Judith Kushner, who had been Kaye's doctoral advisor at Stanford.

Judith Kushner stood just under five and a half feet high, with salted and twisted black hair, a round, wistful face that seemed always on the edge of a smile, and small, slightly protuberant black eyes. She was known internationally as a true wizard, someone who could design experiments and make any apparatus do what it was supposed to do—in other words, to fashion those repeatable experiments necessary to make science actually work.

That she spent most of her time nowadays filling out paperwork and guiding grad students and postdocs was simply the way of modern science.

Kushner's assistant and secretary, a painfully thin young redhead named Fiona Bierce, led Kaye through the maze of labs and down a central elevator.

Kushner's office lay on the zeroth floor, below ground level but above the basement: windowless, concrete walls painted a pleasant light beige. The walls were crammed with neatly arranged texts and bound journals. Four computers hummed faintly in one corner, including a Sim Engine supercomputer donated by Mind Design of Seattle.

"Kaye Lang, I am so *proud*!" Kushner got out of her chair, beamed, and spread her arms to embrace Kaye as she entered. She gave a little squeal and waltzed her former student around the room, smiling in professorial joy. "So tell me—who have you heard from? Lynn? The old man himself?"

"Lynn called yesterday," Kaye said, blushing.

Kushner clasped her hands together and shook them at the ceiling like a prizefighter celebrating victory. "Wonderful!"

"It's really too much," Kaye said, and at Kushner's invitation, took a seat beside the Sim Engine's broad flat display screen.

"Grab it! Enjoy it!" Kushner advised lustily. "You've earned it, dear. I saw you on television three times. Jackie Oniama on Triple C Network trying to talk science—wonderfully funny! Is she so much like a little doll in person?"

"They were all very friendly, really. But I'm exhausted from trying to explain things."

"So much to explain. How's Saul?" Kushner asked, doing well to hide some apprehension.

"He's fine. We're still trying to pin down whether we'll be going into partnership with the Georgians."

"If they don't partner with you now, they have a long way to go before they can become capitalists," Kushner said, and sat beside Kaye.

Fiona Bierce seemed happy just to listen. She grinned toothily.

"So . . ." Kushner said, staring at Kaye intently. "It's been kind of a short road, hasn't it?"

Kaye laughed. "I feel so *young*!"

"I am *so* envious. None of my crackpot theories have gotten nearly as much attention."

"Just gobs of money," Kaye said.

"Gobs and gobs. Need any?"

Kaye smiled. "Wouldn't want to compromise our professional standing."

"Ah, the big new world of cash biology, so important and secret and full of itself. Remember, my dear, women are supposed to do science differently. We listen and slog and listen and slog, just like poor Rosalind Franklin, not at all like brash little boys. And all for motives of the highest ethical purity. So—when are you and Saul to go public? My son is trying to set up my retirement account."

"Probably never," Kaye said. "Saul would hate reporting to stockholders. Besides, we have to be successful first, make some money, and that's a long way down the road."

"Enough small talk," Kushner said with finality. "I have something *interesting* to show you. Fiona, could you run our little simulation?"

Kaye moved her chair to one side. Bierce sat by the Sim Engine keyboard and cracked her knuckles like a pianist. "Judith has slaved on this for three months now," she said. "She based much of it on your papers, and the rest of it on data from three different genome projects, and when the word came out, we were ready."

"We went right to your markers and found the assembly routines," Kushner said. "SHEVA's envelope, and its little universal human delivery system. Here's an infection simulation based on lab results from the fifth floor, John Dawson's group. They infected hepatocytes in dense tissue culture. Here's what came out."

Kaye watched as Bierce played back the simulated assembly sequence. SHEVA particles entered the hepatocytes—liver cells in a lab culture dish—and shut down certain cellular functions, co-opted others, transcribed their RNA to DNA and integrated it into the cells' DNA, then began to replicate. In brilliant simulated colors, new virus particles formed naked within the cytosol—the cell's streaming internal fluid. The viruses migrated to the cell's outer membrane and pushed through to the outside world, each particle neatly wrapped in a bit of the cell's own skin.

"They deplete the membrane, but it's all rather gentle and controlled. The viruses stress the cells, but they don't kill them. And it looks like about one in twenty of the virus particles are viable—five times better than HIV."

The simulation suddenly zoomed in to molecules created along with the viruses, wrapped in cell transport packages called vesicles and pushed out with the new infectious particles. They were labeled in bright orange: PGA? and PGE?

"Hold it there, Fiona." Kushner pointed and tapped her finger on the orange letters. "SHEVA doesn't carry everything it needs to cause Herod's flu. We kept finding a large clump of proteins in SHEVA-infected cells, not coded for in SHEVA, and like nothing I've seen. And then—the clump would break down, there would be all these smaller proteins that shouldn't have been there."

"We looked for proteins that were changing our cell cultures," Bierce said. "Really doing a number on them. We puzzled over this for two weeks, and then we sent some infected cells over to a commercial tissue library for comparison. They separated out the new proteins, and they found—"

"This is my story, Fiona," Kushner said, waggling her finger.

"Sorry," Fiona said, smiling sheepishly. "It is just so cool we could do it this fast!"

"We finally decided that SHEVA turns on a gene in another chromosome. But how? We went looking . . . and found a SHEVA-activated gene on chromosome 21. It codes for our polyprotein, what we call the LPC, the large protein complex. A unique transcription factor specifically controls expression of this gene. We looked for the factor and found it in SHEVA's genome. A locked treasure chest on chromosome 21, and the necessary keys in the virus. They're partners."

"Astonishing," Kaye said.

Bierce ran the simulation through again, this time focusing on the action in chromosome 21—the creation of the polyprotein.

"But Kaye—darling Kaye, that is far from the last of it. We have a mystery here. The SHEVA protease cleaves three novel cyclooxygenases and lipooxygenases from the LPC, which then synthesize three different and unique prostaglandins. Two of them are new to us, really quite astonishing. All look very powerful." Kushner used a pen to point out the prostaglandins being exported from a cell. "This could explain the talk about miscarriages."

Kaye frowned in concentration.

"We calculate that a full-bore SHEVA infection could produce enough of the new prostaglandins to abort any fetus in a pregnant woman within a week."

"As if that isn't strange enough," Bierce said, and pointed to series of glycoproteins, "the infected cells make these as byproducts. We haven't analyzed them completely, but they look a lot like FSH and LH—follicle stimulating hormone and luteinizing hormone. And these peptides appear to be releasing hormones."

"The old familiar masters of female destiny," Kushner said. "Egg maturation and release."

"Why?" Kaye asked. "If they've just caused an abortion . . . why force an ovulation?"

"We don't know which activates first. It could be ovulation, then abortion," Kushner said. "Remember, this is a *liver* cell. We haven't even begun investigating infection in reproductive tissues."

"It doesn't make sense!"

"That's the challenge," Kushner said. "Whatever your little endogenous retrovirus is, it's far from harmless—at least to us women. It looks like something designed to invade, take over, and screw us up royally."

"Are you the only ones who've done this work?" Kaye asked.

"Probably," Kushner said.

"We're sending the results to NIH and the Genome Project today," Bierce said.

"And giving you advance notice," Kushner added, putting her hand on Kaye's shoulder. "I don't want you to get stepped on."

Kaye frowned. "I don't understand."

"Don't be naïve, dear," Kushner said, her eyes bright with concern. "What we're looking at could be Biblical bad news. A virus that kills babies. *Lots* of babies. Someone might regard you as a messenger. And you know what they do to messengers who bring bad news."

14

Atlanta
OCTOBER

Dr. Michael Voight strode ahead of Dicken on long, spidery legs down the hallway to the residents' lounge. "Funny you should ask," Dr. Voight said. "We're seeing lots of obstetrics anomalies. We've had staff discussions already. But not about Herod's. We see all kinds of infections, flu, of course, but we still don't have the test kits for SHEVA." He half-twisted to ask, "Cup of coffee?"

Atlanta's Olympic City Hospital was six years old, built at city and federal expense to take the pressure off other hospitals in the inner city. Private donors and a special set-aside from the Olympics had made it one of the best-equipped hospitals in the state, attracting some of the best and brightest young doctors, and a few disgruntled older ones, as well. The world of HMOs and managed care was taking a toll on skilled specialists, who had seen their incomes plummet in the past decade and their patient care practices controlled by accountants. Olympic City at least gave the specialists respect.

Voight steered Dicken into the lounge and drew a cup of coffee from a stainless-steel urn. Voight explained that interns and residents alike could use this room. "It's usually empty this time of night. It's prime time out there—time for life to lurch on and deliver its careless victims."

"What sort of anomalies?" Dicken prompted.

Voight shrugged, pulled a chair away from a Formica table, and curled up his long legs like Fred Astaire. His greens rustled; they were made of tough paper, completely disposable. Dicken sat and held his cup in his hands. He knew it might keep him awake, but he needed the focus and the energy.

"I handle extreme cases, and most of the weird ones haven't qualified for my care. But in the last two weeks . . . would you believe, seven women who can't explain their pregnancies?"

"I'm all ears," Dicken said.

Voight spread his hands and ticked off the cases. "Two that took birth control pills religiously, so to speak, and they didn't work . . . Not so unusual, maybe. Still, there was one who didn't take birth control, but said she hadn't had sex. And guess what?"

"What?"

"She was *virgo intacta*. Had heavy bleeding for a month, it went away, then morning sickness, period stopped, she went to a doctor, he told her she was pregnant, she comes here when the whole thing goes wrong. A shy young woman living with an elderly man, a real peculiar relationship. She insisted no sex was involved."

"Second coming?" Dicken asked.

"Don't be profane. I'm born again," Voight said with a twitch of his lips.

"Sorry," Dicken said.

Voight smiled half-apologetically. "Then her 'old man' comes in, tells us the real story. Turns out he's very concerned for her—wants us to know the truth so we can treat her. She's been letting him get in bed with her and rub up against her . . . Sympathy, you know. So that's how she gets pregnant the first time."

Dicken nodded. Nothing very shocking here—the versatility of life and love.

Voight continued. "It's a miscarriage. But three months later, she comes back, she's pregnant again. Two months along. Her elderly friend shows up with her, says he hasn't been rubbing against her or anything, and he knows she hasn't been seeing another man. Do we believe him?"

Dicken tilted his head to one side, lifted his eyebrows.

"All sorts of peculiar stuff going on," Voight said softly. "More than usual, I think."

"Did they complain of illness?"

"The usual. Colds, fevers, body aches. I think we may still have a couple of specimens in the lab, if you want to look at them. Have you been over to Northside?"

"Not yet," Dicken said.

"Why not Midtown? Lot more tissue for you over there."

Dicken shook his head. "How many young women with unexplained fever, nonbacterial infections?"

"Dozens. That's not unusual either. We don't keep tests more than a week; if they're negative for bacteria, we dump them."

"All right. Let's see the tissue."

Dicken took his coffee with him as he followed Voight to the elevator. The biopsy and analysis lab was in the basement, just two doors down from the morgue.

"Lab techs go home at nine." Voight switched on the lights and did a quick search in a small steel card file.

Dicken looked the lab over: three long white benches equipped with sinks, two fume hoods, incubators, cabinets neatly arrayed with brown glass and clear glass bottles filled with reagents, neatly ordered stacks of standard test kits in slim orange and green cardboard boxes, two stainless-steel refrigerators and an older white freezer; a computer connected to an ink-jet printer with an OUT OF ORDER note posted on it; and jammed in a back room behind a Dutch door, rolling stock steel storage shelving in standard gray and putty.

"They haven't put these into the computer yet; takes us about three weeks. Looks like we have one left . . . It's procedure now for the hospital, we give mothers the choice, they can have a mortician take the tissue and arrange for a funeral. Better closure that way. But we had an indigent through here, no money, no family . . . Here." He lifted a card, walked into the back room, rotated a wheel, found the shelf number on the card.

Dicken waited by the Dutch door. Voight emerged with a small jar, held it up to the brighter light in the lab room. "Wrong number, but it's the same type. This is from six months ago. I think the one I'm looking for may still be in cold saline." He handed Dicken the jar and walked to the first refrigerator.

Dicken peered at the fetus: at twelve weeks, about the size of his thumb, curled, a tiny pale extraterrestrial that had failed its tryout for life on Earth. The anomalies struck him immediately. The limbs were mere nubs, and there were protuberances around the swollen abdomen he had not seen before even on severely malformed fetuses.

The tiny face seemed unusually pinched and vacant.

"There's something wrong with its bone structure," Dicken said as Voight closed the refrigerator. The resident lifted another fetus in a moisture-frosted glass beaker covered with plastic wrap, sealed with a rubber band, and marked with a tape label.

"Lots of problems, no doubt about it," Voight said, trading jars and peering at the older specimen. "God sets up little checkpoints in every pregnancy. These two did not make the grade." He looked upward significantly. "Back to Heaven's nursery."

Dicken did not know whether Voight was expressing heart-felt philosophy or a more typical medical cynicism. He compared the cold beaker and the room-temperature jar. Both fetuses at twelve weeks, very similar.

"Can I take this one?" he asked, lifting the cold beaker.

"What, and rob our med students?" Voight shrugged. "Sign for it, call it a loan to CDC, shouldn't be a problem." He looked at the jar again. "Something significant?"

"Maybe," Dicken said. He felt a little creep of sadness and excitement. Voight gave him a more secure jar and a small cardboard box, cotton, a piece of ice in a sealed plastic bag to keep the specimen cold. They transferred the specimen quickly with a pair of wooden tongue depressors, and Dicken sealed the box with packing tape.

"If you get any more like these, let me know immediately, okay?" Dicken asked.

"Sure." In the elevator, Voight asked him, "You look a little funny. Is there something I might like to know about early, some little clue to help me better serve the public?"

Dicken knew he had kept his face deadpan, so he smiled at Voight and shook his head. "Keep track of all miscarriages," Dicken said. "Especially this type. Any correlation with Herod's flu would be dandy."

Voight curled his lip, disappointed. "Nothing official yet?"

"Not yet," Dicken said. "I'm working on a real long shot."

15

Boston

The spaghetti and pizza dinner with Saul's old colleagues from MIT was going very well. Saul had flown in to Boston that afternoon, and they had gathered at Pagliacci. Talk early in the evening in the dark old Italian restaurant ranged from mathematical analysis of the human genome to a chaotic predictor for dataflow systole and diastole on the Internet.

Kaye filled up on breadsticks and green peppers even before her lasagna arrived. Saul picked at a piece of buttered bread.

One of MIT's celebrities, Dr. Drew Miller, showed up at nine o'clock, unpredictable as always, to listen and throw in a few comments about the hot topic of bacterial community action. Saul listened intently to the legendary researcher, an expert on artificial intelligence and self-organizing systems. Miller changed seats several times, and finally tapped the shoulder of Saul's old roommate, Derry Jacobs. Jacobs grinned, got up to find another seat, and Miller placed himself beside Kaye. He picked up a breadstick from Jacobs's plate, stared at her with wide, childlike eyes, pursed his lips, and said, "You've really pissed off the old gradualists."

"Me?" Kaye asked, laughing. "Why?"

"Ernst Mayr's kids are sweating ice cubes, if they've got any sense. Dawkins is beside himself. I've been telling them for months that all that was needed was another link in the chain, and we'd have a feedback loop."

Gradualism was the belief that evolution proceeded in small moves, mutations accumulating over tens of thousands or even millions of years, usually detrimental to the individual. Beneficial mutations were selected for by conferring an advantage and increasing opportunities to gather resources and reproduce. Ernst Mayr had been a brilliant spokesman for this belief. Richard Dawkins had eloquently argued the case for the modern synthesis of Darwinism, as well as describing the so-called selfish gene.

Saul heard this and got up to stand behind Kaye, leaning over the table to hear what Miller had to say. "You think SHEVA gives us a loop?" he asked.

"Yes. Complete circle of communication between individuals in a population, outside of sex. Our equivalent of plasmids in bacteria, but of course more like phages."

"Drew, SHEVA only has eighty kb and thirty genes," Saul said. "Can't carry much information."

She and Saul had already gone over this territory before she had published her article in *Virology*. They had spoken to nobody about their particular theories. Kaye found herself a little surprised that Miller should be bringing this up. He was not known as a progressive.

"They don't need to carry all the information," Miller said. "All they need to carry is an authorization code. A key. We still don't know all the things SHEVA does."

Kaye glanced at Saul, then said, "Tell us what you've been thinking, Dr. Miller."

"Call me Drew, please. It's really not my field of endeavor, Kaye."

"It's not like you to be cagey, Drew," Saul said. "And we know you're not humble."

Miller grinned from ear to ear. "Well, I think you suspect something already. I'm sure your wife does. I've read your papers on transposable elements."

Kaye sipped from her almost-empty glass of water. "We can never be sure what to say to whom," she murmured. "We might either offend or give away the farm."

"Don't worry about original thinking," Miller said. "Someone out there is always ahead of you, but they usually haven't done the work. It's someone who's working all the time who will make the discovery. You do good work and write good papers, and this is a big jump."

"We're not sure it's *the* big jump though," Kaye said. "It may just be an anomaly."

"I don't want to push anybody into a Nobel prize," Miller said, "but SHEVA isn't really a disease-causing organism. Doesn't make evolutionary sense for something to hide this long in the human genome, and then express just to cause a mild flu. SHEVA is really just a kind of mobile genetic element, isn't it? A promoter?"

Kaye thought of the talk with Judith about the symptoms that SHEVA could cause.

Miller was perfectly willing to continue talking over her silence. "Everyone thinks that viruses, and in particular retroviruses, could be evolutionary messengers or triggers, or just random goads," Miller said. "Ever since it was found that some viruses carry snippets of genetic material from host to host. I just think there are a couple of questions you should ask yourselves, if you haven't already. What does SHEVA trigger? Let's say gradualism is dead. We get bursts of adaptive speciation whenever a niche opens up—new continents, a meteor clears out the old species. It happens fast, in less than ten thousand years; good old punctuated equilibrium. But there's a real problem. Where is all this proposed evolutionary change stored?"

"An excellent question," Kaye said.

Miller's eyes sparkled. "You've been thinking about this?"

"Who hasn't?" Kaye said. "I've been thinking about virus and retrovirus as contributors to genomic novelty. But it comes down to the same thing. So maybe there's a master biological computer in each species, a processor of some sort that tots up possible beneficial mutations. It makes decisions about what, where, and when something will change . . . Makes guesses, if you will, based on success rates from past evolutionary experience."

"What triggers a change?"

"We know that stress-related hormones can affect expression of genes. This evolutionary library of possible new forms . . ."

Miller grinned broadly. "Go on," he prompted.

"Responds to stress-produced hormones," Kaye continued. "If enough organisms are under stress, they exchange signals, reach a kind of quorum, and this triggers a genetic algorithm that compares sources of stress with a list of adaptations, evolutionary responses."

"Evolution evolving," Saul said. "The species with an adaptive computer can change more rapidly and more efficiently than hackneyed old species that don't control and select their mutations, that rely on randomness."

Miller nodded. "Good. Much more efficient than just allowing any old mutation to be expressed and probably destroy an individual or damage a population. Let's say this adaptive genetic computer, this evolutionary processor, only allows certain kinds of mutations to be used. Individuals store the results of the processor's work—which would, I assume, be . . ." Miller looked at Kaye for help, waggling his hand.

"Mutations that are grammatical," she said, "physiological statements that don't violate any important structural rules in an organism."

Miller smiled beatifically, then held his knee and began rocking gently back and forth. His large square cranium glinted as it caught the reddish gleam of an overhead light. He was thoroughly enjoying himself.

"Where would the evolutionary information be stored—throughout the genome, holographically, in different parts in different individuals, or just in germ-line cells, or . . . elsewhere?"

"Tags stored in a set-aside section of the genome in each individual," Kaye said, and then bit her tongue. Miller—and Saul, for that matter—regarded an idea as a kind of food that needed to be thoroughly shared and chewed over before it could be useful. Kaye preferred certainties before she spoke. She searched for an immediate example. "Like heat-shock response in bacteria, or single-generation climate adaptation in fruit flies."

"But a human set-aside has to be huge. We're so much more complex than fruit flies," Miller said. "Have we found it already, but just don't know what it is?"

Kaye touched Saul's arm, urging caution. They had a reputation now for riding a certain wave, and even with an old-guard scientist like Miller, a gadfly with sufficient accomplishments under his belt for a dozen careers, she felt nervous giving away their most recent thinking. It could get around: *Kaye Lang says such and such . . .*

"Nobody's found it yet," Kaye said.

"Oh?" Miller said, searching her face with a critical gaze. She felt like a deer frozen in headlights.

Miller shrugged. "Maybe not. My guess is, it's expressed only in germ-line cells. Sex cells. Haploid to haploid. It doesn't get expressed, it doesn't start work unless there's confirmation from other individuals. Pheromones. Eye contact, maybe."

"We think otherwise," Kaye said. "We think the set-aside will only carry instructions for the small alterations that lead to a new species. The rest of the details remain encoded in the genome, standard instructions for everything below that level . . . Probably working as well for chimpanzees as for us."

Miller frowned, stopped rocking. "I have to let that run around in my head for a minute." He glanced up at the dark ceiling. "Makes sense. Protect the design that you know works, at a minimum. So will these subtle changes carried in the set-aside express as units, do you think," Miller said, "one change at a time?"

"We don't know," Saul said. He folded his napkin beside his plate and thumped it with his hand. "And that's all we're going to tell you, Drew."

Miller smiled broadly. "Jay Niles has been talking with me. He thinks punctuated equilibrium is on a roll, and he thinks it's a systems problem, a network problem. Selective neural network intelligence at work. I've never much trusted talk about neural networks. Just a way of clouding the issue, of not describing what you need to describe." With complete lack of guile, Miller added, "I think I can help, if you want me to."

"Thanks, Drew. We might call on you," Kaye said, "but for right now, we'd like to have our own fun."

Miller shrugged expressively, tipped his finger to his forehead, and walked back to the other end of the table, where he picked up another breadstick and began another conversation.

On the plane to La Guardia, Saul slumped in his seat. "Drew has no idea, *no* idea."

Kaye looked up from the airplane copy of *Threads*.

"About what?" Kaye asked. "He seemed pretty on track to me."

"If you or I or anybody in biology was to talk about any kind of intelligence behind evolution . . ."

"Oh," Kaye said. She gave a delicate shudder. "The old spooky vitalism."

"When Drew talks about intelligence or mind, he doesn't mean conscious thought, of course."

"No?" Kaye said, deliciously tired, full of pasta. She pushed the magazine into the pouch under the tray table and leaned her seat back. "What *does* he mean?"

"You've already thought about ecological networks."

"Not my most original work," Kaye said. "And what does it let us predict?"

"Maybe nothing," Saul said. "But it orders my thinking in useful ways. Nodes or neurons in a network leading to neural net patterns, feeding back to the nodes the results of any network activity, leading to increased efficiencies for every node and for the network in particular."

"That's certainly clear enough," Kaye said, making a sour face.

Saul wagged his head from side to side, acknowledging her criticism. "You're smarter than I'll ever be, Kaye Lang," Saul said. She watched him closely, and saw only what she admired in Saul. The ideas had taken hold of him; he was not interested in attribution, merely in seeing a new truth. Her eyes misted, and she remembered with an almost painful intensity the emotions Saul had aroused in their first year together. Goading her, encouraging her, driving her nuts until she spoke clearly and understood the full arc of an idea, a hypothesis. "Make it clear, Kaye. That's what you're good at."

"Well . . ." Kaye frowned. "That's the way the human brain works, or a species, or an ecosystem, for that matter. And it's also the most basic definition of thought. Neurons exchange lots of signals. The signals can add or subtract from each other, neutralize or cooperate to reach a decision. They follow the basic actions of all nature: cooperation and competition: symbiosis, parasitism, predation. Nerve cells are nodes in the brain, and genes are nodes in the genome, competing and cooperating to be reproduced in the next generation. Individuals are nodes in a species, and species are nodes in an ecosystem."

Saul scratched his cheek and looked at her proudly.

Kaye waggled her finger in warning. "The Creationists will pop out of the woodwork and crow that we're finally talking about God."

"We all have our burdens." Saul sighed.

"Miller talked about SHEVA closing the feedback loop for individual organisms—that is, individual human beings. That would make SHEVA a neurotransmitter of sorts," Kaye said, mulling this over.

Saul pushed closer to her, his hands working to describe volumes of ideas. "Let's get specific. Humans cooperate for advantage, forming a society. They communicate sexually, chemically, but also socially—through speech, writing, culture. Molecules and memes. We know that scent molecules, pheromones, affect behavior; females in groups come into estrus together. Men avoid chairs where other men have sat; women are attracted to those same chairs. We're just refining the kinds of signals that can be sent, what kinds of messages, and what can carry the messages. Now we suspect that our bodies exchange endogenous virus, just as bacteria do. Is it really all that startling?"

Kaye had not told Saul about her conversation with Judith. She did not want to take the edge off their fun just yet, especially with so little actually known, but it would have to happen soon. She sat up. "What if SHEVA has multiple purposes," she suggested. "Could it also have bad side effects?"

"Everything in nature can go wrong," Saul said.

"What if it actually *has* gone wrong? What if it's been expressed in error, has completely lost its original purpose and just makes us sick?"

"Not impossible," Saul said in a way that suggested polite lack of interest. His mind was still on evolution. "I really think we should work this over in the next week and put together another paper. We have the material almost ready—we could cover all the speculative bases, bring in some of the folks in Cold Spring Harbor and Santa Barbara . . . Maybe even Miller. You just don't turn down an offer from someone like Drew. We should talk to Jay Niles, too. Get a real firm base laid down. Shall we go ahead, put our money on the table, tackle evolution?"

In truth, this possibility scared Kaye. It seemed very dangerous, and she wanted to give Judith more time to learn what SHEVA could do. More to the point, it had no connection with their core business of finding new antibiotics.

"I'm too tired to think," Kaye said. "Ask me tomorrow."

Saul sighed happily. "So many puzzles, so little time."

Kaye had not seen Saul so energetic and content in years. He tapped his fingers in rapid rhythm on the armrest and hummed softly to himself.

16

Innsbruck, Austria

Sam, Mitch's father, found him in the hospital lobby, his single bag packed and his leg wrapped in a cumbersome cast. The surgery had gone well, the pins had been removed two days before, his leg was healing on schedule. He was being discharged.

Sam helped Mitch out to the parking lot, carrying the bag for him. They pushed the seat all the way back on the passenger side of the rented Opel. Mitch fitted his leg in awkwardly, with some discomfort, and Sam drove him through the light midmorning traffic. His father's eyes darted to every corner, nervous.

"This is nothing compared to Vienna," Mitch said.

"Yes, well, I don't know how they treat foreigners. Not as bad as they do in Mexico, I guess," Sam said. Mitch's father had wiry brown hair and a heavily freckled, broad Irish face that looked as if it might smile easily enough. But Sam seldom smiled, and there was a steely edge in his gray eyes that Mitch had never learned to fathom.

Mitch had rented a one-bedroom flat on the outskirts of Innsbruck, but had not been there since the accident. Sam lit up a cigarette and smoked it quickly as they walked up the concrete stairwell to the second floor.

"You handle that leg pretty well," Sam said.

"I don't have much choice," Mitch said. Sam helped him negotiate a corner and stabilize himself on the crutches. Mitch found his keys and opened the door. The small, low-ceilinged flat had bare concrete walls and hadn't been heated for weeks. Mitch squeezed into the bathroom and realized he would have to take his craps from a certain angled altitude; the cast didn't fit between the toilet and the wall.

"I'll have to learn to aim," he told his father as he came out. This made his father grin.

"Get a bigger bathroom next time. Spare-looking place, but clean," Sam commented. He stuffed his hands in his pockets. "Your mother and I assume you're coming home. We'd like you to."

"I probably will, for a while," Mitch said. "I'm a bit of a whipped puppy, Dad."

"Bullshit," Sam murmured. "Nothing's ever whipped you."

Mitch regarded his father with a flat expression, then swiveled around on the crutches and looked at the goldfish Tilde had given him months before. She had provided a little glass bowl and a tin of food and had set it on the counter in the small kitchen. He had cared for it even after the relationship was over.

The fish had died and was now a little raft of mold floating on the surface of the half-filled bowl. Lines marked the levels of scum as the water evaporated. It was pretty gruesome.

"Shit," Mitch said. He had completely forgotten about the fish.

"What was it?" Sam asked, peering at the bowl.

"The last of a relationship that almost killed me," Mitch said.

"Pretty dramatic," Sam said.

"Pretty anticlimactic," Mitch corrected. "Maybe it should have been a shark." He offered his father a Carlsberg from the tiny refrigerator beside the kitchen sink. Sam took the beer and swallowed about a third as he walked around the living room.

"You got any unfinished business here?" Sam asked.

"I don't know," Mitch said, carrying his suitcase into the ridiculously small bedroom with bare concrete walls and a single ceiling light fixture of clear ribbed glass. He tossed it on the sleeping mat, squidgied his way around on the crutches, returned to the living room. "They want me to help them find the mummies."

"Then let them fly you back here," Sam said. "We're going home."

Mitch thought to check the answering machine. The little message counter had gone to its maximum, thirty.

"It's time to come home and get your strength back," Sam said.

That sounded pretty good, actually. Go back home at age thirty-seven and just stay there, let Mom cook and Dad teach him how to tie flies or whatever Sam was into now, visit with their friends, become a little kid again, not responsible for anything very important.

Mitch felt sick to his stomach. He pressed the rewind button on the answering machine tape. As it whirred back onto its spool, the phone chimed and Mitch answered.

"Excuse me," a tenor male voice said in English. "Is this Mitch Rafelson?"

"The very one," Mitch said.

"I just tell you this, then good-bye. Maybe you recognize my voice, but . . . no matter. They have found your bodies in the cave. The University of Innsbruck people. Without your help, I assume. They do not tell anybody yet, I don't know why. I am not joking and this is no prank, *Herr* Rafelson."

There was a distinct click and the line went dead.

"Who was it?" Sam asked.

Mitch sniffed and tried to relax his jaw. "Fuckers," he said. "They're just messing with me. I'm famous, Dad. A famous crackpot chucklehead."

"Bullshit," Sam said again, his face sharp with disgust and anger. Mitch stared at his father with a mix of love and shame; this was Sam at his most involved, his most protective.

"Let's get out of this rat hole," Sam said in disgust.

17

Long Island, New York

Kaye made Saul breakfast just after sunrise. He seemed subdued, sitting at the knotty pine table in the kitchen, slowly sipping a cup of black coffee. He had had three cups already, not a good sign. In a good mood—*Good Saul*—he never drank more than a cup a day. *If he starts smoking again . . .*

Kaye delivered his scrambled eggs and toast and sat beside him. He leaned over, ignoring her, and ate slowly, deliberately, sipping coffee between each bite. As he finished, he made a sour face and pushed the plate back.

"Bad eggs?" Kaye asked quietly.

Saul gave her a long look and shook his head. He was

moving slower, also not a good sign. "I called Bristol-Myers Squibb yesterday," he said. "They haven't cut a deal with Lado and Eliava, and apparently they don't expect to. There's something political going on in Georgia."

"Maybe that's good news?"

Saul shook his head and turned his chair toward the French doors and the gray morning outside. "I also called a friend of mine at Merck. He says there's something cooking with Eliava, but he doesn't know what it is. Lado Jakeli flew to the United States and met with them."

Kaye stopped herself in the middle of a sigh, let it out slowly, inaudibly. *Walking on eggshells again* . . . The body knew, her body knew. Saul was suffering again, worse even than he appeared. She had been through this at least five times. Any hour now he would find a pack of cigarettes, inhale the hot acrid nicotine to straighten out some of his brain chemistry, even though he hated smoking, hated tobacco.

"So . . . we're out," she said.

"I don't know yet," Saul said. He squinted at a brief ray of sun. "You didn't tell me about the grave."

Kaye's face flushed like a girl's. "No," she said stiffly. "I didn't."

"And it didn't make the newspapers."

"No."

Saul pushed his chair back and grabbed the edge of the table, then half-stood and performed a series of angled push-ups, eyes focused on the table top. When he finished, having done thirty, he sat down again and wiped his face with the folded paper towel he was using as a napkin.

"Christ, I'm sorry, Kaye," he said, his voice rough. "Do you know how that makes me feel?"

"What?"

"Having my wife experience something like that."

"You knew about my taking criminal medicine at SUNY."

"It makes me feel funny, even so," Saul said.

"You want to protect me," Kaye said, and put her hand over his, rubbing his fingers. He withdrew his hand slowly.

"Against everything," Saul said, sweeping the hand over the table, taking in the world. "Against cruelty and failure. Stupidity." His speech accelerated. "It *is* political. We're suspect. We're associated with the United Nations. Lado can't go with us."

"It didn't seem to be that way, the politics, in Georgia," Kaye said.

"What, you went with the UN team and you didn't worry it could hurt us?"

"Of course I worried!"

"Right." Saul nodded, then waggled his head back and forth, as if to relieve tension in his neck. "I'll make some more calls. Try and learn where Lado is taking his meetings. He apparently has no plans to visit us."

"Then we go ahead with the people at Evergreen," Kaye said. "They have a lot of the expertise, and some of their lab work is—"

"Not enough. We'll be competing with Eliava and whoever they go with. They'll get the patents and make it to the market first. They'll grab the capital." Saul rubbed his chin. "We have two banks and a couple of partners and . . . lots of people who were expecting this to come through for us, Kaye."

Kaye stood, her hands trembling. "I'm sorry," she said, "but that grave—*they were people,* Saul. Someone needed help finding out how they died." She knew she sounded defensive, and that confused her. "I was there. I made myself useful."

"Would you have gone if they hadn't ordered you to?" Saul asked.

"They did not order me," Kaye said. "Not in so many words."

"Would you have gone if it hadn't been official?"

"Of course not," Kaye said.

Saul reached out his hand and she held it again. He gripped her fingers with almost painful firmness, then his eyes grew heavy-lidded. He let go, stood, poured himself another cup of coffee.

"Coffee doesn't work, Saul," Kaye said. "Tell me how you are. How you feel."

"I feel fine," he said defensively. "Success is the medication I need most right now."

"This has nothing to do with business. It's like the tides. You have your own tides to fight. You told me that yourself, Saul."

Saul nodded but would not face her. "Going to the lab today?"

"Yes."

"I'll call from here after I make my inquiries. Let's put together a bull session with the team leaders this evening, at the lab. Order in pizza. A keg of beer." He made a valiant effort to smile. "We need a fallback position, and soon," he said.

"I'll see how the new work is going," Kaye said. They both knew that any revenue from current projects, including the bacteriocin work, was at least a year down the road. "How soon will we—"

"Let me worry about that," Saul said. He sidled over with a crablike motion, waggling his shoulders, self-mocking in that way only he could manage, and hugged her with one arm, dropping his face to her shoulder. She stroked his head.

"I hate this," he said. "I really, really hate being like this."

"You are very strong, Saul," Kaye whispered into his ear.

"You're my strength," he said, and pushed away, rubbing his cheek like a little boy who has been kissed. "I love you more than life itself, Kaye. You know that. Don't worry about me."

For a moment, there was a lost, feral wildness in his eyes, cornered, nowhere left to hide. Then that passed, and his shoulders drooped and he shrugged.

"I'll be fine. We'll prevail, Kaye. I just have to make some calls."

Debra Kim was a slender woman with a broad face and a smooth bowl of thick black hair. Eurasian, she tended to be quietly authoritarian. She and Kaye got along very well, though she was prickly with Saul and most men.

Kim ran the cholera isolation lab at EcoBacter with a glove of velvet-wrapped steel. The second largest lab in EcoBacter, the isolation lab functioned at level 3, more to protect Kim's supersensitive mice than the workers, though cholera was no joke. She used severe combined immunodeficient, or SCID, mice, genetically shorn of an immune system, in her research.

Kim took Kaye through the outer office of the lab and offered her a cup of tea. They engaged in small talk for several minutes, watching through a pane of clear acrylic the special sterile plastic and steel containers stacked along one wall and the active mice within.

Kim was working to find an effective phage-based therapy against cholera. The SCID mice had been equipped with human intestinal tissues, which they could not reject; they thus became small human models of cholera infection. The project had cost hundreds of thousands of dollars and had produced slim results, but still, Saul kept it going.

"Nicki down in payroll says we may have three months left," Kim said without warning, setting down her cup and smiling stiffly at Kaye. "Is that true?"

"Probably," Kaye said. "Three or four. Unless we seal a partnership with Eliava. That would be sexy enough to bring in some more capital."

"Shit," Kim said. "I turned down an offer from Procter and Gamble last week."

"I hope you didn't burn any bridges," Kaye said.

Kim shook her head. "I like it here, Kaye. I'd rather work with you and Saul than almost anyone else. But I'm not getting any younger, and I have some pretty ambitious work in mind."

"So do we all," Kaye said.

"I'm pretty close to developing a two-pronged treatment," Kim said, walking to the acrylic panel. "I've got the gene connection between the endotoxins and adhesins. The *cholerae* attach to our little intestinal mucus cells and make them drunk. The body resists by shedding the mucus membranes. Rice-water stools. I can make a phage that carries a gene that shuts down pilin production in the cholera. If they can make toxin, they can't make pili, and they can't adhere to mucus cells in the intestine. We deliver capsules of phage to cholera-infected areas, voilà. We can even use them in water treatment programs. Six months, Kaye. Just six more months and we could hand this over to the World Health Organization for seventy-five cents a dose. Just four hundred dollars to treat an entire water purification plant. Make a very tidy profit and save several thousand lives every month."

"I hear you," Kaye said.

"Why is timing everything?" Kim asked softly, and poured herself another cup of tea.

"Your work won't stop here. If we go under, you can take it with you. Go to another company. And take the mice. Please."

Kim laughed, then frowned. "That's insanely generous of you. What about you? Are you just going to bite the bullet and sink under the debts, or declare bankruptcy and go to work for the Squibb? You could get work easily enough, Kaye, especially if you strike before the publicity dies down. But what about Saul? This company is his life."

"We have options," Kaye said.

Kim drew the ends of her lips down in concern. She put her hand on Kaye's arm. "We all know about his cycles," she said. "Is this getting to him?"

Kaye half shuddered, half shivered at this, as if to throw off any unpleasantness. "I can't talk about Saul, Kim. You know that."

Kim threw her hands up in the air. "Christ, Kaye, maybe you could use all the publicity to take the company public, get some funding. Tide us over for another year . . ."

Kim had very little sense of how business worked. She was atypical this way; most biotech researchers in private companies were very savvy about business. *No francs, no Frankenstein's monster,* she had heard one of her colleagues say. "We couldn't convince anybody to back us for a public offering," Kaye said. "SHEVA has nothing to do with EcoBacter, not now at any rate. And cholera is Third World stuff. It isn't sexy, Kim."

"It isn't?" Kim said, and fluttered her hands in disgust. "Well, what in hell *is* sexy in the big old bidness world today?"

"Alliances and high profits and stock value," Kaye said. She stood and tapped the plastic panel near one of the mouse cages. The mice inside reared up and wriggled their noses.

Kaye walked into Lab 6, where she did most of her research. She had handed off her bacteriocin studies a month ago to some postdocs in Lab 5. This lab was being used by Kim's assistants for the time being, but they were at a conference in Houston, and the lab had been closed, the lights turned off.

When she wasn't working on antibiotics, her favorite subjects had been Henle 407 cultures, derived from intestinal cells; she had used them to meticulously study aspects of mammalian genomes and to locate potentially active HERV. Saul had encouraged her, perhaps foolishly; she could have focused completely on the bacteriocin research, but Saul had assured her she was a golden girl. Anything she touched would advance the company.

Now, lots of glory, but no money.

The biotech industry was unforgiving at best. Maybe she and Saul simply did not have what it took.

Kaye sat in the middle of the lab on a rolling chair that had somehow lost a wheel. She leaned to one side, hands on her knees and tears slicking her cheeks. A small and persistent voice in the back of her head told her that this could not go on. The same voice continued to warn her that she had made bad choices in her personal life, but she could not imagine how she could have done otherwise. Despite everything, Saul was not her enemy; far from being a brutal or abusive man, he was simply a victim of tragic biological imbalances. His love for her was pure enough.

What had started her tears was this treasonous inner voice that insisted that she should get out of this situation, abandon Saul, start over again; *no better time*. She could get work in a university lab, apply for funding for a pure research project that suited her, escape this damned and very literal rat race.

Yet Saul had been so loving, so *right* when she had returned from Georgia. The paper on evolution had seemed to rekindle his interest in science over profit. Then . . . the setbacks, the discouragement, the downward spiral. *Bad Saul.*

She did not want to face again what had happened eight months ago. Saul's worst breakdown had tested her own limits. His attempted suicides—two of them—had left her exhausted, and, more than she cared to admit, embittered. She had fantasized about living with other men, calm and normal men, men closer to her own age.

Kaye had never told Saul about these wishes, these dreams; she wondered if perhaps she needed to see her own psychiatrist, but she had decided against it. Saul had spent tens of thousands of dollars on psychiatrists, had gone through five regimens of drug therapy, had once suffered complete loss of sexual function and weeks of being unable to think clearly. For him, the miracle drugs did not work.

What did they have left, what did *she* have left in the way of reserves, if the tide turned again and she lost Good Saul? Being around Saul in the bad times had eaten at some other reserve—a spiritual reserve, generated during her childhood, when her parents had told her, *You are responsible for your life, your behavior. God has given you certain gifts, beautiful tools* . . .

She knew she was good; once, she had been autonomous, strong, inner-directed, and she wanted to feel that way again.

Saul had an outwardly healthy body, and intellectually a fine mind, yet there were times when, through no fault of his own, he could not control his existence. What then did this say about God and the ineffable soul, the self? That so much could be skewed by mere chemicals . . .

Kaye had never been too strong on the God thing, on faith;

the crime scenes in Brooklyn had stretched her belief in any sort of fairy-tale religion; stretched it, then broke it.

But the last of her spiritual conceits, the last tie she had to a world of ideals, was that you controlled your own behavior.

She heard someone come into the lab. The light was switched on. The broken chair scraped as she turned. It was Kim.

"*Here* you are!" Kim said, her face pale. "We've been looking all over for you."

"Where else would I be?" Kaye asked.

Kim held out a portable lab phone. "It's from your house."

18

The Centers for Disease Control and Prevention, Atlanta
"Mr. Dicken, this isn't a baby. It wasn't ever going to be a baby."

Dicken looked over the photos and analysis of the Crown City miscarriage. Tom Scarry's battered old steel desk sat at the end of a small room with pale blue walls, filled with computer terminals, adjacent to Scarry's viral pathology lab in Building 15. The top of the desk was littered with computer disks, photos, and folios filled with papers. Somehow, Scarry managed to keep his projects sorted; he was one of the best tissue analysts in the CDC.

"What is it, then?" Dicken asked.

"It may have started out as a fetus, but nearly all the internal organs are severely underdeveloped. The spine hasn't closed—spina bifida would be one interpretation, but in this case, there's a whole series of nerves branching to a follicular mass in what would otherwise be the abdominal cavity."

"Follicular?"

"Like an ovary. But containing only about a dozen eggs."

Dicken drew his brows together. Scarry's pleasant drawl matched a friendly face, but his smile was sad.

"So—it would have been a female?" Dicken asked.

"Christopher, this fetus miscarried because it is the most screwed up arrangement of cellular material I've ever seen. Abortion was a major act of mercy. It might have been female—but something went very wrong in the first week of the pregnancy."

"I don't understand—"

"The head is severely malformed. The brain is just a nubbin of tissue at the end of a shortened spinal cord. There is no jaw. The eye sockets are open at the side, like a kitten's. The skull looks more like a lemur's, what there is of it. No brain function would have been possible after the first three weeks. No metabolism could have been established after the first month. This thing functions as an organ drawing sustenance, but it has no kidneys, a very small liver, no stomach or intestines to speak of . . . A kind of heart, but again, very small. The limbs are just little fleshy buttons. It's not much more than an ovary with a blood supply. Where in hell did this come from?"

"Crown City Hospital," Dicken said. "But don't spread that around."

"My lips are sealed. How many of these have they had?"

"A few," Dicken said.

"I'd start looking for a major source of teratogens. Forget thalidomide. Whatever caused this is pure nightmare."

"Yeah," Dicken said, and pressed the bridge of his nose with his fingers. "One last question."

"Fine. Then get it out of here and let me get back to a normal existence."

"You say it has an ovary. Would the ovary function?"

"The eggs were mature, if that's what you're asking. And

one follicle appears to have ruptured. I said that in my analysis . . ." He flipped back sheets from the paper and pointed, impatient and a little cross, more with Nature than him, Dicken thought. "Right here."

"So we have a fetus that *ovulated* before it was miscarried?" Dicken asked, incredulous.

"I doubt it got that far."

"We don't have the placenta," Dicken said.

"If you get one, don't bring it to me," Scarry said. "I'm spooked enough. Oh—one more thing. Dr. Branch dropped off her tissue assay this morning." Scarry pushed a single paper across the desk, lifting it delicately to clear the other material.

Dicken picked it up. "Christ."

"You think SHEVA could have done this?" Scarry asked, tapping the analysis.

Branch had found high levels of SHEVA particles in the fetal tissue—well over a million particles per gram. The particles had suffused the fetus, or whatever they might call the bizarre growth; only in the follicular mass, the ovary, were they virtually absent. She had posted a small note at the end of the page.

These particles contain less than 80,000 nucleotides of single-stranded RNA. They all are associated with an unidentified 12,000+ kilodalton protein complex in the host cell nucleus. The viral genome demonstrates substantial homology with SHEVA. Talk to my office. I'd like to obtain fresher samples for accurate PCR and sequencing.

"Well?" Scarry persisted. "Is this caused by SHEVA or not?"

"Maybe," Dicken said.

"Does Augustine have what he needs now?"

Word spread fast at 1600 Clifton Road.

"Not a peep to anyone, Tom," Dicken said. "I mean it."

"No suh, massa." Scarry zipped his lips with a finger.

Dicken shuffled the report and the analysis into a folder and glanced at his watch. It was six o'clock. There was a possibility Augustine was still in his office.

Six more hospitals in the Atlanta area, part of Dicken's network, were reporting high rates of miscarriage, with similar fetal remnants. More and more were testing for, and finding, SHEVA in the mothers.

That was something the surgeon general would definitely want to know.

19

Long Island, New York

A bright yellow fire truck and a red Emergency Response vehicle had parked in the gravel driveway. Their rotating red and blue lights flashed and brightened the afternoon shadows on the old house. Kaye drove past the fire truck and parked behind the ambulance, eyes wide and palms damp, her heart in her throat. She kept whispering, "God, Saul. Not now."

Clouds blew in from the east, breaking up the afternoon sun, raising a gray wall behind the brilliant emergency lights. She opened the car door, stepped out, and stared at two firemen, who blandly returned her look. A slow and warmer breeze gently combed her hair. The air smelled damp, close; there might be thunder this evening.

A young paramedic approached. He looked professionally concerned and held a clipboard. "Mrs. Madsen?"

"Lang," she said. "Kaye Lang. Saul's wife." Kaye turned to gather her wits and saw for the first time the police car parked on the other side of the fire truck.

"Mrs. Lang, we received a call from a Miss Caddy Wilson—"

Caddy pushed open the front screen door and stood on the porch, followed by a police officer. The door slammed woodenly behind them, a familiar, friendly sound suddenly made ominous.

"Caddy!" Kaye waved. Caddy made a little run down the steps, clutching her light cotton skirt in front of her, wisps of pale blond hair flying. She was in her late forties, thin, with strong wiry forearms and manly hands, a handsome stalwart face, large brown eyes that now looked both concerned for Kaye and a little panicked, like a horse about to bolt.

"Kaye! I came to the house this afternoon, like always—"

The paramedic interrupted her. "Mrs. Lang, your husband is not in the house. We haven't found him."

Caddy stared at the medic resentfully, as if, of all people, this was without a doubt her story to tell. "The house is an incredible sight, Kaye. There's blood—"

"Mrs. Lang, perhaps you should talk to the police first—"

"Please!" Caddy shrieked at the paramedic. "Can't you see she's scared?"

Kaye took Caddy's hand and made a small shushing noise. Caddy wiped her eyes with her wrist and nodded, swallowing twice. The police officer joined them, tall and bull-bellied, skin deep black, hair swept neatly back above a high forehead and a patrician face; wise, tired eyes with golden sclera. She thought he was really quite striking, much more prepossessing than the others in the yard.

"Missus . . ." The officer began.

"Lang," the paramedic offered.

"Missus Lang, your house is in something of a state—"

Kaye started up the porch steps. Let them work out the jurisdiction and procedure. She had to see what Saul had done before she could have any idea as to where Saul might be, what he might have done since . . . Might be doing even now.

The police officer followed. "Does your husband have a history of self-mutilation, Missus Lang?"

"No," Kaye said through clenched teeth. "He bites his fingernails."

The house was quiet but for the tread of another police officer descending the stairs. Someone had opened the living room windows. White curtains billowed over the overstuffed couch. The second officer, in his fifties, thin and pale, slouched at the shoulders, his face seamed with perpetual worry, looked more like a mortician or a coroner. He started to talk, his words distant and liquid, but Kaye pushed up the stairs past him. The bull-bellied man followed.

Saul had hit their bedroom hard. The drawers had been pulled out and his clothes were scattered everywhere. She knew without really thinking that he had been searching for the right piece of underwear, the right pair of socks, appropriate to some special occasion.

An ashtray on the window sill was filled with cigarette butts. Camels, unfiltered. The hard stuff. Kaye hated the smell of tobacco.

The bathroom had been lightly sprayed with blood. The tub was half-filled with pinkish water, and bloody footprints went from the yellow bath mat across the black and white checkerboard tile to the old teak floor and then into the bedroom, where they stopped showing traces of blood.

"Theatrical," she murmured, glancing up at the mirror, the thin spray of blood over the glass and across the sink. "God. Not now, Saul."

"Do you have any idea where he might have gone?" the bull-bellied officer asked. "Did he do this to himself, or is there someone else involved?"

This was certainly the worst she had seen. He must have been concealing the worst of his mood, or the break had come with vicious speed, occluding every bit of sense and responsibility. He had once described the arrival of an intense depression as long dark blankets of shadow dragged by slack-faced devils in rumpled clothing.

"It's just him, just him," she said, and coughed into her fist. Surprisingly, she did not feel sick. She saw the bed, neatly made, white cover drawn up and folded precisely under the pillows, Saul trying to make order and sense out of this darkened world, and she stopped by a small circle of splatted drops of blood on the wood beside her nightstand. "Just him."

"Mr. Madsen can be quite sad at times," Caddy said from the bedroom door, long-fingered hand pressed flat and white against the dark maple jamb.

"Does your husband have a history of suicide attempts?" the medic asked.

"Yes," she said. "Never this bad."

"Looks like he cut his wrists in the tub," said the sad thin police officer. He nodded sagely. Kaye decided she would call him Mr. Death, and the other Mr. Bull. Mr. Bull and Mr. Death could tell just as much about the house as she could, possibly more.

"He got out of the tub," Mr. Bull said, "and . . ."

"Bound his wrists again, like a Roman, trying to draw out his time on Earth," Mr. Death said. He smiled apologetically at Kaye. "Sorry, ma'am."

"And then he must have gotten dressed and left the house." Just so, Kaye thought. They were so right.

Kaye sat on the bed, wishing she were the fainting type, blank this scene here and now, let others take charge.

"Mrs. Lang, we might be able to find your husband—"

"He did not kill himself," she said. She waved her hand at the blood, pointed loosely toward the hall and the bathroom. She was looking for a tiny shred of hope, thought for a moment she had grasped it. "This was bad, but he . . . as you said, he stopped himself."

"Missus Lang—" Mr. Bull began.

"We should find him and get him to the hospital," she said, and with this sudden possibility, that he might still be saved, her voice broke and she began to quietly weep.

"The boat's gone," Caddy said. Kaye stood up abruptly and walked to the window. She knelt on the window seat and looked down on the small dock thrusting from the rocky sea wall into the gray-green water of the sound. The small sail-boat was not at its moorage.

Kaye shook as if with chill. She could slowly accept now that this was going to be it. Bravery and denial could no longer compete with blood and things out of place, Saul gone awry, in the control of *Sad/Bad*, blanketed Saul.

"I can't see it," Kaye said shrilly, looking out across the choppy water. "It has a red sail. It's not out there."

They asked her for a description, a photograph, and she provided both. Mr. Bull went downstairs, out the front door, to the police car. Kaye followed him part of the way and turned to go into the living room. She was unwilling to stay in the bedroom. Mr. Death and the paramedic stayed to ask more questions, but she had very few answers. A police photographer and a coroner's assistant went up the stairs with their equipment.

Caddy watched it all with owlish concern and then cattish fascination. Finally, she hugged Kaye and said some more words and Kaye said, automatically, that she would be fine. Caddy wanted to leave but could not bring herself to do so.

At that moment, the orange cat Crickson came into the room. Kaye picked him up and stroked him, suddenly wondered if he had seen, then stooped and slipped him gently back on the floor.

The minutes seemed to last for hours. Daylight faded and rain spatted against the living room windows. Finally, Mr. Bull returned, and it was Mr. Death's turn to leave.

Caddy watched, made guilty by her horror and fascination.

"We can't clean this up for you," Mr. Bull told her. He handed her a business card. "These folks have a little business. They clean up messes like this. It's not cheap, but they do a good job. Husband and wife. Christians. Nice people."

Kaye nodded and took the card. She did not want the house now; thought about just locking the door and leaving it.

Caddy was the last to go. "Where you going to spend the night, Kaye?" she asked.

"I don't know," Kaye said.

"You're welcome to come stay with us, dear."

"Thank you," Kaye said. "There's a cot at the lab. I think I'll sleep there tonight. Could you take care of the cats? I can't . . . think about them now."

"Of course. I'll round them up. You want me to come back?" Caddy asked. "Clean up after . . . you know? The others are done?"

"I'll call," Kaye said, close to breaking down again. Caddy hugged her with painful intensity and then went to find the cats. She left ten minutes later and Kaye was alone in the house.

No note, no message, nothing.

The phone rang. She did not answer for a time, but it continued to ring, and the answering machine had been turned off, perhaps by Saul. Perhaps it *was* Saul, she realized with a shock, hating herself for having briefly lost hope, and instantly picked up the phone.

"Is this Kaye?"

"Yes." Hoarsely. She cleared her throat.

"Mrs. Lang, this is Randy Foster at AKS Industries. I need to speak with Saul. About the deal. Is he home?"

"No, Mr. Foster."

Pause. Awkward. What to say? Who to tell just now? And who was Randy Foster, and what *deal*?

"Sorry. Tell him we've just finished with our lawyers and the contracts are done. They'll be delivered tomorrow. We've scheduled a conference call for four P.M. I look forward to meeting you, Mrs. Lang."

She mumbled something and put the phone down. For a moment she thought now she *would* break, a really big break. Instead, slowly and with great deliberation, she went back up the stairs and packed a large suitcase with the clothes she might need for the next week.

Then she left the house and drove the car to EcoBacter. The building was mostly empty by dinnertime, and she was not hungry. She used her key to open the small side office where

Saul had placed a cot and blankets, then hesitated a moment before opening the door. She pushed it slowly inward.

The small windowless room was dark and empty and cool. It smelled clean. Everything in order.

Kaye undressed and got under the beige wool blanket and crisp white sheets.

That morning, early, before dawn, she awoke in a sweat, shivering, not ill, but horrified by the specter of her new self, a *widow*.

London

The reporters finally found Mitch at Heathrow. Sam sat across from him at a small table in the court around the open seafood bar while five of them, two females and three males, clustered just outside a low barrier of plastic plants surrounding the eating area and peppered him with questions. Curious and irritated travelers watched from the other tables, or brushed past carting their luggage.

"Were you the first to confirm they were prehistoric?" the older woman asked, camera clutched in one hand. She self-consciously pushed back wisps of hennaed hair, her eyes twitching left and right, finally zeroing in on Mitch for his answer.

Mitch picked at his shrimp cocktail.

"Do you think they have any connection with Pasco man in the U.S.A.?" asked one of the males, obviously hoping to provoke.

Mitch could not tell the three men apart. They were all in

their thirties, dressed in rumpled black suits, carrying steno pads and digital recorders.

"That was your last debacle, wasn't it?"

"Were you deported from Austria?" another man asked.

"How much did the dead climbers pay you to keep their secret? What were they going to charge for the mummies?"

Mitch leaned back and stretched ostentatiously, then smiled. The hennaed female duly recorded this. Sam shook his head, hunkered down as if under a rain cloud.

"Ask me about the infant," Mitch said.

"What infant?"

"Ask me about the baby. The normal baby."

"How many sites did you plunder?" Henna-hair asked cheerily.

"We found the baby in the cave with its parents," Mitch said, and stood, pushing back the cast-iron chair with an ugly scraping sound. "Dad, let's go."

"Fine," Sam said.

"Whose cave? The cavemen's cave?" the middle male asked.

"Caveman and cavewoman," the younger woman corrected.

"Do you think they kidnapped it?" Henna-hair asked, licking her lips.

"Kidnapped a baby, killed it, carried it for food perhaps into the Alps . . . Got caught in a storm, died!" Left-side-male enthused.

"What a story that would be!" Number-three-male, on the left, said.

"Ask the scientists," Mitch said, and worked his way to the counter on crutches to pay the check.

"They give out news like it was holy dispensation!" the younger woman shouted after them.

21

Washington, D.C.

Dicken sat beside Mark Augustine in the office of the surgeon general, Doctor Maxine Kirby. Kirby was of medium height, stout, with discerning almond eyes set in chocolate skin that bore only a few character lines and belied her six decades; those lines had deepened in the last hour, however.

It was eleven P.M. and they had gone through the details twice now. For the third time, the laptop automatically cycled through its slide show of charts and definitions, but only Dicken was watching.

Frank Shawbeck, deputy director of the National Institutes of Health, returned to the room through the heavy gray door after having made a visit to the lavatory down the hall. Everyone knew that Kirby did not like others using her private washroom.

The surgeon general stared up at the ceiling and Augustine gave Dicken a small, quick scowl, concerned that the presentation had not been convincing.

She lifted her hand. "Shut that down, please, Christopher. My brain is spinning." Dicken hit the ESCAPE key on the laptop and turned off the overhead projector. Shawbeck turned up the office lights and shoved his hands into his pockets. He took a position of loyal support on the corner of Kirby's broad maple desk.

"These domestic stats," Kirby said, "all from area hospitals—

that's a strong point, it's happening in the neighborhood . . . and we're still getting reports from other cities, other states."

"All the time," Augustine confirmed. "We're trying to be as quiet as we can, but—"

"They're getting suspicious." Kirby grabbed hold of her index finger and stared at a chipped, painted nail. The nail was teal blue. The surgeon general was sixty-one years old, but she wore teenager's enamel on her nails. "It'll be on the news any minute now. SHEVA is more than just a curiosity. It's the same as Herod's flu. Herod's causes mutations and miscarriages. By the way, that name . . ."

"Maybe a bit on the nose," Shawbeck said. "Who made it up?"

"I did," Augustine said.

Shawbeck was acting watchdog. Dicken had seen him play the adversary with Augustine before, and never knew how genuine the role was.

"Well, Frank, Mark, is this my ammunition?" Kirby asked. Before they could answer, she made an approving and speculative face, pouching out her lips, and said, "It's damned scary."

"It is that," Augustine said.

"But it doesn't make any sense," Kirby said. "Something pops out of our genes and makes monster babies . . . with a single huge ovary? Mark, what in *hell*?"

"We don't know what the etiology is, ma'am," Augustine said. "We're way behind, down to minimum staff on any single project as it is."

"We're asking for more money, Mark. You know that. But the mood in Congress is ugly. I do not want to be caught in anything like a false alarm."

"Biologically, the work is top notch. Politically, this is a ticking bomb," Augustine said. "If we don't go public soon—"

"Damn it, Mark," Shawbeck said, "we have no direct connection! People who get this flu—*all* of their tissues are suffused with SHEVA, for weeks after! What if the viruses are old and weak and don't have any oomph? They express because, what," he waved his hand, "there's less ozone and we're all getting more UV or something, like herpes coming out in a lip sore? Maybe they're harmless, maybe they have nothing to do with the miscarriages."

"I don't think it's coincidence," Kirby said. "The figures look too close. What I want to know is, why doesn't the body eat up these viruses, shed them?"

"Because they're released continuously for months," Dicken said. "Whatever the body does with them, they're still being expressed by different tissues."

"Which tissues?"

"We're not sure yet," Augustine said. "We're looking at bone marrow and lymph."

"There's absolutely no sign of viremia," Dicken said. "No swelling of the spleen and lymph nodes. Viruses all over, but no extreme reaction." He rubbed his cheek nervously. "I'd like to go over something again."

The surgeon general returned her gaze to him, and Shawbeck and Augustine, seeing her focus, grew quiet.

Dicken pulled his chair forward a couple of inches. "The women get SHEVA from steady male partners. Women who are single—women without committed partners—don't get SHEVA."

"That's stupid," Shawbeck said, his face curled in disgust. "How in hell does a disease know whether a woman is shacked up with somebody or not?" It was Kirby's turn to frown. Shawbeck apologized. "But you know what I mean," he said defensively.

"It's in the stats," Dicken countered. "We checked this out very thoroughly. It's transmitted from males to their female partners, over a fairly long exposure. Homosexual men do not transmit it to their partners. If there is no heterosexual contact, it is not passed along. It's a sexually transmitted disease, but a selective one."

"Christ," Shawbeck said, whether in doubt or awe, Dicken could not tell.

"We'll accept that for now," the surgeon general said. "What's made SHEVA come out now?"

"Obviously, SHEVA and humans have an old relationship," Dicken said. "It might be the human equivalent of a lysogenic phage. In bacteria, lysogenic phages express themselves when the bacteria are subjected to stimuli that could be interpreted as life-threatening—stress, as it were. Maybe SHEVA reacts to things that cause stress in humans. Overcrowding. Social conditions. Radiation."

Augustine shot him a warning glance.

"We're a hell of a lot more complicated than bacteria," he concluded.

"You think SHEVA is expressing now because of overpopulation?" Kirby asked.

"Perhaps, but that isn't my point," Dicken said. "Lysogenic phages can sometimes serve a symbiotic function. They help bacteria adapt to new conditions and even new sources of nutrition or opportunity by swapping genes. What if SHEVA serves a useful function in us?"

"By keeping the population down?" Shawbeck ventured skeptically. "The stress of overpopulation causes us to express little abortion experts? Wow."

"Maybe, I don't know," Dicken said, nervously wiping his hands on his pants. Kirby saw this, looked up coolly, a little embarrassed for him.

"Who *does* know?" she asked.

"Kaye Lang," Dicken said.

Augustine made a small gesture with his hand, unseen by the surgeon general; Dicken was on very thin ice. They had not discussed this earlier.

"She does seem to have gotten a leg up on SHEVA before everybody else," Kirby said. Her eyes wide, she leaned forward over her desk and gave him a challenging look. "But Christopher, how did you know that . . . Way back in August, in the Republic of Georgia? Your hunter's intuition?"

"I had read her papers," Dicken said. "What she wrote about was intrinsically fascinating."

"I'm curious. Why did Mark send you to Georgia and Turkey?" Kirby asked.

"I seldom send Christopher anywhere," Augustine said. "He has a wolf's instincts when it comes to finding our kind of prey."

Kirby kept her gaze on Dicken.

"Don't be shy, Christopher. Mark had you out scouting for a scary disease. I admire that—like preventive medicine applied to politics. And in Georgia, you encountered Ms. Kaye Lang, by accident?"

"There's a CDC office in Tbilisi," Augustine said, trying to be helpful.

"An office that Mr. Dicken did not visit, even for a social call," the surgeon general said, brows coming together.

"I went looking for her. I admired her work."

"And you said nothing to her."

"Nothing substantive."

Kirby sat back in her seat and looked to Augustine. "Can we bring her in?" she asked.

"She's having some problems," Augustine said.

"What kind of problems?" she asked.

"Her husband is missing, probably a suicide," Augustine said.

"That was over a month ago," Dicken said.

"There seems to be more trouble in store. Before he disappeared, her husband sold their company out from under her, to pay off an investment of venture capital she apparently did not know about."

Dicken had not heard about this. Obviously, Augustine had been conducting his own probe on Kaye Lang.

"Jesus," Shawbeck said. "So, she's what, a wreck, we leave her alone until she heals?"

"If we need her, we need her," Kirby said. "Gentlemen, I don't like the feel of this one. Call it a woman's intuition, having to do with ovaries and such. I want all the expert advice we can get. Mark?"

"I'll call her," Augustine said, giving in with uncharacteristic speed. He had read the breeze, saw the windsock swinging; Dicken had won a point.

"Do that," Kirby said, and swiveled in her chair to face Dicken dead on. "Christopher, for the life of me, I *still* think you're hiding something. What is it?"

Dicken smiled and shook his head. "Nothing solid."

"Oh?" Kirby raised her eyebrows. "The best virus man in the NCID? Mark says he relies on your nose."

"Sometimes Mark is too damned candid," Augustine said.

"Yeah," Kirby said. "Christopher should be candid, too. What's your nose say?"

Dicken was a little dismayed by the surgeon general's question, and reluctant to show his cards while his hand was still weak. "SHEVA is very, very old," he reiterated.

"And?"

"I'm not sure it's a disease."

Shawbeck released a quiet snort of dubiety.

"Go on," Kirby encouraged.

"It's an old part of human biology. It's been in our DNA since long before humans existed. Maybe it's doing what it's supposed to do."

"Kill babies?" Shawbeck suggested tartly.

"Regulate some larger, species-level function."

"Let's go with what's solid," Augustine suggested quickly. "SHEVA is Herod's. It causes gross birth defects and miscarriages."

"The connection is strong enough for me," Kirby said. "I think I can sell the president and Congress."

"I agree," Shawbeck said. "With some deep concerns, however. I wonder if all this mystery could catch up to us down the road a ways and bite us in the butt."

Dicken felt some relief. He had almost blown the game but had managed to hold back an ace to play later; traces of SHEVA from the corpses in Georgia. The results had just come back from Maria Konig at the University of Washington.

"I'm seeing the president tomorrow," the surgeon general said. "I have ten minutes with him. Get me the domestic stats on paper, ten copies, full color."

SHEVA would soon become an official crisis. In the politics of health, a crisis tended to be resolved using familiar science and bureaucratically tried and true routines. Until the situation showed its true strangeness, Dicken did not think anybody would believe his conclusions. He could hardly believe them himself.

Outside, under felt-colored skies, a dull November afternoon, Augustine opened the door to the government Lincoln and said, over the roof, "Whenever anyone asks you what you really think, what do you do?"

"Go with the flow," Dicken said.

"You got it, boy genius."

Augustine drove. Despite Dicken's near fumble, Augustine seemed happy enough with the meeting. "She's only got six weeks left before she retires. She's taking my name in to the White House chief of staff as a suggested replacement."

"Congratulations," Dicken said.

"With Shawbeck as a very close backup," Augustine added. "But this could do it, Christopher. This could be the ticket."

New York City

Kaye sat in a dark brown leather chair in the richly paneled office and wondered why highly paid East Coast lawyers chose such elegantly somber trappings. Her fingers pressed the brass heads of the upholstery nails on the arm.

The lawyer for AKS Industries, Daniel Munsey, stood beside the desk of J. Robert Orbison, her family's lawyer for thirty years.

Her father and mother had died five years before, and Kaye had not paid Orbison's retainer. With Saul's disappearance and the all-too-stunning news from AKS and the corporate attorney for EcoBacter, now sucking up to AKS, she had gone to Orbison in a state of shock. She had found him to be a decent and caring fellow, who said he would charge no more than he had ever charged Mr. and Mrs. Lang in their thirty years of business.

Orbison was thin as a rail, hook-nosed, bald, with age spots all over his head and down his cheeks, whiskers on his moles, loose wet lips, bleary blue eyes, but he dressed in a beautiful custom-fitted pinstripe suit with wide lapels and a tie that almost filled the V of his vest.

Munsey was in his early thirties, darkly handsome, soft-spoken. He wore a smooth tobacco-colored wool suit and knew biotech almost as well as she did; in some ways, better.

"AKS may not be responsible for the failures of Mr. Madsen," Orbison said in a strong, gentle voice, "but under the circumstances, we believe your company owes Ms. Lang due consideration."

"Monetary consideration?" Munsey lifted his hands in puzzlement. "Saul Madsen could not convince his investors to keep funding him. Apparently, he had focused on a deal with a research group in the Republic of Georgia." Munsey shook his head sadly. "My clients bought out the investors. Their price was more than fair, considering what's happened since."

"Kaye put a lot of work into the company. Compensation for intellectual property—"

"She has contributed greatly to science, not to any product a potential purchaser could possibly market."

"Then surely, fair compensation for contributing to the value of EcoBacter as a name."

"Ms. Lang was not a legal co-owner. Saul Madsen apparently never regarded his wife as more than a managerial employee."

"It is a regrettable lapse that Ms. Lang did not inquire," Orbison admitted. "She trusted her husband."

"We believe she's entitled to whatever assets remain in the estate. EcoBacter is simply no longer one of those assets."

Kaye looked away.

Orbison looked down at the glass-covered desktop. "Ms. Lang is a famous biological scientist, Mr. Munsey."

"Mr. Orbison, Ms. Lang, AKS Industries buys and sells going concerns. With Saul Madsen's death, EcoBacter is no longer a going concern. There are no valuable patents in its name, no relationships with other companies or institutions that can't be renegotiated outside our control. The one product that could be marketable, a treatment for cholera, is actually owned by a so-called employee. Mr. Madsen was remarkably generous with his contracts. We'll be lucky if the physical assets recoup ten percent of our costs. Ms. Lang, we can't even make payroll for this month. Nobody's buying."

"We believe that given five months, using her reputation, Ms. Lang could assemble a team of solid financial backers and restart EcoBacter. Employee loyalty is very high. Many have signed letters of intent to stay with Kaye and help rebuild."

Munsey raised his hands again: no go. "My clients follow their instincts. Perhaps Mr. Madsen should have chosen another kind of firm to sell his company to. With all respect to Ms. Lang, and nobody holds her in higher esteem than I do, she has performed no work of immediate commercial interest. Biotech is a highly competitive business, Ms. Lang, as you know."

"The future lies in what we can create, Mr. Munsey," Kaye said.

Munsey shook his head sadly. "You'd have my own investment in a flash, Ms. Lang. But I'm a softy. The rest of the companies . . ." He let his words trail off.

"Thank you, Mr. Munsey," Orbison said, and made a tent with his hands, on which he rested his long nose.

Munsey seemed nonplussed by this dismissal. "I'm very sorry, Ms. Lang. We're still having difficulty with our completion bond and insurance negotiations because of the way Mr. Madsen vanished."

"He's not coming back, if that's what you're worried about," Kaye said, her voice breaking. "They found him, Mr. Munsey. He's not going to come back and have a good laugh with us and tell me how to get on with my life."

Munsey stared at her.

She could not stop. The words poured out. "They found him on the rocks in Long Island Sound. He was in terrible shape. I had to identify him from our wedding ring."

"I'm deeply sorry. I hadn't heard," Munsey said.

"The final identification was made this morning," Orbison told him quietly.

"I'm so very sorry, Ms. Lang."

Munsey backed out and closed the door behind him.

Orbison watched her silently.

Kaye wiped her eyes with the backs of her hands. "I had no idea how much he meant to me, how much we had become one brain, working together. I thought I had my own mind and my own life . . . and now, I find out different. I feel less than half a human being. He's dead."

Orbison nodded.

"This afternoon I'm going back to EcoBacter and I'm going to hold a little wake with all the people there. I'm going to tell them it's time to find work, and that I'll be there right alongside them."

"You're smart and young. You'll make it, Kaye."

"I know I'll make it!" she said fiercely. She hit her knee with her fist. "Goddamn him. The . . . bastard. The *creep*. He had no goddamn right!"

"No goddamn right at all," Orbison said. "It was a cheap and dirty trick to pull on someone like you." His eyes brightened with the kind of anger and sympathy he might have carried into a courtroom, firing up his emotions like a rusty Coleman lantern.

"Yeah," she said, staring wildly around the room. "Oh, God, it is going to be so *hard*. You know what the worst part is?"

"What, dear?" Orbison asked.

"Part of me is *glad*," Kaye said, and she began to weep.

"Now, now," Orbison said, an old and weary man once more.

The Centers for Disease Control and Prevention, Atlanta
Neandertal mummies," Augustine said. He strode across Dicken's small office and shoved a folded paper onto Dicken's desk. "Time marches on. And *Newsweek*, too."

Dicken pushed aside a set of copies of infant and fetal postmortems for the last two months from Northside Hospital in Atlanta and picked up the paper. It was the *Atlanta Journal-Constitution*, and the headline read "Ice Couple Confirmed Prehistoric."

He skimmed the article with little interest, just to be polite, and looked up at Augustine.

"It's getting hot in Washington," the director said. "They've asked me to assemble a taskforce."

"You're in charge?"

Augustine nodded.

"Good news, then," Dicken said warily, sensing storms.

Augustine looked at him, deadpan. "We used the statistics you put together and it scared the hell out of the president. The surgeon general showed him one of the miscarriages. A picture, of course. She says she's never seen him so upset over a national health issue. He wants us to go public right away with the full details. 'Babies are dying,' he says. 'If we can fix it, go fix it, and now.' "

Dicken waited patiently.

"Dr. Kirby thinks this could be a full-time operation. Could bring in additional appropriations, even more funds for international efforts."

Dicken prepared to appear sympathetic.

"They don't want to distract me by appointing me to fill her shoes." Augustine's eyes became beady, hard.

"Shawbeck?"

"Got the nod. But the president can make his own pick. They'll hold a press conference on Herod's flu tomorrow. 'All-out war on an international killer.' Better than polio, and politically it's a slam dunk, unlike AIDS."

"Kiss the babies and make them well?"

Augustine did not find that funny. "Cynicism doesn't become you, Christopher. You're the idealistic type, remember?"

"I blame the charged atmosphere," Dicken said.

"Yeah. I've been told to put together my team for Kirby's and Shawbeck's approval by noon tomorrow. You're my first choice, of course. I'll be conferring with some folks at NIH and some scientific headhunters from New York this evening. Every agency director will want a piece of this. It's my job in part to feed them things they can do before they try to take over the whole problem. Can you get in touch with Kaye Lang and tell her she's going to be drafted?"

"Yes," Dicken said. His heart felt funny. He was short of breath. "I'd like to have a few picks of my own."

"Not a whole army, I hope."

"Not at first," Dicken said.

"I need a *team*," Augustine said, "not a loose bunch of fiefdoms. No prima donnas."

Dicken smiled. "A few divas?"

"If they sing in key. 'Star Spangled Banner' time. I want a background check for any sort of bad smell. Martha and Karen in human resources can arrange that for us. No flag burners, no hotheads. No fringies."

"Of course," Dicken said. "But that would leave me out."

"Boy genius." Augustine wet his finger and made a mark in the air. "I'm allowed just one. Government issue. Be in my office at six. Bring some Pepsi and Dixie cups and a tub of ice from the labs, *clean* ice, okay?"

Long Island, New York

Three moving vans stood outside the front entrance of EcoBacter as Kaye parked her car. She walked past two men dollying a stainless-steel lab refrigerator past the reception desk. Another hefted a microplate counter, and behind him, a fourth carried the body of a PC. EcoBacter was being nibbled to death by ants.

Not that it mattered. It had no blood left anyway.

She went to her office, which had not been touched yet, and closed the door forcefully behind her. Sitting in the blue office chair—worth about two hundred bucks, very comfortable—she switched on her desktop computer and logged in to her account on the International Association of Biotech Firms job board. What her agent in Boston had told her was true. At least fourteen universities and seven companies were interested in her services. She scrolled through the offers. Tenure track, start and run a small virology research lab in New Hampshire . . . professor of biological science at a private college in California, a Christian school, Southern Baptist . . .

She smiled. An offer from UCLA School of Medicine to work with an established professor of genetics—unnamed—in a research group focusing on inherited diseases and their connection with provirus activation. She marked that one.

After fifteen minutes, she leaned back and rubbed her forehead dramatically. She had always hated looking for work. But she could not let her momentum be diverted; she had not won any prizes yet, might not for years to come. It was time to take charge of her life and move out of the shallows.

She had marked three of the twenty-one offers as worth looking into, and already she was exhausted, her armpits wet with sweat.

With a sense of foreboding, she checked her e-mail. It was there that she found a curt message from Christopher Dicken at the NCID. His name sounded familiar; then she remembered, and swore at the monitor, the message it bore, the way her life was going, the whole ugly ball of wax.

Debra Kim knocked on the transparent glass of the door to her office. Kaye swore again, very loudly, and Kim peeked in, eyebrows arched.

"You yelling at me?" she asked innocently.

"I've been asked to join a team at the CDC," Kaye said, and slammed her hand on the desk.

"Government work. Great health plan. Freedom to do your own research on your own schedule."

"Saul hated working in a government lab."

"Saul was a rugged individualist," Kim said, and sat on the edge of Kaye's desk. "They're cleaning out my equipment now. I figure there's nothing left for me to do here. I've got my photos and disks and . . . Christ, Kaye."

Kaye stood up and hugged her as Kim broke into sobs. "I don't know what I'll do with the mice. Ten thousand dollars worth of mice!"

"We'll find a lab that will hold them for you."

"How can we transport them? They're full of *Vibrio*! I'll have to sacrifice them here before they take away the sterilization equipment and the incinerator."

"What do the AKS people say?"

"They're going to leave them in the containment room. They won't do anything."

"That's unbelievable."

"They say they're my patents, they're my problem."

Kaye sat again, then thumbed through her Rolodex, hoping for inspiration, but it was a futile gesture. Kim had no doubt she would find work in a month or two, even be able to carry on with her research using SCID mice. But they would have to be new mice, and she might lose six months or a year of her time.

"I don't know what to tell you," Kaye said, her voice cracking. She held up her hands, helpless.

Kim thanked Kaye—though for what, Kaye hardly knew. They hugged again, and Kim left.

There was little or nothing she could do for Debra Kim or any of the other ex-employees of EcoBacter. Kaye knew she had been as much a part of this disaster as Saul, as responsible for it through her own ignorance. She hated fund-raising, hated finances, hated looking for jobs. Was there anything practical in this world that she *did* like to do?

She reread Dicken's message. She had to find some way to get her wind back, get on her feet, join the race again. A short-term government job might be just what she needed. She could not imagine why Christopher Dicken would want her; she barely remembered the short, plumpish man in Georgia.

Using her cell phone—the lab phone lines had been disconnected—Kaye called Dicken's number in Atlanta.

25

Washington, D.C.

"We have test results from forty-two hospitals around the country," Augustine said to the president of the United States. "All instances of mutation and subsequent rejection of fetuses, of the type we are studying, have been positively associated with the presence of Herod's flu."

The president sat at the head of the large polished maple table in the Situation Room in the White House. Tall and portly, his curly head of white hair stood out like a beacon. He had been affectionately dubbed "Q-Tip" during his campaign, converting a derogatory term used by younger women to describe older men into an expression of pride and affection. Flanking him were the vice president; the Speaker of the House, a Democrat; the Senate majority leader, a Republican; Dr. Kirby; Shawbeck; the secretary of Health and Human Services; Augustine; three presidential aides, including the chief of staff; the White House liaison for public health issues; and a number of people Dicken couldn't identify. It was a very big table, and three hours had been set aside for their discussion.

Dicken had surrendered his cell phone, pager, and palmtop at the security check point before entering, as had all the others. An exploding "cell phone" on a tourist had caused considerable damage in the White House just two weeks before.

He was a little disappointed by the nature of the Situation Room—no state-of-the-art wall screens, computer consoles, threat boards. Just a large, ordinary room with a big table and lots of telephones. Still, the president was listening intently.

"SHEVA is the first confirmed instance of human-to-human transmission of endogenous retroviruses," Augustine continued. "Herod's flu is caused by SHEVA, beyond any shadow of a doubt. In my career in medicine and science, I have never seen anything quite so virulent. If a woman is in the early stages of pregnancy and contracts Herod's, her fetus—her baby—will eventually abort. Our statistics show a possibility of over ten thousand miscarriages that can already be attributed to this virus. According to our present information, men are the only source of Herod's flu."

"Horrible name, that," the president said.

"An effective name, Mr. President," Dr. Kirby said.

"Horrible and effective," the president conceded.

"We do not know what causes expression in males," Augustine said, "though we suspect some sort of pheromone triggering process, perhaps from female partners. We haven't a clue how to stop it." He handed sheets of paper around the table. "Our statisticians tell us that we could see more than two million cases of Herod's flu in the next year. Two million possible miscarriages."

The president absorbed this thoughtfully, having heard most of it from Frank Shawbeck and the secretary of Health and Human Services in earlier meetings. Repetition, Dicken thought, was necessary to help lay politicos understand just how much in the dark the scientists really were.

"I still do not understand how something from inside of us could cause so much harm," the vice president said.

"The devil within," said the Speaker.

"Similar genetic aberrations can cause cancer," Augustine said. Dicken felt that was a little broad, and Shawbeck seemed to agree. Now was the moment to deliver his pep talk, as top candidate for the rank of surgeon general, to replace Kirby.

"We are facing a problem new to medicine, no doubt about it," Shawbeck said. "But we've got HIV on the ropes. With that experience behind us, I have confidence that we can make some breakthroughs within six to eight months. We have major research centers all around the country, the world, poised to take on this problem. We have designed a national program that utilizes the resources of the NIH, CDC, and the National Center for Infectious and Allergic Diseases. We divide the pie to consume it more quickly. Never have we, as a nation, been more ready to tackle a problem of this magnitude. As soon as this program is in place, over five thousand researchers in twenty-eight centers will go to work. We will enlist the aid of private companies and researchers around the world. An international program is being planned right now. It all begins here. All we need is a quick and coordinated response from your respective branches, ladies and gentlemen."

"I don't see anybody on either side of the House who'll stand in the way of an extraordinary funding appropriations bill," the Speaker said.

"Or in the Senate," added the majority leader. "I'm impressed by the work done so far, but gentlemen, I am not as enthusiastic about our scientific ability as I would like to be. Dr. Augustine, Dr. Shawbeck, it's taken us over twenty years to even begin to get a handle on AIDS, despite pouring tens of billions of dollars into research. I know. I lost a daughter to AIDS five years ago." He stared around the table. "If this Herod's flu is so new to us, how can we expect miracles in six months?"

"Not miracles," Shawbeck said. "A beginning to understanding."

"Then how long before we have a treatment? I ask not for a cure, gentlemen. But a *treatment*? A vaccine at the very least?"

Shawbeck admitted he did not know.

"We can only proceed as fast as we can harness the power of science," the vice president said, and looked around the table a little blankly, wondering how this might go over.

"I will say again, I have my doubts," the majority leader said. "I'm wondering if this is a sign. Maybe it's time to get our house in order and look deep into our hearts, make peace with our Maker. Quite clearly, we've disturbed some powerful forces here."

The president touched his nose with his finger, his expression serious. Shawbeck and Augustine knew enough to keep quiet.

"Senator," the president said, "I pray you are wrong."

As the meeting concluded, Augustine and Dicken followed Shawbeck down a side corridor past basement offices to a rear elevator. Shawbeck was clearly angry. "What hypocrisy," he muttered. "I hate it when they invoke God." He shook his arms to loosen the tension in his neck and gave a small, crackling chuckle. "I vote for aliens, myself. Call in the *X-Files*."

"I wish I could laugh, Frank," Augustine said, "but I'm scared out of my wits. We're in uncharted territory. Half the proteins activated by SHEVA are new to us. We have no idea what they do. This could sink like a rock. I keep asking, Why me, Frank?"

"Because you're so *ambitious*, Mark," Shawbeck said. "You found this particular rock and looked under it." Shawbeck smiled a little wolfishly. "Not that you had any choice . . . in the long run."

Augustine cocked his head to one side. Dicken could smell

Augustine's nervousness. He felt a little numb, himself. *Up the wrong creek,* he thought, *and paddling like sons of bitches.*

26

Never one to sit still for long, Mitch spent a day with his parents on their small farm in Oregon, then took Amtrak to Seattle. He rented an apartment on Capitol Hill, dipping into a former retirement fund, and bought an old Buick Skylark for two thousand dollars from a friend in Kirkland.

Fortunately, this far from Innsbruck, the Neandertal mummies aroused only mild curiosity from the press. He gave one interview: to the science editor of the *Seattle Times*, who then turned around and labeled him a two-time offender against the sober, law-abiding world of archaeology.

A week after his return to Seattle, the Five Tribes Confederation in Kumash County reburied Pasco man in an elaborate ceremony on the banks of the Columbia River in eastern Washington. The Army Corps of Engineers capped the burial ground with concrete to prevent erosion. Scientists protested, but they did not invite Mitch to join the protest.

More than anything, he wanted time to be by himself and think. He could live on his savings for six months, but he doubted that would be anywhere near enough time for his reputation to cool, for him to land a new position.

Mitch sat with cast outstretched near the apartment's prominent bay window, looking down on pedestrians on

Broadway. He could not stop thinking about the mummified baby, the cave, the look on Franco's face.

He had placed the small glass tubes containing tissue from the mummies in a cardboard box filled with old photographs and stashed the box in the back of a closet. Before he did something with that tissue, he had to be clear in his own mind about what had actually been discovered.

Self-righteous anger was not productive.

He had seen the association. The female's wound matched the infant's injury. The female had given birth to the infant, or perhaps aborted it. The male had stayed with them, had taken the newborn and wrapped it in furs even though it had likely been born dead. Had the male assaulted the female? Mitch did not think so. They were in love. He was devoted to her. They were escaping from something. And how did he know all this?

It had nothing to do with ESP or channeling spirits. A substantial part of Mitch's career had been spent interpreting the ambiguities of archaeological sites. Sometimes the answers came to him in late night musings, or while sitting on rocks, staring up at the clouds or the starry night skies. Rarely the answers arrived in dreams. Interpretation was a science and an art.

Day in, day out, Mitch drew diagrams, wrote short notes, made entries in a small vinyl-bound diary. He pasted a piece of butcher paper on the wall of the small bedroom and drew a map of the cave as he remembered it. He placed paper cutouts of the mummies on the butcher paper. He sat and stared at the butcher paper and the cutouts. He bit his fingernails to the quick.

One day, he drank a six-pack of Coors in the afternoon—one of his favorite hydrators at the end of long days of digging, but this time, without digging, without purpose, just to try something different. He got sleepy and woke up at three in the morning and went for a walk on the street, past a Jack-in-the-Box, a Mexican restaurant, a bookstore, a magazine rack, a Starbuck's coffee shop.

He returned to the apartment and remembered to check his mail. There was a cardboard box. He carried it up the stairs, shaking it gently.

From a bookstore in New York, he had ordered a back issue of *National Geographic* with an article on Ötzi, the Iceman. The magazine had arrived packed with newspapers.

Devoted. Mitch knew they had been devoted to each other. The way they lay next to each other. The position of the male's arms. The male had stayed with the female when he could have escaped. What the hell—use the words. The *man* had stayed with the *woman*. Neandertals were not subhuman; it was generally recognized now that they had had speech and complex social organizations. Tribes. Nomads, traders, tool-makers, hunters and gatherers.

Mitch tried to imagine what would have driven them to hide in the mountains, in a cave behind the sheets of ice, ten or eleven thousand years ago. Perhaps the last of their kind.

Having given birth to a baby indistinguishable in most respects from a modern infant.

He ripped newspaper wrappings from around the magazine, opened it, and flipped to the multipage spread showing the Alps, the green valleys, the glaciers, the spot where the Iceman had been crudely hacked and chipped from the ice.

The Iceman was now on display in Italy. There had been an international dispute as to where the five-thousand-year-old corpse had been found, and after major research had been completed in Innsbruck, it was Italy that had finally claimed him.

Austria had clear title to the Neandertals. They would be studied at the University of Innsbruck, perhaps in the same facility where they had studied Ötzi; stored in deep cold, under controlled humidity, visible through a little window, lying near each other, as they had died.

Mitch closed the magazine and pressed his nose between two fingers, remembering the awful sense of entanglement after he had found Pasco man. *I lost my temper. I nearly went to jail. I went to Europe to try something new. I found something new. I got trapped and screwed it up. I have no credibility whatsoever. If I believe these impossible things, what can I do? I am a tomb raider. I am a criminal, a rogue, twice over.*

Idly, he smoothed out the crumpled wrappings, taken from the *New York Times*. His eye lit on an article at the bottom righthand corner of a torn sheet of newsprint. The headline read "Old Crimes, New Dawn in the Republic of Georgia." Superstition and death in the shadows of the Caucasus. Pregnant women rounded up from three towns, with their husbands or partners, and taken by soldiers and police to dig their own graves outside a town named Gordi. Seven column inches next to an ad for stock trading on the Internet.

As he finished reading the piece, Mitch shook with anger and excitement.

The women had been shot in the stomach. The men had all been shot in the groin and clubbed. The scandal was rocking the Georgian government. The government claimed the murders had occurred under the regime of Gamsakhurdia, who had been ousted in the early nineties, but some of those alleged to have been involved were still in office.

Why the men and women had been murdered was not at all clear. Some residents of Gordi accused the dead women of having consorted with the devil, asserted that their murder was necessary; they were giving birth to children of the devil, and causing other mothers to miscarry.

There was some speculation these women had suffered from an early appearance of Herod's flu.

Mitch hopped into the kitchen, catching the bare toe at the end of his cast on a chair leg. He swung back and swore, then reached down and pulled from a shallow stack of newspapers in one corner, near the gray, green, and blue plastic recycling bins, the A section of a two-day-old *Seattle Times*. Headline: an announcement about Herod's from the president, the surgeon general, and the secretary of Health and Human Services. A sidebar—by the same science editor who had judged

Mitch so severely—explained the connection between Herod's flu and SHEVA. Illness. Miscarriages.

Mitch sat in the worn chair before the window looking out over Broadway and watched his hands tremble.

"I know something nobody else knows," he said, and clamped his hands on the chair arms. "But I haven't the slightest idea *how I know it, or what in hell to do about it*!"

If ever there was a wrong man to have such an incredible insight, to make such a huge and unsubstantiated leap of judgment, it was Mitch Rafelson. Better for all concerned if he started looking for faces on Mars.

It was time to either give up and lay in several dozen cases of Coors, settle for a slow and boring decline, or to hammer together a platform he could stand on, plank by carefully researched scientific plank.

"You asshole," he said as he stood by the window, scrap of packing newspaper in one hand, front page headlines in the other. "You goddamned . . . immature . . . *asshole*!"

27

The Centers for Disease Control and Prevention, Atlanta
LATE JANUARY

Low lazy clouds, thin sunlight neutral through the windows of the office of the director. Mark Augustine stood back from the scrawl of crisscrossing lines and names on the whiteboard and clasped his elbow in his hand, rubbed his nose. At the bottom of the complex outline, below Shawbeck, the director of the NIH, and the as-yet unannounced replacement for Augustine at the CDC, lay the Taskforce for Human Provirus

Research: THUPR, pronounced like "super" with a lisp. Augustine hated this name and referred to it always as the Taskforce; just the Taskforce.

He swept his hand down the management staircases. "There it is, Frank. I leave here next week and hop on over to Bethesda, at the very bottom of the whiteboard jumble. Thirty-three steps down. This is what it's come to. Bureaucracy at its finest."

Frank Shawbeck leaned back in his chair. "It could have been worse. We spent most of the month trimming it down."

"It could be less of a nightmare. It's still a nightmare."

"At least you know who *your* boss is. I'm answerable to both HHS and the president," Shawbeck said. The news had arrived two days earlier. Shawbeck would remain at NIH, but was moving up to be director. "Right in the middle of the old cyclone. Frankly, I'm glad Maxine has decided not to step down. She's a much better lightning rod than I am."

"Don't fool yourself," Augustine said. "She's a better politician than either of us. We'll take the bolt when it comes."

"If it comes," Shawbeck said, but his face was sober.

"*When,* Frank," Augustine repeated. He gave Shawbeck his characteristic grin-grimace. "WHO wants us to coordinate on all outside investigations—and they want to come into the U.S. and run their own tests. Commonwealth of Independent States is dead in the water . . . Russia lorded it over the republics for too long. No coordination possible there, and Dicken still hasn't been able to get a peep out of Georgia and Azerbaijan. We won't be allowed to investigate there until the political situation stabilizes, whatever that means."

"How bad is it there?" Shawbeck asked.

"Bad, that's all we know. They aren't asking for help. They've had Herod's for ten or twenty years, maybe longer . . . and they've been dealing with it in their own way, on a local level."

"With massacres."

Augustine nodded. "They don't want that to come out, and

they certainly don't want us saying SHEVA originated with them. The pride of fresh nationalism. We're going to keep it quiet as long as we can, just to have some leverage there."

"Jesus. What about Turkey?"

"They've accepted our help, let our inspectors in, but they won't let us look along the borders with either Iraq or Georgia."

"Where's Dicken now?"

"In Geneva."

"He's keeping WHO in the loop?"

"Every step of the way," Augustine said. "Carbon-copy reports to WHO and UNICEF. The Senate's screaming again. They're threatening to delay UN payments until we get a clear picture of who's paying for what on the world scene. They don't want us holding the tab on whatever treatment we come up with—and they can't believe it won't be us who comes up with a treatment."

Shawbeck lifted his hand. "It probably *will* be us. I've got meetings scheduled with four CEOs tomorrow—Merck, Schering Plough, Lilly, Bristol-Myers," he said. "Americol and Euricol next week. They want to talk sharing and subsidies. As if that isn't enough, Dr. Gallo's coming in this afternoon—he wants to have access to all of our research."

"This has nothing to do with HIV," Augustine said.

"He claims there might be similar receptor activity. It's a long shot, but he's famous and he has a lot of clout on the Hill. And apparently he can help us with the French, now that they're cooperating again."

"How are we going to treat this, Frank? Hell, my people have found SHEVA in every ape from green monkeys to highland gorillas."

"It's too early for pessimism," Shawbeck said. "It's only been three months."

"We have forty thousand confirmed cases of Herod's on the Eastern Seaboard alone, Frank! *There is nothing on the horizon!*" Augustine pounded the whiteboard with his fist.

Shawbeck shook his head and held up both hands, making little shushing noises.

Augustine dropped his voice and let his shoulders slump. Then he picked up a cloth and meticulously wiped the edge of his hand where it had smeared across the ink on the board. "On the bright side, the message is getting out," he said. "We've had two million hits on our Herod's web site. But did you hear Audrey Korda on *Larry King Live* last night?"

"No," Shawbeck said.

"She practically calls men devils incarnate. Says women could get along without us, that we should be put in quarantine . . . *Pfft!*" He shot out his hand. "No more sex, no more SHEVA."

Shawbeck's eyes glittered like little wet stones. "Maybe she's right, Mark. Have you seen the surgeon general's list of extreme measures?"

Augustine ran his hand back through his sandy hair. "I hope to hell it never leaks."

Long Island, New York

Toothpaste dribbles lay like little blue tadpoles in the bottom of the sink. Kaye finished washing out her mouth, spat water in an arc to swirl the tadpoles down the drain, and wiped her face on a towel. She stood in the bathroom doorway and glanced down the long upstairs hall at the closed master bedroom door.

This was her last night in the house; she had slept in the guest bedroom. Another moving van—a small one—was arriving at eleven this morning to remove what few belongings she wanted to take with her. Caddy was adopting Crickson and Temin.

The house was up for sale. In a booming market, she would get top dollar. That at least was protected from their creditors. Saul had put the house in her name.

She chose her clothes for the day—plain white panties and bra, a blouse and cream sweater combination, pale blue slacks—and rolled the few items of wardrobe that hadn't already been packed into a suitcase. She was weary of dealing with stuff, apportioning this and that to Saul's sister, marking bags for Goodwill, other bags for trash.

It had taken Kaye almost a week to remove those marks of their life together that she did not want to take with her and that the real estate agent thought might "color" the place for potential buyers. She had gently explained about the detrimental effect of "All these science books, the journals . . . Too abstract. Too cold. Too much the *wrong* color."

Kaye pictured snooty upper-class lookie-loos invading the house in critically mindless pairs, well-dressed in tweeds and penny loafers or draped silk and knee-length microfiber, shunning signs of true individuality or intellect, but finding hints of style from Sunday supplement magazines all too charming. Well, by itself, the house had plenty of that sort of charm. She and Saul had bought furniture and curtains and carpeting that did not overtly offend that sort of charm. Their own life, however, had to be expunged before the house could go on the market.

Their own life. Saul had ended his share of any more life. She was erasing the evidence of their time together; AKS was disbanding and scattering their professional life.

Mercifully, the agent had not mentioned Saul's bloody incident.

How long would the guilt go on? She stopped herself going down the stairs and bit the ball of her thumb. No matter how many times she tired to jerk herself up short and get back on whatever track was left to her, she would wander off into a maze of associations, emotional paths to an even deeper unhappiness. The offer from the Herod's Taskforce was a way back on a single track, her own new path, cool and solid. Nature's oddities would help her heal the oddities of her own life, and that was bizarre, but it was also acceptable, believable; she could see her life working like that.

The doorbell chimed melodiously, "Eleanor Rigby." Saul's touch. Kaye finished the descent and opened the door. Judith Kushner stood on the porch, her face tight. "I came as soon as I saw a pattern," Judith said. She wore a black wool skirt and black shoes and a white blouse, and her London Fog raincoat trailed its buckles on the step.

"Hello, Judith," Kaye said, a little at a loss. Kushner grasped the door, glanced at her to ask a sort of permission to enter, and stepped into the house. She swung off her coat and draped it over a maple silent butler.

"By pattern, I mean that I called eight people I know, and Marge Cross has contacted all of them. She drove out personally to where they live, says she's on her way to a business meeting somewhere—hell, five live around New York, so it's a good excuse."

"Marge Cross—of Americol?" Kaye asked.

"And Euricol, too. Don't think she doesn't pull all the strings overseas. Christ, Kaye, she's a great big bull of a woman—she has Linda and Herb with her now! And they're just the first."

"Please, Judith, slow down."

"Fiona was like a little mooncalf when I turned Cross down, I swear! But I hate this conglomerate shit. I hate it like fury. Call me a socialist—call me a child of the sixties—"

"Please," Kaye said, holding up her hands to stem the torrent. "It's going to take forever if you stay this angry."

Kushner stopped and glared. "You're smart, sweetie. You can figure it out."

Kaye blinked for a second or two. "Marge Cross, Americol, wants a piece of SHEVA?"

"Not only can she fill her hospitals, she can supply directly with any drug 'her' team develops. Treatment programs exclusive to Americol-associated HMOs. Plus, she announces a blue-ribbon team, and her companies' valuations go through the roof."

"She wants me?"

"I got a call from Debra Kim. She said that Marge Cross was going to put her in a lab, house her SCID mice, buy out her patent rights on the cholera treatment—for a very fair figure, enough to make her wealthy. All before there *is* a treatment. Debra wanted to know what she should tell you."

"Debra?" This was going much too fast for Kaye.

"Marge is a master at human psychology. I know. I went to medical school with her in the seventies. She took an MBA at the same time. Lots of energy, ugly as sin, no man trouble, extra time you and I might have wasted on dating . . . She jumped off the gurney in 1987, and now look at her."

"What does she want with me?"

Kushner shrugged. "You're a pioneer, you're a celebrity— Hell, Saul's made you a bit of a martyr, especially to women . . . Women who are going to come looking for treatment. You have great credentials, great publications, credibility just smeared all over you. I thought they might shoot the messenger, Kaye. Now I think they're going to offer you the gold ring."

"My God." Kaye walked into the living room with the blank walls and sat on the freshly cleaned couch. The room smelled soapy, faintly piney, like a hospital.

Kushner sniffed and frowned. "Smells like robots live here."

"The real estate agent said it should smell clean," Kaye said, stalling to buy time enough to get her wits together. "And when they cleaned upstairs . . . after Saul . . . it left a smell. Pine-Sol. Lysol. Something."

"Jesus," Kushner said softly.

"You turned down Marge Cross?" Kaye said.

"I have enough work to keep me happy for the rest of my life, sweetie. I don't need a driven money machine calling the shots. Have you seen her on TV?"

Kaye nodded.

"Don't believe her image."

A car rumbled along the driveway. Kaye looked out the front bay window and saw a large hunter-green Chrysler sedan. A young man in a gray suit stepped out and opened the right rear door. Debra Kim emerged, looked around, shielded her face against a cool wind off the water. A few flakes of snow were starting to fall.

The young man in gray opened the left side door and Marge Cross unfolded, all six feet of her, wearing a dark blue wool overcoat, her graying black hair done up in a dignified bun. She said something to the young man and he nodded, returned to the driver's side, leaned against the car as Cross and Debra Kim walked up to the porch.

"I'm flabbergasted," Kushner said. "She works faster than the speed of thought."

"You didn't know she was coming?"

"Not this soon. Should I run out the back door?"

Kaye shook her head and for the first time in days she could not help laughing. "No. I'd like to see you two argue over my soul."

"I love you, Kaye, but I know better than to argue with Marge."

Kaye stepped quickly to the front door and opened it before Cross could ring the bell. Cross broke into a broad, friendly grin, her blocky face and small green eyes brimming with motherly cheer.

Kim smiled nervously. "Hello, Kaye," she said, her face pinking.

"Kaye Lang? We haven't been introduced," Cross said.

My God, Kaye thought. *She does sound like Julia Child!*

Kaye made instant vanilla-flavored coffee from an old tin and poured it around in the china she was leaving with the house. Not for a moment did Cross make her feel as if she was serving something less than stylish and gourmet to a woman worth twenty billion dollars.

"I'm here to be up front with you. I was out seeing Debra's lab at AKS," Cross said. "She's doing very intriguing work. We have a place for her. Debra mentioned your situation . . ."

Kushner glanced at Kaye, nodded ever so faintly.

"And frankly, I've wanted to meet you for months now. I have five young men who read the literature for me—all very handsome and very smart. One of the handsomest and the smartest told me, 'Read this.' Your piece predicting expression of ancient human provirus. Wow. Now—it's more timely than ever. Kim says you're fielding an offer to work for the CDC. For Christopher Dicken."

"The Herod's Taskforce and Mark Augustine, actually," Kaye said.

"I know Mark. He delegates well. You'll be working for Christopher. He's a bright boy." Cross plowed on as if discussing gardening. "We intend to set up a world-class investigation and research team to work on Herod's. We are going to find a treatment, maybe even a cure. We'll offer the specialized treatments at all Americol hospitals, but we'll sell the kits to anybody. We have the infrastructure, my God, we have the finances . . . We partner with the CDC, and you can act as one of our reps inside HHS and NIH. It'll be like the Apollo program, government and industry working together on a huge scale, but this time, wherever we land, we stay." Cross shifted on the couch to face Kushner. "My offer to you still stands, Judith. I'd love to have you both working for us."

Kushner gave a little laugh, almost girlish. "No thanks, Marge. I'm too old to put on a new harness."

Cross shook her head. "No chafing, guaranteed."

"I'm not at all clear about doing double duty," Kaye said. "I haven't even started work with the Taskforce."

"I'm seeing Mark Augustine and Frank Shawbeck this afternoon. If you want, you can fly with me down to Washington. We can see them together. You're invited, too, Judith."

Kushner shook her head, but this time her laugh was forced.

Kaye sat silently for a few seconds, staring down at her

clasped hands, the knuckles and nails alternating white and pink as she squeezed and relaxed her fingers. She knew what she was going to say, but she wanted to hear more from Cross.

"You will never have to worry about funding for anything you care to work on," Cross said. "We'll put it in your contract. I'm that confident in you."

But do I want to be a jewel in your crown, my queen? Kaye asked herself.

"I work on my instincts, Kaye. I've already had you checked out by my human resources people. They think you'll be doing your best work in the decades to come. Work with us, Kaye. Nothing you ever do will be ignored or trivialized."

Kushner laughed again, and Cross smiled at them both.

"I want to get out of this house as soon as I can," Kaye said. "I wasn't going down to Atlanta until next week . . . I'm looking for an apartment down there now."

"I'll ask my people to take care of it. We'll find you something nice in Atlanta or Baltimore, wherever you settle."

"My God," Kaye said with a small smile.

"Something else I know is important to you. You and Saul did a lot of work in the Republic of Georgia. I may have the contacts to salvage that. I'd like to do a lot more research on phage therapy. I think I can persuade Tbilisi to pull back on the political pressure. It's all ridiculous anyway—a bunch of amateurs trying to run things."

Cross put a hand on her arm and squeezed gently. "Come with me now, fly to Washington, let's see Mark and Frank, meet with anybody else you might want to talk to, get a feel for things. Make your decision in a couple of days. Consult your attorney if you wish. We'll even provide a draft contract. If it doesn't work out, I leave you with the CDC, no gripes, no grudges."

Kaye turned to Kushner and saw on her mentor's face the same expression she had shown when Kaye had told her she was going to marry Saul. "What kind of restrictions are there, Marge?" Kushner asked quietly, folding her hands in her lap.

Cross sat back and pursed her lips. "Nothing out of the ordinary. Scientific credit goes to the team. The company PR office orchestrates all press releases and oversees all papers for timeliness of release of information. No prima donna tactics. Financial rewards are shared in a very generous royalties deal." Cross folded her arms. "Kaye, your lawyer is a little old and not too well versed on these things. Surely Judith can recommend a better one."

Kushner nodded. "I'll recommend a very good one . . . If Kaye is seriously considering your offer." Her voice was a little pinched, disappointed.

"I'm not used to being courted with so many boxes of Godivas and bunches of roses, believe me," Kaye said, staring off at the carpet corner beyond the coffee table. "I would like to know what the Taskforce expects of me before I make any decision."

"If you march into Augustine's office with me, he'll know what I'm up to. I think he'll go along."

Kaye surprised herself by saying, "Then I would like to fly to Washington with you."

"You deserve it, Kaye," Cross said. "And I need you. We're not walking into a funhouse here. I want the best researchers, the best armor I can get."

Outside, the snow was falling much faster. Kaye could see that Cross's chauffeur had moved inside the car and was talking on a cell phone. A different world, so fast, busy, connected, with so little time to actually think.

Maybe this was just what she needed.

"I'll call that attorney," Kushner said. Then, to Cross, she said, "I'd like to speak to Kaye alone for a few minutes."

"Of course," Cross said.

In the kitchen, Judith Kushner took Kaye by the arm and looked at her with a fixed fierceness Kaye had rarely seen in her.

"You realize what's going to happen," she said.

"What?"

"You're going to be a figurehead. You'll spend half your

time in big rooms talking to people with expectant smiles who'll tell you to your face whatever you want to hear, and then gossip behind your back. You'll be called one of Marge's pets, one of her waifs."

"Oh, really," Kaye said.

"You'll think you're doing great work and then one day you'll realize she's had you doing what she wants, and nothing else, all along. She thinks this is *her* world, and it works by her rules. Then someone will have to come along and rescue you, Kaye Lang. I don't know if it could ever be me. And I hope for your sake there will never be another Saul."

"I appreciate your concern. Thank you," Kaye said quietly, but with a touch of defiance. "I work by my instincts, too, Judith. And besides, I want to find out what Herod's is all about. That won't be cheap. I think she's right about the CDC. And what if we can . . . finish our work with Eliava? For Saul. In his memory."

Kushner's intensity melted and she braced herself against the wall, shaking her head. "All right."

"You make Cross sound like the devil," Kaye said.

Kushner laughed. "Not the devil. Not my cup of tea, either."

The kitchen door swung open and Debra Kim entered. She glanced between them nervously, then, pleading, said, "Kaye, it's you she wants. Not me. If you don't come on board, she'll find some way to dump my work . . ."

"I'm doing it," Kaye said, waving her hands. "But my God, I can't leave right now. The house—"

"Marge will take care of that for you," Kushner said, as if having to tutor a slow student on a subject she did not herself enjoy.

"She will," Kim affirmed quickly, her face lighting up. "She's amazing."

Taskforce Primate Lab, Baltimore
FEBRUARY

Good morning, Christopher! How's the continent?" Marian Freedman held open the back door at the top of the concrete steps. A very cold wind rushed down the alley. Dicken pulled up his knitted scarf and made a point of rubbing one bleary eye as he climbed the steps.

"I'm still on Geneva time. Ben Tice sends his regards."

Freedman saluted briskly. "Europe on the case," she called out dramatically. "How is Ben?"

"Dead tired. They did coat proteins last week. Tougher than they thought. SHEVA doesn't crystallize."

"He should have talked to me," Marian said.

Dicken took off his scarf and coat. "Got some hot coffee?"

"In the lounge." She guided him down a concrete corridor painted a bizarre orange and motioned him through a door on the left.

"How's the building?"

"It sucks. Did you hear the inspectors found tritium in the plumbing? This was a medical waste processing facility last year, but somehow or other, they got tritium in their pipes. We didn't have time to object and start looking again. What a market! So . . . It costs us ten grand to put in monitors and retrofit. Plus we have to guide a radiation inspector from the NRC through the building with his sniffer every other day."

Dicken stood by a bulletin board in the lounge. The board was divided into two sections, one a large whiteboard, the smaller, on the left, a corkboard studded with notices. *"Wanted to share: cheaper apartment!" "Can someone pick up my dogs in quarantine at Dulles next Wednesday? I'm on all day." "Anyone know day care in Arlington?" "Need a ride to Bethesda Monday. Someone from metabolic or excretion preferred: we need to talk anyway."*

His eyes misted over. He was tired, but seeing the evidence of this thing coming alive, of people coming together, moving families and changing lives, traveling from around the world, deeply affected him.

Freedman handed him his coffee in a foam cup. "It's fresh. We do good coffee."

"Diuretic," he said. "Should help you shed that tritium."

Freedman made a face.

"Have you induced expression?" Dicken asked.

"No," Freedman said. "But simian scattered ERV is so close to SHEVA in its genome that it's scary. We're just proving what we already assumed: this stuff is old. It entered the simian genome before we and the vervets parted ways."

Dicken drank his coffee quickly and wiped his mouth. "Then it isn't a disease," he said.

"Whoa. I didn't say that." Freedman took his cup and disposed of it for him. "It expresses, it spreads, it infects. That's a disease, wherever it comes from."

"Ben Tice has analyzed two hundred rejected fetuses. Every single one of them contained a large follicular mass, similar to an ovary but containing only about twenty follicles. Every single one—"

"I know, Christopher. Three or fewer erupted follicles. He sent me his report last night."

"Marian, the placentas are tiny, the amnion is just a thin little sack, and after the miscarriage, which is incredibly easy—many of the women don't even feel pain—they don't even shed their endometrium. It's as if they're still pregnant."

Freedman was becoming very agitated. "Please, Christopher—"

Two other researchers, both young black men, came in,

recognized Dicken, though they had not yet met, nodded greetings, then went to the refrigerator. Freedman lowered her voice.

"Christopher, I am not going to stand between you and Mark Augustine when the sparks fly. Yes, you've shown that the Georgian victims had SHEVA in their tissues. But their babies were not these misshapen egg-case things. They were normally developing fetuses."

"I would love to get one of them for analysis."

"Take it somewhere else, then. We are not a criminal lab, Christopher. I've got one hundred and twenty-three people here and thirty vervets and twelve chimpanzees and we are dedicated to a very focused mission. We are exploring endogenous virus expression in simian tissues. That's it." She spoke these last words in a low whisper to Dicken near the door. Then, more loudly, "So come and take a look at what we've done."

She led Dicken through a small maze of cubicle offices, each with its own little flat-screen display. They passed several women in white lab coats and a technician in green overalls. The air smelled of antiseptic until Marian opened the steel door to the main animal lab. Then, Dicken smelled the old-bread smell of monkey chow, the tang of urine and feces, and again, the smells of soap and disinfectant.

She brought him into a large concrete-walled room with three female chimpanzees, each in separate sealed plastic and steel enclosures. Each enclosure was supplied with air by its own ventilation system. A lab worker had inserted a bar clamper into the nearest enclosure, and the chimp was busily trying to push past the restraining steel posts. Slowly, the clamper closed, ratcheted down by the worker, who waited, whistling tunelessly, as the chimp finally acquiesced. The clamper held her almost flat; she could no longer bite, and only one arm waved through the bars, away from where the lab technician was going to do her work.

Marian watched, face blank, as the restrained chimp was withdrawn from the enclosure. The clamper swung around on rubber wheels and a technician took blood and vaginal swabs. The chimp shrieked protests and grimaced. Both the worker and the technician ignored her shrieks.

Marian approached the clamper and touched the chimp's extended hand. "There, Kiki. There, girl. That's my girl. We're sorry, sweety."

The chimp's fingers brushed Marian's palm repeatedly. The chimp grimaced and squirmed but no longer shrieked. When she was returned to her enclosure, Marian swiveled to face the worker and the technician.

"I'll can the next son of a bitch that treats these animals as if they're machines," she said in a low, harsh growl. "You understand? She's socializing. She's been violated and she wants to touch somebody to feel reassured. You're the closest thing she's got to friends and family. Understand me?"

The worker and technician sheepishly apologized.

Marian steamed past Dicken and jerked her head for him to follow.

"I'm sure it's going great," Dicken said, distressed by the scene. "I trust you implicitly, Marian."

Marian sighed. "Then come back to my office and let's talk some more there."

The corridor back to the office was empty, doors closed at both ends. Dicken made broad gestures as he spoke. "I've got Ben on my side. He thinks this is a significant event, not just a disease."

"So will he go up against Augustine? All our funding is predicated on finding a treatment, Christopher! If it isn't a disease, why find a treatment? People are unhappy, sick, and they think they're losing babies."

"These rejected fetuses aren't *babies*, Marian."

"Then what in hell are they? I have to go with what I know, Christopher. If we get all theoretical—"

"I'm canvassing," Dicken said. "I want to know what you think."

Marian stood behind her desk, put her hands on the Formica top, tapped her short fingernails. She looked exasperated. "I am a geneticist and a molecular biologist. I don't know shit about much else. It takes me five hours each night just to read a hundredth of what I need to keep up in my own field."

"Have you logged on to MedWeb? Bionet? Virion?"

"I don't get on the net much except to get my mail."

"Virion is a little informal netzine out of Palo Alto. Private subscription only. It's run by Kiril Maddox."

"I know. I dated Kiril at Stanford."

This brought Dicken up short. "I didn't know that."

"Don't tell anybody, please! He was a brilliant and subversive little shmuck even then."

"Scout's honor. But you should check it out. There are thirty anonymous postings there. Kiril assures me they're all legitimate researchers. The buzz is *not* about disease or treatment."

"Yes, and when they go public, I'll join you and march in to Augustine's office."

"Promise?"

"Not on your life! I am not a brilliant researcher with an international reputation to protect. I'm an assembly-line kind of gal with split ends and a lousy sex life who loves her work and wants to keep her job."

Dicken rubbed the back of his neck. "Something's up. Something really big. I need a list of good people to back me when I tell Augustine."

"Try and set him straight, you mean. He will kick your ass right out of CDC."

"I don't think so. I hope not." Then, with a twinkle and a squint, Dicken asked, "How do you know? Did you date Augustine, too?"

"He was a medical student," Freedman said. "I stayed the hell away from medical students."

Jessie's Cougar was half a flight down from the street, fronted by a small neon sign, a cast faux-wood plaque, and a polished brass handrail. Inside the long, narrow showroom, a burly man in a fake tux and black pants served beer and wine at tiny wooden tables, and seven or eight naked women, one after another, made generally unenthusiastic attempts to dance on a small stage.

A small hand-lettered sign on a music stand beside the empty cage said that the cougar was sick this week, so Jessie wouldn't be performing. Pictures of the limp cat and its pumped-up, smiling blond mistress lined the wall behind the small bar.

The room was cramped, barely ten feet across, and smoky, and Dicken felt bad the moment he sat down. He looked around the gawker's side of the floor and saw older men in business suits in groups of two or three, young men in denims, alone, all white, nursing beers in small glasses.

A man in his late forties approached a dancer just going off stage and whispered something to her and she nodded. He and his companions then filed off to a back room for some private entertainment.

Dicken had not had more than a couple of hours to himself in a month. By chance, he had this evening free, no social connections, nowhere to go but a small room at the Holiday Inn, so he had walked to the club district, past numerous police cars and a few beat cops on bike and on foot. He had spent a few minutes in a big chain bookstore, found the prospect of spending his free night just reading almost unbearable, and his feet had moved him automatically where he knew he had intended to go in the first place, if only to look upon a woman he was not connected with by business.

The dancers were attractive enough, in their early to late twenties, startling in their blunt nudity, breasts rarely natural, as far as he could judge, with pubic hair shaved to a universal small exclamation point. Not one of them looked at him as he entered. In a few minutes it would be money smiles and money eyes, but from the start, there was nothing.

He ordered a Budweiser—the choices were Coors or Bud or Bud Lite—and leaned back against the wall. The woman currently on stage was young, thin, with dramatically projecting breasts that did not match her narrow rib cage. He watched her with little interest, and when she was finished with her ten-minute gyration and a few marble-eyed glances around the room, she donned a rayon thigh-high robe and descended the ramp to mingle.

Dicken had never quite learned the ropes in these clubs. He knew about the private rooms, but not about what was allowed there. He found himself thinking less about the women and the smoke and his beer than about the Howard University Medical Center tour the next morning, and about the meeting with Augustine and the new team members in the late afternoon . . . Another very full day.

He looked at the next woman on stage, shorter and a little more filled out, with small breasts and a very narrow waist, and thought of Kaye Lang.

Dicken finished his beer and dropped a couple of quarters on the scuffed little table and pushed his chair back. A half-naked redheaded woman offered him her stocking for money, her robe draped over a lifted leg. Like a fool, he stuffed twenty into the garter belt and looked up at her with what he hoped was nonchalant command, and what he suspected was nothing more than a stiff little glance of uncertainty.

"That's a start, honey," she said, her voice small but assured. She looked around quickly. He was the biggest unaccompanied fish currently swimming in the pool. "You been working too hard, haven't you?"

"I have," he said.

"A little private dance is all you need, I think," she added.

"That would be nice," he said, his tongue dry.

"We got a place," she said. "But you know the rules, honey? I do all the touching. Management wants you to stay in your seat. It's fun."

It sounded awful. He went with her anyway, into a small room near the back of the building, one of eight or ten on the second floor, each the size of a bedroom and empty of furniture except for a small stage and a folding chair or two. He sat in the folding chair as the woman let slip her robe. She wore a tiny thong.

"My name is Danielle," she said. She put her finger to her lips when he started to speak. "Don't tell me," she said. "I like mystery."

Then, from a small black purse on her arm, she withdrew a limp plastic package and unwrapped it with a practiced little sweep of her wrist. She slipped a surgical mask over her face. "Sorry," she said, voice even smaller now. "You know how it is. The girls say this new flu cuts through everything—the pill, rubbers, you name it. You don't even have to be, you know, nasty to get in trouble anymore. They say all the guys carry it. I got two kids already. I don't need time off from work just to make a little freak."

Dicken was so tired he could hardly move. She got up on stage and took a stance. "You like fast or slow?"

He stood, accidentally kicking the chair over with a loud clatter. She frowned at him, eyes narrowing and brows knitting over her mask. The mask was medicine green.

"Sorry," he said, and handed her another twenty. Then he fled the room, stumbled through the smoke, tripped over a couple of legs near the stage, climbed up the steps, held on to the brass rail for a moment, taking deep breaths.

He wiped his hand vigorously on his pants, as if he were the one who could get infected.

30

The University of Washington, Seattle

Mitch sat on the bench and stretched his arms out in the watery sunshine. He wore a Pendleton wool shirt, faded jeans, scuffed hiking boots, and no coat.

The bare trees lifted gray limbs over a trampled field of snow. Student pathways had cleared the sidewalks and left crisscross trails over the snowy lawns. Flakes fell slowly from the broken gray masses of clouds hustling overhead.

Wendell Packer approached with a narrow smile and a wave. Packer was Mitch's age, in his late thirties, tall and slender, with thinning hair and regular features marred only slightly by a bulbous nose. He wore a thick sweater and a dark blue down vest and carried a small leather satchel.

"I've always wanted to make a film about this quad," Packer said. He clasped his hands nervously.

"What sort?" Mitch asked, his heart aching already. He had had to force himself to make the call and come to the campus. Mitch was trying to learn to ignore the nervousness of former colleagues and scientist friends.

"Just one scene. Snow covering the ground in January; plum blossoms in April. A pretty girl walking, right about there. Slow fade: she's surrounded by falling flakes, and they turn to petals." Packer pointed along the path where students slogged to their classes. He made a swipe at the slush on the bench and sat beside Mitch. "You could have come to my office. You're not a pariah, Mitch. Nobody's going to kick you off campus."

Mitch shrugged. "I've become a wild man, Wendell. I don't get much sleep. I have a stack of textbooks in my apartment . . . I read biology all day long. I don't know where I need to catch up most."

"Yeah, well, say good-bye to *élan vital*. We're engineers now."

"I want to buy you lunch and ask a few questions. And then I want to know if I can audit some classes in your department. The texts just aren't cutting it for me."

"I can ask the professors. Any classes in particular?"

"Embryology. Vertebrate development. Some obstetrics, but that's outside your department."

"Why?"

Mitch stared out over the quad at the surrounding walls of

ochre brick buildings. "I need to learn a lot of things before I shoot my mouth off or make any more stupid moves."

"Like what?"

"If I told you, you'd know for sure that I was crazy."

"Mitch, one of the best times I've had in years was when we went out to Gingko Tree with my kids. They loved it, marching all over, looking for fossils. I was staring down at the ground for hours. The back of my neck got sunburned. I realized that was why you wore a little flap on your hat."

Mitch smiled.

"I'm still a friend, Mitch."

"That really means a lot to me, Wendell."

"It's cold out here," Packer said. "Where are you taking me for lunch?"

"You like Asian?"

They sat in the Little China restaurant, in a booth by the window, waiting for their rice and noodles and curry to be brought out. Packer sipped a cup of hot tea; Mitch, perversely, drank cold lemonade. Steam clouded the window looking out on the gray Ave, so-called, not an avenue in actuality but University Street, flanking the campus. A few young kids in leather jackets and baggy pants smoked and stamped their feet around a chained newspaper rack. The snow had stopped and the streets were shiny black.

"So tell me why you need to audit classes," Packer said.

Mitch spread out three newspaper clippings on Ukraine and the Republic of Georgia. Packer read them with a frown.

"Somebody tried to kill the mother in the cave. And thousands of years later, they're killing mothers with Herod's flu."

"Ah. You think the Neandertals . . . The baby found outside the cave." Packer tilted his head back. "I'm a little confused."

"Christ, Wendell, I was *there*. I saw the baby inside the cave. I'm sure the researchers in Innsbruck have confirmed that by now, they just aren't telling anybody. I've written letters, and they don't even bother to respond."

Packer thought this over, brow deeply wrinkled, trying to

put together a complete picture. "You think you stumbled onto a little bit of punctuated equilibrium. In the Alps."

A short woman with a round pretty face brought their food and laid chopsticks beside their plates. When she left, Packer continued, "You think they've done a tissue match in Innsbruck and just won't release the results?"

Mitch nodded. "It's so far out there, as an idea, that nobody is saying a thing. It's an incredible long shot. Look, I don't want to belabor . . . I don't want to drag you down with all the details. Just give me a chance to find out whether I'm right or wrong. I'm probably so wrong I should start a new career in asphalt management. But . . . *I was there, Wendell.*"

Packer looked around the restaurant, pushed aside the chopsticks, ladled a few spoons of hot pepper sauce onto his plate, and stuck a fork into his curried pork and rice. Around a mouthful, he said, "If I let you audit some classes, will you sit way in the back?"

"I'll stand outside the door," Mitch said.

"I was joking," Packer said. "I think."

"I know you were," Mitch said, smiling. "Now I'm going to ask just one more favor."

Packer lifted his eyebrows. "You're pushing it, Mitch."

"Do you have any postdocs working on SHEVA?"

"You bet," Packer said. "The CDC has a research coordination program and we've signed on. You see all the women wearing gauze masks on campus? We'd like to help shine a little reason on this whole thing. You know . . . *Reason?*" He stared pointedly at Mitch.

Mitch pulled out his two glass vials. "These are very precious to me," he said. "I do not want to lose them." He held them out in his palm. They clinked softly together, their contents like two little snips of beef jerky.

Packer put down his fork. "What are they?"

"Neandertal tissue. One from the male, one from the female."

Packer stopped chewing.

"How much of them would you need?" Mitch asked.

"Not much," Packer said around his mouthful of rice. "If I was going to do anything."

Mitch waggled his hand and the vials slowly back and forth.

"If I were to trust you," Packer added.

"I have to trust *you*," Mitch said.

Packer squinted at the fogged windows, the kids still milling outside, laughing and smoking their cigarettes.

"Test them for what . . . SHEVA?"

"Or something like SHEVA."

"Why? What has SHEVA got to do with evolution?"

Mitch tapped the newspaper articles. "It would explain all this talk about the devil's children. Something very unusual is happening. I think it's happened before, and I found the evidence."

Packer wiped his mouth thoughtfully. "I absolutely do not believe this." He lifted the vials from Mitch's hand, stared at them closely. "They're so damned *old*. Three years ago, two of my postdocs did a research project on mitochondrial DNA sequences from Neandertal bone tissue. All that remained were fragments."

"Then you can confirm these are the real thing," Mitch said. "Dried out, degraded, but probably complete."

Packer gently set the vials on the table. "Why should I do this? Just because we're friends?"

"Because if I'm right, it's going to be the biggest scientific discovery of our time. We may finally learn how evolution works."

Packer removed his wallet and took out a twenty. "I'm paying," he said. "Big discoveries make me very nervous."

Mitch looked at him in dismay.

"Oh, I'll do it," Packer said grimly. "But only because I'm an idiot and a sucker. No more favors, please, Mitch."

31

The National Institutes of Health, Bethesda

Cross and Dicken sat opposite each other at the broad table in a small executive conference room in the Natcher Building, and Kaye sat beside Cross. Dicken fiddled with a pen, staring down at the table like a nervous little boy.

"When's Mark going to make his grand entrance?" Cross asked.

Dicken looked up and grinned. "I'd give him five minutes. Maybe less. He's not very happy about this."

Cross picked her teeth with a long chipped fingernail.

"The only thing you don't have lots of is time, right?" Dicken asked.

Cross smiled politely.

"It doesn't seem that long since Georgia," Kaye said, just to make conversation.

"Not long at all," Dicken said.

"You met in Georgia?" Cross asked.

"Just briefly," Dicken said. Before the conversation could go any further, Augustine entered. He wore an expensive gray suit that was showing a little wrinkling at the back and around the knees. He had been in a good many conferences today, Kaye guessed.

Augustine shook hands with Cross and sat. He clasped his hands loosely in front of him. "So, Marge, this is a done deal? You've got Kaye and we have to share?"

"Nothing's final yet," Cross said cheerfully. "I wanted to talk to you first."

Augustine was not convinced. "What do we get out of it?"

"Nothing you probably wouldn't have gotten anyway, Mark," Cross said. "We can work out the larger features of the picture now, and pencil in the details later."

Augustine colored a little, clamped his jaw for a moment, then said, "I do love bargaining. What do we actually need from Americol?"

"This evening I'll be having dinner with three Republican senators," Cross said. "Bible Belt types. They don't much care what I do, so long as I attend their little fund-raisers. I'll explain to them why I think the Taskforce and the whole research establishment should get even more money, and why we should set up an intranet connection between Americol, Euricol, and selected researchers in the Taskforce and the CDC. Then I'll explain the facts of life to them. About Herod's, that is."

"They're going to shout 'Act of God,' " Augustine said.

"I don't think so, actually," Cross said. "They may be smarter than you think."

"I've already explained this to every senator and most of the House of Representatives," Augustine said.

"Then we'll make a good tag team. I'll make them feel sophisticated and in the loop, something I know you're not good at, Mark. And what we share . . . will lead to a treatment, possibly even a cure, within a year. I guarantee it."

"How can you guarantee anything like that?" Augustine asked.

"As I told Kaye on the flight down here, I took her papers seriously years ago. I set some of my key people in San Diego looking into the possibility. When the news about activation of SHEVA came down, and then Herod's, I was ready. I handed it over to the good folks in our Sentinel program. They kind of parallel what you do, Christopher, but on a corporate level. We already know the structure of SHEVA's capsid coat, how SHEVA crawls into human cells, which receptors it attaches to. The CDC and the Taskforce can take half the credit eventually, and we'll take on the business of getting the treatment to everybody. We'll do it for little or nothing, of course, maybe not even break even."

Augustine looked at her with genuine surprise. Cross chuckled. She leaned over the table as if to throw a punch at him and said, "Gotcha, Mark."

"I don't believe it," Augustine said.

"Mr. Dicken says he wants to work directly with Kaye. That's fine," Cross allowed.

Augustine folded his arms.

"But that intranet will really be something. Direct, fast, best we can put together. We'll chart every damned HERV in the genome to make sure SHEVA is not duplicated somewhere, to catch us by surprise. Kaye can lead that project. The pharmaceutical applications could be wondrous, absolutely *wondrous*." Her voice broke with enthusiasm.

Kaye found herself buzzing with her own enthusiasm. Cross was something else.

"What do your people tell you about these HERV, Mark?" Cross asked.

"A lot," Augustine said. "We've concentrated on Herod's, of course."

"Do you know that the largest gene turned on by SHEVA, the polyprotein on chromosome 21, differs between simian expressions and human? That it's one of only three genes in the whole SHEVA cascade that differ in apes and humans?"

Augustine shook his head.

"We're close to knowing that," Dicken said, then glanced around in some embarrassment. Cross ignored him.

"What we're looking at is an archaeological catalog of human disease, going back millions of years," Cross said. "At least one old damned visionary has seen this already and we're going to beat CDC to the ultimate description ... Leave government research out in the cold, Mark, unless we cooperate. Kaye can help keep the channels open. Together, we can do it a whole lot faster, of course."

"You're going to save the world, Marge?" Augustine asked softly.

"No, Mark. I doubt Herod's is much more than a nasty inconvenience. But it gets us where we live. Down where we make babies. Everyone who watches TV or reads newspapers is scared. Kaye is famous, she's female, and she's presentable. She's just what we both need. That's why Mr. Dicken here and the surgeon general thought she might be useful, isn't it? Besides her obvious expertise?"

Augustine aimed his next question at Kaye. "I assume you didn't approach Ms. Cross yourself, after agreeing to go with us."

"I didn't," Kaye said.

"What do you expect to get out of this arrangement?"

"I think Marge is right," Kaye said, feeling an almost chilly self-confidence. "We need to cooperate and find out what this is and what we can do about it." *Kaye Lang the corporate item, cool and distanced, knowing no doubt. Saul, you would be proud of me.*

"This is an international effort, Marge," Augustine said. "We're putting together a coalition of twenty different countries. WHO is a major player here. No prima donnas."

"I've already set up a crack management team to deal with that. Robert Jackson is going to head our vaccine program. Our functions will be transparent. We've been doing this on the world scene for twenty-five years. We know how to play ball, Mark."

Augustine looked at Cross, then at Kaye. He held out his hands as if to embrace Cross. "Darling," he said, and stood to blow her a kiss.

Cross cackled like an old hen.

The University of Washington, Seattle

Wendell Packer told Mitch to meet him in his office in the Magnuson building. The room in the E wing was small and stuffy, windowless, packed with shelves of books and two computers, one of them connected to equipment in Packer's laboratory. This screen showed a long series of proteins being sequenced, red and blue bands and green columns in pretty disarray, like a skewed staircase.

"I did this one myself," Packer said, holding up a long folded printout for Mitch. "Not that I don't trust my students, but I don't want to ruin their careers, either. And I don't want my department slammed."

Mitch took the printout and thumbed through it.

"I doubt it makes a lot of sense at first glance," Packer said. "The tissues are way too old to get complete sequences, so I looked for small genes unique to SHEVA, and then I looked for products created when SHEVA enters a cell."

"You found them?" Mitch asked, feeling his throat constrict.

Packer nodded. "Your tissue samples have SHEVA. And they're not just contaminants from you or the people you were with. But the virus is really degraded. I used antibody probes sent to us from Bethesda that bind to proteins associated with SHEVA. There's a follicle stimulating hormone that's unique to SHEVA infection. Sixty-seven percent match, not bad considering the age. Then I relied on a little information theory to design and fabricate better probes, in case

SHEVA has mutated slightly, or differs for other reasons. Took me a couple of days, but I got an eighty percent match. To make doubly sure, I did a Southwestern blot test with Herod's provirus DNA. There are definitely bits of activated SHEVA in your specimens. Tissue from the male is thick with it."

"You're sure it's SHEVA? No doubt, even in a court of law?"

"Considering the source, it wouldn't survive in a court of law. But is it SHEVA?" Packer smiled. "Yes. I've been in this department for seven years. We have some of the best equipment money can buy, and some of the best people that equipment can seduce to join us, thanks to three very rich young folks at Microsoft. But . . . Sit down, please, Mitch."

Mitch looked up from the printout. "Why?"

"Just sit."

Mitch sat.

"I have a bonus. Karel Petrovich in Anthropology asked Maria Konig, just down the hall, the best in our lab, to work on a very old tissue sample. Guess where he got the sample?"

"Innsbruck?"

Packer held out another sheet of paper. "They asked Karel specifically to go to us. Our reputation, what can I say? They wanted us to search for specific markers and combinations of alleles most often used to determine parental relationship. We were given one small tissue sample, about a gram. They wanted very precise work, and they wanted it quick. Mitch, you got to swear to absolute secrecy on this."

"I swear," Mitch said.

"Just out of curiosity, I asked one of the analysts about the results. I won't go into boring details. The tissue comes from a newborn. It's at least ten thousand years old. We looked for the markers and found them. And I compared several alleles with *your* tissue samples."

"They match?" Mitch asked, his voice breaking.

"Yes . . . and no. I don't think Innsbruck is going to agree with me, or with what you seem to be implying."

"I don't imply. I *know*."

"Yes, well, I'm intrigued, but in a courtroom, I could wriggle your male out of responsibility. No prehistoric child support. The female, however, yes. The alleles match."

"She's the baby's mother?"

"Beyond a doubt."

"But he's not the father?"

"I just said I could wriggle him out of it in a courtroom. There's some weird genetics going on here. Real spooky stuff that I've never seen before."

"But the baby is one of us."

"Mitch, please don't get me wrong. I'm not going to back you up, I'm not going to help you write any papers. I have a department to protect, and my own career. You of all people should understand that."

"I know, I know," Mitch said. "But I can't go it alone."

"Let me feed you a few clues. You know that *Homo sapiens sapiens* is remarkably uniform, genetically speaking."

"Yes."

"Well, I don't think *Homo sapiens neandertalensis* was all that uniform. It's a real miracle that I can tell you that, Mitch, I hope you understand. Three years ago, it would have taken us eight months to do the analysis."

Mitch frowned. "I'm losing you."

"The infant's genotype is a close match to you and me. She's close to modern. Mitochondrial DNA in the tissue you gave me matches with samples we have from old Neandertal bone. But I'd say, if you did not look at me too critically, that the male and female that supplied your samples are her parents."

Mitch felt dizzy. He bent over on the chair and rested his head between his knees. "Christ," he said, his voice muffled.

"A very late contender to be Eve," Packer said. He held up his hand. "Look at me. Now I'm trembling."

"What *can* you do, Wendell?" Mitch asked, lifting his head to stare up at him. "I'm sitting on the biggest story in modern science. Innsbruck is going to stonewall, I can just smell it.

They'll deny everything. It's the easy way out. What do I do?
Where do I go?"

Packer wiped his eyes and blew his nose into his handker-
chief. "Find some folks who aren't all that conservative," he
said. "People outside of academics. I know people at the
CDC. I talk fairly often with a friend in the labs in Atlanta, a
friend of an old girlfriend, actually. We stayed on good terms.
She's done some cadaver tissue analysis for a CDC virus
hunter named Dicken, on the Herod's Taskforce. Not surprisingly, he's been looking for SHEVA in cadaver tissues."

"From Georgia?"

Packer did not connect this immediately. "Atlanta?"

"No, Republic of."

"Ah . . . yes, as a matter of fact," Packer said. "But he's also
been looking for evidence of Herod's flu in historical records.
Decades, even centuries." Packer tapped Mitch's hand pointedly. "Maybe he'd like to know what you know?"

Magnuson Clinical Center, The National Institutes of Health, Bethesda

Four women sat in the brightly lighted room. The room was
equipped with two couches, two chairs, a television and
video player, books, and magazines. Kaye wondered how
hospital designers always managed to create an atmosphere
of sterility: ash-colored wood, cool off-white walls, sanitary
pastel art of beaches and forests and flowers. A bleached and
calming world.

She watched the women briefly through the window of

the side door as she waited for Dicken and the director of the clinical center project to catch up with her.

Two black women. One, in her late thirties and stout, sitting upright in a chair, inattentively watched something on the television, a copy of *Elle* draped across her lap. The other, in her early twenties, if that, very thin, with small pointy breasts and short cornrowed hair, sat with her cheek propped on her hand and her elbow on a couch arm, staring at nothing in particular. Two white women, both in their thirties, one bottle-blond and haggard and dazed-looking, the other neatly dressed, face expressionless, read battered copies of *People* and *Time*.

Dicken approached along the gray-carpeted hallway with Dr. Denise Lipton. Lipton was in her early forties, small, pretty in a sharp sort of way, with eyes that looked as if they could shoot sparks when she was angry. Dicken introduced them.

"Ready to see our volunteers, Ms. Lang?" Lipton asked.

"As ready as I'll ever be," Kaye said.

Lipton smiled bloodlessly. "They're not very happy. They've undergone enough tests in the last few days to . . . Well, to make them not very happy."

The women within the room looked up at the sound of voices. Lipton smoothed her lab coat and pushed the door open.

"Good afternoon, ladies," she greeted them.

The meeting went well enough. Dr. Lipton escorted three of the women to their private rooms and left Dicken and Kaye to talk more extensively to the fourth, the older black woman, Mrs. Luella Hamilton, of Richmond, Virginia.

Mrs. Hamilton wondered if she could get some coffee. "I've been drained so many times. If it isn't blood samples, it's my kidneys acting cross." Dicken said he would get them each a cup and left the room.

Mrs. Hamilton focused on Kaye and narrowed her eyes. "They told us you found this bug."

"No," Kaye said. "I wrote some papers, but I didn't actually find it."

"It's just a little fever," Mrs. Hamilton said. "I've had four children, and now they tell me this one won't really be a baby. But they won't take it out of me. They say, let the disease take its course. I'm just a big lab rat, aren't I?"

"Seems like it. Are they treating you well?"

"I'm eating," she said with a shrug. "The food's good. I don't like the books or the movies. The nurses are nice, but that Dr. Lipton—she's a hard case. She acts nice, but I think she doesn't like *anybody* very much."

"I'm sure she's doing a good job."

"Yeah, well, lady, Miz Lang, you sit in my seat for a while and tell me you don't want to bitch a little."

Kaye smiled.

"It pisses me off, there's this black nurse, a man, he keeps treating me like some sort of example. He wants me to be *strong* like his mammy." She regarded Kaye with steady wide eyes and shook her head. "I don't want to be strong. I want to cry when they do their tests, when I think about this baby, Miz Lang. You understand?"

"Yes," Kaye said.

"It feels like all my others did around this time. I say maybe it *is* a baby and they're wrong. Does that make me a fool?"

"If they've done the tests, they know," Kaye said.

"They won't let me visit my husband. That's part of the contract. He gave me the flu and he gave me this baby, but I miss him. It wasn't his fault. I talk to him on the phone. He sounds all right, but I know he misses me. Makes me nervous, being away, you know?"

"Who's taking care of your children?" Kaye said.

"My husband. They let the children come and see me. That's okay. My husband brings them by and they come in and see me and he stays out in the car. Four months it will be, four months!" Mrs. Hamilton twisted the thin gold wedding band on her finger. "He says he gets so lonely, and the kids, they ain't easy to be with sometimes."

Kaye grasped Mrs. Hamilton's hand. "I *know* how brave you are, Mrs. Hamilton."

"Call me Luella," she said. "I say it again, I ain't brave. What's your first name?"

"Kaye."

"I am scared, Kaye. You find out what's really going on, come and tell me first, all right?"

Kaye left Mrs. Hamilton. She felt dried out and cold. Dicken walked with her to the ground floor and outside the clinical center. He kept looking at her when he thought she would not notice.

She asked to stop for a minute. She crossed her arms and stared at a stand of trees across a short stretch of manicured lawn. The lawn was surrounded by trenches. Most of the NIH campus was a maze of detours and construction sites, holes filled with raw earth and concrete and jutting forests of rebar.

"Everything all right?" Dicken asked.

"No," she said. "I feel scattered."

"We have to get used to it. It's happening all over," Dicken said.

"All of the women volunteered?" Kaye said.

"Of course. We pay for all their medical expenses and a per diem. We can't compel this sort of thing, even in a national emergency."

"Why can't they see their husbands?"

"Actually, that may be my fault," Dicken said. "I presented some evidence at our last meeting that Herod's will lead to a second pregnancy, without sexual activity. They're going to hand the bulletin out this evening to all researchers."

"*What* evidence? My God, are we talking immaculate conception here?" Kaye put her hands on her hips and swung around to face him. "You've been tracking this thing since we ran into each other in Georgia, haven't you?"

"Since before Georgia. Ukraine, Russia, Turkey, Azerbaijan,

Armenia. Herod's started hitting those countries ten, twenty years ago, maybe even earlier."

"Then you read my papers, and it all fell into place? You're a kind of scientific stalker?"

Dicken made a face, shook his head. "Hardly."

"Am I the catalyst?" Kaye asked in disbelief.

"It's not simple, Kaye."

"I wish they'd keep me in the loop, Chris!"

"Christopher, please." He looked uncomfortable, apologetic.

"I wish *you'd* keep me in the loop. You act like a shadow around here, always following, so why do I think you may be one of the most important people in the Taskforce?"

"Thank you, it's a common misperception," he said with a wry smile. "I try to keep out of trouble, but I'm not sure I'm succeeding. They listen sometimes, when the evidence is strong—as it actually is in this case, reports from Armenian hospitals, even a couple of hospitals in Los Angeles and New York."

"Christopher, we've got two hours before the next meeting," Kaye said. "I've been stuck in SHEVA conferences for two weeks now. They think they've found my niche. A safe little cubbyhole, looking for other HERV. Marge has put together a nice lab for me in Baltimore, but . . . I don't think the Taskforce has much use for me."

"Going with Americol really irritated Augustine," Dicken said. "I could have warned you."

"I'll have to focus on doing work with Americol, then."

"Not a bad idea. They have the resources. Marge seems to like you."

"Let me know more of what it's like . . . on the front? Is that what it's called?"

"The front," Dicken affirmed. "Sometimes we say we're going to meet the real troops, the people who are getting sick. We're just workers; they're the soldiers. They do most of the suffering and the dying."

"I feel like I'm on the sidelines here. Will you talk to an outsider?"

"Love to," Dicken said. "You know what I'm up against here, don't you?"

"A bureaucratic juggernaut. They think they know what Herod's is. But . . . a second pregnancy, without sex!" Kaye felt a quick little chill.

"They've rationalized that," Dicken said. "We're going to discuss the possible mechanism this afternoon. They don't think they're hiding anything." He screwed up his face like a boy with a dark secret. "If you ask questions I'm not prepared to answer . . ."

Kaye dropped her hands from her hips, exasperated. "What kind of questions is *Augustine* not asking? What if we're getting this completely wrong?"

"Exactly," Dicken said. His face reddened and he sliced the air with his hand. "*Exactly*. Kaye, I knew you would understand. While we're talking what ifs . . . would you mind if I spill my guts to you?"

Kaye leaned back at this prospect.

"I mean, I admire your work so much—"

"I was lucky, and I had Saul," Kaye said stiffly. Dicken looked vulnerable and she did not like that. "Christopher, what in hell are you hiding?"

"I'd be surprised if you didn't already know. We're all just hanging back from the obvious—what is obvious to a few of us, at any rate." He searched her face closely through squinted eyes. "I'll tell you what I think, and if you agree that it's possible—that it's probable—you have to let me decide when to make the case. We wait until we have all the evidence we need. I've been living in a land of guesswork for a year, and I know for a fact neither Augustine nor Shawbeck want to hear me out. Sometimes I think I'm not much more than a glorified errand boy. So—" He shifted on one foot. "Our secret?"

"Of course," Kaye said, leveling her gaze on him. "Tell me what you think is going to happen to Mrs. Hamilton."

34

Seattle

Mitch knew he was asleep, or rather, half-asleep. On rare occasions his mind would process the facts of his existence, his plans, his suppositions, separately and with stubborn independence, and always on the edge of sleep.

Many times he had dreamed of the site where he was currently digging, but with mixed frames of time. This morning, his body numb, his conscious mind an observer in a wraparound theater, he saw a young man and woman wrapped in light furs, wearing ragged reed and skin sandals laced up their ankles. The woman was pregnant. He saw them first in profile, as if in some rotating display, and amused himself for a while viewing them from different angles.

Gradually, this control came to an end, and the man and woman walked over fresh snow and windswept ice, in bright daylight, the brightest he had even seen in a dream. The ice glared and they shielded their eyes with their hands.

At first, he looked upon them as people just like himself. Soon, however, he realized these people were *not* like him. Their facial features were not what aroused this suspicion at first. It was the intricate patterns of beard and facial hair on the man, and a thick soft mane of hair circling the woman's face, leaving her cheeks, receding chin, and low forehead clear, but drawing from temple to temple through her brows. Beneath the furred brow, her eyes were soft and deep brown, almost black, and her skin had a rich olive color. Her fingers were gray and pink, heavily callused. Both had broad heavy noses.

They are not my people, Mitch thought. *But I know them.*

The man and woman were smiling. The woman reached down to scoop up snow. Slyly, she started to nibble at it, then, when the man was not looking, she formed it into a quick hard ball and threw it at his head. It hit with a thwack and he reeled, yelped, his voice clear and bell-toned, almost like a beagle's. The woman made as if to cower, then ran away, and the man chased her. He pulled her down despite her repeated grunts of supplication, then stood back and raised his arms to heaven and heaped loud words upon her. Despite the gravelly timbre of his voice, deep and rolling, she did not seem impressed. She flapped her hands at him and pouched out her lips, making loud smacking sounds.

With the lazy editing of a dream, he saw them walking single file down a muddy trail in drizzling rain and snow. Through slow cloud cover, he could see patches of forest and meadow in a valley below them, and a lake, upon which floated broad flat rafts of logs bearing reed huts.

They're doing all right, a voice in his head told him. *You look at them now and you don't know them, but they're doing all right.*

Mitch heard a bird and realized this was no bird, but his cell phone. It took him some seconds to put away the paraphernalia of his dream. The clouds and valley floor broke like a soap bubble and he groaned as he lifted his head. His body was numb. He had been sleeping on his side with one arm curled under his head and his muscles were stiff.

The phone persisted. He answered on the sixth ring.

"I hope I'm speaking to Mitchell Rafelson, the anthropologist," said a male voice with a British accent.

"One of them, anyway," Mitch said. "Who's this?"

"Merton, Oliver. I'm a science editor for the *Economist.* I'm doing a piece on the Innsbruck Neandertals. It's been tough finding your phone number, Mr. Rafelson."

"It's unlisted. I'm getting tired of being chastised."

"I can imagine. Listen, I think I can show that Innsbruck has bollixed up the whole case, but I need some details. Chance for you to explain things to a sympathetic ear. I'll be out in Washington state day after tomorrow—to speak with Eileen Ripper."

"Okay," Mitch said. He considered simply closing the phone and trying to bring back the remarkable dream.

"She's working on another dig in the gorge . . . Columbia Gorge? Do you know where Iron Cave is?"

Mitch stretched. "I've done some digs near there."

"Yes, well, it hasn't leaked to the press yet, but it will next week. She's found three skeletons, very old, not nearly as remarkable as your mummies, but still quite interesting. Principally, my story is going to focus on her tactics. In an age of sympathy for indigenes, she's put together a really canny consortium to protect science. Ms. Ripper solicited support from the Five Tribes Confederation. You know them, of course."

"I do."

"She's got a team of pro bono lawyers and she's kept some congressmen and senators in the loop as well. Not at all like your experience with Pasco man."

"I'm glad to hear it," Mitch said with a scowl. He picked a piece of sleep from his eye. "That's a day's drive from here."

"Is it that far? I'm in Manchester now. England. Just packed my bags and drove over from Leeds. My plane goes out in an hour. I'd love to talk."

"I'm probably the last person Eileen wants out there."

"She was the one who gave me your phone number. You're not the outcast you might think, Mr. Rafelson. She'd like to have you look at the dig. I gather she's the motherly type."

"She's a whirlwind," Mitch said.

"I'm very excited, really. I've seen digs in Ethiopia, South Africa, Tanzania. I've been to Innsbruck twice to see what they'd let me see, which isn't much. Now—"

"Mr. Merton, I hate to disappoint you—"

"Yes, well, what about the baby, Mr. Rafelson? Can you

tell me more about this remarkable infant the woman had in her backpack?"

"I had a blinding headache at the time." Mitch was about to put down the phone, Eileen Ripper or not. He'd been through this too many times. He held the phone away from his ear. Merton's voice sounded tinny and harsh.

"Do you know what's going on in Innsbruck? Did you know they've actually had fistfights in the labs there?"

Mitch brought the phone back to his ear. "No."

"Did you know they've sent tissue samples to other labs in other countries to try to build some sort of consensus?"

"No-oo," Mitch said slowly.

"I'd love to bring you up to date. I think there's a good chance you could come out of this smelling like a fresh apple tree or whatever it is that blooms in Washington state. If I ask Eileen to call you, invite you out, if I tell her you're interested . . . Could we meet?"

"Why not just meet at SeaTac? That's where you're coming in, isn't it?"

Merton made a small blat with his lips. "Mr. Rafelson. I can't see you turning down the chance to sniff some dirt and sit under a canvas tent. A chance to talk about the biggest archaeological story of our time."

Mitch found his watch and looked at the date. "All right," he said. "If Eileen invites me."

When he hung up the phone, he went to the bathroom, brushed his teeth, looked in the mirror.

He had spent several days moping around the apartment, unable to decide what to do next. He had obtained the e-mail address and a phone number for Christopher Dicken, but had not yet built up sufficient courage to call him. His money was running out faster than he had expected. He was putting off hitting up his parents for a loan.

As he fixed breakfast, the phone rang again. It was Eileen Ripper.

When Mitch finished speaking to her, he sat for a moment on the ragged chair in the living room, then stood and looked out the window at Broadway. It was getting light outside. He opened the window and leaned out. People were walking up and down the street, and cars were stopped at the red light on Denny.

He called home. His mother answered.

The National Institutes of Health, Bethesda

"It's happened before," Dicken said. He broke a sweet roll in half and dunked it into the foamy top of his latte. The huge modern cafeteria of the Natcher Building was nearly empty at this hour of the morning, and served better food than the cafeteria in Building 10. They sat near the tall tinted glass windows, well away from the few other employees. "Specifically, it happened in Georgia, in Gordi, or nearby."

Kaye's mouth made an O. "My God. The massacre . . ." Outside, sun broke through low morning clouds, sending shadows and bright patches over the campus and into the cafeteria.

"Their tissues all show SHEVA. I only got samples from three or four, but they all had it."

"And you haven't told Augustine?"

"I've been relying on clinical evidence, fresh reports from hospitals . . . What in hell difference would it make if I put SHEVA back a few years, a decade at most? But two days ago I got some files from a hospital in Tbilisi. I helped a young intern there make some contacts in Atlanta. He told me about some people in the mountains. Survivors of another massacre, this one almost sixty years ago. During the war."

"Germans never got into Georgia," Kaye said.

Dicken nodded. "Stalin's troops. They wiped out most of an isolated village near Mount Kazbeg. Some survivors were found two years ago. The government in Tbilisi protected them. Maybe they were fed up with purges, maybe . . . Maybe they didn't know anything about Gordi, or the other villages."

"How many survivors?"

"A doctor named Leonid Sugashvili made it his own little crusade to investigate. It was his report the intern sent me—a report that was never published. But pretty thorough. Between 1943 and 1991, he estimated, about thirteen thousand men, women, and even children were killed in Georgia, Armenia, Abkhazi, Chechnya. They were killed because somebody thought they spread a disease that caused pregnant women to abort. Those who survived the first purges were hunted down later . . . because the women were giving birth to mutated children. Children with spots all over their faces, with weird eyes, children who could speak from the moment they were born. In some villages, the local police did the killing. Superstition dies hard. The men and women—mothers and fathers—they were accused of consorting with the devil. There weren't that many of them, over four decades. But . . . Sugashvili estimates there might have been instances of this sort of thing going back hundreds of years. Tens of thousands of murders. Guilt, shame, ignorance, silence."

"You think the children were mutated by SHEVA?"

"The doctor's report says that many of the women who were killed pleaded that they had cut off sexual relations with their husbands, their boyfriends. They did not want to bear the devil's offspring. They had heard about the mutated children in other villages, and once they had their fever, their miscarriage, they tried to avoid getting pregnant. Almost all the women who had the miscarriages were pregnant thirty days later, no matter what they did or did not do. Just as some of our hospitals are reporting now."

Kaye shook her head. "That is so completely unbelievable!"

Dicken shrugged. "It's not going to get any more believable, or any easier," he said. "For some time now, I just haven't been convinced that SHEVA is any known kind of disease."

Kaye's lips tightened. She put down her cup of coffee and folded her arms, remembering the conversation with Drew Miller in the Italian restaurant in Boston, and Saul saying it was time they tackle the problem of evolution. "Maybe it's a signal," she said.

"What sort of signal?"

"A code-key that opens up a genetic set-aside, instructions for a new phenotype."

"I'm not sure I understand," Dicken said, frowning.

"Something built up over thousands of years, tens of thousands of years. Guesses, hypotheses having to do with this or that trait, elaborations on a pretty rigid plan."

"To what end?" Dicken asked.

"Evolution," Kaye said.

Dicken backed his chair away and placed his hands on his legs. "Whoa."

"You said it wasn't a disease," Kaye reminded him.

"I said it wasn't like any disease I know. It's still a retrovirus."

"You read my papers, didn't you?"

"Yes."

"I dropped a few hints."

Dicken pondered this. "A catalyst."

"You make it, we get it, we suffer," Kaye said.

Dicken's cheeks reddened. "I'm trying not to turn this into a man-woman thing," he said. "There's enough of that going on already."

"Sorry," Kaye said. "Maybe I just want to avoid the real issue."

Dicken seemed to reach a decision. "I'm stepping out of line by showing this to you." He dug into his valise and produced a printout of an e-mail message from Atlanta. Four small pictures had been pasted on the bottom of the message.

"A woman died in an automobile accident outside Atlanta. An autopsy was performed at Northside Hospital, and one of our pathologists found she was in her first trimester. He examined the fetus, clearly a Herod's fetus. Then he examined the woman's uterus. He found a second pregnancy, very early, at the base of the placenta, protected by a thin wall of laminar tissue. The placenta had already started to separate, but the second ovum was secure. It would have survived the miscarriage. A month later . . ."

"A grandchild," Kaye said. "Released by the . . ."

"Intermediate daughter. Really just a specialized ovary. She creates a second ovum. That ovum attaches to the wall of the mother's uterus."

"What if her eggs, the daughter's eggs, are different?"

Dicken's throat had grown dry and he coughed. "Excuse me." He got up to pour himself a cup of water, then walked back between the tables to sit beside Kaye.

He continued, speaking slowly. "SHEVA provokes the release of a complex of polyproteins. They break down in the cytosol outside the nucleus. LH, FSH, prostaglandins."

"I know. Judith Kushner told me," Kaye said, her voice little more than a squeak. "Some of them are responsible for causing the miscarriages. Others could change an ovum substantially."

"Mutate it?" Dicken asked, still clinging to the tatters of an old paradigm.

"I'm not sure that's the right word," Kaye said. "It sounds kind of vicious and random. No. We may be talking about a different kind of reproduction here."

Dicken finished his cup of water.

"This isn't exactly new to me," Kaye mused quietly. She clenched her fingers into fists, then lightly, nervously, rapped her knuckles on the table. "Are you willing to argue that SHEVA is part of human evolution? That we're about to make a new kind of human?"

Dicken examined Kaye's face, her mixed wonder and excitement, the peculiar terror of coming upon the intellectual equivalent of a raging tiger. "I wouldn't dare to put it so bluntly. But maybe I'm a coward. Maybe it *is* something like that. I value your opinion. God knows I need an ally here."

Kaye's heart thudded in her chest. She lifted her cup of coffee and the cold liquid sloshed. "My God, Christopher." She gave a small, helpless laugh. "What if it's true? What if we're *all* pregnant? The whole human race?"

PART TWO

SHEVA SPRING

Eastern Washington State

Wide and slow, the Columbia River glided like a plain of polished jade between black basalt walls.

Mitch pulled off state route 14, drove for half a mile on a dirt and gravel road through scrub trees and bushes, then turned at a bent and rusted sheet-metal sign that read IRON CAVE.

Two old Airstream trailers gleamed in the sun a few yards from the edge of the gorge. Wooden benches and tables heaped with burlap sacks and digging tools surrounded the trailers. He parked the car off the road.

A chill breeze picked at his felt Stetson. He gripped the hat with one hand as he walked from the car to the edge and stared down upon Eileen Ripper's encampment, fifty feet below.

A short young blond woman in frayed and faded jeans and a brown leather jacket stepped down from the door of the nearest trailer. In the moist air off the river, he instantly picked up the young woman's scent: Opium or Trouble or some such perfume. She looked remarkably like Tilde.

The woman paused under the outstretched awning, then stepped out and shaded her eyes against the sun. "Mitch Rafelson?" she asked.

"None other," he said. "Is Eileen down there?"

"Yeah. It's falling apart, you know."

"Since when?"

"Since three days ago. Eileen worked real hard to make her case. Didn't make much difference in the long run."

Mitch grinned sympathetically. "Been there," he said.

"The woman from Five Tribes packed up two days ago. That's why Eileen thought it would be okay for you to come out here. Nobody gets mad now if you show up."

"Nice to be popular," Mitch said, and tipped his hat.

The woman smiled. "Eileen is feeling low. Give her some encouragement. I think you're a hero, myself. Except maybe for those mummies."

"Where is she?"

"Just below the cave."

Oliver Merton sat on a folding chair in the shadow of the largest canvas canopy. About thirty, with flaming red hair, a pale broad face and short pushed-up nose, he wore a look of utter and almost fierce concentration, his lips drawn back as he punched the keyboard of a laptop computer with his index fingers.

Hunt-and-peck, Mitch thought. *A self-taught typist.* He checked out the man's clothes, distinctly out of place at a dig: tweed slacks, red suspenders, a white linen dress shirt with a banded collar.

Merton did not look up until Mitch was within touching distance of the canopy.

"Mitchell Rafelson! What a pleasure!" Merton shifted the computer to the table, jumped to his feet, and held out his hand. "It's damned gloomy here. Eileen is up the slope by the dig. I'm sure she's eager to see you. Shall we?"

The six other workers on the site, all young interns or graduate students, looked up in curiosity as the two men passed. Merton walked ahead of Mitch and climbed over natural shelves cut by centuries of river erosion. They paused twenty feet below the bluff where an old, rust-streaked cave dug into an outcrop of basalt. Above and east of the outcrop, part of an overlying ledge of weathered stone had collapsed, scattering large blocks down the gentle slope to the shore.

Eileen Ripper stood at the outside of a posted series of carefully excavated square pits marked with topometric grids—wire and string—on the western side of the slope. In her late forties, small and dark, with deep-set black eyes and a thin nose, Ripper's most conspicuous beauty lay in her generous lips, which contrasted appealingly with a short, unruly cap of peppered black hair.

She turned at Merton's hail. She did not smile or call out. Instead, she put on a determined face, walked gingerly down the talus, and held out her hand to Mitch. They shook firmly.

"We got radiocarbon figures back yesterday morning," she said. "They're thirteen thousand years old, plus or minus five hundred . . . and if they ate a lot of salmon, they're twelve thousand five hundred years old. But the Five Tribes folks say that Western science is trying to strip them of the last of their dignity. I thought I could reason with them."

"At least you made the effort," Mitch said.

"I apologize for judging you so harshly, Mitch. I kept my cool for so long, despite little signs of trouble, and then this woman, Sue Champion . . . I thought we were friends. She advises the tribes. She comes back here yesterday with two men. The men were . . . so *smug*, Mitch. Like little boys who can piss higher up the barn door. They tell me I am fabricating evidence to support my lies. They say they have the government and the law on their side. Our old nemesis, NAGPRA."

That stood for the Native American Graves Protection and Repatriation Act. Mitch was very familiar with the details of this legislation.

Merton stood on the loose slope, trying to keep from slipping, and made little darting glances between them.

"What evidence did you fabricate?" Mitch asked lightly.

"Don't joke." But Ripper's expression loosened and she held Mitch's hand between hers. "We took collagen from the bones and sent it to Portland. They did a DNA analysis. Our bones are from a different population, not at all related to modern Indians, only loosely related to the Spirit Cave mummy. Caucasoid, if we can use that loose term. But hardly Nordic. More Ainu, I believe."

"That's historic, Eileen," Mitch said. "That's excellent. Congratulations."

Once started, Ripper couldn't seem to stop. They walked down the trail to the tents. "We can't even begin to make modern racial comparisons. That is what is so infuriating! We let our screwball notions of race and identity cloud the truth. Populations were so different back then. But modern Indians did not come from the people our skeletons belonged to. They may have competed with the ancestors of modern Indians. And they lost."

"The Indians won?" Merton said. "They should be glad to hear it."

"They think I'm trying to divide their political unity. They don't care about what really happened. They want their own little dream world and the hell with truth!"

"You're telling me?" Mitch asked.

Ripper smiled through tears of discouragement and exhaustion. "The Five Tribes have got counsel petitioning in federal court in Seattle to take the skeletons."

"Where are the bones now?"

"In Portland. We packed them up in situ and shipped them out yesterday."

"Across state lines?" Mitch asked. "That's kidnapping."

"It's better than waiting around for a bunch of lawyers." She shook her head and Mitch put an arm around her shoulders. "I tried to do it right, Mitch." She wiped at her cheeks with a dusty hand, leaving muddy streaks, and forced a laugh. "Now I've even got the Vikings mad at us!"

The Vikings—a small group of mostly middle-aged men calling themselves the Nordic Worshippers of Odin in the New World—had come to Mitch as well, years before, to conduct their ceremonies. They had hoped that Mitch could prove their claims that Nordic explorers had populated much of North America thousands of years ago. Mitch, ever the philosopher, had let them conduct a ritual over the bones of Pasco man, still in the ground, but ultimately he had had to disappoint them. Pasco man was in fact quite thoroughly Indian, closely related to the Southern Na-dene.

After Ripper's tests on her skeletons, the Worshippers of Odin had once again left in disappointment. In a world of fragile self-justification, the truth made no one happy.

Merton brought out a bottle of champagne and vacuum packs of smoked salmon and fresh bread and cheese as the daylight waned. Several of Ripper's students built a large fire that snapped and crackled on the shore as Mitch and Eileen toasted their mutual insanity.

"Where'd you get this feed?" Ripper asked Merton as he spread the camp's battered Melmac plates on the bare pine table beneath the largest canopy.

"At the airport," Merton said. "Only place I had time to stop. Bread, cheese, fish, wine—what more does one need? Though I could use a good pint of bitter."

"I've got Coors in the trailer," a burly, balding male intern said.

"Breakfast of diggers," Mitch said approvingly.

"Spare me," Merton said. "And pardon me if I tell everyone to *dig in*. Everyone has a story to tell." He took a plastic cup of champagne from Ripper. "Of race and time and migration and what it means to be a human being. Who wants to be first?"

Mitch knew he had only to keep silent for a couple of seconds and Ripper would start in. Merton took notes as she talked about the three skeletons and local politics. An hour and a half later, it was getting bitterly cold and they moved closer to the fire.

"The Altai tribes resent having ethnic Russians dig up their dead," Merton said. "It's an indigenous revolt everywhere. A slap on the wrist to the colonial oppressors. Do you think the Neandertals have their spokespersons in Innsbruck picketing right now?"

"Nobody wants to be a Neandertal," Mitch said dryly.

"Except me." He turned to Eileen. "I've been dreaming about them. My little nuclear family."

"Really?" Eileen leaned forward, intrigued.

"I dreamed their people lived on a big raft in a lake."

"Fifteen thousand years ago?" Merton asked, raising an eyebrow.

Mitch caught something in the reporter's tone and looked at him suspiciously. "Is that your guess?" he asked. "Or have they got a date?"

"None they're releasing to the public," Merton said with a sniff. "I have a contact at the university, however . . . and he tells me they've definitely settled on fifteen thousand years. If, that is," and he smiled at Ripper, "they didn't eat a lot of fish."

"What else?"

Merton punched the air dramatically. "Pugilism," he said. "Raging arguments in the back rooms. Your mummies violate everything known in anthropology and archaeology. They're not strictly Neandertal, so claim a few in the main research team; they're a new subspecies, *Homo sapiens alpinensis,* according to one scientist. Another is betting they're late stage gracile Neandertals who lived in a large community, got less stocky and robust, looked more like you and me. They hope to explain away the infant."

Mitch lowered his head. *They don't feel this the way I do. They don't know the way I know.* Then he drew back and blanketed these emotions. He had to keep some level of objectivity.

Merton turned toward Mitch. "Did you see the baby?"

This made Mitch jerk upright in his folding chair. Merton's eyes narrowed. "Not clearly," Mitch said. "I just assumed, when they said it was a modern infant . . ."

"Could Neandertal traits be masked by infant features?" Merton asked.

"No," Mitch said. Then, with a squint, "I don't think so."

"I don't think so, either," Ripper agreed. The students had gathered close around this discussion. The fire snapped and hissed and flung up tall yellow arms that grabbed at the cold, still sky. The river lapped the gravelly shore with a sound like a clockwork dog licking a hand. Mitch felt the champagne mellowing him after a long, tiring day of driving.

"Well, implausible as it might be, it's easier than arguing against a genetic association," Merton said. "The people in Innsbruck pretty much have to agree that the female and the infant are related. But there are anomalies, pretty serious ones, that no one can explain. I was hoping Mitchell might be able to enlighten me."

Mitch was saved from having to feign ignorance when a woman's strong voice called from the top of the bluff.

"Eileen? You there? It's Sue Champion."

"Hell," Ripper said. "I thought she was back in Kumash by now." She cupped her hands to her mouth and yelled upward, "We're down here, Sue. We're getting drunk. Want to join us?"

One of the male students ran up the trail to the top of the bluff with a flashlight. Sue Champion followed him back down to the tent.

"Nice fire," she observed. Over six feet tall, slender to the point of thin, with long black hair arranged in a braid draped down the front shoulder of her brown corduroy jacket, Champion looked smart, classy, and a little stiff. She might have had a ready smile, but her face was lined with fatigue. Mitch glanced at Ripper, saw the fix in her expression.

"I'm here to say I'm sorry," Champion said.

"We're all sorry," Ripper said.

"Have you been out here all night? It's cold."

"We're dedicated."

Champion walked around the canopy to be near the fire. "My office got your call about the tests. The chair of the board of trustees doesn't believe it."

"I can't help that," Ripper said. "Why did you just pull out all of a sudden and sic your attorney on me? I thought we had an agreement, and if they turned out to be Indian, we'd do basic science, with minimum invasion, then turn them over to the Five Tribes."

"We let our guard down. We were tired after the mess over Pasco man. It was wrong." She looked again at Mitch. "I know you."

"Mitch Rafelson," he said, and held out his hand.

Champion did not accept it. "You ran us a merry chase, Mitch Rafelson."

"I feel the same way," Mitch said.

Champion shrugged. "Our people gave in against their deeper feelings. We felt sandbagged. We need the folks in Olympia and last time we upset them. The trustees sent me here because I'm trained in anthropology. I didn't do such a good job. Now everybody's angry."

"Is there anything more that we can do, out of court?" Ripper asked.

"The chairman told me that knowledge isn't worth disturbing the dead. You should have seen the pain in the board meeting when I described the tests."

"I thought we explained the whole procedure," Ripper said.

"You disturb the dead everywhere. We ask only that you leave our dead alone."

The women stared at each other sadly.

"They aren't your dead, Sue," Ripper said, her eyes drooping. "They aren't your people."

"The council thinks NAGPRA still applies."

Ripper lifted her hand; no use going over old battles. "Then there's nothing we can do but spend more money on lawyers."

"No. This time you are going to win," Champion said. "We have other troubles now. Many of our young mothers are ill with Herod's." Champion brushed the edge of the canvas cover with one hand. "Some of us thought it was confined to the big cities, maybe to the whites, but we were wrong."

Merton's eyes gleamed like eager little lenses in the flickering firelight.

"I'm sorry to hear that, Sue," Ripper said. "My sister has Herod's, too." She stood and put her hand on Champion's shoulder. "Stay for a while. We have hot coffee and cocoa."

"Thank you, no. It's a long drive back. We will not bother with the dead for a while. We need to take care of the living." A slight change came over Champion's features. "Some who are ready to listen, like my father and my grandmother, say that what you have learned is interesting."

"Bless them, Sue," Ripper said.

Champion looked down at Mitch. "People come and go, all of us come and go. Anthropologists know that."

"We do," Mitch said.

"It will be hard to explain to others," Champion said. "I will let you know what our people decide to do about the illness, if we know any medicine. Maybe we can help your sister."

"Thank you," Ripper said.

Champion looked around the group under the canvas canopy, nodded deeply, then gave several additional shallow nods, showing she had had her say and was prepared to leave. She climbed the trail to the lip of the bluff with the burly intern lighting the way.

"Extraordinary," Merton said, eyes still gleaming. "Privileged insight. Maybe even native wisdom."

"Don't let it get to you," Ripper said. "Sue's good people, but she doesn't know what's happening any more than my sister does." Ripper turned to Mitch. "God, you look ill," she said.

Mitch did feel a little queasy.

"I've seen that look on cabinet ministers," Merton observed quietly. "When they were stuffed full of too many secrets."

37

Baltimore

Kaye swung her small bag out of the backseat of the cab and slipped her credit card through the driver's-side reader. She craned her head to look at Baltimore's newest tower condo development, Uptown Helix, thirty floors poised on two broad quadrangles of shops and theaters, all in the shadow of the Bromo-Seltzer Tower.

The remains of a dusting of snow from earlier in the morning lingered in slushy patches along the sidewalk. To Kaye, it seemed this winter was lasting forever.

Cross had told her that the condo on the twentieth floor would be fully furnished, that her belongings would be moved in and arranged, there would be food in the refrigerator and pantry, a running tab at several restaurants downstairs: everything she desired and needed, a home just three blocks from Americol's corporate headquarters.

Kaye presented herself to the doorman in the resident's lobby. He smiled the way servants smile at rich people and gave her an envelope containing her key. "I don't own this, you know," she said.

"Doesn't matter a bit to me, ma'am," he replied with the same cheerful deference.

She rode the sleek steel and glass elevator through the atrium of the shopping arcade to the residential floors, tapping her fingers on the handrail. She was alone in the elevator. *I am protected, provided for, kept busy going from meeting to meeting, no time to think. I wonder who I am anymore.*

She doubted that any scientist had ever felt so rushed as she felt now. Her conversation with Christopher Dicken at the NIH had pushed her onto a sidetrack having little to do with the development of SHEVA therapies. A hundred different elements of her research since postgraduate days had suddenly floated to the surface of her mind, shuffled around like swimmers in a water ballet, arranged themselves in enchanting patterns. Those patterns had nothing to do with disease and death, everything to do with the cycles of human life—or every kind of life, for that matter.

She had less than two weeks before Cross's scientists would present their first candidate vaccine, out of twelve—at last count—being developed around the country, at Americol and elsewhere. Kaye had underestimated the speed with which Americol could work—and had overestimated the extent to which they would keep her informed. *I'm still just a figurehead,* she thought.

In that time, she had to make up her mind about what was actually happening—what SHEVA actually represented. What would finally happen to Mrs. Hamilton and the other women at the NIH clinic.

She emerged on the twentieth floor, found her number, 2011, fitted the electronic key into the lock, and opened the heavy door. A rush of clean, cool air, smelling of new carpet and furniture, of something else rosy and sweet, wafted out to greet her. Soft music played: Debussy, she could not remember the name of the piece, but she liked it a lot.

A bouquet of several dozen yellow roses spilled over from a crystal vase on the top of the low étagère in the hall.

The condominium was bright and cheerful, with elegant wood accents, beautifully furnished with two couches and a chair in suede and sunset gold fabric. *And Debussy.* She dropped the bag onto a couch and walked into the kitchen. Stainless-steel refrigerator, stove, dishwasher, gray granite countertops edged with rose-colored marble, expensive jewel-like track lighting throwing little diamond glows around the room . . .

"Damn it, Marge," Kaye said under her breath. She carried the bag into the bedroom, unzipped it on the bed, pulled out her skirts and blouses and one dress to be hung in the closet, opened the closet, and stared at the wardrobe. Had she not already met two of Cross's handsome young male companions, she would have been sure, at this point, that Marge Cross had designs on her other than corporate. She quickly flicked through the dresses, suits, silk and linen blouses, looked down at shoe racks supporting at least eight pairs for all occasions—even hiking boots—and that was enough.

Kaye sat on the edge of the bed and let out a deep, quavering sigh. She was in way over her head socially as well as scientifically. She turned to look at the reproduction Whistler prints over the maple dresser, at the oriental scroll beautifully framed in ebony with brass finials that hung on the wall over the bed.

"Little hothouse posy in the big city." She felt her face screwing up in anger.

The phone in her purse rang. She jumped, walked into the living room, opened the purse, answered.

"Kaye, this is Judith."

"You were right," Kaye said abruptly.

"Beg pardon?"

"You were right."

"I'm always right, dear. You know that." Judith paused for effect, and Kaye knew she had something important to say. "You asked about transposon activity in my SHEVA-infected hepatocytes."

Kaye felt her spine stiffen. This was the stab in the not-so-dark she had made two days after speaking with Dicken. She had pored over the texts and refreshed herself with a dozen articles in six different journals. She had gone through her notebooks, where she had scribbled down mad little moments of extreme speculation.

She and Saul had counted themselves among the biologists who suspected that transposons—mobile lengths of DNA within the genome—were far more than just selfish genes.

Kaye had written a solid twelve pages in the notebook on the possibility that these were very important phenotype regulators, not selfish but selfless; they could, under certain circumstances, guide the way proteins became living tissue. *Change* the way proteins created a living plant or animal. Retrotransposons were very similar to retroviruses—and thus the genetic link with SHEVA.

All together, they could be the handmaids of evolution.

"Kaye?"

"Just a moment," Kaye said. "Let me catch my breath."

"Well you should, dear, dear former student Kaye Lang. Transposon activity in our SHEVA-infected hepatocytes is mildly enhanced. They shuffle around with no apparent effect. That's interesting. But we've gone beyond the hepatocytes. We've been doing tests on embryonic stem cells for the Taskforce."

Embryonic stem cells could become any sort of tissue, very much like early growth cells in fetuses.

"We've sort of encouraged them to behave like fertilized human ova," Kushner said. "They can't grow up to be fetuses, but please don't tell the FDA. In these stem cells, the transposon activity is extraordinary. After SHEVA, the transposons jump around like bugs on a hot griddle. They're active on at least twenty chromosomes. If this were random churning, the cell should die. The cell survives. It's as healthy as ever."

"It's regulated activity?"

"It's triggered by something in SHEVA. My guess is, something in the LPC—the large protein complex. The cell reacts as if it's being subjected to extraordinary stress."

"What do you think that means, Judith?"

"SHEVA has designs on us. It wants to change our genome, maybe radically."

"Why?" Kaye grinned expectantly. She was sure Judith would see the inevitable connection.

"This kind of activity can't be benign, Kaye."

Kaye's smile collapsed. "But the cell survives."

"Yes," Kushner said. "But as far as we know, the babies don't. It's too much change all at once. For years I've been waiting for nature to react to our environmental bullshit, tell us to stop overpopulating and depleting resources, to shut up and stop messing around and just *die*. Species-level apoptosis. I think this could be the final warning—a real species killer."

"You're passing this on to Augustine?"

"Not directly, but he'll see it."

Kaye looked at the phone for a moment, stunned, then thanked Judith and told her she would call her later. Kaye's hands tingled.

Not evolution, then. Perhaps Mother Nature had judged humans to be a malignant growth, a cancer.

For a horrible moment, that made more sense than what she and Dicken had talked about. Yet what about the new children, the ones born of the ova released by the intermediate daughters? Were they going to be genetically damaged, born apparently normal, but dying soon after? Or would they simply be rejected during the first trimester, like the interim daughters?

Kaye looked through the wide glass doors over the city of Baltimore, the late morning sun glittering on wet rooftops, asphalt streets. She imagined every pregnancy leading to another equally futile pregnancy, to wombs clogged with endless, horribly distorted first-trimester fetuses.

Shutting down human reproduction.

If Judith Kushner was correct, the bell had just tolled for the whole human race.

38

Marge Cross stood at stage left of the auditorium as Kaye formed a line with six scientists, prepared to field questions on the announcement.

Four hundred and fifty reporters filled the auditorium to capacity. Americol's public relations director for the eastern U.S., Laura Nilson, young, black, and very intent, tugged at the hem of the jacket of her trim olive wool suit, then took over the questions.

The health and science reporter for CNN was first in the queue. "I'd like to direct my question to Dr. Jackson."

Robert Jackson, head of the Americol SHEVA vaccine project, lifted his hand.

"Dr. Jackson, if this virus has had so many millions of years to evolve, how is it possible that Americol can announce a trial vaccine after less than three months of research? Are you smarter than Mother Nature?"

The room buzzed for a moment with mixed laughter and whispered comment. The excitement was palpable. Most of the young women in the room wore gauze masks, though that precaution had been proven ineffective. Others sucked on special mint and garlic lozenges claimed to prevent SHEVA from gaining a hold. Kaye could smell this peculiar odor even on the stage.

Jackson came to the microphone. At fifty, he looked like a well-preserved rock musician, loosely handsome, with suits

213

only barely pressed and unruly brown hair graying at the temples.

"We began our work years before Herod's flu," Jackson said. "We've always been interested in HERV sequences, because, as you imply, there's a lot of cleverness hidden there." He paused for effect, favoring the audience with a small smile, showing his strength by expressing admiration for the enemy. "But in truth, in the last twenty years, we've learned how most diseases do their dirty work, how the agents are constructed, how they are vulnerable. By creating empty SHEVA particles, increasing the retrovirus failure rate to one hundred percent, we make a harmless antigen. But the particles are not strictly empty. We load them with a ribozyme, a ribonucleic acid with enzymatic activity. The ribozyme locks on to, and cleaves, several fragments of SHEVA RNA not yet assembled in an infected cell. SHEVA becomes the delivery system for a molecule that blocks its own disease-causing activity."

"Sir—" the CNN reporter tried to break in.

"I'm not done answering your question," Jackson said. "It is *such* a good one!" The audience chuckled. "Our problem until now has been that humans do not react in any strong fashion to SHEVA antigen. So our breakthrough came when we learned how to emphasize the immune response by attaching glycoproteins associated with other pathogens for which the body automatically mounts a strong defense."

The CNN reporter tried to ask another question, but Nilson had already moved on down the long list. Next up was Sci-Trax's young on-line correspondent. "Again for Dr. Jackson. Do you know why we are so vulnerable to SHEVA?"

"Not all of us are vulnerable. Men demonstrate a strong immune response to SHEVA they do not themselves produce. This explains the course of Herod's flu in men— a quick, forty-eight-hour sort of thing, when it happens at all. Women, however, are almost universally open to the infection."

"Yes, but why are women so vulnerable?"

"We believe that SHEVA's strategy is incredibly long-term, on the order of thousands of years. It may be the first virus we've seen that relies on the growth of populations rather than individuals for its own propagation. To provoke a strong immune response would be counterproductive, so SHEVA emerges only when it seems that populations are either under stress, or because of some other triggering event we don't yet understand."

The science correspondent for the *New York Times* was next. "Drs. Pong and Subramanian, you've specialized in understanding Herod's flu in Southeast Asia, which is reporting over a hundred thousand cases so far. There has even been rioting in Indonesia. There were rumors last week that this was a different provirus—"

"Completely wrong," Subramanian said, smiling politely. "SHEVA is remarkably uniform. May I make a slight correction? 'Provirus' refers to the viral DNA inserted into the human genetic material. Once expressed, it is simply a virus or a retrovirus, although in this case, a very interesting one."

Kaye wondered how Subramanian could focus solely on the science, when her ears caught the singular and frightening word "riots."

"Yes, but my next question is, why do human males mount a strong immune response to the viruses of other males, but not to their own, if the glycoproteins in the envelope, the antigens, according to your press announcement, are so simple and invariant?"

"A very good question," Dr. Pong said. "Do we have time for a daylong seminar?"

Mild laughter. Pong continued, "We believe that male response begins after cell invasion, and that at least one gene within SHEVA contains subtle variations or mutations, which cause production of antigens on the surfaces of certain cells prior to a full-bore immune response, thereby acclimating the body to—"

Kaye listened with half her mind. She kept thinking of Mrs. Hamilton and the other women in the NIH clinic.

Human reproduction shutting down. There had to be extreme reactions to any failure; the burden on the scientists was going to be enormous.

"Oliver Merton, from the *Economist*. Question for Dr. Lang." Kaye looked up and saw a young red-haired man in a tweed coat holding the remote microphone. "Now that the genes coding for SHEVA, on their different chromosomes, have all been patented by Mr. Richard Bragg . . ." Merton glanced at his notes. "Of Berkeley, California . . . Patent number 8,564,094, issued by the United States Patent and Trademark Office on February 27, just yesterday, how will any company hoping to create a vaccine proceed without licensing and paying royalties?"

Nilson leaned toward her podium microphone. "There is no such patent, Mr. Merton."

"There is indeed," Merton said with an irritated wrinkle of his nose, "and I was hoping Dr. Lang could explain her deceased husband's involvement with Richard Bragg, and how that figures in her current association with Americol and the CDC?"

Kaye stood in dumfounded silence.

Merton grinned proudly at the confusion.

Kaye entered the green room after Jackson, followed by Pong, Subramanian, and the rest of the scientists. Cross sat in the middle of a large blue couch, her expression grave. Four of her top attorneys stood in a half circle around the couch.

"What in the hell was that all about?" Jackson demanded, swinging his arm out to poke in the general direction of the stage.

"The little rooster out there is right," Cross said. "Richard Bragg convinced somebody at the PTO that he isolated and sequenced the SHEVA genes before anyone else. He started the patent process last year."

Kaye took a faxed copy of the patent from Cross. Listed among the inventors was Saul Madsen; EcoBacter was on the list of assignees, along with AKS Industries—the company that had purchased and then liquidated EcoBacter.

"Kaye, tell me now, tell me straight," Cross said, "did you know anything about this?"

"Nothing," Kaye said. "I'm at a loss, Marge. I specified locations, but I did *not* sequence the genes. Saul never mentioned Richard Bragg."

"What does it mean for our work?" Jackson stormed. "Lang, how could you not know?"

"We're not done with this," Cross said. "Harold?" She glanced at the nearest gray-haired man in his immaculate pinstripe suit.

"We'll challenge with *Genetron v. Amgen*, 'Random patenting of retrogenes in mouse genome,' " the attorney said. "Give us a day and we'll have a dozen more reasons to overturn." He pointed to Kaye and asked her, "Does AKS or any subsidiary use federal funds?"

"EcoBacter applied for a small federal grant," Kaye said. "It was approved, but never funded."

"We could get NIH to invoke Bayh-Dole," the attorney mused happily.

"What if it's solid?" Cross interrupted, her voice low and dangerous.

"It's possible we can get Ms. Lang an interest in the patent. Unlawful exclusion of primary inventor."

Cross thumped the couch cushions with a fist. "Then we'll think positive," she said. "Kaye, honey, you look like a stunned ox."

Kaye held up her hands in defense. "I swear, Marge, I didn't—"

"Why my own people didn't weed this out, I'd like to know. I want to talk with Shawbeck and Augustine right away." She turned to the attorneys. "See where else Bragg has poked his finger. Where there's scum, there's bound to be a slipup."

Bethesda

MARCH

"It was a very short trip," Dicken said as he dropped a paper report and a diskette on Augustine's desk. "The WHO folks in Africa told me they were handling things their way, thank you. They said cooperation on past investigations could not be assumed here. They only have one hundred and fifty confirmed cases in all of Africa, so they say, and they don't see any reason for panic. At least they were kind enough to give me some tissue samples. I shipped them out of Cape Town."

"We got them," Augustine said. "Odd. If we believe their figures, Africa's being hit much more lightly than Asia or Europe or North America." He looked troubled—not angry, but sad. Dicken had never seen Augustine look so down before. "Where are we going with this, Christopher?"

"The vaccine, right?" Christopher asked.

"I mean you, me, the Taskforce. We're going to have over a million infected women by the end of May in North America alone. The national security advisor has called in sociologists to tell them how the public's going to react. The pressure is increasing every week. I've just come from a meeting with the surgeon general and the vice president. Just the veep, Christopher. The president considers the Taskforce a liability. Kaye Lang's little scandal was *completely* unexpected. The only joy I got out of that was watching Marge Cross chug around this room like a derailed freight train. We're getting

218

pasted in the press—'Incompetent Bungling in an Age of Miracles.' That's the general tone."

"Not surprising," Dicken said, and sat in the chair across from the desk.

"You know Lang better than I do, Christopher. How could she have let this happen?"

"I was under the impression that NIH was getting the patent reversed. Some technicality, inability to exploit a natural resource."

"Yes—but in the meanwhile, this son of a bitch Bragg is making us look like donkeys. Was Lang so stupid as to sign *every* paper her husband thrust in front of her?"

"She signed?"

"She signed," Augustine said. "Plain as day. Handing over control of any discovery based on primordial human endogenous retrovirus to Saul Madsen and any partners."

"Partners not specified?"

"Not specified."

"Then she's not really culpable, is she?" Dicken said.

"I don't enjoy working with fools. She crossed me quite literally with Americol, and now she's brought ridicule down on the Taskforce. Any wonder the president won't meet with me?"

"It's temporary." Dicken bit at a fingernail but stopped when Augustine looked up.

"Cross says we go ahead with the trials and let Bragg sue us. I agree. But for the time being, I'm burying our relationship with Lang."

"She could still be useful."

"Then let her be anonymously useful."

"Are you saying I should stay away from her?"

"No," Augustine said. "Keep everything hunky-dory between you. Make her feel wanted and in the loop. I don't want *her* going to the press—unless it's to complain about Cross's treatment. Now . . . for the next bit of unpleasantness."

Augustine reached into his desk drawer and pulled out a

glossy black-and-white photo. "I hate this, Christopher, but I see why it's being done."

"What?" Dicken felt like a little boy about to be scolded.

"Shawbeck asked the FBI to keep tabs on our key people."

Dicken leaned forward. He had long since developed a civil servant's instinct for keeping his reactions in check. "Why, Mark?"

"Because there's talk about declaring a national emergency and invoking martial law. No decision has been made yet . . . it may be months away . . . But under the circumstances, we all need to be pure as the driven snow. We're angels of healing, Christopher. The public is relying on us. No flaws allowed."

Augustine handed him the photo. It showed him standing in front of Jessie's Cougar in Washington, D.C. "It would have been very embarrassing if you had been recognized."

Dicken's face flushed with both guilt and anger. "I went there once, months ago," he said. "I stayed fifteen minutes and left."

"You went into a back room with a girl," Augustine said.

"She wore a surgical mask and treated me like a leper!" Dicken said, showing more heat than he had intended. The instinct was wearing very thin. "I didn't even want to touch her!"

"I hate this shit as much as anybody, Christopher," Augustine said stonily, "but it's just the beginning. We're all of us facing pretty intense public scrutiny."

"So I'm under probation and review, Mark? The FBI is going to ask for my little black book?"

Augustine did not feel the need to answer this.

Dicken stood and threw the photograph down on the desk. "What next? Shall I tell you the name of everyone I'm dating, and what we do together?"

"Yes," Augustine said softly.

Dicken stopped in midtirade and felt his anger fly out of him like a loose burp. The implications were so broad and frightening that he suddenly felt nothing more than cold anxiety.

"The vaccine won't be through clinical trials for at least four months, even on emergency fast track. Shawbeck and the VP are taking a new policy to the White House this evening. We're recommending quarantine. It's a good bet we're going to need to invoke some sort of martial law to enforce it."

Dicken sat down again. "Unbelievable," he said.

"Don't tell me you haven't thought about this," Augustine said. His face was gray with strain.

"I don't have that kind of imagination," Dicken said bitterly.

Augustine swiveled to look out the window. "Springtime soon. Young men's fancy and all that. A really good time to announce segregation of the sexes. All women of child-bearing age, all men. OMB will have a ball figuring out how much this will slow down the GNP."

They sat in silence for a long moment.

"Why did you lead with Kaye Lang?" Dicken asked.

"Because I know what to do with her," Augustine said. "This other stuff . . . Don't quote me, Christopher. I see the necessity, but I don't know how in hell we can survive it, politically." He pulled another print from the folder and held it up for Dicken to see. It showed a man and a woman on a porch in front of an old brownstone, illuminated by a single overhead light. They were kissing. Dicken could not see the man's face, but he dressed like Augustine and had the same physique.

"Just so you don't feel bad. She's married to a freshman congressman," Augustine said. "We're finished. Time for all of us to grow up."

Dicken stood outside the Taskforce center in Building 51, feeling a little ill. Martial law. Segregation of the sexes. He hunched his shoulders and walked to the parking lot, avoiding the cracks in the sidewalk.

In his car, he found a message on the cell phone. He dialed in and retrieved it. An unfamiliar voice tried to overcome a real antipathy toward leaving messages, and after a few false starts, suggested they had mutual acquaintances—two or three removed—and possibly some mutual interests.

"My name is Mitch Rafelson. I'm in Seattle now but I hope to fly East soon and meet with some people. If you're interested . . . in historical incidents of SHEVA, ancient examples, please get in touch with me."

Dicken closed his eyes and shook his head. Unbelievable. It seemed everyone knew about his crazy hypothesis. He took down the phone number on a small notepad, then stared at it quizzically. The man's name sounded familiar. He marked it through once with his pen.

He rolled down the window and took a deep breath of air. The day was warming and the clouds over Bethesda were clearing. Winter would be over soon.

Against his better judgment, against any judgment worthy of the name, he punched in Kaye Lang's number. She was not at home.

"I hope you're good at dancing with the big girls," Dicken murmured to himself, and started the car. "Cross is a very big girl indeed."

Baltimore

The attorney's name was Charles Wothering. He sounded pure Boston, dressed with rumpled flair, wore a rough-knit wool cap and a long purple muffler. Kaye offered him coffee and he accepted.

"Very nice," he commented, looking around the apartment. "You have taste."

"Marge set it up for me," Kaye said.

Wothering smiled. "Marge has no taste in decoration at all. But money does wonderful things, doesn't it?"

Kaye smiled. "No complaints," she said. "Why did she send you here? To . . . amend our agreements?"

"Not at all," Wothering said. "Your father and mother are dead, aren't they?"

"Yes," Kaye said.

"I'm a middling lawyer, Ms. Lang—may I call you Kaye?" Kaye nodded.

"Middling at law, but Marge values me as a judge of character. Believe it or not, Marge is not a very good judge of character. Lots of bravado, but a string of bad marriages, which I helped untangle and pack away into the distant past, never to be heard from again. She thinks you need my help."

"How?" Kaye asked.

Wothering sat on the couch and took three spoons of sugar from the bowl on the serving tray. He stirred them deliberately into his cup. "Did you love Saul Madsen?"

"Yes," Kaye said.

"And how do you feel now?"

Kaye thought this over, but did not look down from Wothering's steady gaze. "I realize how much Saul was hiding things from me, just to keep our dream afloat."

"How much did Saul contribute to your work, intellectually?"

"That depends which work."

"Your endogenous virus work."

"Only a little. Not his specialty."

"What was his specialty?"

"He likened himself to yeast."

"Beg your pardon?"

"He contributed to the ferment. I brought in the sugar."

Wothering laughed. "Did he stimulate you, intellectually, I mean?"

"He challenged me."

"Like a teacher, or a parent, or . . . a partner?"

"Partner," Kaye said. "I don't see where we're going, Mr. Wothering."

"You attached yourself to Marge because you did not feel yourself adequate to deal with Augustine and his people alone. Am I right?"

Kaye stared at him.

Wothering lifted a bushy eyebrow.

"Not exactly," Kaye said. Her eyes stung from not blinking. Wothering blinked luxuriously and set down his cup.

"To be brief, Marge sent me here to separate you from Saul Madsen every way I can. I need your permission to conduct a thorough investigation of EcoBacter, AKS, and your contracts with the Taskforce."

"Is that necessary? I'm sure there aren't any more skeletons in my closet, Mr. Wothering."

"We can never be too cautious, Kaye. You understand that things are getting very serious. Embarrassments of any sort can have a real impact on public policy."

"I know," Kaye said. "I've said I'm sorry."

Wothering held out his hand and made a soothing face as he patted the air with his fingers. In a different age, he might have patted her knee in a fatherly fashion. "We'll clean up the mess." Wothering's eyes took on a flinty look. "I don't want to replace your own growing sense of individual responsibility with the automatic personal housekeeping of a good lawyer," he said. "You're a grown woman now, Kaye. But what I will do is untangle the strings, and then . . . I'll cut them. You will owe nothing to anybody."

Kaye bit her lip. "I'd like to make one thing clear, Mr. Wothering. My husband was sick. He was mentally ill. What Saul did or did not do is no reflection on me—nor on him. He was trying to keep his balance and get on with his life and work."

"I understand, Ms. Lang."

"Saul was very helpful to me, in his own way, but I resent any implication that I am not my own woman."

"No such implication intended."

"Good," Kaye said, feeling her way through a subtle mine-field of irritation, threatening to flare into anger. "What I need to know now is, does Marge Cross still find me useful?"

Wothering smiled and gave a tilt of his head in a way that expertly expressed acknowledgment of her irritation and the need to continue his task. "Marge never gives more than she takes, as I'm sure you will learn soon. Can you explain this vaccine to me, Kaye?"

"It's a combination antigen coat carrying a tailored ribozyme. Ribonucleic acid with enzymelike properties. It attaches to part of the SHEVA code and splits it. Breaks its back. The virus can't replicate."

Wothering shook his head in amazement. "Technically wonderful," he said. "For most of us, incomprehensible. Tell me, how do you think Marge will get women all over the world to consider using it?"

"Advertising and promotion, I suppose. She said she'd practically give it away."

"Who will the patients *trust*, Kaye? You are a brilliant woman whose husband deceived her, kept her in the dark. Women can feel this unfairness in their very wombs. Believe me, Marge will go to great lengths to keep you on her team. Your story just gets better and better."

41

Seattle

Mitch pushed up in bed, in a sweat and shouting. The words leaped out in a guttural tumble even as he realized he was awake. He sat on one side of the bed, leg still tangled in the covers, and shivered. "Nuts," he said. "I am nuts. Nuts to *this*."

He had dreamed of the Neandertals again. This time, he had flowed in and out of the male's point of view, a fluid sort of freedom that had at once immersed him in a very clear and unpleasant set of emotions, and then lofted him away to observe a jumbled flow of events. Crowds had formed at the edge of the village—not on a lake this time, but in a clearing surrounded by deep and ancient woods. They had shaken sharpened, fire-hardened sticks at the female, whose name he could almost remember . . . *Na-lee-ah* or *Ma-lee*.

"Jean Auel, here I come," he murmured as he extricated his foot from the covers. "Mowgli of the Stone Tribe saves his woman. Jesus."

He walked into the kitchen to get a glass of water. He was fighting off some virus—a cold, he was sure, and not SHEVA, considering the state of his relationships with women. His mouth tasted dry and foul and his nose was dripping. He had caught the cold somewhere on his trip to Iron Cave the week before. Maybe Merton had given it to him. He had driven the British journalist to the airport for a flight to Maryland.

The water tasted terrible, but it cleaned out his mouth. He looked out over Broadway and the post office, nearly deserted now. A March snowstorm was throwing small crystal flakes down on the streets. The orange sodium vapor streetlights turned the accumulated snow into scattered piles of gold.

"They were kicking us off the lake, out of the village," he murmured. "We were going to have to fend for ourselves. Some hotheads were getting ready to follow us, maybe try to kill us. We . . ."

He shuddered. The emotions had been so raw and so real he could not easily shake them. Fear, rage, something else . . . a helpless kind of love. He felt his face. They had been shedding some sort of skin from their faces, little masks. The mark of their crime.

"Dear Shirley MacLaine," he said, pressing his forehead against the cold glass of the window. "I'm channeling cavemen who don't live in caves. Any advice?"

He looked at the clock on the VCR perched precariously on top of the small TV. It was five in the morning. It would be eight o'clock in Atlanta. He would try that number again, and then try to log on with his repaired laptop and send an e-mail message.

In the bathroom, he stared at himself in the mirror. Hair awry, face sweaty and oily, two days' growth of beard, wearing a ripped T-shirt and BVDs. "A regular Jeremiah," he said.

Then he started another general cleanup by blowing his nose and brushing his teeth.

Atlanta

Christopher Dicken had returned to his small house on the outskirts of Atlanta at three in the morning. He had worked at his CDC office until two, preparing papers for Augustine on the spread of SHEVA in Africa. He had lain awake for an hour, wondering what the world was going to be like in the next six months. When he finally drifted off into sleep, he was awakened it seemed moments later by the buzzing of his cell phone. He sat up in the queen-size bed that had once belonged to his parents, wondered for a moment where he was, decided quickly he was not in the Cape Town Hilton, and switched on the light. Morning was already glowing through the window shutters. He managed to pull the phone out of his coat pocket in the closet by the fourth ring and answered it.

"Is this Dr. Chris Dicken?"

"Christopher. Yeah." He looked at his watch. It was eight fifteen. He had managed to sleep a mere two hours, and he was sure he felt worse than if he had had no sleep at all.

"My name is Mitch Rafelson."

This time, Dicken remembered the name and its association. "Really?" he said. "Where are you, Mr. Rafelson?"

"Seattle."

"Then it's even earlier where you are. I need to get back to sleep."

"Wait, please," Mitch said. "I'm sorry if I woke you up. Did you get my message?"

"I got *a* message," Dicken said.

"We need to talk."

"Listen, if you *are* Mitch Rafelson, *the* Mitch Rafelson, I need to talk to you . . . about as much as . . ." He tried to come up with a witty comparison, but his mind wouldn't work. "I don't need to talk with you."

"Point made . . . but please listen anyway. You've been tracking SHEVA all over the world, right?"

"Yeah," Dicken said. He yawned. "I get very little sleep thinking about it."

"Me, too," Mitch said. "Your bodies in the Caucasus tested positive for SHEVA. My mummies . . . in the Alps . . . the mummies at Innsbruck test positive for SHEVA."

Dicken pressed the phone closer to his ear. "How do you know that?"

"I have the lab reports from the University of Washington. I need to show what I know to you and to whoever else is open-minded about this."

"Nobody is open-minded about this," Dicken said. "Who gave you my number?"

"Dr. Wendell Packer."

"Do I know Packer?"

"You work with a friend of his. Renée Sondak."

Dicken scratched at a front tooth with a fingernail. Thought very seriously about hanging up. His cell phone was digitally scrambled, but somebody could decode the conversation if they had a mind to. This made him flash hot with anger. Things were out of control. Everyone had lost perspective and it was not going to get better if he just played along.

"I'm pretty lonely," Mitch said into the silence. "I need someone to tell me I'm not completely nuts."

"Yeah," Dicken said. "I know what that's like." Then, screwing up his face and stamping his foot on the floor, knowing this was going to give him far more trouble than any windmill he had ever tilted at before, he said, "Tell me more, Mitch."

43

San Diego, California
MARCH 28

The title of the international conference, arranged in black plastic letters on the convention center billboard, gave Dicken a brief thrill—brief and very necessary. Nothing much had thrilled him in the good old way of work satisfaction in the past couple of months, but the name of the conference was easily sufficient.

CONTROLLING THE EN-VIRON-MENT:
NEW TECHNIQUES TOWARD THE CONQUEST OF VIRAL ILLNESS

The sign was not overly optimistic or off base. In a few more years, the world might not need Christopher Dicken to chase down viruses.

The problem they all faced was that in disease time, a few years could be very long indeed.

Dicken walked just outside the shadow of the center's concrete overhang, near the main entrance, reveling in the bright sun on the sidewalk. He had not experienced this kind of heat since Cape Town, and it gave him a furnace boost of energy. Atlanta was finally warming, but the cold gripping the East had kept snow on the streets in Baltimore and Bethesda.

Mark Augustine was in town already, staying at the U.S. Grant, away from the majority of the five thousand predicted attendees, most of whom were filling the hotels along the waterfront. Dicken had picked up his convention package—a thick spiral-bound program book with a companion DVD-ROM disk—just this morning to get an early glimpse at the schedule.

Marge Cross would deliver a keynote address tomorrow morning. Dicken would sit on five panels, two of them dealing with SHEVA. Kaye Lang would be on one panel with Dicken, and on seven others beside, and she would deliver a talk before the plenary session of the World Retrovirus Eradication Research Group, held in conjunction with this conference.

The press was already hailing Americol's ribozyme vaccine as a major breakthrough. It looked good in a petri dish—very good indeed—but the human trials had not yet begun. Augustine was under considerable pressure from Shawbeck, and Shawbeck was under considerable pressure from the administration, and they were all using a very long spoon to sup with Cross.

Dicken could smell eight different kinds of disaster in the winds.

He had not heard from Mitch Rafelson for several days, but suspected the anthropologist was already in town. They had not yet met, but the conspiracy was on. Kaye had agreed to join them for a talk this evening or tomorrow, depending on when Cross's people would let her loose from a round of public relations interviews.

They would have to find a place away from prying eyes. Dicken suspected the best place would be right in the middle of everything, and to that end, he carried a second bag with a blank convention badge—"Guest of CDC"—and program book.

Kaye walked through the crowded suite, eyes darting nervously from face to face. She felt like a spy in a bad movie, trying to hide her true emotions, certainly her opinions—though she, herself, hardly knew what to think now. She had spent much of the afternoon in Marge Cross's suite—rather, her entire floor—upstairs, meeting with men and women representing wholly owned subsidiaries, professors from UCSD, the mayor of San Diego.

Marge had taken her aside and promised even more impressive VIPs near the end of the conference. "Keep bright and shiny," Cross had told her. "Don't let the conference wear you down."

Kaye felt like a doll on display. She did not like the sensation.

She took the elevator to the ground floor at five-thirty and boarded a charter bus to the opener. The event was being held at the San Diego Zoo, hosted by Americol.

As she stepped down from the bus in front of the zoo, she breathed in a scent of jasmine and the soil-rich wetness of evening sprinklers. The line at the entrance booth was busy; she queued up at a side gate and showed the guard her invitation.

Four women dressed in black carried signs and marched solemnly in front of the zoo entrance. Kaye saw them just before she was allowed in; one of their signs read OUR BODIES, OUR DESTINY: SAVE OUR CHILDREN.

Inside, the warm twilight felt magical. She had not had anything like a vacation in over a year, the last time with Saul. Everything since had been work and grief, sometimes both together.

A zoo guide took charge of a group of Americol's guests and gave them a brief tour. Kaye spent a few seconds watching the pink flamingos in their wading pool. She admired four centenarian sulfur-crested cockatoos, including the zoo's current mascot, Ramesses, who regarded the departing crowds of day visitors with sleepy indifference. The guide then showed them to a side pavilion and court surrounded by palm trees.

A mediocre band played forties' favorites under the pavilion as men and women carried food on paper plates and found tables.

Kaye stopped by a buffet table laden with fruit and vegetables, picked up a generous helping of cheese, cherry tomatoes, cauliflower, and pickled mushrooms, then ordered a glass of white wine from the no-host bar.

As she was taking money from her purse to pay for the wine, she spotted Christopher Dicken out of the corner of her eye. He had in tow a tall, rugged-looking man dressed in a denim jacket and faded gray jeans and carrying a scuffed leather satchel under his arm. Kaye took a deep breath, fumbled her change back into her purse, and turned in time to meet Dicken's stealthy glance. In return, she gave him a surreptitious tilt of her head.

Kaye could not help giggling as Dicken pulled aside a canvas and they strolled casually away from the closed court. The zoo was nearly empty. "I feel so sneaky," she said. She still carried her glass of wine, but had managed to ditch the plate of vegetables. "What in the *world* do we think we're doing?"

There was little conviction in Mitch's smile. She found his eyes disconcerting—at once boyish and sad. Dicken, shorter and plumper, seemed more immediate and accessible, so Kaye focused on him. He carried a gift-shop bag and with a flourish pulled from it a folding map of the world's largest zoo.

"We may be here to save the human race," Dicken said. "Subterfuge is justified."

"Damn," Kaye said. "I'd hoped it was something more sensible. I wonder if anyone's listening?"

Dicken swept his hand toward the low arches of the Spanish-style reptile house as if waving a magic wand. Only a few straggling tourists remained on the zoo grounds. "All clear," he said.

"I'm serious, Christopher," Kaye said.

"If the FBI is bugging Komodo dragons or men in Hawaiian shirts, then we're goners. This is the best I can do."

Loud shrieks from howler monkeys greeted the last of the daylight. Mitch led them down a concrete path through a tropical rain forest. Footlights illuminated the pathway and misters sprayed the air over their heads. The charm of the setting held them all for the moment, and no one was willing to break the spell.

To Kaye, Mitch seemed all legs and arms, the kind of man who did not fit indoors. His silence bothered her. He turned, regarded her with his steady green eyes. Kaye noticed his shoes: hiking boots, the thick-treaded soles well-worn.

She smiled awkwardly and Mitch returned her smile.

"I'm out of my league," he said. "If anybody's going to start our conversation, it should be you, Ms. Lang."

"But you're the man with the revelation," Dicken said.

"How much time do we have?" Mitch asked.

"I'm free for the rest of the evening," Kaye said. "Marge wants us in tow by eight tomorrow morning. There's going to be an Americol breakfast."

They descended an escalator into a canyon and paused by a cage occupied by two Scottish wildcats. The domestic-looking brindled felines paced back and forth, grumbling softly in the dusk.

"I'm the odd man out here," Mitch said. "I know very little microbiology, barely enough to get along. I stumbled onto something wonderful, and it almost ruined my life. I'm disreputable, known to be eccentric, a two-time loser in the science game. If you were smart, you wouldn't even be seen with me."

"Remarkably candid," Dicken said. He raised his hand. "Next. I've chased diseases over half the Earth. I have a feel for how they spread, what they do, how they work. From almost the very beginning, I suspected I was tracking something new. Up until just recently, I've tried to lead a double life, tried to believe two contradictory things at once, and I can't do it anymore."

Kaye finished her glass of wine with one gulp. "We sound like we're working through a twelve-step program," she said. "All right. My turn. I'm an insecure female research scientist who wants to be kept out of all the dirty little details, so I cling to anybody who'll give me a place to work and protect me . . . and now it's time to be independent and make my own decisions. Time to grow up."

"Hallelujah," Mitch said.

"Go, sister," Dicken said.

She looked up, ready to be angry, but they were both smiling in just the right way, and for the first time in many months—since the last good time with Saul—she felt she was among friends.

Dicken reached into the shopping bag and produced a bottle of merlot. "Zoo security could bust us," he said, "but this is the least of our sins. Some of what needs to be said may only be said if we're properly drunk."

"I gather you two have shared ideas already," Mitch said to Kaye as Dicken poured the wine. "I've tried to read everything I could just to get ready for this, but I'm still way behind."

"I don't know where to begin," Kaye said. Now that they were more relaxed, the way Mitch Rafelson looked at her—direct, honest, assessing her without being obvious about it—stirred something she had thought almost dead.

"Begin with where you two met," Mitch said.

"Georgia," Kaye said.

"The birthplace of wine," Dicken added.

"We visited a mass grave," Kaye said. "Though not together. Pregnant women and their husbands."

"Killing the children," Mitch said, his eyes suddenly losing their focus. "Why?"

They sat at a plastic table near a closed refreshment stand, deep in the shadows of a canyon. Brown and red roosters pecked through the bushes beside the asphalt road and beige concrete walkways. A big cat coughed and snarled in its cage and the sound echoed eerily.

Mitch pulled a file folder from his small leather satchel and laid the papers neatly on the plastic table. "This is where it all comes together." He laid his hand on two papers on the right. "These are analyses made at the University of Washington.

Wendell Packer gave me permission to show them to you. If somebody blabs, however, we could all be in deep zoo-doo."

"Analyses of what?" Kaye asked.

"The genetics of the Innsbruck mummies. Two sets of tissue results from two different labs at the University of Washington. I gave tissue samples of the two adults to Wendell Packer. Innsbruck, as it turned out, sent a set of samples of all three mummies to Maria Konig in the same department. Wendell was able to make comparisons."

"What did they find?" Kaye asked.

"That the three bodies were really a family. Mother, father, daughter. I knew that already—I saw them all together in the cave in the Alps."

Kaye frowned in puzzlement. "I remember the story. You went to the cave at the request of two friends . . . Disturbed the site . . . And the woman with you took the infant in her backpack?"

Mitch looked away, jaw muscles tight. "I can tell you what actually happened," he said.

"That's all right," Kaye said, suddenly wary.

"Just to straighten things out," Mitch insisted. "We need to trust each other if we're going to continue."

"Then tell me more," Kaye said.

Mitch went through the whole story in brief. "It was a mess," he concluded.

Dicken watched them both intently, arms folded.

Kaye used the pause to look through the analyses spread on the plastic table top, making sure the papers did not get stained by leftover catsup. She studied the results of carbon 14 dating, the comparisons of genetic markers, and finally, Packer's successful search for SHEVA.

"Packer says SHEVA hasn't changed much in fifteen thousand years," Mitch said. "He finds that astonishing, if they're junk DNA."

"They're hardly junk," Kaye said. "The genes have been conserved for as much as thirty million years. They're constantly refreshed, tested, conserved . . . Locked up in tight-packed chromatin, protected by insulators ... They have to be."

"If you'll indulge me, I'd like to tell you both what I think," Mitch said, with a touch of boldness and shyness Kaye found both puzzling and appealing.

"Go ahead," she said.

"This was an example of subspeciation," he said. "Not extreme. A nudge to a new variety. A modern-type infant born to late-stage Neandertals."

"More like us," Kaye said.

"Right. There was a reporter named Oliver Merton in Washington state a few weeks ago. He's investigating the mummies. He told me about fights breaking out at the University of Innsbruck—" Mitch looked up and saw Kaye's surprise.

"Oliver Merton?" she asked, frowning. "Working for *Nature*?"

"For the *Economist*, at the time," Mitch said.

Kaye turned to Dicken. "The same one?"

"Yeah," Dicken said. "He does science journalism, some political reporting. Has one or two books published." He explained to Mitch. "Merton started a big ruckus at a press conference in Baltimore. He's dug pretty deeply into Americol's relationship with the CDC and the SHEVA matter."

"Maybe it's two different stories," Mitch said.

"It would have to be, wouldn't it?" Kaye asked, looking between the two men. "We're the only ones who have made a connection, aren't we?"

"I wouldn't be at all sure," Dicken said. "Go on, Mitch. Let's agree that there is a connection before we get fired up about interlopers. What were they arguing about in Innsbruck?"

"Merton says they've connected the infant to the adult mummies—which Packer confirms."

"It's ironic," Dicken said. "The UN sent some of the samples from Gordi to Konig's lab."

"The anthropologists at Innsbruck are pretty conservative," Mitch said. "To actually come across the first direct evidence of human speciation . . ." He shook his head in sympathy. "I'd be scared if I were them. The paradigm doesn't just shift—it snaps in two. No gradualism, no modern Darwinian synthesis."

"We don't need to be so radical," Dicken said. "First of all, there's been a lot of talk about punctuations in the fossil record—millions of years of steady state, then sudden change."

"Change over a million or a hundred thousand years, in some cases maybe as little as ten thousand years," Mitch said. "Not overnight. The implications are damned scary to any scientist. But the markers don't lie. And the baby's parents had SHEVA in their tissues."

"Um," Kaye said. Again, the howler monkeys let loose with continuous musical whoops, filling the night air.

"The female was injured by something sharp, perhaps a spear point," Dicken said.

"Right," Mitch said. "Causing the late-term infant to be born either dead or very near death. The mother died shortly after, and the father . . ." His voice hitched. "Sorry. I don't find it easy to talk about."

"You sympathize with them," Kaye said.

Mitch nodded. "I've been having weird dreams about them."

"ESP?" Kaye asked.

"I doubt it," Mitch said. "It's just the way my mind works, putting things together."

"You think they were pushed out of their tribe?" Dicken asked. "Persecuted?"

"Someone wanted to kill the woman," Mitch said. "The man stayed with her, tried to save her. They were different. They had something wrong with their faces. Little flaps of skin around their eyes and nose, like masks."

"They were shedding *skin*? I mean, when they were alive?" Kaye asked, and her shoulders shuddered.

"Around the eyes, the face."

"The bodies near Gordi," Kaye said.

"What about them?" Dicken asked.

"Some of them had little leathery masks. I thought it might have been . . . some bizarre product of decay. But I've never seen anything like it."

"We're getting ahead of ourselves," Dicken said. "Let's focus on Mitch's evidence."

"That's all I have," Mitch said. "Physiological changes substantial enough to place the infant in a different sub-species, all at once. In one generation."

"This sort of thing had to have been going on for over a hundred thousand years before your mummies," Dicken said. "So populations of Neandertals were living with or around populations of modern humans."

"I think so," Mitch said.

"Do you think the birth was an aberration?" Kaye asked.

Mitch regarded her for several seconds before saying "No."

"It's reasonable to conclude that you found something representative, not singular?"

"Possibly."

Kaye lifted her hands in exasperation.

"Look," Mitch said. "My instincts are conservative. I feel for the guys in Innsbruck, I really do! This is weird, totally unexpected."

"Do we have a smooth, gradual fossil record leading from Neandertals to Cro-Magnons?" Dicken asked.

"No, but we do have different stages. The fossil record is usually far from smooth."

"And . . . that's blamed on the fact that we can't find all the necessary specimens, right?"

"Right," Mitch said. "But some paleontologists have been at loggerheads with the gradualists for a long time now."

"Because they keep finding leaps, not gradual progression," Kaye said. "Even when the fossil record is better than it is for humans or other large animals."

They sipped from their glasses reflectively.

"What are *we* going to do?" Mitch asked. "The mummies had SHEVA. We have SHEVA."

"This is very complicated," Kaye said. "Who's going to go first?"

"Let's all write down what we believe is actually happening." Mitch reached into his satchel and brought out three legal pads and three ballpoint pens. He spread them out on the table.

"Like schoolkids?" Dicken asked.

"Mitch is right. Let's do it," Kaye said.

Dicken pulled a second bottle of wine from the gift shop bag and uncorked it.

Kaye held the cap of her pen between her lips. They had been writing for ten or fifteen minutes, switching pads and asking questions. The air was getting chilly.

"The party will be over soon," she said.

"Don't worry," Mitch said. "We'll protect you."

She smiled ruefully. "Two half-drunk men dizzy with theories?"

"Exactly," Mitch said.

Kaye had been trying to avoid looking at him. What she was feeling was hardly scientific or professional. Writing down her thoughts was not easy. She had never worked this way before, not even with Saul; they had shared notebooks, but had never looked at each other's notes in progress, as they were being written.

The wine relaxed her, took away some of the tension, but did not clarify her thinking. She was hitting a block. She had written:

Populations as giant networks of units that both compete and cooperate, sometimes at the same time. Every evidence of communication between individuals in populations. Trees communicate with chemicals. Humans use pheromones. Bacteria exchange plasmids and lysogenic phages.

Kaye looked at Dicken, writing steadily, crossing out entire paragraphs. Plump, yes, but obviously strong and motivated, accomplished; attractive features.

She now wrote:

Ecosystems are networks of species cooperating and competing. Pheromones and other chemicals can cross species. Networks can have the same qualities as brains; human brains are networks of neurons. Creative thinking is possible in any sufficiently complicated functional neural network.

"Let's take a look at what we've got," Mitch suggested. They exchanged notebooks. Kaye read Mitch's page:

Signaling molecules and viruses carry information between people. The information is gathered by the individual human in life experience; but is this Lamarckian evolution?

"I think this networking stuff confuses the issue," Mitch said.

Kaye was reading Dicken's paper. "It's how all things in nature work," she said. Dicken had scratched out most of his page. What remained was:

Chase disease all my life; SHEVA causes complex biological changes, unlike any disease ever seen. Why? What does it gain? What is it trying to do? What is the end result? If it pops up once every ten thousand or hundred thousand years, how can we defend that it is, in any sense, a separate organic concern, a purely pathogenic particle?

"Who's going to buy that all things in nature function like neurons in a brain?" Mitch asked.

"It answers your question," Kaye said. "Is this Lamarckian evolution, inheritance of traits acquired by an individual? No.

It's the result of complex interactions of a network, with emergent thoughtlike properties."

Mitch shook his head. "Emergent properties confuse me."

Kaye glared at him for a moment, both challenged and exasperated. "We don't have to posit self-awareness, conscious thought, to have an organized network that responds to its environment and issues judgments about what its individual nodes should look like," Kaye said.

"Still sounds like the ghost in the machine to me," Mitch said, making a sour face.

"Look, trees send out chemical signals when they're attacked. The signals attract insects that prey on the bugs that attack them. Call the Orkin man. The concept works at all levels, in the ecosystem, in a species, even in a society. All individual creatures are networks of cells. All species are networks of individuals. All ecosystems are networks of species. All interact and communicate with one another to one degree or another, through competition, predation, cooperation. All these interactions are similar to neurotransmitters crossing synapses in the brain, or ants communicating in a colony. The colony changes its overall behavior based on ant interactions. So do we, based on how our neurons talk to each other. And so does all of nature, from top to bottom. It's all connected."

But she could see Mitch still wasn't buying it.

"We have to describe a method," Dicken said. He looked at Kaye with a small, knowing smile. "Make it simple. You're the thinker on this one."

"What packs the punch in punctuated equilibrium?" she asked, still irritated at Mitch's density.

"All right. If there's a mind of some sort, where's the memory?" Mitch asked. "Something that stores up the information on the next model of human being, before it's turned loose on the reproductive system."

"Based on what stimulus?" Dicken asked. "Why acquire information at all? What starts it? What mechanism triggers it?"

"We're getting ahead of ourselves," Kaye said, sighing. "First, I don't like the word mechanism."

"All right, then . . . organ, organon, magic architect," Mitch said. "We know what we're talking about here. Some sort of memory storage in the genome. All the messages have to be kept there until they're activated."

"Would it be in the germ-line cells? The sex cells, sperm and egg?" Dicken asked.

"You tell me," Mitch said.

"I don't think so," Kaye said. "Something modifies a single egg in each mother, so it produces an interim daughter, but it's what's in the daughter's ovary that may produce a new phenotype. The other eggs in the mother are out of the loop. Protected, not modified."

"In case the new design, the new phenotype is a bust," Dicken said, nodding agreement. "Okay. A set-aside memory, updated over thousands of years by . . . hypothetical modifications, somehow tailored by . . ." He shook his head. "Now I'm confused."

"Every individual organism is aware of its environment and reacts to it," Kaye said. "The chemicals and other signals exchanged by individuals cause fluctuations in internal chemistry that affect the genome, specifically, movable elements in a genetic memory that stores and updates sets of hypothetical changes." Her hands waved back and forth, as if they could clarify or persuade. "This is so clear to me, guys. Why can't you see it? Here's the complete feedback loop: the environment changes, causing stress on organisms—in this case, on humans. The types of stress alter balances of stress-related chemicals in our bodies. The set-aside memory reacts and movable elements shift based on an evolutionary algorithm established over millions, even billions of years. A genetic computer decides what might be the best phenotype for the new conditions that cause the stress. We see small changes in individuals as a result, prototypes, and if the stress levels are reduced, if the offspring are healthy and many, the changes are kept. But every now and then, when a problem in the environment is intractable . . . long-term social stress in humans, for example . . . there's a major shift. Endogenous retroviruses express, carry a signal, coordinate the activation of specific elements in the genetic memory storage. Voilà. Punctuation."

Mitch pinched the bridge of his nose. "Lord," he said.

Dicken frowned deeply. "That's too radical for me to swallow all at once."

"We have evidence for every step along the way," Kaye said hoarsely. She took another long swallow of merlot.

"But how does it get passed along? It *has* to be in the sex cells. Something has to be passed along from parent to child for hundreds, thousands of generations before it gets activated."

"Maybe it's zipped, compacted, in shorthand code," Mitch said.

Kaye was startled by this. She looked at Mitch with a little chill of wonder. "That's so crazy it's brilliant. Like overlapping genes, only more devious. Buried in the repeats."

"It doesn't have to carry the whole instruction set for the new phenotype . . ." Dicken said.

"Just the parts that are going to be changed," Kaye said. "Look, we know that between a chimp and humans, there's maybe a two percent difference in the genome."

"And different numbers of chromosomes," Mitch said. "That makes a big difference ultimately."

Dicken frowned and held his head. "God, this is getting deep."

"It's ten o'clock," Mitch said. He pointed to a security guard walking down the middle of the road through the canyon, clearly heading in their direction.

Dicken threw the empty bottles into a trash can and returned to the table. "We can't afford to stop now. Who knows when we'll be able to get together again?"

Mitch studied Kaye's notes. "I see your point about change in the environment causing stress on individual humans.

Let's get back to Christopher's question. What triggers the signal, the change? Disease? Predators?"

"In our case, crowding," Kaye said.

"Complex social conditions. Competition for jobs," Dicken added.

"Folks," the guard called out as he drew close. His voice echoed in the canyon. "Are you with the Americol party?"

"How'd you guess?" Dicken asked.

"You're not supposed to be out here."

As they walked back, Mitch shook his head dubiously. He wasn't going to give either of them any breaks: a real hard case. "Change usually occurs at the edge of a population, where resources are scarce and competition is tough. Not in the center, where everything's cushy."

"There are no 'edges,' no boundaries for humans anymore," Kaye said. "We cover the planet. But we're under stress all the time just to keep up with the Joneses."

"There's always war," Dicken said, suddenly thoughtful. "The early Herod's outbreaks might have occurred just after World War II. Stress of a social cataclysm, society going horribly wrong. Humans must change or else."

"Says who? Says what?" Mitch asked, slapping his hip with his hand.

"Our species-level biological computer," Kaye said.

"There we go again—a computer network," Mitch said dubiously.

"THE MIGHTY WIZARD IN OUR GENES," Kaye intoned in a deep, fruity announcer's voice. Then, marking the air with her finger, "The Master of the Genome."

Mitch grinned and jabbed his finger back at her. "That's what they're going to say, and then they'll laugh us out of town."

"Out of the whole damned zoo," Dicken said.

"That'll cause stress," Kaye said primly.

"Focus, focus," Dicken insisted.

"Screw that," Kaye said. "Let's go back to the hotel and

open the next bottle." She swung her arms out and pirouetted. *Damn,* she thought. *I'm showing off. Hey, guys, I'm available, look at me.*

"Only as a reward," Dicken said. "We'll have to take a cab if the bus is gone. Kaye . . . what's wrong with the center? What's wrong with being in the middle of the human population?"

She dropped her arms. "Every year more and more people . . ." She stopped herself and her expression hardened. "The competition is so intense." Saul's face. Bad Saul, losing and not accepting it, and good Saul, enthusiastic as a child, but still painted with that indelible marker that said, *You're going to lose. There are tougher, smarter wolves than you.*

The two men waited for her to finish.

They walked toward the gate. Kaye wiped her eyes quickly and said, in as steady a voice as she could manage, "Used to be one or two or three people would come up with a brilliant, world-shaking idea or invention." Her voice grew stronger; now she felt resentment and even anger, on behalf of Saul. "Darwin and Wallace. Einstein. Now, there's a hundred geniuses for every challenge, a *thousand* people competing to topple the castle walls. If it's that bad in the sciences, up in the stratosphere, what's it like down in the trenches? Endless nasty competition. Too much to learn. Too much bandwidth crowding the channels of communication. We can't listen fast enough. We're left standing on our tiptoes all the time."

"How is that any different from fighting a cave bear or a mammoth?" Mitch asked. "Or from watching your kids die of plague?"

"They result in different sorts of stress, affecting different chemicals, maybe. We've long since given up on growing new claws or fangs. We're social. All our major changes are pointed in the direction of communication and social adaptation."

"Too much change," Mitch said thoughtfully. "Everyone hates it, but we have to compete or we end up out on the streets."

They stood in front of the gate and listened to the crickets.

Back in the zoo, a macaw squawked. The sound carried all over Balboa Park.

"Diversity," Kaye murmured. "Too much stress could be a sign of impending catastrophe. The twentieth century has been one long, frenetic, extended catastrophe. Let loose with a major change, something stored up in the genome, before the human race fails."

"Not a disease, but an upgrade," Mitch said.

Kaye looked at him again with the same brief chill. "Precisely," she said. "Everyone travels everywhere in just hours or days. What gets triggered in a neighborhood is suddenly spread all over the world. The Wizard is overwhelmed with signals." She stretched out her arms again, more restrained, but hardly sober. She knew Mitch was looking at her, and Dicken was watching them both.

Dicken peered up the drive beside the broad zoo parking lot, trying to find a cab. He saw one making a U-turn several hundred feet away and thrust out his hand. The cab pulled up at the loading zone.

They climbed in. Dicken took the front seat. As they drove, he turned to say, "All right, so some stretch of DNA in our genome is patiently building up a model of the next type of human. Where is it getting its ideas, its suggestions? Who's whispering, 'Longer legs, bigger brain case, brown eyes are best this year?' Who's telling us what's handsome and what's ugly?"

Kaye spoke rapidly. "The chromosomes use a biological grammar, built into the DNA, a kind of high-level species blueprint. The Wizard knows what it can say that will make sense for an organism's phenotype. The Wizard includes a genetic editor, a grammar checker. It stops most nonsense mutations before they ever get included."

"We're off into the wild blue yonder here," Mitch said, "and they'll shoot us down in the first minute of any dogfight." He whipped his hands through the air like two airplanes, making the cabby nervous, then dramatically plunged his left hand into his knee, crumpling his fingers. "Scrunch," he said.

The cabby regarded them curiously. "You folks biologists?" he asked.

"Grad students in the university of life," Dicken said.

"Got ya," the cabby said solemnly.

"Now we've earned this." Dicken took the third bottle of wine from the bag and pulled out his Swiss Army knife.

"Hey, not in the cab," the cabby said sternly. "Not unless I go off duty and you share."

They laughed. "In the hotel, then," Dicken said.

"I'll be drunk," Kaye said, and shook her hair down around her eyes.

"We'll have an orgy," Dicken said, and then flushed bright pink. "An intellectual orgy," he added sheepishly.

"I'm worn out," Mitch said. "Kaye's got laryngitis."

She gave a small squeak and grinned.

The cab pulled up in front of the Serrano Hotel, just southwest of the convention center, and let them out.

"My treat," Dicken said. He paid the fare. "Like the wine."

"All right," Mitch said. "Thanks."

"We need some sort of conclusion," Kaye said. "A prediction."

Mitch yawned and stretched. "Sorry. Can't think another thought."

Kaye watched him through her bangs: the slim hips, the jeans tight around his thighs, the square rugged face with its single line of eyebrow. Not beautifully handsome, but she heard her own chemistry, a low breathy singing in her loins, and it cared little about that. The first sign of the end of winter.

"I'm serious," she said. "Christopher?"

"It's obvious, isn't it?" Dicken said. "We're saying the interim daughters are not diseased, they're a stage of development we've never seen before."

"And what does that mean?" Kaye asked.

"It means the second-stage babies will be healthy, viable. And different, maybe just a little," Dicken said.

"That would be amazing," Kaye said. "What else?"

"Enough, please. We can't possibly finish it tonight," Mitch said.

"Pity," Kaye said.

Mitch smiled down on her. Kaye offered him her hand and they shook. Mitch's palm was dry as leather and rough with calluses from long years of digging. His nostrils dilated as he was near her, and she could have sworn she saw his irises grow large, as well.

Dicken's face was still pink. He slurred his words slightly. "We don't have a game plan," he said. "If there's going to be a report, we have to get all our evidence together—and I mean all of it."

"Count on it," Mitch said. "You have my number."

"I don't," Kaye said.

"Christopher will give it to you," Mitch said. "I'll be around for a few more days. Let me know when you're available."

"We will," Dicken said.

"We'll call," Kaye said as she and Dicken walked toward the glass doors.

"Interesting fellow," Dicken said on the elevator.

Kaye agreed with a small nod. Dicken was watching her with some concern.

"Seems bright," he continued. "How in the world did he get in so much trouble?"

In her room, Kaye took a hot shower and crawled into bed, exhausted and more than a little drunk. Her body was happy. She twisted the sheets and blanket around her head and rolled on her side, and almost immediately, she was asleep.

44

San Diego, California
APRIL 1

Kaye had just finished washing her face, whistling through the dripping water, when her room phone rang. She dabbed her face dry and answered it.

"Kaye? This is Mitch."

"I remember you," she said lightly, she hoped not *too* lightly.

"I'm flying north tomorrow. Hoped you might have some time this morning to get together."

She had been so busy giving talks and serving on panels at the conference that there had been little time to even think about the evening at the zoo. Each night, she had fallen into bed, completely exhausted. Judith Kushner had been right; Marge Cross was absorbing every second of her life.

"That would be good," she said cautiously. He was not mentioning Christopher. "Where?"

"I'm at the Holiday Inn. There's a nice little coffee shop in the Serrano. I could walk over and meet you there."

"I've got an hour before I have to be somewhere," Kaye said. "Downstairs in ten minutes?"

"I'll jog," Mitch said. "See you in the lobby."

She laid out her clothes for the day—a trim blue linen suit from the ever-tasteful Marge Cross collection—and was considering whether to block a small sinus headache with a couple of Tylenol when she heard muted yelling through the double-pane window. She ignored it for a moment and reached to the bed to flip a page on the convention program. As she carried the program to the table and fumbled for the badge in her purse, she grew tired of her tuneless whistling. She walked around the bed again to pick up the TV remote and pushed the power button.

The small hotel TV made the necessary background noise. Commercials for tampons, hair restorer. Her mind was full of other things; the closing ceremonies, her appearance on the podium with Marge Cross and Mark Augustine.

Mitch.

As she looked for a good pair of nylons, she heard the woman say, ". . . first full-term infant. To bring all our listeners up to date, this morning, an unidentified woman in Mexico City gave birth to the first scientifically recognized second-stage Herod's baby. Reporting live from—"

Kaye flinched at the sound of metal crunching, glass breaking. She pulled back the window's gauze curtain and looked north. West Harbor Drive outside the Serrano and the convention center was covered by a thick shag of people, a packed and streaming mass flowing over curbs and lawns and plazas, absorbing cars, hotel vans, shuttle buses. The sound they made was extraordinary, even through the double panes of glass: a low, grinding roar, like an earthquake. White squares flopped about over the mass, green ribbons flexed and rippled: placards and banners. From this angle, ten floors up, she could not read the messages.

"—Apparently born dead," the TV announcer continued. "We're trying to get an update from—"

Her phone rang again. She pulled the receiver from its cradle and stretched the cord to reach the window. She could not stop watching the living river below her window. She saw cars being rocked, flipped on their backs as the crowd surged, heard more sounds of glass breaking.

"Ms. Lang, this is Stan Thorne, Marge Cross's chief of security. We want you up here on the twentieth, in the penthouse."

The writhing mass below cheered with one animal voice.

"Take the express elevator," Thorne said. "If that's blocked, take the stairs. Just get up here *now*."

"I'll be right there," she said.

She put on her shoes.

"This morning, in Mexico City—"

Even before she boarded the elevator, the bottom seemed to fall out of Kaye's stomach.

Mitch stood across the street from the convention center, shoulders hunched, hands in pockets, trying to look as uninvolved and anonymous as possible.

The crowd sought out scientists, official representatives, anyone involved in the convention, flowing toward them, waving signs, shouting at them.

He had removed the badge Dicken had provided him, and with his faded denims, suntanned face, and windblown, sandy hair, did not at all resemble the hapless pasty-skinned scientists and pharmaceutical representatives.

The demonstrators were mostly women, all colors, all sizes, but nearly all young, between the ages of eighteen and forty. They seemed to have lost all sense of discipline. Anger was quickly taking over.

Mitch was terrified, but for the moment, the crowd was moving south, and he was free. He walked with quick, stiff steps away from Harbor Drive and ran down a parking ramp, jumped a wall, and found himself in a planter strip between high-rise hotels.

Out of breath, more from alarm than exertion—he had always hated crowds—he trudged through the ice plant, climbed another wall, and lowered himself onto the concrete floor of a parking garage. A few women with stunned expressions ran awkwardly to their cars. One of them carried a drooping and battered placard. Mitch read the words as they swept by: OUR DESTINY OUR BODIES.

The aching sound of sirens echoed through the garage. Mitch pushed through a door to the elevator cubicle just as three uniformed security guards came thumping down the stairs. They rounded the corner, guns drawn, and glared at him.

Mitch held up his hands and hoped he looked innocent. They swore and locked the double glass doors. "Get up there!" one shouted at him.

He climbed the stairs with the guards close behind.

From the lobby, looking out upon West Harbor Drive, he saw small riot trucks skirt the crowd, pushing slowly and steadily into the women. The women cried out in chorus, compressed and angry voices like a crashing wave. Water cannons twisted on top of a truck like antennae on a bug's head.

The lobby's glass doors opened and closed as guests waggled keys at staff and were allowed in. Mitch walked to the middle of the lobby, standing in an atrium, feeling the air from outside brush past. A sharp tang caught his attention: odors of fear and rage and something else, acrid, like dog piss on a hot sidewalk.

It made his hair stand on end.

The smell of the mob.

Dicken met Kaye on the penthouse floor. A man in a dark blue suit held open the door to the penthouse level and checked their badges. Tiny voices chattered in his earplug.

"They're already in the lobby downstairs," Dicken told her. "They're going nuts out there."

"Why?" Kaye asked, baffled.

"Mexico City," Dicken said.

"But why riot?"

"Where's Kaye Lang?" a man shouted.

"Here!" Kaye held up her hand.

They pushed through a line of confused and chattering men and women. Kaye saw a woman in a swimsuit laughing, shaking her head, clutching a large white terry cloth towel. A man in a hotel bathrobe sat in a chair with his legs drawn up, eyes wild. Behind them, the guard yelled, "Is she the last one?"

"Check," another answered. Kaye had never known there were so many of Marge's security people in the hotel—she guessed twenty. Some wore sidearms.

Then she heard Cross's high-pitched bellow.

"For Christ's sake, it's just a bunch of women! Just a bunch of frightened women!"

Dicken took Kaye's arm. Cross's personal secretary, Bob Cavanaugh, a slender man of thirty-five or forty with thinning blond hair, grabbed both of them and ushered them through the last cordon into Cross's bedroom. She was sprawled across a king-size bed, still in her silk pajamas, watching closed circuit television. Cavanaugh draped a fringed cotton wrap over her shoulders. The view on the screen swayed back and forth. Kaye guessed the camera was on the third or fourth floor.

Riot control vehicles sprayed selective shots from water cannons and forced the mass of women farther down the street, away from the convention center entrance. "They're mowing 'em down!" Cross shouted angrily.

"They trashed the convention floor," the secretary said.

"We never expected this kind of reaction," Stan Thorne said, thick arms folded across a substantial belly.

"No," Cross said, her voice like a low flute. "And why in hell not? I always said it was a gut issue. Well, here's the gut response! It's a goddamned disaster!"

"They didn't even present their demands," said a slender woman in a green suit.

"What in hell do they hope to accomplish?" someone else said, not visible to Kaye.

"Dropping a big fat message on our doorstep," Cross grumbled. "Something's kicked the body politic in the groin. They want fast, fast relief, and screw the *process*."

"This could be just what we needed," said a small, thin man whom Kaye recognized: Lewis Jansen, the marketing director for Americol's pharmaceutical division.

"The hell you say." Cross cried out, "Kaye Lang, I want you!"

"Here," Kaye said, stepping forward.

"Good! Frank, Sandra, get Kaye on the tube as soon as they clear the streets. Who's the talent here?"

An older woman in a bathrobe, carrying an aluminum briefcase, named from memory the local television commentators and affiliates.

"Lewis, have your folks work up some talking points."

"My folks are at another hotel."

"Then call them! Tell the people we're working as fast as we can, don't want to move too fast on a vaccine or we'll harm folks—shit, tell them all the stuff we were saying down on the convention floor. When in hell will people ever learn to sit back and listen? Are the phones out of order?"

Kaye wondered whether Mitch had been caught in the riot, if he was okay.

Mark Augustine entered the bedroom. It was getting crowded. The air was thick and hot. Augustine nodded to Dicken, smiled genially at Kaye. He seemed cool and collected, but there was something about his eyes that betrayed this camouflage.

"Good!" Cross roared. "The gang's all here. Mark, what's up?"

"Richard Bragg was shot to death in Berkeley two hours ago," Augustine said. "He was out walking his dog." Augustine tilted his head to one side and drew his lips together into a wry expression for Kaye's benefit.

"Bragg?" someone asked.

"The patent asshole," another answered.

Cross stood up from the bed. "Related to the news about the baby?" she asked Augustine.

"You might think so," Augustine said. "Somebody at the hospital in Mexico City leaked the news. *La Prensa* reported the baby was severely malformed. It was on every channel by six A.M."

Kaye turned to Dicken. "Born dead," he said.

Augustine pointed to the window. "That might explain the mob. This was supposed to be a peaceful demonstration."

"Let's get to it, then," Cross said, subdued. "We have work to do."

Dicken looked downcast as they walked to the elevator. He spoke in an undertone to Kaye. "Let's forget the zoo," he said.

"The discussion?"

"It was premature," he said. "Now is no time to stick our necks out."

Mitch walked along the littered street, boots crunching through shards of glass. Police barricades marked by yellow ribbon closed off the convention center and the front entrances of three hotels. Overturned cars were wrapped in yellow ribbon like presents. Signs and banners littered the asphalt and sidewalks. The air still smelled of tear gas and smoke. Police in skintight dark green pants and khaki shirts and National Guard troops in camouflage stood with folded arms along the street while city officials disembarked from vans and were led off to tour the damage. The police watched the few unofficial bystanders through dark glasses, silently challenging.

Mitch had tried to get back to his hotel room at the Holiday Inn and had been turned away by unhappy clerks working with the police. His luggage—one bag—was still in his room, but he had the satchel with him, and that was all he really cared about. He had left messages for Kaye and Dicken, but there was no fixed place for them to return his calls.

The convention appeared to be finished. Cars were being released from hotel garages by the dozens, and long lines of taxis waited a few blocks south for passengers dragging wheeled suitcases.

Mitch could not pin down how he felt about all this. Anger, jerks of adrenaline, a bitter surge of animal exultation at the damage—typical residues of being so near mob violence. Shame, the single thin coating of social veneer; after hearing about the dead baby, guilt at perhaps being so wrong. In the middle of these flashing emotions, Mitch felt most acutely a wretched sense of displacement. Loneliness.

After this morning and afternoon, what he regretted most was missing his breakfast with Kaye Lang.

She had smelled so good to him in the night air. No perfume, hair freshly washed, richness of skin, breath smelling of wine, but flowery and hardly offensive. Her eyes a little drowsy, her parting warm and tired.

He could picture himself lying next to her on the bed in her hotel room with a clarity more like memory than imagination. *Forward memory.*

He reached into his jacket pocket for his airline tickets, which he always carried with him.

Dicken and Kaye made up a lifeline, an extended purpose in his life. Somehow, he doubted Dicken would encourage that continued connection. Not that he disliked Dicken; the virus hunter seemed straightforward and very sharp. Mitch would like to work with him and get to know him better. However, Mitch could not picture that at all. Call it instinct, more forward memory.

Rivalry.

He sat on a low concrete wall across from the Serrano, gripping his satchel in two broad hands. He tried to summon the patience he had used to stay sane on long and laborious digs with contentious postdocs.

With a start, he saw a woman in a blue suit coming out of the Serrano lobby. The woman stood for a moment in the shade, speaking with two doormen and a police officer. It was Kaye. Mitch walked slowly across the street, around a Toyota with all its windows smashed. Kaye saw him and waved.

They met on the plaza in front of the hotel. Kaye had circles under her eyes.

"It's been awful," she said.

"I was out here, I saw it," Mitch said.

"We're going into high gear. I'm doing some TV interviews,

then we're flying back East, to Washington. There has to be an investigation."

"This was all about the first baby?"

Kaye nodded. "We got some details an hour ago. NIH was tracking a woman who got Herod's flu last year. She aborted an interim daughter, got pregnant a month later. She gave birth a month premature and the baby is dead. Severe defects. Cyclopia, apparently."

"God," Mitch said.

"Augustine and Cross . . . well, I can't talk about that. But it looks as if we're going to have to rework all the plans, maybe even conduct human tests on an accelerated schedule. Congress is screaming bloody murder, pointing fingers everywhere. It's a mess, Mitch."

"I see. What can we do?"

"We?" Kaye shook her head. "What we talked about at the zoo just doesn't make sense now."

"Why not?" Mitch asked, swallowing.

"Dicken has done a turnabout," Kaye said.

"What kind of turnabout?"

"He feels miserable. He thinks we've been completely wrong."

Mitch cocked his head to one side, frowning. "I don't see that."

"It's more politics than science, maybe," Kaye said.

"Then what about the science? Are we going to let one premature birth, one defective baby—"

"Steamroll us?" Kaye finished for him. "Probably. I don't know." She looked up and down the drive.

"Are any other full-term babies due?" Mitch asked.

"Not for several months," Kaye said. "Most of the parents have been choosing abortion."

"I didn't know that."

"It's not been talked about much. The agencies involved aren't releasing names. There'd be a lot of opposition, you can imagine."

"How do you feel about it?"

Kaye touched her heart, then her stomach. "Like a punch in the gut. I need time to think things over, do some more work. I asked him, but Dicken never gave me your phone number."

Mitch smiled knowingly.

"What?" Kaye asked, a little irritated.

"Nothing."

"Here's my home number in Baltimore," she said, handing him a card. "Call me in a couple of days."

She put her hand on his shoulder and squeezed gently, then turned and walked back into the hotel. Over her shoulder, she shouted, "I mean it! Call."

45

The National Institutes of Health, Bethesda

Kaye was hustled out of the Baltimore airport in a nondescript brown Pontiac lacking government license plates. She had just spent three hours in TV studios and six hours on the plane and her skin felt as if it had been varnished.

Two Secret Service agents sat in polite silence, one in front and one in back. Kaye sat in the back. Between Kaye and the agent sat Farrah Tighe, her newly assigned aide. Tighe was a few years younger than Kaye, with pulled-back blond hair, a pleasant broad face, brilliant blue eyes, and broad hips that challenged her companions in these tight quarters.

"We have four hours before you meet with Mark Augustine," Tighe said.

Kaye nodded. Her mind was not in the car.

"You requested a meeting with two of the NIH mothers-in-residence. I'm not sure we can fit that in today."

"Fit it in," Kaye said forcefully, and then added, "Please."

Tighe looked at her solemnly.

"Take me to the clinic before we do anything else."

"We have two TV interviews—"

"Skip them," Kaye said. "I want to talk with Mrs. Hamilton."

Kaye walked through the long corridors from the parking lot to the elevators of Building 10.

On the drive from the airport to the NIH campus, Tighe had briefed her on the events of the past day. Richard Bragg had been shot seven times in the torso and head while leaving his house in Berkeley and had been declared dead at the scene. Two suspects had been arrested, both male, both husbands of women carrying first-stage Herod's babies. The men had been captured a few blocks away, drunk, their car packed with empty cans of beer.

The Secret Service, on orders from the president, had been assigned to protect key members of the Taskforce.

The mother of the first full-term, second-stage infant born in North America, known as Mrs. C., was still in a hospital in Mexico City. She had emigrated to Mexico from Lithuania in 1996; she had worked for a relief agency in Azerbaijan between 1990 and 1993. She was currently being treated for shock and what the first medical reports described as an acute case of seborrhea on her face.

The dead infant was being shipped from Mexico City to Atlanta and would arrive tomorrow morning.

Luella Hamilton had just finished a light lunch and was sitting in a chair by the window, looking out over a small garden and the windowless corner of another building. She shared a room with another mother who was down the hall in an examination room. There were now eight mothers in the Task-force study.

"I lost my baby," Mrs. Hamilton told Kaye as she walked in. Kaye stepped around the bed and hugged her. She returned Kaye's embrace with strong hands and arms and a little moan.

Tighe stood with arms folded near the door.

"She just slipped out one night." Mrs. Hamilton held her eyes steady on Kaye's. "I hardly felt her. My legs were wet. Just a little blood. They had a monitor on my stomach and the little alarm started to beep. I woke up and the nurses were there and they put up a tent. They didn't show her to me. A minister came in, Reverend Ackerley, from my church, she was right there for me, wasn't that nice?"

"I'm so sorry," Kaye said.

"The reverend told me about that other woman, in Mexico, with her second baby . . ."

Kaye shook her head in sympathy.

"I am so scared, Kaye."

"I'm sorry I wasn't here. I was in San Diego and I didn't know you had rejected."

"Well, it's not like you're my doctor, is it?"

"I've been thinking about you a lot. And the others." Kaye smiled. "But mostly you."

"Yeah, well, I'm a strong black woman, and we make an impression." Mrs. Hamilton did not smile as she said this. Her expression was drawn, her skin verging on olive. "I talked to my husband on the telephone. He's coming by today and we'll see each other, but we'll be separated by glass. They told me they'd let me go after the baby was born. But now they say they want to keep me here. They tell me I'm going to be pregnant again. They know it's coming. My own little baby Jesus. How can the world get along with millions of little baby Jesuses?" She started to cry. "I haven't been with my husband or anyone else! I swear!"

Kaye held her hand tightly. "This is so difficult," she said.

"I want to help, but my family, they're having a hard time.

My husband is half crazy, Kaye. They could run this damned railroad so much better." She stared out the window, held on to Kaye's hand tightly, then waved it gently back and forth, as if listening to some inner music. "You've had some time to think. Tell me what's happening?"

Kaye fixed her eyes on Mrs. Hamilton and tried to think of something to say. "We're still trying to figure that out," she finally managed. "It's a challenge."

"From God?" Mrs. Hamilton asked.

"From inside," Kaye said.

"If it's from God, all the little Jesuses are going to die except one, then," Mrs. Hamilton said. "That's not good odds for me."

"I hate myself," Kaye said as Tighe escorted her to Dr. Lipton's office.

"Why?" Tighe said.

"I wasn't here."

"You can't be everywhere."

Lipton was in a meeting, but interrupted it long enough to talk with Kaye. They went to a side office filled with filing cabinets and a computer.

"We did scans last night and checked out her hormone levels. She was almost hysterical. The miscarriage didn't hurt much if at all. I think she wanted it to hurt more. She had a classic Herod's fetus."

Lipton held up a series of photographs. "If this is a disease, it's a damned organized disease," she said. "The pseudo-placenta is not very different from a normal placenta, except that it's much reduced. The amnion is something else, however." Lipton pointed to a process curled on one side of the shrunken shriveled amnion, which had been expelled with the placenta. "I don't know what you'd call it, unless it's a little fallopian tube."

"And the other women in the study?"

"Two should reject within a few days, the rest over the next two weeks. I've brought in ministers, a rabbi, psychiatrists, even their friends—as long as they're female. The mothers are deeply unhappy. No surprises there. But they've agreed to stay with the program."

"No male contact?"

"Not from any male past puberty," Lipton said. "By order of Mark Augustine, co-signed by Frank Shawbeck. Some of the families are sick of this treatment. I don't blame them."

"Any rich women staying here?" Kaye asked, deadpan.

"No," Lipton said. She chuckled humorlessly. "Need you even ask?"

"Are you married, Dr. Lipton?" Kaye said.

"Divorced six months ago. And you?"

"A widow," Kaye said.

"We're the lucky ones, then," Lipton said.

Tighe tapped her watch. Lipton glanced between them. "Sorry to be keeping you," the doctor said sharply. "My people are waiting, too."

Kaye held up the photographs of the pseudo-placenta and amniotic sac. "What do you mean when you say this is a terribly *organized* disease?"

Lipton leaned on the top of a filing cabinet. "I've dealt with tumors and lesions and buboes and warts and all the other little horrors diseases can build in our bodies. There's organization, to be sure. Rearranging the blood flow, subverting cells. Sucking greed. But this amniotic sac is a highly specialized organ, different from any I've ever studied."

"It's not a product of disease, in your opinion?"

"I didn't say that. The results are distortion, pain, suffering, and miscarriage. The infant in Mexico . . ." Lipton shook her head. "I won't waste my time by characterizing this as anything else. It's a new disease, a hideously inventive one, that's all."

46

Atlanta

Dicken climbed the gentle slope from the parking garage on Clifton Way, glancing up with a squint at clear skies with low fat-bellied puffs of cloud. He hoped the fresh cool air would clear his head.

Dicken had returned to Atlanta the night before and bought a bottle of Jack Daniels and holed up in his house, drinking until four in the morning. Walking from the living room to the bathroom, he had stumbled over a pile of textbooks, slammed his shoulder against a wall, and fallen to the floor. His shoulder and leg were bruised and sore, and his back felt as if he had been kicked, but he could walk and he was pretty sure he did not have to go to the hospital.

Still, his arm hung half-bent, and his face was ashen. His head hurt from the whiskey. His stomach hurt from not eating breakfast. And in his soul he felt like shit, confused and angry at just about everything, but mainly angry at himself.

The memory of the intellectual jam session at the San Diego Zoo felt like a burning brand. The presence of Mitch Rafelson, a loose cannon, saying little substantive but still seeming to guide the conversation, at once challenging their sophomoric theories and spurring them on; Kaye Lang, lovelier than he had ever seen her before, almost radiant, with her patented look of puzzled concentration *and no goddamned interest in Dicken beyond the professional*.

Rafelson clearly outclassed him. Once again, after having spent his entire adult life braving the worst that Earth could throw at a human male, he was coming up short in the eyes of a woman he thought he might care for.

And what the hell did it matter? What did his masculine ego, his sex life, matter in the face of Herod's?

Dicken came around the corner onto Clifton Road and stopped, confused for a moment. The attendant at the garage booth had mentioned something about picketing, but had given no hint of the scale.

Demonstrators filled the street from the small plaza and tree planter fronting the redbrick entrance of Building 1 to the American Cancer Society headquarters and the Emory Hotel across Clifton Road. Some were standing in the beds of purple azaleas; they had left a path open to the main entrance but blocked the visitor center and the cafeteria. Dozens sat around the pillar that held the bust of Hygeia, their eyes closed, swaying gently from side to side as if in silent prayer.

Dicken estimated there were two thousand men, women, and children, in vigil, waiting for something; salvation or word at least that the world was not about to end. Many of the women and more than a few of the men still wore masks, colored orange or purple, guaranteed by half a dozen fly-by-night manufacturers to kill all viruses, including SHEVA.

The organizers of the vigil—it was not called a protest— walked among their people with water coolers and paper cups, leaflets, advice, and instructions, but those holding the vigil never spoke.

Dicken walked to the entrance of Building 1, through the crowd, attracted to them despite his sense of the danger in the situation. He wanted to see what the troops were thinking and feeling—the people on the front line.

Cameramen moved around and through the crowds slowly, or more deliberately along the pathways, cameras held at waist level to capture the immediacy, then being lifted to shoulders for the panorama, the scale.

* * *

"Jesus, what happened?" Jane Salter asked as Dicken passed her in the long hall to his office. She carried a briefcase and an armload of files in green folders.

"Just an accident," Dicken said. "I fell. Did you see what's going on outside?"

"I saw," Salter said. "Creeps me out." She followed him and stood in the open door. Dicken glanced over his shoulder at her, then pulled out the old rolling chair and sat down, his face like a disappointed little boy's.

"Down about Mrs. C.?" Salter asked. She pushed back a wisp of brown hair with the corner of a folder. The wisp fell back and she ignored it.

"I suppose," Dicken said.

Salter bent to set down the briefcase, then stepped forward and laid the files on his desk. "Tom Scarry has the baby," she said. "It was autopsied in Mexico City. I guess they did a thorough job. He'll do it all over again, just to be sure."

"Have you seen it?" Dicken asked.

"Just a video feed when they took it from the ice chest in Building 15."

"Monster?"

"Major," Salter said. "A real mess."

"For whom the bell tolls," Dicken said.

"I've never figured out your position on this, Christopher," Salter said, leaning against the door jamb. "You seem surprised that this is a really nasty disease. We knew that going in, didn't we?"

Dicken shook his head. "I've chased diseases so long . . . this one seemed different."

"What, more sympathetic?"

"Jane, I got drunk last night. I fell in my house and cracked my shoulder. I feel like hell."

"A bender? That sounds more appropriate to a bad love life, not a misdiagnosis."

Dicken made a sour face. "Where are you going with all that?" he asked, and shoved his left forefinger at the files.

"I'm moving some stuff over to the new receiving

lab. They've got four more tables. We're putting together personnel and procedures for a round-the-clock autopsy mission, L3 conditions. Dr. Sharp is in charge. I'm helping the group doing neural and epithelial analysis. I'll keep their records straight."

"Keep me in the loop? If you find something?"

"I don't even know why you're here, Christopher. You flew way above us when you went with Augustine."

"I miss the front lines. News always gets here first." He sighed. "I'm still a virus hunter, Jane. I came back to look over some old papers. See if I forgot something crucial."

Jane smiled. "Well, I did hear this morning that Mrs. C had genital herpes. Somehow it got to little Baby C early in its development. It was covered with lesions."

Dicken looked up in surprise. "Herpes? They didn't tell us that before."

"I told you it was a mess," Jane said.

Herpes could change the whole interpretation of what happened. How did the infant contract the genital herpes while still protected in the womb? Herpes was usually passed from mother to infant in the birth canal.

Dicken was severely distracted.

Dr. Denby passed by the office, smiled briefly, then doubled back and peered through the open door. Denby was a bacterial growth specialist, small and very bald, with a cherub's face and a natty plum shirt and red tie. "Jane? Did you know they've blocked the cafeteria from outside? Hello, Christopher."

"I heard. It's impressive," Jane said.

"Now they're up to something else. Want to go look?"

"Not if it's violent," Salter said with a shudder.

"That's what's spooky. It's peaceful and absolutely silent! Like a drill team without the band."

Dicken walked with them and took the elevator and stairs to the front of the building. They followed other employees and doctors to the lobby beside the public display of CDC history. Outside, the crowd was milling in an orderly fashion. Leaders were using megaphones to shout orders.

A security guard stood with his hands on his hips, glaring at the crowd through the glass. "Will you look at that," he said.

"What?" Jane asked.

"They're breaking up, boy-girl. Segregating," he said with a mystified look.

Banners stretched in plain view of the lobby and the dozens of cameras arrayed outside. A breeze rippled one banner. Dicken caught what it said in two sinuous flaps: VOL-UNTEER. SEPARATE. SAVE A CHILD.

Within a few minutes, the crowd had parted before their leaders like the Red Sea before Moses, women and children on one side, men on the other. The women looked grimly·determined. The men looked somber and shamefaced.

"Christ," the guard muttered. "They're telling me to leave my wife?"

Dicken felt as if he were being whipsawed. He returned to his office and called Bethesda. Augustine had not arrived yet. Kaye Lang was visiting the Magnuson Clinical Center.

Augustine's secretary added that protesters were also on the NIH campus, several thousand of them. "Look on the TV," she said. "They're marching all over the country."

The National Institutes of Health, Bethesda

Augustine drove around the campus on the Old Georgetown Road to Lincoln Street and made his way to a temporary employee parking lot near the Taskforce Center. The Taskforce had been assigned a new building at the surgeon general's request just two weeks before. The protesters apparently did not know of this change, and were marching on the old headquarters, and on Building 10.

Augustine walked quickly in the warming sun to the ground floor entrance. NIH campus police and newly-hired private security guards stood outside the building, talking in low voices. They were eyeing knots of protesters a few hundred yards away.

"Don't worry, Mr. Augustine," the building's chief of security told him as he carded himself in through the main entrance. "We've got the National Guard coming in this afternoon."

"Oh, goodie." Augustine drew in his chin and punched the elevator button. In the new office, three assistants and his personal secretary, Mrs. Florence Leighton, matronly and very efficient, were trying to reestablish a network link with the rest of the campus.

"What's wrong, sabotage?" Augustine asked, a little savagely.

"No," Mrs. Leighton said, handing him a sheaf of printouts. "Stupidity. The server decided not to recognize us."

Augustine slammed the door to his office, pulled out his rolling chair, slapped the brief on the desktop. The phone cheeped. He reached over to punch the button.

"Five minutes uninterrupted, please, Florence, to put my thoughts in order?" he pleaded.

"It's Kennealy for the vice president, Mark," Mrs. Leighton said.

"Double goodie. Put him on."

Tom Kennealy, the vice president's chief of technical communications—another new position, established the week before—was first on the line, and asked Augustine if he had been told about the scale of the protests.

"I'm seeing it through my window now," he replied.

"They're at four hundred and seventy hospitals at last count," Kennealy said.

"God bless the Internet," Augustine said.

"Four demonstrations have gotten out of hand—not including the riot in San Diego. The vice president is very concerned, Mark."

"Tell him I'm more than concerned. It's the worst news I could imagine—a dead full-term Herod's baby."

"What about the herpes angle?"

"Screw that. Herpes doesn't infect an infant until it's born. They must not have taken any precautions in Mexico City."

"That's not what we're hearing. Maybe we can offer some reassurance on this? If it is a diseased infant?"

"Quite clearly it is *diseased*, Tom. It's Herod's we should be focusing on here."

"All right. I've briefed the vice president. He's here now, Mark."

The vice president came on the line. Augustine composed his voice and greeted him calmly. The vice president told him that the NIH was being afforded military security, high-security protected status, as were the CDC and five Taskforce research centers around the country. Augustine could visualize the result now—razor wire, police dogs, concussion grenades, and tear gas. A fine atmosphere in which to conduct delicate research.

"Mr. Vice President, don't push them off campus," Augustine said. "Please. Let them stay and let them protest."

"The president gave the order an hour ago. Why change it?"

"Because it looks like they're venting steam. It's not like San Diego. I want to meet with the leaders here on campus."

"Mark, you aren't a trained negotiator," the VP argued.

"No, but I'd be a hell of a lot better than a phalanx of troops in camouflage."

"That's the jurisdiction of the director of NIH."

"Who *is* negotiating, sir?"

"The director and chief of staff are meeting with the protest leaders. We shouldn't divide our effort or our voice, Mark, so don't even consider going out there to talk."

"What if we have another dead baby, sir? This one came at us out of nowhere—we only knew it was on its way six days ago. We tried to send a team down to help, but the hospital refused."

"They've sent you the body. That seems to show a spirit of cooperation. From what Tom tells me, nobody could have saved it."

"No, but we could have known ahead of time and coordinated our media release."

"No division on this, Mark."

"Sir, with all due respect, the international bureaucracy is killing us. That's why these protests are so dangerous. We'll be blamed whether we're culpable or not—and frankly, I feel pretty sick to my stomach right now. I can't be responsible where I don't have input!"

"We're soliciting your input now, Mark." The VP's voice was measured.

"Sorry. I know that, sir. Our involvement with Americol is causing all sorts of problems. Announcing the vaccine . . . prematurely, in my opinion—"

"Tom shares that opinion, and so do I."

What about the president? he thought. "I appreciate that, but the cat is out of the bag. My people tell me there's a fifty-fifty chance the preclinical trials will fail. The ribozyme is depressingly versatile. It seems to have an affinity for thirteen or fourteen different messenger RNAs. So we stop SHEVA, but we end up with myelin degradation . . . multiple sclerosis, for God's sake!"

"Ms. Cross reports that they've refined it and it's more specific now. She personally assured me there was never any chance of MS. That was just a rumor."

"Which version is FDA going to let them test, sir? The paperwork has to be refiled—"

"FDA is bending on this one."

"I'd like to set up a separate evaluation team. NIH has the people, we have the facilities."

"There's no time, Mark."

Augustine closed his eyes and rubbed his forehead. He

could feel his face turning beet red. "I hope we draw a good hand," he said quietly. His heart was hammering.

"The president is announcing speedier trials tonight," the vice president said. "If the preclinical trials are successful, we'll go to human trials within a month."

"I wouldn't approve that."

"Robert Jackson says they can do it. The decision's been made. It's done."

"Has the president talked to Frank about this? Or the surgeon general?"

"They're in constant touch."

"Please have the president call me, too, sir." Augustine hated to be put in the position of having to ask, but a smarter president would not have needed the reminder.

"I will, Mark. As for your response . . . follow what the NIH brass says, no division, no separation, understood?"

"I'm not a rogue, Mr. Vice President," Augustine said.

"Talk with you soon, Mark," the VP said.

Kennealy came back on the line. He sounded miffed. "Troops are being trucked in now, Mark. Hold on a second." His hand cupped over the receiver. "The VP is out of the room. Jesus, Mark, what did you do, chew him out?"

"I asked him to have the president call me," Augustine said.

"That's a hell of a note," Kennealy said coldly.

"Will someone please tell me if we learn about another baby, out of the country?" Augustine said. "Or in? Could the State Department please coordinate with my office on a daily basis? I hope I am not treading water here, Tom!"

"Please don't ever talk to the VP like that again, Mark," Kennealy said, and hung up.

Augustine pressed the call button. "Florence, I need to write a cover letter and a memo. Is Dicken in town? Where's Lang?"

"Dr. Dicken is in Atlanta and Kaye Lang is on campus. At the clinic, I believe. You're supposed to meet with her in ten minutes."

Augustine opened his desk drawer and took out a legal

pad. On it he had sketched the thirty-one levels of command above him, thirty between him and the president—a bit of an obsession with him. He sharply slashed off five, then six, then worked his way up to ten names and offices, tearing the paper. If worst came to worst, he thought that with a little careful planning he could possibly eliminate ten of those levels, maybe twenty.

But first he had to stick out his neck and send them his report and a coverage memo, and make sure it was on everybody's desk before the shit was airborne.

Not that he would be sticking his neck out very far. Before some White House lackey—maybe Kennealy, greasing for a promotion—whispered in the president's ear that Augustine was not a team player, he strongly suspected there would be another incident.

A very bad incident.

48

The National Institutes of Health, Bethesda

Burying herself in work was the only thing Kaye could think of to do right now. Confusion blocked any other option. As she left the clinic, walking briskly past the outdoor tables full of Vietnamese and Korean vendors selling toiletries and knickknacks, she looked at the task list in her daybook and ticked off the meetings and calls—Augustine first, then ten minutes in Building 15 with Robert Jackson to ask about the ribozyme binding sites, a cross-check with two NIH researchers in Buildings 5 and 6 helping her in her search for additional SHEVA-like HERV; then to half a dozen other researchers in her backup list to solicit their opinions—

She was halfway between the clinic and the Taskforce center when her cell phone rang. She pulled it out of her purse.

"Kaye, this is Christopher."

"I don't have any time and I feel like shit, Christopher," she snapped. "Tell me something that will make me feel good."

"If it's any consolation, I feel like shit, too. I got drunk last night and there are demonstrators out front."

"They're here, too."

"But listen to this, Kaye. We have Infant C in pathology now. It was born at least a month premature."

"*It? It* had a sex, didn't it?"

"He. He's riddled inside and out with herpes lesions. He had no protection against herpes in the womb—SHEVA induces some sort of opportunistic opening through the placental barrier for herpes virus."

"So they're in league—all out to cause death and destruction. That's cheerful."

"No," Dicken said. "I don't want to talk about it on the phone. I'm coming up to NIH tomorrow."

"Give me something to go on, Christopher. I don't want another night like the last two."

"Infant C might not have died if his mother hadn't contracted herpes. They may be separate issues, Kaye."

Kaye closed her eyes, stood still on the sidewalk. She looked around for Farrah Tighe; in her distraction, she had apparently walked out without her, against instructions. No doubt Tighe was frantically searching for her right now. "Even if they are, who will listen to us now?"

"None of the eight women at the clinic have any herpes or HIV. I called Lipton and checked. They're excellent test cases."

"They aren't due for ten months," Kaye said. "If they follow the one-month rule."

"I know. But I'm sure we'll find others. We need to talk again—seriously."

"I'll be in meetings all day, then at the Americol labs in Baltimore tomorrow."

"This evening, then. Or doesn't the truth mean much now?"

"Don't lecture me about truth, damn it," Kaye said. She could see National Guard trucks moving in along Center Drive. So far, the protesters had kept to the northern end; she could see their signs and banners from where she stood beside a low grassy hill. She missed Dicken's next few words. She was fascinated by the distant crowds on the move.

"—I want to give your idea a fair chance," Dicken said. "The LPC carries no possible benefit for a simple virus— why use it?"

"Because SHEVA's a messenger," Kaye said, her voice soft, between dreamy and distracted. "It's Darwin's radio."

"What?"

"You've seen the afterbirth from the Herod's first-stage fetuses, Christopher. Specialized amniotic sacs . . . Very sophisticated. Not diseased."

"Like I said, I want to work on this more. Convince me, Kaye. God, if this Infant C is just a fluke!"

Three blunt little popping sounds came from the north end of the campus, small, toylike. She heard the crowd let out a startled moan, then a distant, high scream.

"I can't talk, Christopher." She shut the phone with a plastic clack and ran. The crowd was about a quarter of a mile away, breaking up, people pushing back and scattering along the roads, the parking lots, the brick buildings. No more pops. She slowed to a walk for several steps, considering the danger, then ran again. She had to know. Too much uncertainty in her life. Too much hanging back and inaction, with Saul, with everything and everybody.

Fifty feet from her she saw a stocky man in a brown suit dash out of a building's rear service door, arms and legs going like windmills. His coat flapped up over a bulging white shirt and he looked ridiculous, but he was quick as a bat out of hell and heading right for her.

For a moment she was alarmed and veered to avoid him.

"Damn it, Dr. Lang," he shouted. "Hold on there! Stop!"

She slowed to a grudging walk, out of breath. The man in the brown suit caught up with her and flashed a badge. He was from the Secret Service and his name was Benson and that was all she managed to catch before he closed the case and pocketed it again. "What in hell are you doing? Where's Tighe?" he asked her, his face beefy red, sweat pouring down his pockmarked cheeks.

"They need help," she said. "She's back at the—"

"That's gunfire. You will stay right here if I have to hold you down personally. Goddamn it, Tighe was not supposed to let you out alone!"

At that moment, Tighe came running to catch up with them. She was red-faced with anger. She and Benson exchanged quick, harsh whispers, then Tighe positioned herself beside Kaye. Benson broke into a speedy trot toward the broken clumps of protesters. Kaye continued walking, but slower.

"Stop right here, Ms. Lang," Tighe said.

"Somebody's been shot!"

"Benson will take care of it!" Tighe insisted, standing between her and the crowd.

Kaye peered over Tighe's shoulders. Men and women clutched their hands to their faces, crying. She saw dropped banners, drooping signs. The crowd swirled in complete confusion.

National Guard soldiers in camouflage, automatic rifles held at ready, took positions between brick buildings along the closest road.

A campus police car drove over the lawn and between two tall oak trees. She saw other men in suits, some talking on cell phones, walkie-talkies.

Then she noticed the lone man in the middle, arms held straight out as if he wanted to fly. Beside him, a motionless woman sprawled on the grass. Benson and a campus security officer reached them simultaneously. Benson kicked a dark object across the grass: a pistol. The security officer pulled out his own pistol and aggressively pushed back the flying man.

Benson knelt beside the woman, checked the pulse at her neck, looked up, around, his face saying it all. Then he glared at Kaye, mouthed emphatically, *Get back.*

"It wasn't my baby," the flying man shouted. Skinny, white, short fuzzy blond hair, in his late twenties, he wore a black T-shirt and black jeans slung low on his hips. He tossed his head back and forth as if surrounded by flies. "She made me come here. She goddamn *made me*. It wasn't my baby!"

The flying man danced back from the guard, jerking like a marionette. "I can't take this shit anymore. *NO MORE SHIT!*"

Kaye stared at the injured woman. Even from twenty yards she could see the blood staining her blouse around her stomach, sightless eyes staring up with a blank kind of hope at the sky.

Kaye ignored Tighe, Benson, the flying man, the troops, the security guards, the crowd.

All she could see was the woman.

49

Baltimore

Cross entered the Americol executive dining room on a pair of crutches. Her young male nurse pulled out a chair, and Cross sat with a relieved puff of breath.

The room was empty but for Cross, Kaye, Laura Nilson, and Robert Jackson.

"How'd it happen, Marge?" Jackson asked.

"Nobody shot me," she piped cheerfully. "I fell in the bathtub. I have always been my own worst enemy. I am a clumsy ox. What do we have, Laura?"

Nilson, whom Kaye had not seen since the disastrous vaccine press conference, wore a stylish but severe blue three-piece suit. "The surprise of the week is RU-486," she said. "Women are using it—a lot of it. The French have come forward with a solution. We've spoken to them, but they say they are tendering their offer directly to the WHO and to the Taskforce, that their effort is humanitarian, and they aren't interested in any business liaisons."

Marge ordered wine from the steward and wiped her forehead with the napkin before spreading it on her lap. "How generous of them," she mused. "They'll supply all the world needs, and no new R&D costs. Does it work, Robert?"

Jackson took up a Palmbook and poked his way through his notes with a stylus. "Taskforce has unconfirmed reports that RU-486 aborts the second-stage implanted ovum. No word yet on first-stage. It's all anecdotal. Street research."

Cross said, "Abortion drugs have never been to my taste." To the steward, she said, "I'll have the Cobb salad, side of vinaigrette, and a pot of coffee."

Kaye ordered a club sandwich, though she was not hungry in the least. She could feel thunderheads building—an unpleasant personal awareness that she was in a very dangerous mood. She was still numb from witnessing the shooting at NIH, two days before.

"Laura, you look unhappy," Cross said, with a glance at Kaye. She was going to save Kaye's complaints for last.

"One earthquake after another," Nilson said. "At least I didn't have to experience what Kaye did."

"Horrible," Cross agreed. "It's a whole barrel of worms. So, what kind of worms are they?"

"We've ordered our own polls. Psych profiles, cultural

profiles, across the board. I'm spending every penny you gave me, Marge."

"Insurance," Cross said.

"Scary," Jackson said simultaneously.

"Yes, well it might buy you another Perkin-Elmer machine, that's all," Nilson said defensively. "Sixty percent of married or involved males surveyed do not believe the news reports. They believe it is necessary for the women to have sex to be pregnant a second time. We're coming up against a wall of resistance here, denial, even among the women. Forty percent of married or otherwise involved women say they would abort any Herod's fetus."

"That's what they tell a pollster," Cross murmured.

"They'd certainly go for an easy out in large numbers. RU-486 is tried and proven. It could become a household remedy for the desperate."

"It isn't prevention," Jackson said, uneasy.

"Of those who wouldn't use an abortion pill, fully half believe the government is trying to force wholesale abortion on the nation, maybe the world," Nilson said. "Whoever chose the name 'Herod's' has really skewed the issue."

"Augustine chose it," Cross said.

"Marge, we're heading for a major social disaster: ignorance mixed with sex and dead babies. If large numbers of women with SHEVA abstain from sex with their partners—and get pregnant anyway—then our social science people say we're going to see more domestic violence, as well as a huge rise in abortions, even of normal pregnancies."

"There are other possibilities," Kaye said. "I've seen the results."

"Go ahead," Cross encouraged.

"The 1990s cases in the Caucasus. Massacres."

"I've studied those, as well," Nilson said efficiently, flipping through her legal pad. "We don't actually know much even now. There was SHEVA in the local populations—"

Kaye interrupted. "It's far more complicated than any of us here can deal with," she said, her voice cracking. "We are not looking at a disease profile. We're looking at lateral transmission of genomic instructions leading to a transition phase."

"Come again? I don't understand," Nilson said.

"SHEVA is not an agent of disease."

"Bullshit," Jackson said in astonishment. Marge waved her hand at him in warning.

"We keep building walls around this subject. I can't hold back anymore, Marge. The Taskforce has denied this possibility from the very beginning."

"I don't know what's being denied," Cross said. "In brief, Kaye."

"We see a virus, even one that comes from within our own genome, and we assume it's a disease. We see everything in terms of disease."

"I've never known a virus that didn't cause problems, Kaye," Jackson said, his eyes heavy-lidded. If he was trying to warn her she was treading on thin ice, this time it wasn't going to work.

"We keep seeing the truth but it doesn't fit into our primitive views on how nature works."

"Primitive?" Jackson said. "Tell that to smallpox."

"If this had hit us thirty years from now," Kaye persisted, "maybe we'd be prepared—but we're still acting like ignorant children. Children who have never been told the facts of life."

"What are we missing?" Cross asked patiently.

Jackson drummed his fingers on the table. "It's been discussed."

"What?" Cross asked.

"Not in any serious forum," Kaye countered.

"What, please?"

"Kaye is about to tell us that SHEVA is part of a biological reshuffling. Transposons jumping around and affecting phenotype. It's the buzz among the interns who've been reading Kaye's papers."

"Which means?"

Jackson grimaced. "Let me anticipate. If we let the new babies be born, they're all going to be big-headed super-humans. Prodigies with blond hair and staring eyes and telepathic abilities. They'll kill us all and take over the Earth."

Stunned, near tears, Kaye stared at Jackson. He smiled half-apologetically, half in glee at having warded off any possible debate. "It's a waste of time," he said. "And we don't have any time to waste."

Nilson watched Kaye with cautious sympathy. Marge lifted her head and glared at the ceiling. "Will someone please tell me what I've just stepped into?"

"Pure bullshit," Jackson said under his breath, adjusting his napkin.

The steward brought them their food.

Nilson put her hand on Kaye's. "Forgive us, Kaye. Robert can be very forceful."

"It's my own confusion I'm dealing with, not Robert's defensive rudeness," Kaye said. "Marge, I have been trained in the precepts of modern biology. I've dealt with rigid interpretations of data, but I've grown up in the middle of the most incredible ferment imaginable. Here's the solid foundation wall of modern biology, built brick by careful brick . . ." She drew the wall with her outstretched hand. "And here's a tidal wave called genetics. We're mapping the factory floor of the living cell. We're discovering that nature is not just surprising, but shockingly unorthodox. Nature doesn't give a damn *what* we think or what our paradigms are."

"That's all very well," Jackson said, "but science is how we organize our work and avoid *wasting time.*"

"Robert, this is a discussion," Cross said.

"I can't apologize for what I feel in my gut is true," Kaye persisted. "I will lose everything rather than lie."

"Admirable," Jackson said. " 'Nevertheless, it moves,' is that it, dear Kaye?"

"Robert, don't be an asshole," Nilson said.

"I am outnumbered, *ladies,*" Jackson said, pushing back his chair in disgust. He draped his napkin over his plate but did not leave. Instead, he folded his arms and cocked his head, as if encouraging—or daring—Kaye to continue.

"We're behaving like children who don't even know how babies are made," Kaye said. "We're witnessing a different kind of pregnancy. It isn't new—it's happened many times before. It's evolution, but it's directed, short-term, immediate, not gradual, and I have no idea what kind of children will be produced," Kaye said. "But they will not be monsters and they won't eat their parents."

Jackson lifted his arm high like a boy in a classroom. "If we're in the hands of some fast-acting master craftsman, if *God* is directing our evolution now, I'd say it's time to hire some cosmic lawyers. It's malpractice of the lowest order. Infant C was a complete botch."

"That was herpes," Kaye said.

"Herpes doesn't work that way," Jackson said. "You know that as well as I."

"SHEVA makes fetuses particularly susceptible to viral invasion. It's an error, a natural error."

"We have no evidence of that. Evidence, Ms. Lang!"

"The CDC—" Kaye began.

"Infant C was a Herod's second-stage monstrosity with herpes added on, as a side dish," Jackson said. "Really, ladies, I've had it. We're all tired. I for one am exhausted." He stood, bowed quickly, and stalked out of the dining room.

Marge picked through her salad with a fork. "This sounds like a conceptual problem. I'll call a meeting. We'll listen to your evidence, in detail," she said. "And I'll ask Robert to bring in his own experts."

"I don't think there are many experts who would openly support me," Kaye said. "Certainly not now. The atmosphere is charged."

"This is all-important with regard to public perception," Nilson said thoughtfully.

"How?" Cross asked.

"If some group or creed or corporation decides that Kaye is right, we'll have to deal with that."

Kaye suddenly felt very exposed, very vulnerable.

Cross picked up a strip of cheese with her fork and examined it. "If Herod's isn't a disease, I don't know how we'd deal with it. We'd be caught between a natural event and an ignorant and terrified public. That makes for horrible politics and nightmarish business."

Kaye's mouth went dry. She had no answer to that. It was true.

"If there are no experts who support you," Cross said thoughtfully, pushing the cheese into her mouth, "how do you make a case?"

"I'll present the evidence, the theory," Kaye said.

"By yourself?" Cross asked.

"I could probably find a few others."

"How many?"

"Four or five."

Cross ate for a few moments. "Jackson's an asshole, but he's brilliant, he's a recognized expert, and there are hundreds who would agree with his point of view."

"Thousands," Kaye said, straining to keep her voice steady. "Against just me and a few crackpots."

Cross waggled a finger at Kaye. "You're no crackpot, dear. Laura, one of our companies developed a morning-after pill some years ago."

"That was in the nineties."

"Why did we abandon it?"

"Politics and liability issues."

"We had a name for it . . . what were we calling it?"

"Some wag code-named it RU-Pentium," Nilson said.

"I recall that it tested well," Marge said. "We still have the formulae and samples, I assume."

"I made an inquiry this afternoon," Nilson said. "We could bring it back and get production up to speed in a couple of months."

Kaye clutched the tablecloth where it crossed her lap. She had once campaigned passionately for a woman's right to choose. Now, she could not work her way through the conflicting emotions.

"No reflection on Robert's work," Cross said, "but there's a better than fifty-fifty chance the trials on the vaccine are going to fail. And that statement does not leave this room, ladies."

"We're still getting computer models predicting MS as a side effect for the ribozyme component," Kaye said. "Will Americol recommend abortion as an alternative?"

"Not all on our lonesome," Cross said. "The essence of evolution is survival. Right now, we're standing in the middle of a minefield, and anything that clears a path, I'm certainly not going to ignore."

Dicken took the call in the equipment room next to the main receiving and autopsy lab. He slipped off his latex gloves while a young male computer technician held the phone. The technician was there to adjust a balky old workstation used to record autopsy results and track the specimens through the rest of the labs. He stared at Dicken, in his green robe and surgical mask, with some concern.

"Nothing catching, for you," Dicken told him as he took the phone receiver. "Dicken here. I'm elbow deep."

"Christopher, it's Kaye."

"Hello-o-o, Kaye." He did not want to put her off; she sounded gloomy but however she sounded, to Dicken, hearing her voice was a disturbing pleasure.

"I've screwed things up big time," Kaye said.

"How's that?" Dicken waved his hand at Scarry, still in the pathology lab. Scarry wagged his arms impatiently.

"I had a tiff with Robert Jackson . . . a conversation with Marge and Jackson. I couldn't hold back. I told them what I thought."

"Oh," Dicken said, making a face. "How'd they react?"

"Jackson pooh-poohed it. Treated me with contempt, actually."

"Arrogant bastard," Dicken said. "I always thought so."

"He said we need evidence about the herpes."

"That's what Scarry and I are looking for now. We have an accident victim in our pathology lab. Prostitute from Washington, D.C., pregnant. Tests positive for *Herpes labialis* and for hepatitis A and HIV as well as SHEVA. Rough life."

The young technician grimly folded his tool kit and left the room.

"Marge is going to match the French on their morning-after pill."

"Shit," Dicken said.

"We have to move fast."

"I don't know how fast we can go. Dead young women with the right mix of problems just don't come rolling in off the street every day."

"I don't think any amount of evidence is going to convince Jackson. I'm close to my wit's end, Christopher."

"I hope Jackson doesn't go to Augustine. We aren't ready yet, and thanks to me, Mark is already touchy," Dicken said. "Kaye, Scarry is dancing around in the lab. I've got to go. Keep your chin up. Call me."

"Has Mitch spoken to you?"

"No," Dicken said, a deceptive truth. "Call me later at my office. Kaye—I'm here for you. I'll support you every way I can. I mean that."

"Thank you, Christopher."

Dicken put the receiver in its cradle and stood for a moment, feeling stupid. He had never been comfortable with these emotions. Work became all because everything else important was too painful.

"Not very good at this, are we?" he asked himself in a low voice.

Scarry tapped angrily on the glass between the office and the lab.

Dicken lifted his surgical mask and put on a new pair of gloves.

50

Baltimore

Mitch stood in the apartment building lobby, hands in his pockets. He had shaved very carefully this morning, staring into the long mirror in the communal bathroom at the YMCA, and just last week he had gone to a barber and had his hair styled—managed was more like it.

His jeans were new. He had dug through his suitcase and pulled out a black blazer. He had not dressed to impress in over a year, but here he was, thinking of little else but Kaye Lang.

The doorman was not impressed. He leaned on his pedestal and watched Mitch closely out of the corner of his eye. The phone rang at the pedestal and he answered it.

"Go on up," he said, waving his hand at the elevator. "Twentieth floor. 2011. Check in with the guard up there. Serious beef."

Mitch thanked him and stood in the elevator. As the door closed, he wondered for a panicky moment what the hell he thought he was doing. The last thing he needed in this mess was emotional involvement. Where women were concerned, however, Mitch was guided by secret masters reticent to divulge either their goals or their immediate plans. These secret masters had caused him a lot of grief.

He closed his eyes, took a deep breath, and resigned himself to the next few hours, come what may.

On the twentieth floor, he stepped out of the elevator and

saw Kaye speaking to a man in a gray suit. He had short black hair, a strong thick face, a hooked nose. The man had spotted Mitch before Mitch saw them.

Kaye smiled at Mitch. "Come on in. The coast is clear. This is Karl Benson."

"Glad to meet you," Mitch said.

The man nodded, folded his arms, and stepped back, allowing Mitch to pass, but not without a sniff, like a dog trying for a scent.

"Marge Cross gets about thirty death threats every week," Kaye said as she led Mitch into the apartment. "I've had three since the incident at NIH."

"The game is getting tough," Mitch said.

"I've been so busy since the RU-486 mess," Kaye said.

Mitch lifted his thick brows. "The abortion pill?"

"Didn't Christopher tell you?"

"Chris hasn't returned any of my calls," Mitch said.

"Oh?" Dicken had not told her the precise truth. Kaye found that interesting. "Maybe it's because you call him Chris."

"Not to his face," Mitch said, grinned, and sobered. "As I said, I'm ignorant."

"RU-486 removes the secondary SHEVA pregnancy if it's used at an early stage." She looked for his reaction. "You don't approve?"

"Under the circumstances, it seems wrong." Mitch peered at the simple, elegant furniture, the art prints.

Kaye closed the door. "Abortion in general . . . or this?"

"This." Mitch sensed her tension and felt for a moment as if she were putting him through a quick exam.

"Americol is going to make its own abortion pill available. If it's a disease, we're close to stopping it," Kaye said.

Mitch strolled to the large plate glass window, pushed his hands into his pockets, looked over his shoulder at Kaye. "You're helping them do this?"

"No," Kaye said. "I'm hoping to convince some key

people, rearrange our priorities. I don't think I'm going to succeed, but it has to be done. I'm glad you came here, though. Maybe it's a sign my luck is improving. What brings you to Baltimore?"

Mitch pulled his hands out of his pockets. "I'm not a very promising sign. I can barely afford to travel. I got some money from my father. I'm on the parental dole big time."

"Are you going on to somewhere else?" Kaye asked.

"Just to Baltimore," Mitch said.

"Oh." Kaye stood a long step behind him. He could see her reflection in the glass, her bright beige suit, but not her face.

"Well, that's not strictly true. I'm going to New York, SUNY. A friend in Oregon arranged for an interview. I'd like to teach, do field research in the summer. Maybe start over again on a different coast."

"I went to SUNY. I'm afraid I don't know anybody there now. Nobody influential. Please sit." Kaye motioned toward the couch, the armchair. "Water? Juice?"

"Water, please."

As she went to the kitchen, Mitch sniffed the flowers on the étagère, roses and lilies and baby's breath, then circled around the couch and sat at one end. His long legs seemed to have no place to go. He folded his hands over his knees.

"I can't just scream and shout and resign," Kaye said. "I owe it to the people I work with."

"I see. How's the vaccine coming?"

"We're well into preclinical trials. Some fast-track clinical trials in Britain and Japan, but I'm not happy about them. Jackson—he's in charge of the vaccine project—wants me moved out of his division."

"Why?"

"Because I spoke out in the dining room three days ago. Marge Cross couldn't use our theory. Doesn't fit the paradigm. Not defensible."

"Quorum sensing," Mitch said.

Kaye brought him a glass of water. "How's that?"

"A chance discovery in my reading. When there's enough

bacteria, they change their behavior, get coordinated. Maybe we do the same thing. We just don't have enough scientists to make a quorum."

"Maybe," Kaye said. She stood, once more, about a step away from him. "I've been working in the HERV and genome labs at Americol most of the time. Finding out where other endogenous virus like SHEVA might express, and under what conditions. I'm a little surprised that Christopher—"

Mitch looked up at her and interrupted. "I came to Baltimore to see you," he said.

"Oh," Kaye said softly.

"I can't stop thinking about our evening at the zoo."

"It doesn't seem real now," Kaye said.

"It does to me," Mitch said.

"I think Marge is moving me off the press conference schedule," Kaye said, perversely trying to shift the conversation, or to see if he would allow it to be shifted. "Wean me away from being a spokeswoman. It'll take me some time to earn her trust again. Frankly, I'm glad to be away from the public eye. There's going to be a—"

"In San Diego," he interrupted, "I reacted pretty strongly to your presence."

"That's sweet," Kaye said, and half turned, as if to run away. She did not run, but she walked around the table and stopped on his other side, again, just a step away.

"Pheromones," Mitch said, and stood tall beside her. "The way people smell is important to me. You aren't wearing perfume."

"I never do," Kaye said.

"You don't need it."

"Hold it," Kaye said, and backed off one more step. She raised her hands and stared at him intently, lips pressed together. "I can be easily confused now. I need to keep my focus."

"You need to relax," Mitch said.

"Being around you is not relaxing."

"You're not sure about things."

"I'm certainly not sure about *you*."

He held out his hand. "Want to smell my hand first?"

Kaye laughed.

Mitch sniffed his palm. "Dial soap. Taxi cab doors. I haven't dug a hole in years. My calluses are smoothing over. I'm out of work, in debt, and I have a reputation as a crazy and unethical son of a bitch."

"Stop being so hard on yourself. I read your papers, and old news stories. You don't cover up and you don't lie. You're interested in the truth."

"I'm flattered," Mitch said.

"And you confuse me. I don't know what to think about you. You're not much like my husband."

"Is that good?" Mitch asked.

Kaye looked him over critically. "So far."

"The customary thing would be to try things out slowly. I'd ask you out to dinner."

"Dutch treat?"

"My expense account," Mitch said wryly.

"Karl would have to come with us. He'd have to approve the restaurant. I usually eat up here, or at Americol's cafeteria."

"Does Karl eavesdrop?"

"No," Kaye said.

"The doorman said he was serious beef," Mitch said.

"I am still a kept woman," Kaye said. "I don't like it, but that's the way it is. Let's stay here and eat. We can walk in the roof garden later, if it's stopped raining. I stock some really good frozen entrées. I get them from a market in the mall down below. And salad in a bag. I'm a good cook when there's time, but there hasn't been any time." She walked back to the kitchen.

Mitch followed, looking at the other pictures on her walls, the little ones in cheap frames that were probably her own contribution to the décor. Small prints of Maxfield Parrish, Edmund Dulac, Arthur Rackham; photos of family groups.

He did not see any pictures of her dead husband. Perhaps she kept them in the bedroom.

"I'd like to cook for *you* some time," Mitch said. "I'm pretty handy with a camp stove."

"Wine? With dinner?"

"I need some now," Mitch said. "I'm very nervous."

"So am I," Kaye said, and held up her hands to show him. They were trembling. "Do you have this effect on all women?"

"Never," Mitch said.

"Nonsense. You smell good," Kaye said.

They were less than a step apart. Mitch closed the gap, touched her chin, lifted it. Kissed her gently. She pushed back a few inches, then grasped his own chin between thumb and forefinger, tugged it down, kissed him more forcefully.

"I think it's okay to be playful with you," she said. With Saul, she could never be sure how he would react. She had learned to limit her range of behaviors.

"Please," he said.

"You're solid," she said. She touched the sun wrinkles in his face, premature crow's feet. Mitch had a young face and bright eyes but wise and experienced skin.

"I'm a madman, but a solid one."

"The world goes on, our instincts don't change," Kaye said, eyes losing their focus. "We're not in charge." A part of her she had not heard from in a long time liked his face very much.

Mitch tapped his forehead. "Do you hear it? From the deep inside?"

"I think so," Kaye said. She decided to fish. "What do I smell like?"

Mitch leaned into her hair. Kaye gave a little gasp as his nose touched her ear. "Clean and alive, like a beach in the rain," he said.

"You smell like a lion," Kaye said. He nuzzled her lips, laid his ear against her temple, as if listening. "What do you hear?" she asked.

"You're hungry," Mitch said, and smiled, a full-bore, thousand-watt, little-boy smile.

This was so obviously unrehearsed that Kaye touched his lips with her fingers, in wonder, before his face returned to that protective, endearing, but ultimately disguising, casual grin. She stepped back. "Right. Food. Wine first, please," she said, and opened the refrigerator. She handed him a bottle of semillon blanc.

Mitch pulled a Swiss Army knife out of his pants pocket, extended the corkscrew, extracted the cork deftly. "We drink beer on a dig, wine when we finish," he said, pouring her a glass.

"What kind of beer?"

"Coors. Budweiser. Anything not too heavy."

"All the men I've known preferred ales or microbrews."

"Not in the sun," Mitch said.

"Where are you staying?" she asked.

"The YMCA," he said.

"I've never met a man who stayed at the YMCA."

"It isn't so bad."

She sipped her wine, wet her lips, moved up closer, lifted on her toes, and kissed him. He tasted the wine on her tongue, still slightly chilled.

"Stay here," she said.

"What will serious beef think?"

She shook her head, kissed him again, and he wrapped his arms around her, still holding his glass and the bottle. A little wine spilled on her dress. He turned her and put the glass on the counter, then the bottle.

"I don't know where to stop," she said.

"I don't either," Mitch said. "I know how to be careful, though."

"It's that kind of age, isn't it?" Kaye said regretfully, and tugged his shirt from his pants.

In Mitch's experience, Kaye was neither the most beautiful woman he had seen naked, nor the most dynamic in bed. That would have to have been Tilde, who, despite her distance, had been very exciting. What struck him most about Kaye was his complete acceptance of every feature, from her small and slightly pendulous breasts, her narrow rib cage, wide hips, thickly flossed pubis, long legs—better than Tilde's, he thought—to her steady and examining gaze as he made love to her. Her scent filled his nose, filled his brain, until he felt as if he were drifting on a warm and supportive ocean of necessary pleasure. Through the condom, he could feel very little, but all his other senses compensated, and it was the touch of her breasts, her cherry-pit-hard nipples, on his own chest that propelled him up and over the wave. He was still moving in her, instinctively still supplying the last of his flow, when she looked very startled, thrashed underneath, squeezed her eyes shut, and cried, "Oh, God, fuck, fuck!"

She had been mostly silent until that moment, and he looked down on her in surprise. She turned her face away and hugged him tight against her, pulling him down, wrapped her legs around him, rubbed against him vigorously. He wanted to pull out before the condom spilled, but she kept moving, and he found himself firming again, and he obliged until she gave a small shriek, this time with eyes open, her face contorted as if in great need or pain. Then her expression went slack, her body relaxed, and she closed her eyes. Mitch withdrew and checked: the condom was still secure. He removed it and deftly tied it, dropped it over the side of the bed for disposal later.

"I can't talk," Kaye whispered.

Mitch lay beside her, savoring their mingled scents. He did not want anything more. For the first time in years, he was happy.

"What was it like to be one of the Neandertals?" Kaye asked. The twilight deepened outside. The apartment was quiet but for the far and muffled sound of traffic on the streets below.

Mitch lifted up on his elbow. "We talked about that already."

Kaye lay on her back, naked from the waist up, a sheet pulled to her navel, listening for something much farther away than the traffic.

"In San Diego," she said. "I remember. We talked about them having masks. About the man staying with her. You thought he must have loved her very much."

"That's right," Mitch said.

"He must have been rare. Special. The woman on the NIH campus. Her boyfriend didn't believe it was his baby." The words started to pour out of her. "Laura Nilson—PR manager for Americol—told us that most men won't believe it's their baby. Most women will probably abort rather than take the risk. That's why they're going to recommend the morning-after pill. If the vaccine has problems, they can still stop this."

Mitch looked uncomfortable. "Can't we forget for a little while?"

"No," Kaye said. "I can't stand it anymore. We're going to slaughter all the firstborn, just like Pharaoh in Egypt. If we keep this up, we'll never know what the next generation looks like. They'll all be dead. Do you want that to happen?"

"No," Mitch said. "But that doesn't mean I'm not as frightened as the next guy." He shook his head. "I wonder what I would have done if I were that man, back then, fifteen thousand years ago. They must have been thrown out of their tribe. Or maybe they ran away. Maybe they were just walking and they came upon a raiding party and she got hurt."

"Do you believe that?"

"No," Mitch said. "I really don't know. I'm not psychic."

"I'm spoiling the mood, aren't I?"

"Mmm hmm," he said.

"Our lives are not our own," Kaye said. She ran her finger around his nipples, stroked the stiff hairs on his chest. "But we can build a wall for a little while. You're going to stay here tonight?"

Mitch kissed her forehead, then her nose, her cheeks. "The accommodations are much nicer than the YMCA."

"Come here," Kaye said.

"I can't get much closer."

"Try."

Kaye Lang lay trembling in the dark. She was certain Mitch was asleep, but to make sure, she poked his back lightly. He squirmed but did not respond. He was comfortable. Comfortable with her.

She had never taken such a risk; from the time of her first dates she had always looked for safety and, she hoped, security, planning her safe haven where she could do her work, think her thoughts with minimal interference from the outside world.

Marrying Saul had been the ultimate achievement. Age, experience, money, business acumen—so she had thought. Now, to swing so far in the opposite direction, was all too obviously an overreaction. She wondered what she would do about it.

When he woke up in the morning, to simply tell Mitch it was all a mistake . . .

Terrified her. Not that she thought he would hurt her; he was the gentlest of men and showed few if any signs of the internal strife that had so troubled Saul.

Mitch was not as handsome as Saul.

On the other hand, Mitch was completely open and honest.

Mitch had sought her out, but she was fairly sure she had seduced *him*. Kaye certainly did not feel anything had been forced upon her.

"What in the hell are you doing?" she muttered in the dark. She was talking to another self, the stubborn Kaye that so seldom told her what was really going on. She got out of bed, put on her robe, went to the desk in the living room and opened the middle drawer, where she kept her record books.

She had six hundred thousand dollars, adding together income from the sale of her home and her personal retirement account. If she resigned from Americol and the Taskforce, she could live in moderately comfortable circumstances for years.

She spent a few minutes working out expenses, emergency budgets, food allowances, monthly bills, on a small piece of note paper, then stiffened in her chair. "This is stupid," she said. "What am I planning?" Then, to that stubborn and secretive self, she added, "What in hell are *you* up to?"

She would not tell Mitch to go away in the morning. He made her feel good. Around him, her mind became quieter, her fears and worries less pressing. He looked as if he knew what he was doing, and maybe he did know. Maybe it was the world that was screwy, that set traps and snares and forced people to make bad choices.

She tapped the pen on the paper, pulled another sheet from the pad. Her fingers pushed the pen over the paper almost without conscious thought, sketching a series of open reading frames on chromosomes 18 and 20 that might bear a relation to the SHEVA genes, previously identified as possible HERVs but turning out not to have the defining characteristics of retrovirus fragments. She needed to look into these loci, these scattered fragments, to see if they might possibly fit together and be expressed; she had been putting this off for some time. Tomorrow would be the proper moment.

Before she followed through with anything, she needed ammunition. She needed armor.

She returned to the bedroom. Mitch seemed to be dreaming. Fascinated, she lay down quietly beside him.

At the top of a snow-covered rise, the man saw the shamans and their helpers following him and his woman. They could not avoid leaving tracks in the snow, but even on the lower grasslands, through the forest, they had been tracked by experts.

The man had brought his woman, heavy and slow with her child, to such heights in hope of crossing over into another valley where he had once gone as a child.

He glanced back at the figures a few hundred steps behind. Then the man looked at the crags and peaks ahead, like so many tumbled flints. He was lost. He had forgotten the way into the valley.

The woman said little now. The face he had once looked upon with so much devotion was hidden by her mask.

The man was filled with such bitterness. This high, the wet snow soaked through his thin shoes with their grass pads. The chill worked up his calves to his knees and made them ache. The wind cut through his skins, even with the fur turned inside, and sapped his strength, shortened his breath.

The woman plodded on. He knew he might escape if he abandoned her. The prospect made his anger darken. He hated the snow, the shamans, the mountains; he hated himself. He could not bring himself to hate the woman. She had suffered the blood on her thighs, the loss, and hidden it from him so as not to bring shame; she had daubed her face with mud to hide the marks, and then, when she could not hide, she had tried to save him by offering herself to the Great Mother, carved into the grass hillside of the valley. But the Great Mother had refused her, and she had come back to him, moaning and mewing. She could not kill herself.

His own face showed the marks. That puzzled and angered him.

The shamans and sisters of the Great Mother, of the Goat Mother, of the Grass Mother, the Snow Woman, Leopard the Loud Killer, Chancre the Soft Killer, Rain the Weeping Father, had all gathered and made their decision during the cooling times, taking painful weeks while the others—the others who had the marks—stayed in their huts.

The man had decided to run. He could not convince himself to trust the shamans and the sisters.

As they fled, they had heard the cries. The shamans and sisters had begun to kill the mothers and the fathers with the marks.

Everyone knew how the flatfaces were brought forth by the people. The women might hide, their men might hide, but all knew. Those who would bear flatface children could only make things worse.

Only the sisters of the gods and goddesses bred true, never bred flatfaces, because they trained the young men of the tribe. They had many men.

He should have let the shamans take his wife as a sister, let her train the boys, too, but she had wanted only him.

The man hated the mountains, the snow, the running. He plodded on, roughly grabbed the woman's arm, pushed her around a rock so they could find a place to hide. He was not watching closely. He was too full of this new truth, that the mothers and fathers of the sky and the ghost world around them were all blind or just lies.

He was alone, his woman was alone, no tribe, no people, no helpers. Not even Long Hairs and Wet Eyes, the most frightening of the dead visitors, the most harmful, cared about them. He was beginning to think none of the dead visitors were real.

The three men surprised him. He did not see them until they came from a cleft in the mountain and thrust their sticks at his woman. He knew them but no longer belonged to them. One had been a brother, another a Wolf Father. They were none of these things now and he wondered how he even recognized them.

Before they could run, one thrust a burned and sharpened stick and pushed it into the woman's full stomach. She spun around, reaching under the skins with scrabbling hands, cried out, and he had rocks in his hand and was throwing them, grabbed a stick from one man and thrust blindly with it, poked one in the eye, drove them off whining and yelping like pups.

He yelled at the sky, held his woman while she kept trying to catch her breath, then carried her and dragged her higher. The woman told him with her hands and her eyes that behind the blood, behind the pain, it was her time. The new one wanted to come.

He looked higher for a place to hide and watch the new one

come. There was so much blood, more than he had ever seen except from an animal. As he walked and carried the woman, he looked over his shoulder. The shamans and the others were not following now.

Mitch cried out, thrashing through the covers. He threw his legs off the bed, hands clutching the sheets, confused by the curtains and the furniture. For a moment he did not know who or where he was.

Kaye sat beside him and held him.

"A dream?" she asked, rubbing his shoulders.

"Yeah," he said. "My God. Not psychic. No time travel. He didn't carry any firewood. But there was a fire in the cave. The masks didn't seem right, either. But it felt real."

Kaye laid him back on the bed and smoothed his damp hair, touched his bristled cheek. Mitch apologized for waking her.

"I was already awake," she said.

"Hell of a way to impress you," Mitch murmured.

"You don't need to impress me," Kaye said. "Do you want to talk about it?"

"No," he said. "It was only a dream."

51

Richmond, Virginia

Dicken pushed open the car door and stepped out of the Dodge. Dr. Denise Lipton handed him a badge. He shaded his eyes against the bright sun and looked up at the small sign over the clinic's bare concrete wall: VIRGINIA CHATHAM

WOMEN S HEALTH AND FAMILY CENTER. A face briefly peered at them through a tiny wire-mesh glass window in the heavy blue-painted metal door. The intercom switched on, and Lipton gave her name and her contact at the clinic. The door opened.

Dr. Henrietta Paskow stood with thick legs planted wide apart, her calf-length gray skirt and white blouse emphasizing a strong stout plainness that made her seem older than she actually was. "Thanks for coming, Denise. We've been very busy."

They followed her through the yellow and white hallway, past the doors of eight waiting rooms, to a small office in the rear. Brass-framed portraits of a large family of young children hung on the wall behind the plain wooden desk.

Lipton sat in a metal folding chair. Dicken remained standing. Paskow pushed two boxes of folders at them.

"We've done thirty since Infant C," she said. "Thirteen D and Cs, seventeen morning-afters. The pills work for five weeks after the rejection of the first-stage fetus."

Dicken looked through the case reports. They were straightforward, concise, with attending physician and nurse practitioner notes.

"There were no severe complications," Paskow said. "The laminal tissue protects against saltwater lavage. But by the end of the fifth week, the laminal tissue has dissolved, and the pregnancy appears to be vulnerable."

"How many requests so far?" Lipton asked.

"We've had six hundred appointments. Nearly all of them are in their twenties and thirties and living with a man, married or otherwise. We've referred half of them to other clinics. It's a significant increase."

Dicken laid the folders facedown on the desk.

Paskow scrutinized him. "You don't approve, Mr. Dicken?"

"I'm not here to approve or disapprove," he said. "Dr. Lipton and I are doing field interviews to see how our figures match the real world."

"Herod's is going to decimate an entire generation," Paskow said. "A third of the women coming to us don't even test positive for SHEVA. They haven't had a miscarriage. They just want the baby out, then wait a few years and see what happens. We're doing a land-office business in birth control. Our clinic classes are full. We've put on a third and fourth classroom upstairs. More men are coming with their wives and their girlfriends. Maybe that's the only good thing about all this. Men are feeling guilty."

"There's no reason to terminate every pregnancy," Lipton said. "The SHEVA tests are highly accurate."

"We tell them that. They don't care," Paskow said. "They're scared and they don't trust us to know what might happen. Meanwhile, every Tuesday and Thursday, we have ten or fifteen Operation Rescue pickets outside yelling that Herod's is a secular humanist myth, that there is no disease. Only pretty babies being needlessly killed. They claim it's a worldwide conspiracy. They're getting shrill and they're very scared. The millennium is young."

Paskow had copied key statistical records. She handed Lipton these papers.

"Thank you for your time," Dicken said.

"Mr. Dicken," Paskow called after them. "A vaccine would save everyone a lot of grief."

Lipton saw Dicken to his car. A black woman in her thirties walked past them and stood at the blue door. She had wrapped herself in a long wool coat, though the day was warm. She was more than six months pregnant.

"I've had enough for one day," Lipton said, her face pale. "I'm going back to the campus."

"I have to pick up some samples," Dicken said.

Lipton put her hand on the door and said, "The women at our clinic have to be told. None of them have STDs, but they've all had chicken pox and one has had hepatitis B."

"We don't know that chicken pox causes problems," Dicken said.

"It's a herpes virus. Your lab results are scary, Christopher."

"They're incomplete. Hell, almost everyone has had chicken pox, or mono, or cold sores. So far, we're only positive about genital herpes and hepatitis and possibly AIDS."

"I still have to tell them," she said, and closed the door for him with a definite slam. "It's about ethics, Christopher."

"Yeah," Dicken said. He kicked at the emergency brake release and started the engine. Lipton walked toward her own car. After a few seconds, he made a disgusted face, shut the engine off again, and sat with his arm out the window, trying to decide how he could best spend his time in the next few weeks.

Things were not going at all well in the labs. Fetal tissue and placenta analysis on samples sent from France and Japan showed vulnerability to all manner of herpes infections. Not a single second-stage pregnancy had survived birth, of the 110 studied thus far.

It was time to make up his mind. Public health policy was in a critical state. Decisions and recommendations would have to be made, and politicians would have to react to those recommendations in ways that could be explained to clearly divided constituencies.

He might not be able to salvage the truth. And the truth seemed remarkably remote at this point. How could something as important as a major evolutionary event be sidetracked so effectively?

On the seat beside him he had dumped a pile of mail from his office in Atlanta. There had been no time to read it on the plane. He pulled out an envelope and swore under his breath. How had he not seen it right away? The postmark and handwriting were clear enough: Dr. Leonid Sugashvili, writing from Tbilisi in the Republic of Georgia.

He tore open the envelope. A snapshot-size black-and-white photograph on slick paper fell into his lap. He picked it up and examined the image: figures standing before a ramshackle old wood-frame house, two women in dresses, a man in overalls. They looked slender, perhaps even slight, but there was no way to be sure. The faces were indistinct.

Dicken pulled open the folded letter accompanying the photo.

> *Dear Dr. Christopher Dicken,*
> *I have been sent this photograph from Atzharis AR, you call perhaps Adjaria. It was taken near Batumi ten years ago. These are putative survivors from the purges you have shown such interest in. There is little to be seen here. Some say they are still alive. Some say they are really from UFO but these people I do not believe.*
>
> *I will look for them and inform you when the time comes. Finance is in very short supply. I would appreciate financial assistance from your organization, the NCID. Thank you for your interest. I feel they may not be "Abominable Snow People" at all, but real! I have not informed the CDC in Tbilisi. You are the one I have been told to entrust.*
>
> *Sincerely,*
> *Leonid Sugashvili*

Dicken examined the photograph again. Less than no evidence. Will-o'-the-wisps.

Death rides in on a pale horse, slicing babies right and left, he thought. *And I'm teamed up with crackpots and money-grubbing eccentrics.*

52

Baltimore

Mitch called his apartment in Seattle while Kaye was taking a shower. He punched in his code and retrieved his messages. There were two calls from his father, a call from a man who did not identify himself, and then a call from Oliver Merton in London. Mitch wrote the number down as Kaye came out of the bathroom, loosely wrapped in a towel.

"You delight in provoking me," he said. She dried her short hair with another towel, gazing at him with an appraising steadiness that was unnerving.

"Who was that?"

"Picking up my messages."

"Old girlfriends?"

"My father, somebody I don't know—a man—and Oliver Merton."

Kaye lifted her eyebrow. "An old girlfriend might make me happier."

"Mmm hmm. He wonders if I would a make a trip to Beresford, New York. He wants me to meet somebody interesting."

"A Neandertal?"

"He says he can arrange for my expenses and accommodations."

"Sounds wonderful," Kaye said.

"I haven't said I'll go. I haven't the slightest idea what he's up to."

"He knows quite a bit about my business," Kaye said.

"You could come with me," Mitch said with a squint that showed he knew this was too hopeful.

"I'm not done here, not by a long shot," she said. "I'll miss you if you go."

"Why don't I call him and ask what he's got in his bag of tricks?"

"All right," Kaye said. "Do that, and I'll fix us two bowls of cereal."

The call took a few seconds to go through. The low trill of an English phone was quickly interrupted by a breathless, "Fuck it's late and I'm busy. Who's this?"

"Mitch Rafelson."

"Indeed. Pardon me while I wrap myself. I hate talking half-naked."

"Half!" exclaimed a perturbed woman in the same room. "Tell them I'm soon to be your wife, and you are *completely* naked."

"Shush." Louder, phone half-muffled, Merton called to the woman, *"She's getting her essentials and going into the next room."* Merton removed his hand and brought his mouth closer to the phone. "We need to talk in private, Mitchell."

"I'm calling from Baltimore."

"How far from Bethesda is that?"

"A ways."

"NIH have you in the loop yet?"

"No," Mitch said.

"Marge Cross? Ah . . . Kaye Lang?"

Mitch winced. Merton's instincts were uncanny. "I'm a simple anthropologist, Oliver."

"All right. The room's empty. I can tell you. The situation in Innsbruck has hotted up considerably. It's gone beyond fistfights. Now they don't even like each other. There's been a falling-out, and one of the principals wants to talk to you."

"Who?"

"Actually, he says he's been a sympathizer since the beginning. Says he called you to tell you they'd found the cave."

Mitch remembered the call. "He didn't leave a name."

"Nor will he now. But he's on the level, he's important, and he wants to talk. I'd like to be there."

"Sounds like a political move," Mitch said.

"I'm sure he'd like to spread some rumors and see what the repercussions are. He wants to meet in New York, not Innsbruck or Vienna. At the home of an acquaintance in Beresford. Do you know anybody there?"

"Can't say that I do," Mitch replied.

"He hasn't told me what he's thinking yet, but . . . I can put a few links together and it all makes a very nice chain."

"I'll think about it and call you back in a few minutes."

Merton did not sound happy about waiting even that length of time.

"Just a few minutes," Mitch assured him. He hung up. Kaye emerged from the kitchen with two bowls of cereal and a pitcher of milk on a tray. She had put on a calf-length black robe tied with a red cord. The robe showed off her legs, and, when she bent over, neatly revealed a breast. "Rice Chex or Raisin Bran?"

"Chex, please."

"Well?"

Mitch smiled. "May I share breakfast with you for a thousand years."

Kaye looked both confused and pleased. She placed the tray on the coffee table and smoothed her robe over her hips, primping with a kind of awkward self-consciousness that Mitch found very endearing. "You know what I like to hear," she said.

Mitch gently pulled her down to the couch beside him. "Merton says there's a breakdown in Innsbruck, a schism. An important member of the team wants to talk to me. Merton's going to write a story about the mummies."

"He's interested in the same things we are," Kaye said speculatively. "He thinks something important is happening. And he's following every angle, from me to Innsbruck."

"I don't doubt it," Mitch said.

"Is he intelligent?"

"Reasonably. Maybe very intelligent. I don't know; I've only spent a few hours with him."

"Then you should go. You should find out what he knows. Besides, it's closer to Albany."

"That's true. Ordinarily, I'd pack my small bag and hop the next train."

Kaye poured her milk. "But?"

"I don't just love and run. I want to spend the next few weeks with you, uninterrupted. Never leave your side." Mitch stretched his neck, rubbed it. Kaye reached out to help him rub. "That sounds clinging," he said.

"I want you to cling," she said. "I feel very possessive and very protective."

"I can call Merton and tell him no."

"But you won't." She kissed him thoroughly and bit at his lip. "I'm sure you'll have some amazing tales to tell. I did a lot of thinking last night, and now I have a lot of very focused work to do. When it's all done, I may have some amazing tales to tell *you*, Mitch."

Washington, D.C.

Augustine jogged briskly along the Capitol mall, following the dirt jogging path beneath the cherry trees, now dropping the last of their blossoms. An agent in a dark blue suit followed at a steady lope, turning to run backward for a moment and scan the trail behind.

Dicken stood with his hands in his jacket pockets, waiting for Augustine to approach. He had driven in from Bethesda an hour earlier, braving rush-hour traffic, hating this clandestine nonsense with something approaching fury. Augustine stopped beside him and jogged in place, stretching his arms.

"Good morning, Christopher," he said. "You should jog more often."

"I like being fat," Dicken said, his face coloring.

"Nobody likes being fat."

"Well, in that case, I'm not fat," Dicken said. "What are we today, Mark, secret agents? Informers?" He wondered why they had not yet assigned an agent to him. He concluded it was because he was not as yet a public figure.

"Goddamn damage control experts," Augustine said. "A man named Mitchell Rafelson spent the night with dear Ms. Kaye Lang at her lovely condominium in Baltimore."

Dicken's heart sank.

"You walked around the San Diego Zoo with the two of them. Got him a badge into a closed Americol party. All very convivial. Did you introduce them, Christopher?"

"In a manner of speaking," Dicken said, surprised at how miserable he felt.

"That wasn't wise. Do you know his record?" Augustine asked pointedly. "The body snatcher from the Alps? He's a nut case, Christopher."

"I thought he might have something to contribute."

"To support whose view in this mess?"

"A defensible view," Dicken said vaguely, looking away. The morning was cool, pleasant, and there were quite a few joggers on the mall, getting in a little outdoors activity before sealing themselves into their government offices.

"The whole thing smells. It looks like some kind of an end run to refocus the whole project, and that concerns me."

"We had a point of view, Mark. A defensible point of view."

"Marge Cross tells me there's talk about *evolution*," Augustine said.

"Kaye has been putting together an explanation that involves evolution," Dicken said. "It's all predicted in her papers, Mark—and Mitch Rafelson has been doing some research along those lines, as well."

"Marge thinks there will be severe fallout if this theory gets publicized," Augustine said. He stopped windmilling his arms and performed neck-stretch exercises, grabbing each upper arm with the opposite hand, applying tension, sighting along the extended arm as he bent it back as far as it would go. "No reason for it to get that far. I'll stop it right here and now. We got a preprint from the Paul-Ehrlich-Institut in Germany this morning that they've found mutated forms of SHEVA. Several of them. Diseases mutate, Christopher. We'll have to withdraw the vaccine trials and start all over again. That pushes all our hopes onto a really bad option. My job might not survive that kind of upheaval."

Dicken watched Augustine prance in place, pounding the ground with his feet. Augustine stopped and caught his breath. "There could be twenty or thirty thousand people demonstrating on the mall tomorrow. Somebody's leaked a report from the Taskforce on the RU-486 results."

Dicken felt something twist inside him, a small little pop, combined disappointment with Kaye and with all the work he had done. All the time he had wasted. He could not see a way around the problem of a messenger that mutated, changing its message. No biological system would ever give a messenger that kind of control.

He had been wrong. Kaye Lang had been wrong.

The agent tapped his watch, but Augustine screwed up his face and shook his head in annoyance.

"Tell me all about it, Christopher," Augustine said, "and then I'll decide whether I'm going to let you keep your goddamned job."

54

Baltimore

Kaye walked with steady confidence from her building to Americol, looking up at the Bromo-Seltzer Tower—so named because it had once carried a huge blue antacid bottle on its peak. Now it carried just the name; the bottle had been removed decades ago.

Kaye could not shake Mitch from her thoughts, but oddly, he was not a distraction. Her thoughts were focused; she had a much clearer idea of what to look for. The play of sun and shadow pleased her as she walked past the alleys between the buildings. The day was so pretty she could almost ignore the presence of Benson. As always, he accompanied her to the lab floor, then stood by the elevators and the stairs, where everyone would have to pass his inspection.

She entered her lab and hung her purse and coat on a glassware drying rack. Five of her six assistants were in the next room, checking the results of last night's electrophoresis analysis. She was glad to have some privacy.

She sat at her small desk and pulled up the Americol intranet on the computer. It was just a few seconds from the first screen to Americol's proprietary Human Genome Project site. The database was beautifully designed and easy to poke through, with key genes identified and functions highlighted and explained in detail.

Kaye plugged in her password. In her original work, she had tracked down seven potential candidates for the expression and reassembly of complete and infectious HERV particles. The candidate genes she had thought most likely to be viable had turned out—luckily, she would have thought—to be associated with SHEVA. In her months at Americol, she had begun to study the six other candidates in detail, and had planned to move on to a list of thousands of possibly related genes.

Kaye was considered an expert, but what she was an expert in, compared to the huge world of human DNA, was a series of broken-down and seemingly abandoned shacks in a number of small and almost forgotten towns. The HERV genes were supposed to be fossils, fragments scattered through stretches of DNA less than a million base pairs long. Within such small distances, however, genes could recombine—jump from position to position—with some ease. The DNA was constantly in ferment—genes switching locations, forming little knots or fistulas of DNA, and replicating, a series of churning and twisting chains constantly being rearranged, for reasons no one could yet completely fathom. And yet SHEVA had remained remarkably stable over millions of years. The changes she was looking for would be both slight and very significant.

If she was right, she was about to overturn a major scientific paradigm, injure a lot of reputations, cause the scientific fight of the twenty-first century, a war actually, and she did not want to be an early casualty because she had come to the battlefield in half a suit of armor. Speculation about the cause was not sufficient. Extraordinary claims required extraordinary evidence.

Patiently, hoping it would be at least an hour before anyone else entered the lab, she once again compared the sequences found in SHEVA with the six other candidates. This time she looked closely at the transcription factors that triggered expression of the large protein complex. She rechecked the sequences several times before she spotted what she had known since yesterday must be there. Four of the candidates carried several such factors, all subtly different.

She sucked in her breath. For a moment she felt as if she

stood on the brink of a tall cliff. The transcription factors would have to be specific for different varieties of LPC. That meant there would be more than one gene coding for the large protein complex.

More than one station on Darwin's radio.

Last week Kaye had asked for the most accurate available sequences of over a hundred genes on several chromosomes. The manager of the genome group had told her they would be available this morning. And he had done his work well. Even scanning by eye, she was seeing interesting similarities. With so much data, however, the eye was not good enough. Using an in-house software package called METABLAST, she searched for sequences roughly homologous with the known LPC gene on chromosome 21. She requested and was authorized to use most of the computing power of the building's mainframe for over three minutes.

When the search was completed, Kaye had the matches she had hoped for—and hundreds more besides, all buried in so-called junk DNA, each subtly different, offering a different set of instructions, a different set of strategies.

LPC genes were common throughout the twenty-two human autosomes, the chromosomes that did not code for sex.

"Backups," Kaye whispered, as if she might be overheard, "alternates," and then she felt a chill. She pushed back from the desk and paced around the lab. "Oh, my God. What in hell am I thinking here?"

SHEVA in its present form was not working properly. The new babies were dying. The experiment—the creation of a new subspecies—was being thwarted by outside enemies, other viruses, not tame, not co-opted ages ago and made part of the human tool kit.

She had found another link in the chain of evidence. If you wanted a message delivered, you would send many messengers. And the messengers could carry different messages. Surely a complex mechanism that governed the shape of a species would not rely on one little messenger and one fixed message. It would automatically alternate subtle designs, hoping to dodge whatever bullets might be out there, problems it could not directly sense or anticipate.

What she was looking at could explain the vast quantities of HERV and other mobile elements—all designed to guarantee an efficient and successful transition to a new phenotype, a new variety of human. *We just don't know how it works. It's so complicated . . . it could take a lifetime to understand!*

What chilled her was that in the present atmosphere, these results would be completely misinterpreted.

She pushed her chair back from the computer. All of the energy she had had in the morning, all the optimism, the glow from her night with Mitch, seemed hollow.

She could hear voices down the hall. The hour had passed quickly. She stood and folded the printout of the candidate sites. She would have to take these to Jackson; that was her first duty. Then she had to talk with Dicken. They had to plan a response.

She pulled her coat from the drying rack and slipped it on. She was about to leave when Jackson stepped in from the hall. Kaye looked at him with some shock; he had never come down to her lab before. He looked tired and deeply concerned. He, too, held a slip of paper.

"I thought I should be the first to let you know," he said, waving the paper under her nose.

"Let me know what?" Kaye asked.

"How wrong you can possibly be. SHEVA is mutating."

Kaye finished the day in a three-hour round of meetings with senior staff and assistants, a litany of schedules, deadlines, the day-to-day minutiae of research in a small part of a very large corporation, mind-numbing at the best of times, but now almost intolerable. Jackson's smug condescension at the delivery of the news from Germany had almost goaded her into a sharp rejoinder, but she had simply smiled, said she was already working on the problem, and left . . . To stand for five minutes in the women's rest room, staring at herself in a mirror.

She walked from Americol to the condominium tower, accompanied by the ever-watchful Benson, and wondered if last night had just been a dream. The doorman opened the big glass door, smiled politely at them both, and then gave the agent a brotherly nod. Benson joined her in the elevator car. Kaye had never been at ease with the agent, but had managed in the past to keep up polite conversation. Now she could only grunt to his inquiry about how her day had gone.

When she opened the door at 2011, for a moment she thought Mitch was not there, and let out her breath with a small whistle. He had gotten what he wanted and now she was alone again to face her failures, her most brilliant and devastating failures.

But Mitch came out of the small side office with a most pleasing haste and stood in front of her for a moment, searching her face, estimating the situation, before he held her, a little too gently.

"Squeeze me until I squeak," she said. "I'm having a really bad day."

That did not stop her from wanting him. Again the love was both intense and wet and full of a marvelous grace she had never felt before. She held on to these moments and when they could go on no more, when Mitch lay beside her covered with beads of sweat and the sheets beneath her were uncomfortably damp, she felt like crying.

"It's getting really tough," she said, her chin quivering.

"Tell me," he said.

"I think I'm wrong, we're wrong. I know I'm not but everything is telling me I'm wrong."

"That doesn't make sense," Mitch said.

"No!" she cried. "I predicted this, I saw it happening, but not soon enough, and they aced me. Jackson aced me. I haven't talked with Marge Cross, but . . ."

It took Mitch several minutes to work the details out of her, and even then, he could only half follow what she was saying.

The short form was that she felt new expressions of SHEVA were stimulating new varieties of LPCs, large protein complexes, in case the first signal on Darwin's radio had not been effective or had met with problems. Jackson and nearly everyone else believed they were encountering a mutated form of SHEVA, perhaps even more virulent.

"Darwin's radio," Mitch repeated, mulling over the term.

"The signaling mechanism. SHEVA."

"Mmm hmm," he said. "I think your explanation makes more sense."

"Why does it make more sense? Please tell me I'm not just being pigheaded and *wrong*."

"Put the facts together," Mitch said. "Run it through the science mill again. We know speciation sometimes occurs in small leaps. Because of the mummies in the Alps, we know SHEVA was active in humans who were producing new kinds of babies. Speciation is rare even on a historical time scale—and SHEVA was unknown in medical science until just recently. There are far too many coincidences if SHEVA and evolution in small leaps aren't connected."

She rolled to face him, and ran her fingers along his cheeks, around his eyes, in a way that made him flinch.

"Sorry," she said. "It is so marvelous that you're here. You restore me. This afternoon—I have never felt so lost . . . not since Saul was gone."

"I don't think Saul ever knew what he had, with you," Mitch said.

Kaye let this lie between them for a moment, to see if she quite understood what it meant. "No," she said finally. "He wasn't capable of knowing."

"I know who and what you are," Mitch said.

"Do you?"

"Not yet," he confessed, and smiled. "But I'd like to try."

"Listen to us," Kaye said. "Tell me what you did today."

"I went to the YMCA and cleared out my locker. I took a cab back here and lounged around like a gigolo."

"I mean it," Kaye said, gripping his hand tighter.

"I made some phone calls. I'm going to take a train to New York tomorrow to meet with Merton and our mysterious stranger from Austria. We're getting together at a place that Merton describes as a 'wonderful, thoroughly corrupting old mansion upstate.' Then I'll take the train to Albany for my interview at SUNY."

"Why a mansion?"

"I have no idea," Mitch said.

"You're coming back?"

"If you want me to."

"Oh, I want you to. You don't need to worry about that," Kaye said. "We're not going to have much time to think, much less worry."

"Wartime romance is the sweetest," Mitch said.

"Tomorrow is going to be much worse," Kaye said. "Jackson is going to make a stink."

"Let him," Mitch said. "In the long run, I don't think anybody is going to be able to stop this. Slow it down, maybe, but not stop it."

Washington, D.C.

Dicken stood on the Capitol steps. It was a warm evening, but he could not help but feel a little cold, listening to a sound like the sea, broken by waves of echoing voices. He had never felt so isolated, so distant, as he did now, staring out over what must have been fifty thousand human beings, stretching from the Capitol to the Washington Monument and beyond. The fluid mass pushed against the barricades along the bottom of the steps, streamed around the tent pavilions and speakers' stands, listened intently to a dozen different speeches being delivered, milling slowly like stirred soup in a huge tureen. He caught bits and pieces of breeze-tattered speeches, incomplete but suggestive: bits of raw language charging the mass.

Dicken had spent his life hunting down and trying to understand the diseases that affected these people, acting as if in some way he were invulnerable. Because of skill and a little luck he had never caught anything but a bout of dengue fever, bad enough but not fatal. He had always thought of himself as separate, a little superior perhaps but infinitely sympathetic. The self-delusion of an educated and intellectually isolated fool.

He understood better now. The mass called the shots. If the mass could not understand, then nothing he did, or Augustine did, or the Taskforce, would much matter. And the mass quite clearly understood nothing. The voices drifting his direction spoke of outrage at a government that would slaughter children, voices angrily denouncing "morning-after genocide."

He had thought about calling Kaye Lang earlier, to regain his composure, his sense of balance, but he hadn't. That was done with, finished in a very real way.

Dicken descended the steps, passing news crews, cameras, clumps of office workers, men in blue and brown suits and dark glasses and wearing microphones in their ears. The police and National Guard troops were determined to keep people away from the Capitol, but did not prevent individuals from joining the crowd.

He had already seen a few senators descend in a tight-packed group and join the mass. They must have sensed they could not be separate, superior, not now. They belonged with their people. He had thought them both opportunistic and courageous.

Dicken climbed over the barricades and pushed into the crowd. It was time to catch this fever and understand the symptoms. He had looked deep inside himself and did not like what he saw. Better to be one of the troops on the front line, part of the mass, ingest its words and smells, and come back infected so that he could in turn be analyzed, understood, made useful again.

That would be a kind of conversion. An end to the pain of separation. And if the mass should kill him, maybe that was what he deserved for his previous aloofness and his failures.

Younger women in the crowd wore colored masks. All the men wore white or black masks. Many wore gloves. More than just a few men wore tight-fitting black jumpers with industrial fume masks, so-called "filter" suits, guaranteed by various enterprising merchants to prevent the shedding of "devil virus."

People in the crowd at this end of the mall were laughing, half listening to a speaker under the nearest pavilion—a civil rights leader from Philadelphia sounding out in deep, rich tones, like caramel. The speaker talked of leadership and responsibility, what the government should do to control this plague, and possibly, just possibly, where the plague had arisen, inside the secret bowels of the government itself.

"Some cry out it has its birth in Africa, but *we* are sick, not Africa. Others cry out it is the devil's disease that strikes us, that it is foretold, to punish—"

Dicken moved on until he came under the more frantic voice of a television evangelist. The evangelist was brightly illuminated, a large and sweating man with a square head wearing a straining black business suit. He pointed and danced around his stage, exhorting the crowd to pray for guidance, to look deep inside.

Dicken thought of his grandmother, who had liked this sort of thing. He moved on again.

It was getting dark, and he could sense a growing tension in the crowd. Somewhere, out of earshot, something had happened, something had been said. The dark triggered a change of mood. Lights turned on around the mall, casting the crowd in etched and lurid orange. He looked up and saw helicopters at a respectful altitude, buzzing like insects. For a moment, he wondered if they were all going to be tear-gassed, shot, but the disruption was not from the soldiers, the police, the helicopters.

The impulse came in a wave.

He experienced an expectant hunger, felt its advancing tide, hoped whatever was disturbing the crowd would reveal something to him. But it was not really news at all. It was simply a propulsion, first this way, then that, and he walked with the tight-packed crowd ten feet north, ten feet south, as if caught in a bizarre dance step.

Dicken's survival instincts now told him it was time to cut the personal angst, cut the psychological crap and get out of the flow. From a speaker nearby, he heard a voice of caution. From the man next to him, dressed in a filter suit, he heard, muffled through the filters, "It's not just one disease now. It's on the news. There's a new plague."

A middle-aged woman in a flower print dress carried a small Walkman TV. She held it out for those around her, showing a tiny framed head speaking in tinny tones. Dicken could not hear these words.

He worked toward the edge, slowly and politely, as if wading through nitroglycerin. His shirt and light jacket were soaked with sweat. A few scattered others, born observers, like him, sensed the change, and their eyes flashed. The crowd smothered in its own confusion. The night was deep and humid, and stars could not be seen, and the orange lights along the mall and around the tents and platforms made everything look bitter.

Dicken stood near the Capitol steps again, within twenty or thirty people of the barricades, where he had stood an hour before. Mounted police, men and women on beautiful brown horses now rich amber in the unreal light, moved back and forth along the perimeter, dozens of them, more than he had ever seen before. The National Guard troops had pulled back, forming a line, but not a dense line. They were not ready. They did not expect trouble; they had no helmets or shields.

Voices immediately around him, whispering, subdued—

"Can't"

"Children have the"

"My grandchildren will"

"The last generation"

"Book"

"Stop"

Then, an eerie quiet. Dicken was five people from the edge. They would not let him move any farther. Faces dull and resentful, like sheep, eyes blank, hands shoving. Ignorant. Frightened.

He hated them, wanted to smash their noses. He was a fool; he did not want to be among the sheep. "Excuse me." No response. The mob's mind had been made up; he could feel it deliberately pulsing. The mob waited, intent, vacant.

Light flared in the east and Dicken saw the Washington Monument turn white, brighter than the floodlights. From the dark muggy sky came a loose rumble. Drops of rain touched the crowd. Faces looked up.

He could smell the mob's eagerness. Something had to change. They were being pressed by a single concern: *something had to change.*

The rain came pouring. People raised their hands over their heads. Smiles broke out. Faces accepted the rain and people spun as best they could. Others shoved the spinners and they stopped, dismayed.

The crowd spasmed and suddenly expelled him and he made it to the barricades and confronted a policeman. "Jesus," the policeman said, dancing back three steps, and the mob shoved over the barricades. The horsemen tried to push them back, weaving through. A woman screamed. The mob surged and swallowed the policemen mounted and on foot, before they could raise their batons or unholster their guns. A horse was pushed up onto the steps and stumbled, falling over into the mob, its rider rolling off, a boot flung high.

Dicken shouted "Staff!" and ran up the Capitol steps, between the guardsmen, who ignored him. He was shaking his head and laughing, glad to be free, waiting for the melee to really begin. But the mob was right behind him, and there was barely time to start running again, ahead of the people, the scattered gunshots, the wet and spreading and stinking mass.

Mitch saw the morning headlines on a rack of *Daily News* at Penn Station:

RIOT IN FRONT OF CAPITOL
Senate Stormed
Four Senators Die; Dozens Dead,
Thousands Injured

He and Kaye had spent the night eating by candlelight and making love. Very romantic, very out of touch. They had parted just an hour ago; Kaye was getting dressed, choosing her colors carefully, expecting a difficult day.

He picked up a paper and boarded the train. As he took his seat and spread the paper open, the train began to pull out, picking up speed, and he wondered if Kaye was safe, whether the riot had been spontaneous or organized, whether it really mattered.

The people had spoken, or rather, snarled. They had had enough of failure and inaction in Washington. The president was meeting with security advisors, the joint chiefs of staff, the heads of select committees, the chief justice. To Mitch, that sounded like a soft approach preliminary to declaring martial law.

He did not want to be on the train. He could not see what

Merton could do for him, or for Kaye; and he could not picture himself lecturing on bonehead bone-ology to college students and never setting foot on a dig again.

Mitch slipped the folded paper onto his seat and made his way down the aisle to the public phone box at the end of the car. He called Kaye's number, but she had already left, and he did not think it would be politic to call her at Americol.

He took a deep breath, tried to calm himself, and returned to his seat.

Baltimore

Dicken met Kaye in the Americol cafeteria at ten. The conference was scheduled for six o'clock, and a number of visitors had been added: the vice president and the president's science advisor among them.

Dicken looked terrible. He had not slept all night. "My turn to be a basket case," he said. "I think the debate is over. We're down, we're out. We can do some more shouting, but I don't know anyone who will listen."

"What about the science?" Kaye asked plaintively. "You tried hard to bring us back in line after the herpes disaster."

"SHEVA mutates," Dickens said. He beat his hand rhythmically on the table.

"I've explained that to you."

"You've only shown that SHEVA mutated a long time ago. It's just a human retrovirus, an old one, with a slow but very clever way of reproducing."

"Christopher . . ."

"You're going to get your hearing," Dicken said. He finished his cup of coffee and stood up from the table. "Don't explain it to me. Explain it to *them*."

Kaye looked up at him, angry and puzzled. "Why change your mind after so long?"

"I started out looking for a virus. Your papers, your work, suggested it might be something else. We can all be misled. Our job is to look for evidence, and when it's compelling, we have to give up our most cherished little notions."

Kaye stood beside him and poked her finger. "Tell me this is entirely about science."

"Of course not. I was on the Capitol steps, Kaye. I could have been one of those poor bastards who got shot or beaten to death."

"That's not what I'm talking about. Tell me you returned Mitch's call, after our meeting in San Diego."

"I didn't."

"Why not?"

Dicken glared back at her. "After last night, anything personal is trivial, Kaye."

"Is it?"

Dicken folded his arms. "I could never present someone like Mitch to someone like Augustine and hope to build our case. Mitch had some interesting information, but it only proves that SHEVA has been with us for a long time."

"He believed in both of us."

"He believes in you more, I think," Dicken said, his eyes darting away.

"Has that affected your judgment?"

Dicken flared. "Has it affected *yours*? I can't take a pee without someone telling someone else how long I spent in the john. But you, you bring Mitch up to your *apartment*."

Kaye crowded in on Dicken. "Augustine told you I slept with Mitch?"

Dicken would not be crowded. He pushed Kaye gently back and sidestepped. "I hate this as much as anyone, but it's the way we have to be!"

"According to whom? Augustine?"

"Augustine's been burned, too. We're in a crisis. Goddamn it, Kaye, that should be obvious to everyone by now."

"I never said I was a saint, Christopher! I trusted you not to abandon me when you brought me into this."

Dicken lowered his head and looked to one side, then the other, his misery and anger tearing him. "I thought you might be a partner."

"What sort of partner, Christopher?"

"A . . . supporter. An intellectual equal."

"A girlfriend?"

For a moment, Dicken's face put on the expression of a small boy handed a crushing bit of news. He looked at Kaye with both longing and sadness. He could hardly stand up straight he was so tired.

Kaye pulled back and reconsidered. She had done nothing to lead him on; she had never regarded herself as a raving beauty whose attractions were irresistible to men. She could not fathom the depth of this man's feeling.

"You never told me you felt anything more than curiosity," Kaye said.

"I never move fast enough, and I never say what I mean," Dicken said. "I don't blame you for not suspecting."

"But it hurt you that I chose Mitch."

"I can't deny it hurts. But it doesn't affect my scientific judgment."

Kaye walked around the table, shaking her head. "What can we salvage from this?"

"You can present your evidence. I just don't believe it's going to be compelling." He swung around and walked out of the cafeteria.

Kaye bused her tray and dishes to the kitchen conveyer belt. She glanced at her watch. She needed a strong dose of the personal, the face-to-face; she wanted to speak with Luella Hamilton. She could make it out to NIH and be back before the meeting.

At the floor security desk, she called for a company car.

58

Mitch stepped out under the soaring white tent pavilion that covered the antique train station of the small town of Beresford. He shaded his eyes against the morning sun and glanced at a planter loud with yellow daffodils, near a bright red garbage can. He was the only one getting off the train.

The air smelled of hot grease and pavement and fresh-cut grass. He looked for someone to meet him, expecting Merton. The town, visible across the tracks, accessible by a pedestrian bridge, was little more than a row of shops and the Amtrak parking lot.

A black Lexus pulled into the parking lot, and Mitch saw a redheaded man step out, look through the chicken-wire fencing at the station, and wave.

"His name is William Daney. He owns most of Beresford— his family does, that is. They have an estate about ten minutes from here that rivals Buckingham Palace. I was naïve enough to forget what kind of royalty America cherishes—old money spent in strange ways."

Mitch listened to Merton as the journalist drove him down a winding two-lane road between splendid hardwood trees, maple and oak, new leaves so intensely green he felt as if he were in a movie. The sun threw dazzles of gold across the road. They hadn't seen another car in five minutes.

"Daney used to be a yachtsman. Spent millions perfecting

325

a graceful big boat, lost a few races. That was more than twenty years ago. Then he discovered anthropology. Problem is, he hates dirt. Loves water, hates dirt, hates to dig. I love driving in America. But this is almost like driving in England. I could even"—Merton swerved briefly over the center line into the left lane—"Follow my instincts." He quickly corrected, smiled at Mitch. "Pity about the riots. England's still relatively calm, but I'm expecting a change of government any minute. Dear old PM doesn't get it yet. Still thinks switching to the Euro is his biggest worry. Hates the gynecological aspect of this whole mess. How's Mr. Dicken? Ms. Lang?"

"They're fine," Mitch said, unwilling to talk much until he saw what he was being dragged into. He liked Merton well enough, found him interesting, but did not trust him one bit. He resented that the man seemed to know so much about his private life.

Daney's mansion made a three-story, gray stone curve at the end of a redbrick drive flanked by beautifully manicured lawns, perfect as a putting green. A few gardeners were out trimming hedges, and an elderly woman in jodhpurs and a broad and ragged straw hat waved at them as Merton drove past. "Mrs. Daney, our host's mum," Merton said, waving out the window. "Lives in the housekeeper's cottage. Nice old woman. Doesn't go into her son's rooms very often."

Merton parked in front of the brownstone steps leading to the huge, double-door entrance.

"Everybody's here," he said. "You, me, Daney, and *Herr Professor* Friedrich Brock, formerly of the University of Innsbruck."

"Brock?"

"Yes." Merton smiled. "He says he met you once."

"He did," Mitch said. "Once."

The entry way of the Daney mansion was shadowy, a huge hall paneled with dark wood. Three parallel beams of sun dropped through a skylight onto the age-darkened limestone floor, cutting over a huge Chinese silk rug, in the middle of which rose a round table covered with a hemisphere of flowers. Just to one side of the table, in shadow, stood a man.

"William, this is Mitch Rafelson," Merton said, taking Mitch's elbow and leading him forward.

The man in shadow stuck out his hand into one of the shafts of sun, and three gold rings gleamed on thick, strong fingers. Mitch shook the hand firmly. Daney was in his early fifties, tanned, with yellow-white hair receding from a Wagnerian forehead. He had small, perfect lips quick to smile, dark brown eyes, baby-smooth cheeks. His shoulders were broadened by a padded gray blazer, but his arms looked well-muscled.

"It's an honor to meet you, sir," Daney said. "I'd have bought them from your friends if they had been offered, you know. And then I would have turned them over to Innsbruck. I've told this to *Herr Professor* Brock, and he has given me absolution."

Mitch smiled to be polite. He was here to meet Brock.

"Actually, William doesn't own any human remains," Merton said.

"I'm happy with duplicates, casts, sculptures," Daney said. "I'm not a scientist, merely a hobbyist, but I hope I honor the past by trying to understand it."

"Into the Hall of Humanity," Merton said with a flourish of his hand. Daney tossed his head proudly and led the way.

The hall filled a former ballroom in the eastern curve of the mansion. Mitch had seen nothing like it outside of a museum: dozens of glass cases arranged in rows, with carpeted aisles in between, each case containing casts and replicas of every major specimen of anthropology. *Australopithecus afarensis* and *robustus*; *Homo habilis* and *erectus*. Mitch counted sixteen different Neandertal skeletons, all professionally mounted, and six of them had waxwork reconstructions of how the individuals might have looked in life. There was no attempt to avoid offending modesty: All the models were nude and hairless, avoiding any speculation on clothing or hair patterns.

Row upon row of hairless apes, illuminated by elegant and respectfully softened spotlights, stared blankly at Mitch as he walked past.

"Incredible," Mitch said, despite himself. "Why have I never heard of you before, Mr. Daney?"

"I only talk to a few people. The Leakey family, Björn Kurtén, a few others. My close friends. I'm eccentric, I know, but I don't like to flaunt it."

"You're among the elect now," Merton said to Mitch.

"Professor Brock is in the library." Daney pointed the way. Mitch would have enjoyed spending more time in the hall. The wax sculptures were superb and the reproductions of the specimens first rate, almost indistinguishable from the specimens themselves.

"No, actually, I am here. I couldn't wait." Brock stepped around a case and advanced. "I feel as if I know you, Dr. Rafelson. And we do have mutual acquaintances, do we not?"

Mitch shook hands with Brock, under Daney's beaming and approving inspection. They walked several dozen yards to an adjacent library, furnished in the epitome of Edwardian elegance, three levels with railed walkways connected by two wrought-iron bridges. Huge paintings of Yosemite and the Alps in dramatic moods flanked the single high north-facing window.

They took seats around a large, low round table in the middle of the room. "My first question," Brock said, "is, do you dream of them, Dr. Rafelson? Because I do, and frequently."

Daney served the coffee himself, after it was rolled into the library by a stout, somber young woman in a black suit. He poured each of them a cup in Flora Danica china, botanical patterns in this series displaying the microscopic plants native to Denmark, based on nineteenth-century scientific art. Mitch examined his saucer, adorned with three beautifully rendered dinoflagellates, and wondered what he would do if he had all the money he could ever hope to spend.

"I myself do not believe these dreams," Brock picked up the conversation. "But these individuals do haunt me."

Mitch looked around the group, completely unsure what was expected of him. It seemed distinctly possible that associating with Daney, Brock, and even Merton, could somehow be turned to his disadvantage. Perhaps he had been battered once too often in this arena.

Merton sensed his unease. "This meeting is completely private, and will be kept secret," he said. "I don't plan to report anything said here."

"At my request," Daney said, lifting his brows emphatically.

"I wanted to tell you that you must be correct in your judgments, the judgments you have shown by seeking out certain people, and learning certain things about our own researches," Brock said. "But I have just been released from my responsibilities with regard to the Alpine mummies. The arguments have become personal, and more than a little dangerous to all our careers."

"Dr. Brock believes the mummies represent the first clear evidence of a human speciation event," Merton said, hoping to move things along.

"Subspeciation, actually," Brock said. "But the idea of a species has become so fluid in past decades, has it not? The presence of SHEVA in their tissues is most evocative, don't you think?"

Daney leaned forward in his chair, cheeks and forehead pink with the intensity of his interest.

Mitch decided he could not be reticent among such fellow travelers. "We've found other instances," he said.

"Yes, so I hear, from Oliver and from Maria Konig at the University of Washington."

"Not me, actually, but people I've talked to. I've been ineffectual, to say the least. Compromised by my own actions."

Brock dismissed this. "When I called your apartment in

Innsbruck, I had forgiven you your lapse. I could sympathize, and your story rang true."

"Thank you," Mitch said, and found himself genuinely affected.

"I apologize for not revealing myself at the time, but you understand, I hope."

"I do," Mitch said.

"Tell me what's going to happen," Daney said. "Are they going to release their findings about the mummies?"

"They are," Brock said. "They are going to claim contamination, that the mummies are in fact not related. The Neandertals are going to be labeled *Homo sapiens alpinensis*, and the infant is going to be sent to Italy for study by other specialists."

"That's ridiculous," Mitch said.

"Yes, and they will not get away with this pretense forever, but for the next few years, the conservatives, the hardliners, will rule. They will mete out information at will, to those they trust not to rock the boat, to agree with them, like zealous scholars defending the Dead Sea Scrolls. They are hoping to see their careers through without having to deal with a revolution that would topple both them and their views."

"Incredible," Daney said.

"No, *human,* and we all study the human, no? Was not our female injured by someone who didn't want her baby to be born?"

"We don't know that," Mitch said.

"I know that," Brock said. "I reserve my own irrational domains of belief, if only to defend myself against the zealots. Is this not the sequence that you dream, in some form or another, as if we have these events buried in our very blood?"

Mitch nodded.

"Perhaps this was the original sin of our kind, that our Neandertal ancestors wished to stop progress, hold on to their unique position . . . By killing the new children.

Those who would become us. Now we do the same thing, perhaps?"

Daney shook his head, quietly growling. Mitch observed this with some interest, then turned to Brock. "You must have examined the DNA results," he said. "It must be available for criticism by others."

Brock reached down by his seat and brought up a briefcase. He tapped it meaningfully. "I have all the material here, on DVD-ROM, massive graphics files, tabulations, the results from different labs around the world. Oliver and I are going to make it available on the Web, announce the coverup, and let the chips fall where they may."

"What we'd really like to do is make this relevant in the broadest way imaginable," Merton added. "We'd like to present conclusive evidence that evolution is knocking on our door again."

Mitch bit his lip, thinking this over. "Have you talked with Christopher Dicken?"

"He told me he can't help me," Merton said.

This shook Mitch. "Last time I spoke with him, he seemed enthusiastic, even gung ho," Mitch said.

"He's had a change of heart," Merton said. "We need to bring Dr. Lang onboard. I think I can convince some of the University of Washington people, certainly Dr. Konig and Dr. Packer, perhaps even an evolutionary biologist or two."

Daney nodded enthusiastically.

Merton turned to Mitch. His lips straightened, and he cleared his throat. "Your look says you don't approve?"

"We can't exactly go at this like we were college freshmen in a debating society."

"I thought you were a rough-and-tumble fellow," Merton said archly.

"Wrong," Mitch said. "I love it smooth and by the book. It's life that's rough-and-tumble."

Daney grinned. "Well put. Myself, I love to be on the ground floor."

"How's that?" Merton asked.

"This is a marvelous opportunity," Daney said. "I'd like to find a willing woman and bring one of these new people into my family."

For a long moment, neither Merton, Brock, nor Mitch could find the right words to reply.

"Interesting idea," Merton said quietly, and glanced quickly at Mitch, eyebrow raised.

"If we try to kick up a storm outside the castle, we might close more doors than we open," Brock admitted.

"Mitch," Merton said, subdued, "tell us, then, how should we go about this . . . more by the book?"

"We put together a group of true experts," Mitch said, and thought intently for a moment. "Packer and Maria Konig make a fine start. We recruit from their colleagues and contacts—the geneticists and molecular biologists at the University of Washington, NIH, and half a dozen other universities, research centers. Oliver, you probably know whom I'm referring to . . . maybe better than I do."

"The more progressive evolutionary biologists," Merton said, and then frowned, as if that might be an oxymoron. "Right now, that's pretty well limited to molecular biologists and a select few paleontologists, like Jay Niles."

"I know only conservatives," Brock said. "I have been drinking coffee with the wrong crowd in Innsbruck."

"We need a scientific foundation," Mitch said. "An overwhelming quorum of respected scientists."

"That'll take weeks, even months," Merton said. "Everyone has careers to protect."

"What if we fund more research in the private sector?" Daney said.

"That's where Mr. Daney could be helpful," Merton said, looking from beneath shaggy red eyebrows at their host. "You have the resources to put together a first-class conference, and that's just what we need now. Counter the public pronouncements from the Taskforce."

Daney's expression dimmed. "How much would that cost? Hundreds of thousands, or millions?"

"The former rather than the latter, I suspect," Merton said with a chuckle.

Daney gave them a troubled glance. "That much money, and I'll have to ask Mother," he said.

The National Institutes of Health, Bethesda

"I let her go," Dr. Lipton said, sitting down behind her desk. "I let them all go. The head of clinic research said we had enough information to make our patient recommendations and bring the experiments to a halt."

Kaye stared at her, dumfounded. "You just . . . let them out of the clinic, to go home?"

Lipton nodded, jaw lightly dimpled. "It wasn't my call, Kaye. But I have to agree. We were beyond our ethical limits."

"What if they need help at home?"

Lipton looked down at the desk. "We advised them that their infants were likely to be born with severe defects, and that they would not survive. We referred them to outpatient treatment at their nearest hospitals. We're picking up all their expenses, even if there are complications. Especially if there are complications. They're all within the period of efficacy."

"They're taking RU-486?"

"It's their choice."

"It isn't policy, Denise."

"I know that. Six of the women asked for the opportunity. They wanted to abort. At that point, we can't continue."

"Did you tell them—?"

"Kaye, our guidelines are crystal clear. If there's a judgment that the infants could endanger the mother's health, we give them the means to terminate. I support their freedom to choose."

"Of course, Denise, but . . ." Kaye turned around, examining the familiar office, the charts, the pictures of fetuses at different stages of development. "I can't believe this."

"Augustine asked us to hold off giving them the RU-486 until a clear policy could be established. But the head of clinical research calls the shots."

"All right," Kaye said. "Who *didn't* ask for the drug?"

"Luella Hamilton," Lipton said. "She took it with her, promised to check in with her pediatrician regularly, but she did not take it under our supervision."

"It's over, then?"

"We've pulled our finger out of the pie," Lipton said softly. "We don't have a choice. Ethically, politically, we're going to get hit whatever we do. We chose ethics and support for our patients. If it were today, however . . . We have new orders from the secretary of Health and Human Services. No recommendations to abort and no dispensing of RU-486. We got out of the baby business just under the wire."

"I don't have Mrs. Hamilton's home address or phone number," Kaye said.

"You won't get it from me, either. She has a right to privacy." Lipton stared at her. "Don't go outside the system, Kaye."

"I think the system is going to eject me any minute now," Kaye said. "Thanks, Denise."

New York

On the train to Albany, surrounded by the musty smells of passengers, sun-warmed fabric, disinfectant, plastic, Mitch sank into his seat. He felt as if he had just escaped from Wonderland. Daney's enthusiasm for bringing a "new person" into the family both fascinated and frightened him. The human race had grown so cerebral, and had assumed so much control of its biology, that this unexpected and ancient form of reproduction, of creating variety in the species, could be stopped in its tracks, or engaged in as if it were some kind of game.

He stared out the window at small towns, forests of young trees, bigger towns with gray expanses of warehouses, factories dull and dirty and productive.

Americol Headquarters, Baltimore

Kaye picked up the papers she had ordered from Medline through the library, twenty copies each of eight different papers, all neatly collated. She shook her head and skimmed one of the folios as she boarded the elevator.

She took an additional five minutes going through the security checkpoints on the tenth floor. Agents waved wands, scanned her photo ID, and then passed sniffers over her hands and purse. Finally, the head of the vice president's Secret Service detail asked for someone inside the executive dining room to vouch for her. Dicken emerged, said that he knew her, and she entered the dining room fifteen minutes into the meeting.

"You're late," Dicken whispered.

"Caught in traffic. Did you know they've ended the special study?"

Dicken nodded. "They're dancing around each other now, trying to avoid making any commitments. Nobody wants to take the blame for anything."

Kaye saw the vice president sitting near the front, the science advisor beside him. The room held at least four Secret Service agents, which made her glad Benson had stayed outside.

Soft drinks, fruit, crackers, cheese, and vegetables had been set out on a table at the back, but no one was eating. The vice president clutched a can of Pepsi.

As Dicken led Kaye to a folding chair on the left side of the room, Frank Shawbeck finished a briefing on the findings of the NIH studies.

"That took just five minutes," Dicken whispered to Kaye.

Shawbeck tapped his papers on the lectern, stepped aside, and Mark Augustine walked forward. He leaned on the lectern.

"Dr. Lang is here," he announced neutrally. "Let's move on to social issues. We have suffered twelve major riots across the U.S. Most seem to have been triggered by announcements that we are going to pass out free RU-486. No such plans were ever completed, but they were of course under discussion."

"None of these drugs are illegal," Cross said irritably. She sat to the right of the VP. "Mr. Vice President, I invited the senate majority leader to attend this meeting, and he declined. I will not be held responsible for—"

"Please, Marge," Augustine said. "We'll air our grievances in a few minutes."

"Sorry," Cross said, and folded her arms. The vice president glanced over his shoulder, surveyed the audience. His eye fell on Kaye and he seemed troubled for a moment, then turned again to face front.

"The U.S. is not alone in having to deal with civil unrest," Augustine continued. "We're heading toward a social disaster of major proportions. Plainly speaking, the general public does not understand what is going on. They react according to gut instincts, or according to the dictates of demagogues. Pat Robertson, bless him, has already recommended that God blast Washington, D.C., with Hell's hottest fires if the Taskforce is allowed to go ahead with RU-486 testing. He's not alone. There's a real likelihood that the public will knock around until they find something, anything, more palatable than the truth, and then they'll flock behind that banner, and it's likely to have a religious aspect, and science will go right out the window."

"Amen," Cross said. Nervous laughter rippled through the small audience. The VP did not smile.

"This meeting was scheduled three days ago," Augustine continued. "The events of yesterday and today make it even more urgent that we keep our ducks in a row."

Kaye thought she could see where this was going. She looked for Robert Jackson and located him seated behind Cross. He angled his head, and his eyes swung left for the briefest moment, looking right at her. Kaye felt her face grow hot.

"This is about me," she whispered to Dicken.

"Don't be arrogant," Dicken warned. "We're all here to eat a little crow today."

"We're already tabling the research on RU-486 and what

has very loosely, and in very bad taste, been labeled RU-Pentium," Augustine said. "Dr. Jackson."

Jackson stood. "Preclinical trials show no efficacy by any of our vaccines or ribozyme inhibitors against newly located strains of SHEVA, loosely referred to as SHEVA-X. We have reason to believe that all new incidents of Herod's in the last three months can be attributed to lateral infection by SHEVA-X, which may come in at least nine different varieties, all with different coat glycoproteins. We can't target the LPC messenger RNA in the cytoplasm because our current ribozymes do not recognize the mutated form. In short, we're dead in the water on a vaccine. We probably won't come up with alternatives for six more months."

He sat down again.

Augustine pressed his fingers together symmetrically, making a flexible polygon. The room was silent for a long interval, absorbing the news and its implications. "Dr. Phillips."

Gary Phillips, science advisor to the president, stood and approached the lectern. "The president wishes me to convey his appreciation. We had hoped for so much more, but no research effort in any other nation has done better than the NIH and the CDC Taskforce. We have to realize we face an extremely clever and versatile opponent, and we have to speak with one voice, with resolve, to avoid pushing our nation into anarchy. That is why I have listened to Dr. Robert Jackson and to Mark Augustine. Our situation now is very sensitive, publicly sensitive, and they tell me there is a potentially divisive disagreement between some members of the Taskforce, especially within the Americol contingent."

"Not a split," Jackson said acidly. "A *schism*."

"Dr. Lang, I have been informed you do not share some of the opinions expressed by Dr. Jackson and Mark Augustine. Could you please express and clarify your point of view now, so that we may judge them?"

Kaye sat in shock for a few seconds, then stood up and managed to say, "I don't believe a fair hearing can be given now, sir. I am apparently the only person in this room whose opinion differs from the official statement you're obviously preparing."

"We need solidarity, but we need to be fair," the science advisor said. "I've read your papers on HERV, Ms. Lang. Your work was seminal and brilliant. You could very well be nominated for a Nobel prize. Your disagreements have to be listened to, and we're prepared to listen. I regret nobody has the luxury of sufficient time. I wish we did."

He motioned for her to come forward. Kaye walked to the lectern. Phillips stepped aside.

"I've expressed my opinions in numerous conversations with Dr. Dicken, and in one conversation with Ms. Cross and Dr. Jackson," Kaye said. "This morning, I put together a folder of supporting articles, some of them my own, and evidence gleaned from studies in the Human Genome Project, evolutionary biology, even paleontology." She opened her briefcase and handed the stack of folders to Nilson, who passed them to her left.

"I do not yet have the conclusive linchpin that holds my theories together," Kaye continued, then sipped from a cup of water handed to her by Augustine. "Scientific evidence from the Innsbruck mummies has not yet been released to the public."

Jackson rolled his eyes.

"I do have preliminary reports on evidence gathered by Dr. Dicken in Turkey and the Republic of Georgia—"

She spoke for twenty minutes, focusing on specifics and on her work with transposable elements and HERV-DL3. She came to an uncertain close by describing her successful search for different versions of the LPC on the same day she heard from Jackson that mutations in SHEVA had been located. "I believe SHEVA-X is a backup or alternate response to the failure of initial lateral transmissions to produce viable children. Second-stage pregnancies induced by SHEVA-X will not be open to herpes viral interference. They will produce healthy and viable infants. I have no direct evidence for this; no such infants have been born that I'm aware of. But I doubt we'll have to wait long. We should be prepared."

Kaye was surprised that she had spoken as coherently as she had, yet she was miserably aware she could not possibly succeed in turning the tide. Augustine watched her closely, with some admiration, she thought, and he gave her a quick smile.

"Thank you, Dr. Lang," Phillips said. "Questions?"

Frank Shawbeck raised his hand. "Does Dr. Dicken support your conclusions?"

Dicken stepped forward. "I did for a time. Recent evidence convinced me I was wrong."

"What evidence?" Jackson called out. Augustine waggled his finger in warning, but allowed the question.

"I believe SHEVA is mutating as a disease organism mutates," Dicken said. "Nothing convinces me it is not acting as a human pathogen."

"Isn't it true, Dr. Lang, that previous supposedly noninfectious forms of HERV have been associated with some kinds of tumors?" Shawbeck asked.

"Yes, sir. But they're also expressed in noninfectious form in many other tissues, including placenta. We only now have the opportunity to understand the many roles these endogenous retroviruses may play."

"We don't understand why they are in our genome, in our tissues, do we, Dr. Lang?" Augustine asked.

"Until now, we knew of no theory that could explain their presence."

"Other than their actions as disease-causing organisms?"

"Many substances in our bodies are both positive and necessary and yet, on occasion, are implicated in disease," Kaye responded. "Oncogenes are necessary genes that can also be provoked to cause cancer."

Jackson raised his hand. "I'd like to scotch this argument with an approach from an evolutionary perspective," he said. "While I'm not an evolutionary biologist, and I've never even played one on TV . . ."

Chuckles from all in the crowd but Shawbeck and the VP, still stony faced.

". . . I believe I had enough of the paradigm drummed into me in school and university. The paradigm is that evolution proceeds by random mutations within the genome. These mutations alter the nature of the proteins or the other components expressed by our DNA, and are usually detrimental, causing the organism to sicken or die. Yet over deep time, and under changing conditions, mutations may also create novel forms that confer positive advantages. Am I correct so far, Dr. Lang?"

"That is the paradigm," Kaye acknowledged.

"What you seem to be implying, however, is a hitherto undiscovered mechanism whereby the genome takes control of its own evolution, somehow sensing the right time to bring about change. Correct?"

"As far as it goes," Kaye said. "I believe our genome is much more clever than we are. It's taken us tens of thousands of years to get to the point where we have a hope of understanding how life works. The Earth's species have been evolving, both competing and cooperating, for billions of years. They've learned how to survive under conditions we can barely imagine. Even the most conservative biologist knows different kinds of bacteria can cooperate and learn from each other—but many now understand that different species of metazoans, plants and animals like us, do much the same thing when they play their roles in any ecosystem. The Earth's species have learned how to anticipate climate change and respond to it in advance, get a head start, and I believe, in our case, our genome is now responding to social change and the stress it causes."

Jackson pretended to work these ideas through in his head before asking, "If you were a graduate advisor and one of your students were to propose doing a thesis on this possibility, would you encourage them?"

"No," Kaye said bluntly.

"Why not?" Jackson pursued.

"It is not a widely defended point of view. Evolution has

been a very closed-minded field in biology, and only the brave few challenge the paradigm of the Darwinian Modern Synthesis. No grad student should try it alone."

"Charles Darwin was wrong, and you're right?"

Kaye turned to Augustine. "Is Dr. Jackson conducting this inquisition all by himself?"

Augustine stepped forward. "This is an opportunity to answer your opponents, Dr. Lang."

Kaye swung back and faced Jackson and the audience, eyes narrowed. "I do not challenge Charles Darwin, I have immense respect for him. Darwin would have recommended we not set our ideas in stone before we understood all the principles. I do not even reject many of the principles of the modern synthesis; quite clearly, whatever the genome devises has to pass the test of survival. Mutation is a source of unexpected and sometimes useful novelty. But there has to be more to explain what we see in nature. The modern synthesis was devised during a period when we were just beginning to learn the nature of DNA and establish the roots of modern genetics. Darwin would have been fascinated to know what we know today, about plasmids and exchange of free DNA, about error correction within the genome, about editing and transposition and hidden viruses, about markers and gene structure, about all manner of genetic phenomena, many of which do not fit at all neatly into the most rigid interpretations of the modern synthesis."

"Does any reputable scientist support the proposition that the genome is a self-aware 'mind,' able to judge the environment and determine the course of its own evolution?"

Kaye took a deep breath. "It would take me several hours to correct and expand upon that proposition as you state it, but, loosely, the answer is yes. None of them are here, unfortunately."

"Are their views noncontroversial?"

"Of course not," Kaye said. "Nothing in this field is noncontroversial. And I try to avoid the word 'mind,' because it has personal and religious connotations that are not productive. I use the term network; a perceptive and adaptive network of cooperating and competing individuals."

"Do you believe this mind, or network, could in some way be the equivalent of God?" Jackson stated this without smugness or contempt, to her surprise.

"No," Kaye said. "Our own brains function as perceptive and adaptive networks, but I don't believe we are gods."

"But our own brains produce *minds*, do they not?"

"I believe the word applies, yes."

Jackson held up his hands in puzzled query. "So we come full circle. Some sort of Mind—perhaps with a capital *M*—determines evolution?"

"Again, emphasis and semantics are important here," Kaye said slowly, and then realized she should have simply dismissed the question with silence.

"Have you ever had the larger scope of your theories peer-reviewed and published in a major journal?"

"No," Kaye said. "I have expressed some aspects in my published articles on HERV-DL3, which were peer-reviewed."

"Many of your articles were rejected by other journals, were they not?"

"Yes," Kaye said.

"By *Cell*, for example."

"Yes."

"Is *Virology* the most respected journal in the field?"

"It's an important journal," Kaye said. "It has published very important papers."

Jackson let this go. "I haven't had time to read all of the material in your handout. I apologize," he continued, getting to his feet. "To the best of your knowledge, would any of the authors whose papers you have included in your handout agree with you completely on the subject of how evolution occurs?"

"Of course not," Kaye said. "It's a developing field."

"It's not just developing, it's infantile, isn't that right, Dr. Lang?"

"In its infancy, yes," Kaye shot back. "Infantile would

apply to those who deny compelling evidence." She could not help looking at Dicken. He returned her look with unhappy resolve.

Augustine stepped forward again and held out his hand. "We could go on like this for days. I'm sure it would be an interesting conference. What we must do, however, is judge whether views such as those held by Dr. Lang could prove detrimental to the goals of the Taskforce. Our mission is to protect public health, not debate rarefied issues in science."

"That isn't exactly fair, Mark," Marge Cross said, rising. "Kaye, does this seem like a kangaroo court to you?"

Kaye let out a small explosion of breath, half chuckle, half sigh, looked down, and nodded.

"I wish there was time," Marge said. "I surely do. These views are fascinating, and I share many of them, dear, but we are hopelessly mired in business and politics, and we must go with what we can all support, and with what the public will understand. I do not see the support in this room, and I know we do not have time or the will to engage in a highly public debate. Unfortunately, we are stuck with science by committee, Dr. Augustine."

Augustine was obviously not pleased by this characterization.

Kaye looked at the vice president. The vice president stared at the folio on his lap, which he had not opened, clearly embarrassed by being stuck in a race in which he had no horse he could hope to ride. He was waiting for the debate to end.

"I understand, Marge," Kaye said. She could not keep her voice from quavering. "Thank you for making things so clear. I see no alternative but to resign from the Taskforce. My value to Americol is probably reduced by doing that, so I offer my resignation to you, as well."

Augustine took Dicken aside in the hallway after the meeting. Dicken had tried to catch up with Kaye, but she was far down the hall toward the elevator.

"This didn't turn out the way I would have liked," Augustine told him. "I don't want her out of the Taskforce. I just don't want her going public with these ideas. Christ, Jackson may have done us a greater disservice—"

"I know Kaye Lang well enough," Dicken said. "She's gone for good, and yes, she's pissed off, and I'm as responsible as Jackson."

"Then what in hell can you do to put things right?" Augustine asked.

Dicken shrugged loose from his grip. "Nada, Mark. Zip. And don't ask me to try."

Shawbeck approached them, his face grim. "There's another march on Washington planned for tonight. Women's groups, Christians, blacks, Hispanics. They're evacuating the Capitol and the White House."

"Jesus H.," Augustine said. "What are they trying to do, shut the country down?"

"The president's agreed to a full defense. Regular Army as well as National Guard. I think the mayor is going to declare a state of emergency in the city. The VP is being flown to Los Angeles this evening. Gentlemen, we should get out of here, too."

Dicken heard Kaye arguing with her bodyguard. He walked briskly down the hall to see what was happening, but they were in the elevator and the door had closed by the time he arrived.

Kaye stood in the ground floor lobby, hands on her hips, shouting at the top of her lungs. "I don't *want* your protection! I don't want any of this! I told you—"

"I don't have any choice, ma'am," Benson said, standing his ground like a small bull. "We are on full alert. You can't go back to your apartment until we get more agents here, and that's going to take at least an hour."

The building security guards were locking the front doors and moving barricades into position. Kaye twirled, saw the barricades, the curious people beyond the glass doors. Steel barriers dropped slowly over the outside entrance.

"Can I make a phone call?"

"Not now, Ms. Lang," Benson said. "I'd apologize all over if this were my fault, you know that."

"Yes, like when you told Augustine who was in my apartment!"

"They asked the doorman, Ms. Lang, not me."

"So what is it now, *us* versus *them*? I want to be outside with real people, not in here—"

"Not if they recognize you, you don't," Benson said.

"Karl, for God's sake, I've *resigned*!"

The agent held up his hands and shook his head firmly: no matter.

"Then where am I going to stay?"

"We're putting you with the other researchers in the executive lounge."

"With Jackson?" Kaye bit her lip and stared at the ceiling, shaking with helpless laughter.

The State University of New York, Albany

Mitch stared out of the taxi window at the students marching along the tree-lined avenue. People poured out of homes and office buildings along the path of the march. This time, they carried no signs, no banners, but all held their left hands high, fingers stretched out, palms forward.

The driver, a Somali immigrant, lowered his head and peered through the window to his right. "What does that mean, raised hand?"

"I don't know," Mitch said.

The march had cut them off at an intersection. The university campus lay just a few blocks away, but Mitch doubted they would get that far today.

"It is scary," the driver said, glancing over his shoulder at Mitch. "They want something to be done, yes?"

Mitch nodded. "I suppose."

The driver shook his head. "I won't cross that line. It's a long line. Mister, I take you back to the station, where you'll be safe."

"No," Mitch said. "Let me out here."

He paid the driver and walked to the curb. The taxi swung around and drove away just before other cars could block it in.

Mitch's jaw clenched. He could feel and smell the tension, the social electricity, in the long line of men and women, mostly young at first, but now more and more older, emerging from the buildings, all marching with left hands held high.

Not fists; hands. Mitch found that significant.

A police car parked just a few yards from him. Two patrol officers stood by their open doors, just watching.

Kaye had joked about wearing a mask, the day they had first made love. They had made love so few times. Mitch's throat constricted. He wondered how many of the women in the march were pregnant, how many had had their tests for exposure to SHEVA return positive, and how that had affected their relationships.

"You know what's going on?" an officer called to Mitch.

"No," Mitch said.

"Think it's going to get ugly?"

"I hope not," Mitch said.

"We weren't told a damned thing," the officer grumbled, then climbed back into the patrol car. The car backed up but was hemmed in by other cars and could go no farther. Mitch thought it was wise they did not turn on their sirens.

This march was different from the march in San Diego. The people here were tired, traumatized, almost past hope. Mitch wished he could tell them all that their fear was unnecessary, that this was not a disaster, not a plague, but he was no longer sure what to believe. All belief and opinion faded in the presence of this massive tide of emotion, of fear.

He did not want the job at SUNY. He wanted to be with Kaye and protect her; he wanted to help her get through this, professionally and personally, and he wanted her to help him, as well.

It was no time to be alone. The whole world was in pain.

Baltimore

Kaye opened the door to the condominium and walked in slowly. She kicked the heavy door shut with two bangs of her foot, then leaned into it with her hand to get it latched. She dropped her purse and valise on the chair and stood for a moment as if to get her bearings. She had not slept in twenty-eight hours.

It was late morning outside.

The phone message light blinked at her. She retrieved three messages. The first was from Judith Kushner, asking her to call back. The second was from Mitch, leaving an Albany phone number. The third was from Mitch also. "I've managed to get back to Baltimore, but it wasn't easy. They won't let me in the building to use the key you gave me. I tried Americol but the switchboard says they're not transferring outside calls, or you're not available, or something. I'm worried sick. It's hell out here, Kaye. I'll call in a few hours and see if you're home."

Kaye wiped her eyes and swore under her breath. She could hardly see straight. She felt as if she were stuck in molasses and no one would let her clean her shoes.

Americol had been surrounded by four thousand protesters for nine hours, shutting off traffic all around the building. Police had moved in and succeeded in roiling the crowds, breaking them into smaller and less controlled groups, and riots had broken out. Fires had been started, cars overturned.

"Where do I call, Mitch?" she murmured, taking the phone out of its recharging cradle. She was paging through the phone book, looking for the number of the YMCA, when the phone rang in her hand.

She fumbled it to her ear. "Hello?"

"Dark Intruder again. How are you?"

"Mitch, oh God, I'm okay, but I'm so tired."

"I've been walking all over downtown. They burned part of the convention center."

"I know. Where are you?"

"A block away. I can see your building and the Pepto-Bismol Tower."

Kaye laughed. "Bromo-Seltzer. Blue, not pink." She took a deep breath. "I don't want you here anymore. I mean, I don't want to be with you *here* anymore. Mitch, I'm not making sense. I need you so badly. Please come. I want to pack and get out. The bodyguard is still here, but he's down in the lobby. I'll tell him to let you in."

"I didn't even try to get the job at SUNY," Mitch said.

"I quit Americol and the Taskforce. We're equal now."

"We're both bums?"

"Shiftless and rootless and with no visible means of support. Other than a large bank account."

"Where will we go?" Mitch asked.

Kaye reached into her purse and pulled out the two small boxes containing SHEVA test kits. She had taken them from the common stores area on the seventh floor at Americol. "How about Seattle? You have an apartment in Seattle, don't you?"

"Yes."

"Exquisite. I want you, Mitch. Let's go live forever and ever in your bachelor apartment in Seattle."

"You're nuts. I'm coming right over."

He hung up and she laughed in relief, then broke into sobs. She smoothed the phone against her cheek, realized how crazy that was, put it down. "I am really strung out," she told herself, walking to the kitchen. She kicked off her shoes, pulled a Parrish print that had belonged to her mother from the wall, laid it on the dining room table, then all the other prints that belonged to her, her family, her past.

In the kitchen, she drew a glass of cold water from the refrigerator tap. "Screw luxury, screw security. Screw propriety." She worked through a list of ten other items to screw, and at the end of the list came "goddamned stupid *me*."

Then she remembered she had better let Benson know Mitch was coming.

Atlanta

Dicken walked toward his old office in the subbasement of Building 1 at 1600 Clifton Road. As he walked, he fingered his way through a vinyl packet of new material—special federal-grade security pass, fresh-printed instructions on new security procedures, talking points for arranged interviews later in the week.

He could not believe it had come to this. National Guard troops patrolled the perimeter and the grounds, and while there had not yet been any violent incidents at the CDC, phone threats arrived at the main switchboard as often as ten times a day.

He opened his office door and stood for a moment in the small room, savoring the cool and quiet. He wished he could be in Lagos or Tegucigalpa. He was much more at home working under rugged conditions in remote places; even the Republic of Georgia had been a bit too civilized, and therefore a bit too dangerous, for his tastes.

He much preferred viruses to out-of-control humans.

Dicken dropped the packet on his desk. For a moment, he could not remember why he was here. He had come to pick up something for Augustine. Then he recalled: the Northside Hospital autopsy reports on first-stage pregnancies. Augustine was working on a plan so top-secret Dicken knew nothing about it, but all the files pertaining to HERV and SHEVA in the building were being copied for his benefit.

He found the reports, then stood pensively, remembering the conversation with Jane Salter months ago, about the screaming of the monkeys in these old subbasement rooms.

He tapped his toe on the floor to the rhythm of an old and morbid child's song and murmured, "The bugs go in and the bugs go out, the monkeys will scream and the apes will shout . . ."

No doubt about it anymore. Christopher Dicken was a team player, hoping just to survive with his wits and his emotions in a few well-ordered pieces.

He picked up the vinyl packet and the folders and left the office.

Baltimore
APRIL 28

Kaye swung the garment bag to her shoulder. Mitch grabbed two suitcases and stood in the door, held open by a rubber chock. They had already loaded three boxes into the car in the condo garage.

"They tell me to keep in touch," Kaye said, and held up a black cell phone for Mitch's inspection. "Marge pays for this. And Augustine tells me not to give any interviews. That I can live with. What about you?"

"My lips are sealed."

"With kisses?" Kaye bumped him with her hip.

Benson followed them down to the garage. He watched them load Mitch's car with a plain expression of disapproval.

"You don't like my idea of freedom?" Kaye asked the agent with a piquant expression as she slammed the trunk. The car's rear springs groaned.

"You're taking everything with you, ma'am," Benson responded stonily.

"He doesn't approve of the company you keep," Mitch said.

"Well," Kaye said, standing beside Benson, brushing back her hair. "That's because he's a man of taste."

Benson smiled. "You're a fool to leave without protection."

"Maybe," Kaye said. "Thanks for your vigilance. Pass along my gratitude."

"Yes, ma'am," Benson said. "Good luck."

Kaye hugged him. Benson blushed.

"Let's go," Kaye said.

Kaye fingered the door frame of the Buick, its dusty blue finish powdery and matte with wear. She asked Mitch how old the car was.

"I don't know," Mitch said. "Ten, fifteen years."

"Find a dealership," Kaye said. "I'm going to buy you a brand-new Land Rover."

"That's roughing it, all right," Mitch said, lifting an eyebrow. "I'd prefer we be less obvious."

"I love the way you do that," Kaye said, lifting her much less impressive eyebrow dramatically. Mitch laughed.

"Screw it, then," she said. "Drive the Buick. We'll camp out under the stars."

66

Approaching Washington, D.C.

The Air Force Falcon passenger jet rolled gently to the east. Augustine sipped a Coke and glanced frequently through the window, clearly nervous about flying. Dicken had not known this about Augustine until now; they had never flown together before.

"We can make a strong case that even should second-stage SHEVA fetuses survive birth, they'll be carriers of a wide variety of infectious HERVs," Augustine said.

"Whose evidence?" Jane Salter asked. Her face was a little flushed from the heat in the airplane before takeoff; she was at best mildly unimpressed by these military trappings.

"I've had Taskforce researchers putting together biopsy results for the last two weeks, just on a hunch. We know HERVs express under all sorts of conditions, but the particles have never been infectious until now."

"We still don't know what the hell purpose the noninfectious particles serve, if any," Salter said. The other staffers, younger and less experienced, sat quietly in their seats, content to listen.

"No good purpose," Augustine said, tapping the seat arm. He swallowed hard and looked out the window again. "The HERV continue to produce viral particles that aren't infectious . . . Until SHEVA codes for a complete tool kit, everything necessary for a virus to assemble and escape a cell. I have six expert opinions, including Jackson's, that SHEVA may 'teach' other HERV how to be infectious again. They'll be most active in individuals with rapidly dividing cells, and that means SHEVA fetuses. We could have to deal with diseases we haven't seen in millions of years."

"Diseases that may no longer be pathogenic in humans," Dicken said.

"Can we take that chance?" Augustine asked. Dicken shrugged.

"So what are you going to recommend?" Salter asked.

"Washington is already under curfew, and they'll have it under martial law the instant someone decides to break a plate glass window or roll a car. No demonstrations, no inflammatory comments . . . Politicians hate to be lynched. It won't be long. The common folk are like cows in a herd, and there's been more than enough lightning to make even the cowboys nervous."

"Infelicitous comparison, Dr. Augustine," Salter said dryly.

"Well, I'll refine it," Augustine said. "I'm not at my best when I'm at twenty thousand feet."

"You think we're going to be under martial law," Dicken said, "and we can sequester all pregnant women and take their babies away from them . . . for testing?"

"It's horrible," Augustine admitted. "Most if not all of the fetuses will probably die. But if they do survive, I think we can make a case that we'll have to sequester them."

"Talk about throwing gas on a fire," Dicken said.

Augustine thoughtfully agreed. "I've been racking my brains trying to find a different solution. I will entertain alternatives."

"Maybe we shouldn't muddy the waters right now," Salter said.

"I have no intention of saying or doing anything now. The work goes on."

"We'd better be on firm ground," Dicken said.

"Damned right," Augustine said with a grimace. "*Terra firma*, and the sooner the better."

67

Leaving Baltimore

Everyone has a bitch," Mitch observed as he steered them along state route 26 out of the city, staying away from the main highways. Too many demonstrations—by truckers, motorists, even bicyclists, all claiming a shot at civil disobedience—had shut down the main routes. As it was, they had to wait twenty minutes in the middle of downtown as police cleared tons of garbage dumped by protesting sanitation workers.

"We failed them," Kaye said.

"You didn't fail them," Mitch said as he tried to find an alley to turn into.

"I screwed up and didn't make my case." Kaye hummed nervously to herself.

"Something wrong?" Mitch asked.

"Nothing," she said briskly. "Just the whole damned planet."

In West Virginia, they pulled into a KOA campground and paid thirty dollars for a tent site. Mitch set up the lightweight dome tent he had bought in Austria before he met Tilde, and a small camp stove, under a young oak tree looking out over a low valley where two tractors sat idle in a carefully furrowed field.

The sun had gone down twenty minutes before and the sky was mottled with light clouds. The air was just beginning to cool. Kaye's hair was sticky, the elastic of her panties chafed.

One other family had set up two tents about a hundred yards away, otherwise the campground was empty.

Kaye climbed through the rainflap into the tent. "Come in here," she told Mitch. She pulled off her dress and lay back on the sleeping bag Mitch had unrolled. Mitch set the campstove down and poked his head into the tent.

"My God, woman," he said admiringly.

"Do you smell me?" she asked.

"I surely do, ma'am," he said in agent Benson's fine North Carolina accent. He slipped in beside her. "It's still a little warm."

"I smell you," Kaye said. She had a needful and serious look on her face. She helped him out of his shirt, and he kicked aside his pants before reaching for the shaving kit where he was keeping the condoms. As he started to rip open the foil package, she bent over and kissed his erect penis. "Not this time," she said. She licked him swiftly, looked up. "I want you now, nothing in between."

Mitch took hold of her head and lifted her mouth away from him. "No," he said.

"Why not?" she asked.

"You're fertile," he said.

"How the hell do you know?" Kaye asked.

"I can see it in your skin. I can smell it."

"I bet you can," she said admiringly. "Can you smell anything else?" She pushed closer to him, lifted over his head, swung her knee to the other side.

"Spring," Mitch said, returning the favor.

She arched her back, half-twisted, and deftly fondled him, as he nuzzled between her legs.

"Ballet dancer," Mitch said, his voice muffled.

"You're fertile, too," she said. "You didn't say otherwise."

"Mm."

She lifted her torso again, rolled off him, and swung around to face him. "You're shedding," she said.

Mitch screwed up his face in puzzlement. "What?"

"You're shedding SHEVA. I test positive."

"Good Christ, Kaye. You sure know how to trash a mood." Mitch pushed back and sat with his legs pulled up in the corner of the tent. "I didn't think it could happen so fast."

"Something thinks I'm your woman," Kaye said. "Nature says we're going to be together a long time. I want that to be true."

Mitch was at a complete loss. "I do, too, but we don't need to act like idiots."

"Every man wants to make love to a fertile woman. It's in their genes."

"That is complete bullshit," Mitch said, and pushed back from her. "What in hell are you doing?"

Kaye hunkered across from him and rested on her knees. She made his head throb. The entire tent smelled of both of them and he could not think straight. "We can prove them wrong, Mitch."

"About what?"

"I once worried that work and family wouldn't fit together. Now, there's no conflict. I am my own laboratory."

Mitch shook his head vehemently. "No."

Kaye lay down beside him, pillowing her head on her arms. "Pretty forward and up front, no?" she asked softly.

"We haven't the slightest idea what's going to happen," Mitch said. His eyes were brimming, warm, half from fear, half from another emotion he could not define—something close to pure physical joy. His body wanted her so intensely, wanted her *now*. If he gave in, he knew it would be the supreme sexual act of his entire life. And if he gave in now, he worried he would never forgive himself.

"I know you believe we're right, and I know you'd be a good father," Kaye said, eyes narrowed to slits. She slowly lifted one leg. "If we don't do something now, maybe it will never happen, and we'll never know. Be my man. Please."

The tears came in a rush and Mitch hid his face. She rose beside him and held him and apologized, feeling his shaking. He mumbled a confused and jerking series of words about how women simply did not understand, never could understand.

Kaye soothed him and lay down beside him and for a while the breeze blew the rain flap gently over their silence.

"It's nothing wrong," she said. She wiped his face and looked down on him, frightened at what she had provoked. "It's the only right thing there is, maybe."

"I'm sorry," Kaye said stiffly as they loaded the car. A cool current of morning air slopped up from the flat farmland below the campsite. The leaves on the oak trees whispered. The tractors stood motionless on their perfect and empty furrows.

"No reason to be sorry," Mitch said, shaking out the tent. He folded it and rolled it into its long fabric sheath, then, with Kaye's help, unsocketed the tent poles and clapped them together into a fasces connected top to bottom by their stretching cords.

They had not made love during the night, and Mitch had slept very little.

"Any dreams?" Kaye asked as they sipped hot coffee from the pot on the camp stove.

Mitch shook his head. "You?"

"I didn't sleep more than a couple of hours," Kaye said. "I dreamed of working at EcoBacter. All these people were coming in and out. You were there." Kaye did not want to tell Mitch that in the dream she did not recognize him.

"Not very exciting," Mitch said.

As they traveled, they saw little out of the ordinary, out of place. They drove west on the two-lane road through small towns, coal towns, old towns, tired towns, towns repainted and repaired, gussied up, with their grand old homes in the rich old neighborhoods made into bed-and-breakfasts for well-to-do young people from Philadelphia and Washington and even New York.

Mitch switched on the radio and they heard about candle-light vigils in the Capitol, ceremonies honoring the dead senators, funerals for others killed in the riot. There were stories on the vaccine effort, how scientists now believed the torch had been passed to James Mondavi or perhaps a team at Princeton. Jackson seemed on the descent, and despite all that had happened, Kaye felt sorry for him.

They ate at the High Street Grill in Morgantown, a new restaurant designed to look old and established, with Colonial décor and thick wood tables coated with clear plastic resin. The sign out front declared the restaurant to be "Just a bit older than the Millennium, and a hell of a lot less significant."

Kaye watched Mitch closely as she picked at her club sandwich.

Mitch avoided her gaze and looked around at the customers, all stolidly involved in fueling their bodies. Older couples sat in silence; a lone man dropped his wool cap on the table next to a foam cup of coffee; three teenage girls in a booth picked at sundaes with long steel spoons. The staff was young and friendly and none of the women wore masks.

"Makes me believe I'm just an ordinary guy," Mitch said quietly, looking down at the bowl of chili before him. "I never thought I'd make a good father."

"Why?" Kaye asked, equally quiet, as if they were sharing a secret.

"I've always focused on my work, on wandering around and going places where there was interesting stuff. I'm pretty self-centered. I never thought any intelligent woman would want me to be a father, or a husband, for that matter. Some made it perfectly clear that wasn't why they were with me."

"Yeah," Kaye said, completely tuned in on him, as if every word might contain an answer essential to solving something that puzzled her.

The waitress asked if they needed more tea or dessert. They declined.

"This is so ordinary," Mitch said, lifting his spoon and swinging it through a small arc to measure the restaurant. "I feel like a big bug in the middle of a Norman Rockwell living room."

Kaye laughed. "There," she said.

"What do you mean, 'there'?"

"That was you, saying that. And I just felt my insides quiver."

"It's the food," Mitch said.

"It's you."

"I need to be a husband before I can be a father."

"It certainly isn't the food. I'm shaking, Mitch." She held out her hand and he let go of the spoon to grasp it. Her fingers were cold and her teeth were chattering though the interior was warm.

"I think we should get married," Mitch said.

"That's a lovely idea," Kaye said.

Mitch held out his hand. "Will you marry me?"

Kaye held her breath for a moment. "Oh, God, yes," she said with a short puff of resolve.

"We're crazy and we don't know what we're in for."

"We don't," Kaye agreed.

"We're on the edge of trying to make someone new, different from us," Mitch said. "Don't you find that terrifying?"

"Utterly," Kaye said.

"And if we're wrong, it's just going to be disaster after disaster. Pain. Grief."

"We are not wrong," Kaye said. "Be my man."

"I am your man."

"Do you love me?"

"I love you in ways I've never felt before."

"So fast. That's incredible."

Mitch nodded emphatically. "But I love you too much not to be a little critical."

"I'm listening."

"I'm troubled by you calling yourself a laboratory. That sounds cold and maybe a little out of it, Kaye."

"I hope you see through the words. See what I hope to say and do."

"I might," Mitch said. "Just barely. The air feels very thin where we are, right now."

"Like being on a mountain," Kaye said.

"I don't like mountains much," Mitch said.

"Oh, I do," Kaye said, thinking of the slopes and white peaks of Mount Kazbeg. "They give you freedom."

"Yeah," Mitch said. "You jump off, and you get ten thousand feet of pure freedom."

As Mitch was paying their bill, Kaye walked toward the rest rooms. On impulse, she pulled her phone card and a piece of paper from her wallet and lifted the receiver on a pay phone.

She was calling Mrs. Luella Hamilton at her home in Richmond, Virginia. She had persuaded the number out of the hospital switchboard at the clinic.

A deep, smooth male voice answered.

"Excuse me, is Mrs. Hamilton in?"

"We're having an early supper," the man said. "Who wants her?"

"Kaye Lang. Dr. Lang."

The man mumbled something, then called out "Luella!" and a few seconds passed. More voices. Luella Hamilton picked up the phone, her breath briefly pounding on the mouthpiece, then familiar and calm. "Albert says this is Kaye Lang, that right?"

"It's me, Mrs. Hamilton."

"Well, I'm at home now, Kaye, and don't need no checking up on."

"I wanted to let you know I'm no longer with the Task-force, Mrs. Hamilton."

"Please call me Lu. Whyever not, Kaye?"

"A parting of the ways. I'm heading west and I was worried about you."

"There's nothing to be worried about. Albert and the kids are all right and I'm just fine."

"I was just concerned. I've been thinking about you a lot."

"Well, Dr. Lipton gave me these pills that kill babies before they're very big, inside. You know about the pills."

"Yes."

"I didn't tell anybody, and we thought about it, but Albert and me, we're going ahead. He says he believes some of what the scientists say, but not all, and besides, he says I'm too ugly to be messing around behind his back." She let out a rich, disbelieving laugh. "He don't know us women and our opportunities, does he, Kaye?" Then, in an undertone, to someone beside her, "Stop that. I'm talking here."

"No," Kaye said.

"We're going to have this baby," Mrs. Hamilton said, coming down heavy on *have*. "Tell Dr. Lipton and the folks at the clinic. Whatever he or she is, he or she is *ours*, and we're going to give him or her a fighting chance."

"I'm glad to hear that, Lu."

"You are, huh? You curious, too, Kaye?"

Kaye laughed and felt her laughter catch, threaten to reverse to tears. "I am."

"You want to see this baby when he comes, don't you?"

"I would like to buy you both a present," Kaye said.

"That's nice. Then why not go find yourself a man and get this flu, and we'll visit together and compare, you and me, our two fine youngsters, all right? And I'll buy *you* a present." The suggestion carried not a hint of anger, absurdity, or resentment.

"I might do that, Lu."

"We get along, Kaye. Thanks for caring about me and you know, looking at me like I was people and not a lab rat."

"May I call you again?"

"We're moving soon, but we'll find each other, Kaye. We will. You take care."

Kaye walked down the long corridor from the rest rooms. She touched her forehead. She was hot. Her stomach was unsettled, as well. *Get this flu and we'll visit and compare.*

Mitch stood outside the restaurant with his hands in his pockets, squinting at the passing cars. He turned and smiled at her as he heard the heavy wood door open.

"I called Mrs. Hamilton," she said. "She's going to have her baby."

"Very brave of her."

"People have been having babies for millions of years," Kaye said.

"Yeah. Piece of cake. Where do you want to get married?" Mitch asked.

"How about Columbus?"

"How about Morgantown?"

"Sure," Kaye said.

"If I think about this much longer, I'm going to be completely useless."

"I doubt it," Kaye said. The fresh air made her feel better.

They drove to Spruce Street, and there, at the Monongahela Florist Company, Mitch bought Kaye a dozen roses. Walking around the County Magistrates Building and a senior center, they crossed High Street, heading toward the tall clock tower and flagpole of the county courthouse. They stopped beside a spreading canopy of maples to examine the inlaid and inscribed bricks arranged across the courthouse square.

" 'In loving memory, James Crutchfield, age 11,' " Kaye

read. The wind rustled through the maple branches, making the green leaves flutter with a sound like soft voices or old memories. " 'My love for fifty years, May Ellen Baker,' " Mitch read.

"Do you think we'll be together that long?" Kaye asked.

Mitch smiled and clasped her shoulder. "I've never been married," he said. "I'm naïve. I'd say, yes, we will." They walked beneath the stone arch to the right of the tower and through the double doors.

Inside, in the Office of the County Clerk, a long room filled with bookshelves and tables supporting huge, scuffed black and green volumes of land transactions, they received paperwork and were told where to get their blood tests.

"It's a state law," the elderly clerk told them from behind her broad wooden desk. She smiled wisely. "They test for syphilis, gonorrhea, HIV, herpes, and this new one, SHEVA. A few years ago, they tried to get the blood test removed as a requirement, but that's all changed now. You wait three days, then you can get married at a church or by a circuit court judge, any county in the state. Those are beautiful roses, honey." She lifted her glasses where they hung on a gold chain around her neck and scanned them shrewdly. "Proof of age will not be required. What took you so long?"

She handed them their application and test papers.

"We won't get our license here," Kaye said to Mitch as they left the building. "We'll fail the test." They rested on a wooden bench beneath the maples. It was four in the afternoon and the sky was clouding over swiftly. She laid her head on his shoulder.

Mitch stroked her forehead. "You're hot. Something wrong?"

"Just proof of our passion."

Kaye smelled her flowers, then, as the first drops of rain fell, held up her hand and said, "I, Kaye Lang, take you, Mitchell Rafelson, to be my wedded husband, in this age of confusion and upheaval."

Mitch stared at her.

"Raise your hand," Kaye said, "if you want me."

Mitch swiftly realized what was required, clasped her hand, braced himself to rise to the occasion. "I want you to be my wife, come hell or high water, to have and to hold, to cherish and to honor, whether they have any room at the inn or not, amen."

"I love you, Mitch."

"I love you, Kaye."

"All right," she said. "Now I'm your wife."

As they left Morgantown, heading southwest, Mitch said, "You know, I believe it. I believe that we're married."

"That's what counts," Kaye said. She moved closer to him across the broad bench seat.

That evening, on the outskirts of Clarksburg, they made love on a small bed in a dark motel room with cinder block walls. Spring rain fell on the flat roof and dripped from the eaves with a steady, soothing rhythm. They never pulled back the bedcover, lying instead naked together, limbs for blankets, lost in each other, needing nothing more.

The universe became small and bright and very warm.

68

West Virginia and Ohio

Rain and mist followed them from Clarksburg. The old blue Buick's tires made a steady hum on wet roads pushing and curling through limestone cuts and low round green hills. The wipers swung short black tails, taking Kaye back to Lado's whining little Fiat on the Georgian Military Road.

"Do you still dream about them?" Kaye asked as Mitch drove.

"Too tired to dream," Mitch said. He smiled at her, then focused on the road.

"I'm curious to know what happened to them," Kaye said lightly.

Mitch made a face. "They lost their baby and they died."

Kaye saw she had touched a nerve and drew back. "Sorry."

"I told you, I'm a little wacko," Mitch said. "I think with my nose and I care what happened to three mummies fifteen thousand years ago."

"You are far from being wacko," Kaye said. She shook her hair, then let out a yell.

"Whoa!" Mitch cringed.

"We're going to travel across America!" Kaye cried. "Across the heartland, and we're going to make *love* every time we stop somewhere, and we're going to *learn* what makes this great nation tick."

Mitch pounded the wheel and laughed.

"But we aren't doing this right," she said, suddenly prim. "We don't have a big poodle dog."

"What?"

"Travels with Charley," Kaye said. "John Steinbeck had a truck he called Rocinante, with a camper on the back. He wrote about traveling with a big poodle. It's a great book."

"Did Charley have attitude?"

"Damn right," Kaye said.

"Then I'll be the poodle."

Kaye buzzed his hair with mock clippers.

"Steinbeck took more than a week, I bet," Mitch said.

"We don't have to hurry," Kaye said. "I don't want this to ever end. You've given me back my life, Mitch."

West of Athens, Ohio, they stopped for lunch at a small diner in a bright red caboose. The caboose sat on a concrete pad and two rails off a frontage road beside the state highway, in a region of low hills covered with maples and dogwood. The food served in the dim interior, illuminated by tiny bulbs in railway lanterns, was adequate and nothing more: a chocolate malt and cheeseburger for Mitch and patty melt and bitter instant iced tea for Kaye. A radio in the kitchen in the back of the caboose played Garth Brooks and Selay Sammi. All they could see of the short-order cook was a white chef's hat bobbing to the music.

As they left the diner, Kaye noticed three shabbily dressed adolescents wandering beside the frontage road: two girls wearing black skirts and torn gray leggings and a boy in jeans and a travel-stained windbreaker. Like a lagging and downcast puppy, the boy walked several steps behind the girls. Kaye seated herself in the Buick. "What are they doing out here?"

"Maybe they live here," Mitch said.

"There's just the house up the hill behind the diner," Kaye said with a sigh.

"You're getting a motherly look," Mitch warned.

Mitch backed the car out of the gravel lot and was about to swing out onto the frontage road when the boy waved vigorously. Mitch stopped and rolled down the window. A light drizzle filled the air with silvery mist scented by trees and the Buick's exhaust.

"Excuse me, sir. You going west?" the boy asked. His ghostly blue eyes swam in a narrow, pale face. He looked worried and exhausted and beneath his clothes he seemed to be made of a bundle of sticks, and not a very large bundle.

The two girls hung back. The shorter and darker girl covered her face with her hands, peeping between her fingers like a shy child.

The boy's hands were dirty, his nails black. He saw Mitch's attention and rubbed them self-consciously on his pants.

"Yeah," Mitch said.

"I'm really *really* sorry to bother you. We wouldn't ask, sir, but it's tough finding rides and it's getting wet. If you're going west, we could use a lift for a while, hey?"

The boy's desperation and a goofy gallantry beyond his

years touched Mitch. He examined the boy closely, his answer snagged somewhere between sympathy and suspicion.

"Tell them to get in," Kaye said.

The boy stared at them in surprise. "You mean, now?"

"We're going west." Mitch pointed at the highway beyond the long chain-link fence.

The boy opened the rear door and the girls jogged forward. Kaye turned and rested her arm on the back of the seat as they jumped in and slid across. "Where are you heading?" she asked.

"Cincinnati," the boy said. "Or as far past as we can go," he added hopefully. "Thanks a million."

"Put on your seat belts," Mitch said. "There's three back there."

The girl who hid her face appeared to be no more than seventeen, hair black and thick, skin coffee-colored, fingers long and knobby with short and chipped nails painted violet. Her companion, a white blond, seemed older, with a broad, easygoing face worn down to vacancy. The boy was no more than nineteen. Mitch wrinkled his nose involuntarily; they hadn't bathed in days.

"Where are you from?" Kaye asked.

"Richmond," the boy said. "We've been hitchhiking, sleeping out in the woods or the grass. It's been hard on Delia and Jayce. This is Delia." He pointed to the girl covering her face.

"I'm Jayce," said the blond absently.

"My name is Morgan," the boy added.

"You don't look old enough to be out on your own," Mitch said. He brought the car up to speed on the highway.

"Delia couldn't stand it where she was," Morgan said. "She wanted to go to L.A. or Seattle. We decided to go with her."

Jayce nodded.

"That's not much of a plan," Mitch said.

"Any relatives out west?" Kaye asked.

"I have an uncle in Cincinnati," Jayce said. "He might put us up for a while."

Delia leaned back in the seat, face still hidden. Morgan licked his lips and craned his neck to look up at the car's headliner, as if to read a message there. "Delia was pregnant but her baby was born dead," he said. "She got some skin problems because of it."

"I'm sorry," Kaye said. She held out her hand. "My name is Kaye. You don't have to hide, Delia."

Delia shook her head, hands following. "It's ugly," she said.

"I don't mind it," Morgan said. He sat as far to the left-hand side of the car as he could, leaving a foot of space between himself and Jayce. "Girls are more sensitive. Her boyfriend told her to get out. Real stupid. What a waste, hey."

"It's too ugly," Delia said softly.

"Come on, sweetie," Kaye said. "Is it something a doctor could help with?"

"I got it before the baby came," Delia said.

"It's okay," Kaye said soothingly, and reached back to stroke the girl's arm. Mitch caught glimpses in the rearview mirror, fascinated by this aspect of Kaye. Gradually, Delia lowered her hands, her fingers relaxing. The girl's face was blotched and mottled, as if splattered with reddish-brown paint.

"Did your boyfriend do that to you?" Kaye asked.

"No," Delia said. "It just came, and everybody hated it."

"She got a mask," Jayce said. "It covered her face for a few weeks, and then it fell off and left those marks."

Mitch felt a chill. Kaye faced forward and lowered her head for a moment, composing herself.

"Delia and Jayce don't want me touching them," Morgan said, "even though we're friends, because of the plague. You know. Herod's."

"I don't want to get pregnant," Jayce said. "We're really hungry."

"We'll stop and get some food," Kaye said. "Would you like to take a shower, get cleaned up?"

"Oh, wow," Delia said. "That would be so great."

"You two look decent, hey, real nice," Morgan said, staring up at the headliner again, this time for courage. "But I have to tell you, these girls are my friends. I don't want you doing this just so *he* can see them without their clothes on. I won't put up with that."

"Don't worry," Kaye said. "If I were your mom, I'd be proud of you, Morgan."

"Thanks," Morgan said, and dropped his gaze to the window. The muscles on his narrow jaw clenched. "Hey, it's just the way I feel. They've gone through enough shit. Her boyfriend got a mask, too, and he was really mad. Jayce says he blamed Delia."

"He did," Jayce said.

"He was a white boy," Morgan continued, "and Delia is partly black."

"I *am* black," Delia said.

"They were living in a farmhouse for a while until he made her leave," Jayce said. "He was hitting her, after the miscarriage. Then she was pregnant again. He said she was making him sick because he had a mask and it wasn't even his baby." This came out in a mumbled rush.

"My second baby was born dead," Delia said, her voice distant. "He only had half his face. Jayce and Morgan never showed him to me."

"We buried it," Morgan said.

"My God," Kaye said. "I'm so sorry."

"It was hard," Morgan said. "But hey, we're still here." He clamped his teeth together and his jaw again tensed rhythmically.

"Jayce shouldn't have told me what he looked like," Delia said.

"If it was God's baby," Jayce said flatly, "He should have taken better care of it."

Mitch wiped his eyes with a finger and blinked to keep the road clear.

"Have you seen a doctor?" Kaye asked.

"I'm okay," Delia said. "I just want these marks to go away."

"Let me see them up close, sweetie," Kaye said.

"Are you a doctor?" Delia asked.

"I'm a biologist, but not a medical doctor," Kaye said.

"A scientist?" Morgan asked, interest piqued.

"Yeah," Kaye said.

Delia thought this through for a few seconds, then leaned forward, eyes averted. Kaye touched her chin to steady her. The sun had come out but a big panel truck growled by on the left and the wide tires showered the windshield. The watery light cast a wavering gray pall over the girl's features.

Her face bore a pattern of demelanized, teardrop-shaped dapples, mostly on her cheeks, with several symmetrical patches at the corners of her eyes and lips. As she turned away from Kaye, the marks shifted and darkened.

"They're like freckles," Delia said hopefully. "I get freckles sometimes. It's my white blood, I guess."

69

Athens, Ohio
MAY 1

Mitch and Morgan stood on the wide white-painted porch outside the office of James Jacobs, MD.

Morgan was agitated. He lit up the last of his pack of cigarettes and puffed with slit-eyed intent, then walked over to a rough-barked old maple and leaned against it.

Kaye had insisted after a lunch stop that they look up a

family practice doctor in the white pages and take Delia in for a checkup. Delia had reluctantly agreed.

"We didn't do anything criminal," Morgan said. "We didn't have no money, hey, and she had her baby and there we were." He waved his hand up the road.

"Where was that?" Mitch asked.

"West Virginia. In the woods near a farm. It was pretty. A nice place to be buried. You know, I am so tired. I am so sick of them treating me like a flea-bitten dog."

"The girls do that?"

"You know the attitude," Morgan said. "Men are contagious. They *rely* on me, I'm always here for them, then they tell me I have real boy cooties, and that's it, hey. No *thanks*, ever."

"It's the times," Mitch said.

"It's lame. Why are we living now and not some other time, not so lame?"

In the main examining room, Delia perched on the edge of the table, legs dangling. She wore a white flower-print open-backed robe. Jayce sat in a chair across from her, reading a pamphlet on smoking-related illnesses. Dr. Jacobs was in his sixties, thin, with a close-cut and tightly curled patch of graying hair around a tall and noble dome. His eyes were large, and both wise and sad. He told the girls he would be right back, then let his assistant, a middle-aged woman with a bun of fine auburn hair, enter the room with a clipboard and pencil. He closed the door and turned to Kaye.

"No relation?" he asked.

"We picked them up east of here. I thought she should see a doctor."

"She says she's nineteen. She doesn't have any ID, but I don't think she's nineteen, do you?"

"I don't know much about her," Kaye said. "I'm trying to help them, not get them in trouble."

Jacobs cocked his head in sympathy. "She gave birth less than a week or ten days ago. No major trauma, but she tore some tissue, and there's still blood on her leggings. I don't like to see kids living like animals, Ms. Lang."

"Neither do I."

"Delia says it was a Herod's baby and that it was born dead. Second-stage, by the description. I see no reason not to believe her, but these things should be reported. The baby should have undergone a postmortem. Laws are being put in place right now, at the federal level, and Ohio is going along . . . She said she was in West Virginia when she delivered. I understand West Virginia is showing some resistance."

"Only in some ways," Kaye said, and told him about the blood test requirements.

Jacobs listened, then pulled a pen from his pocket and nervously clicked it with one hand. "Ms. Lang, I wasn't sure who you were when you came in this afternoon. I had Georgina get on the Web and find some news pictures. I don't know what you're doing in Athens, but I'd say you know more about this sort of thing than I do."

"I might not agree," Kaye said. "The marks on her face . . ."

"Some women acquire dark markings during pregnancy. It passes."

"Not like these," Kaye said. "They tell us she had other skin problems."

"I know." Jacobs sighed and sat on the corner of his desk. "I have three patients who are pregnant, probably with Herod's second-stage. They won't let me do amnio or any kind of scans. They're all churchgoing women and I don't think they want to know the truth. They're scared and they're under pressure. Their friends shun them. They aren't welcome in church. The husbands won't come in with them to my office." He pointed to his face. "They all have skin stiffening and coming loose around the eyes, the nose, the cheeks, the corners of the mouth. It won't just peel away . . . not yet. They're shedding several layers of facial corium and epidermis." He made a face and pinched his fingers together, tugging at an imaginary flap of skin. "It's a little leathery.

Ugly as sin, very scary. That's why they're nervous and that's why they're shunned. This separates them from their community, Ms. Lang. It *hurts* them. I make my reports to the state and to the feds, and I get no response back. It's like sending messages into a big dark cave."

"Do you think the masks are common?"

"I follow the basic tenets of science, Ms. Lang. If I'm seeing it more than once, and now this girl comes along and I see it again, from out of state . . . I doubt it's unusual." He looked at her critically. "Do you know anything more?"

She found herself biting her lip like a little girl. "Yes and no," she said. "I resigned from my position on the Herod's Taskforce."

"Why?"

"It's too complicated."

"It's because they've got it all wrong, isn't it?"

Kaye looked aside and smiled. "I won't say that."

"You've seen this before? In other women?"

"I think we're going to see more of it."

"And the babies will all be monsters and die?"

Kaye shook her head. "I think that's going to change."

Jacobs replaced his pen in his pocket, put his hand on the desktop blotter, lifted its leather corner, dropped it slowly. "I won't file a report on Delia. I'm not sure what I'd say, or who I'd say it to. I think she'd vanish before any authorities could come along to help her. I doubt we'd ever find the infant, where they buried it. She's tired and she needs steady nourishment. She needs a place to stay and rest. I'll give her a vitamin shot and prescribe antibiotics and iron supplements."

"And the marks?"

"Do you know what chromatophores are?"

"Cells that change color. In cuttlefish."

"These marks can change color," Jacobs said. "They're not just a hormonally induced melanosis."

"Melanophores," Kaye said.

Jacobs nodded. "That's the word. Ever seen melanophores on a human?"

"No," Kaye said.

"Neither have I. Where are you going, Ms. Lang?"

"All the way west," she said. She lifted her wallet. "I'd like to pay you now."

Jacobs gave her his saddest look. "I'm not running a goddamned HMO, Ms. Lang. No charge. I'll prescribe the pills and you pick them up at a good pharmacy. You buy her food and find her a clean place to get a good night's sleep."

The door opened and Delia and Jayce emerged. Delia was fully dressed.

"She needs clean clothes and a good soak in a hot tub," Georgina said firmly.

For the first time since they had met, Delia smiled. "I looked in the mirror," she said. "Jayce says the marks are pretty. The doctor says I'm not sick, and I can have children again if I want."

Kaye shook Jacobs's hand. "Thank you very much," she said.

As the three of them left through the front office, joining Mitch and Morgan on the front porch, Jacobs called out, "We live and we learn, Ms. Lang! And the faster we learn, the better."

The little motel sported a huge red sign with TINY SUITES and $50 crowded onto it, clearly visible from the freeway. It had seven rooms, three of them vacant. Kaye rented all three and gave Morgan his own key. Morgan lifted the key, frowned, then pocketed it.

"I don't like being alone," he said.

"I couldn't think of another arrangement," Kaye said.

Mitch put his arm around the boy's shoulder. "I'll stay with you," he said, and gave Kaye a level look. "Let's get cleaned up and watch TV."

"We'd like you to stay in our room," Jayce told Kaye. "We'd feel a lot safer."

The rooms were just on the edge of being dirty. Draped on beds with distinct hollows, thin and worn quilted coverlets showed unraveled nylon threads and cigarette burns. Coffee tables bore multiple ring marks and more cigarette burns. Jayce and Delia explored and settled in as if the accommodations were royal. Delia took the single orange chair beside a table-lamp combo hung with black metal cone-shaped cans. Jayce lounged on the bed and switched on the TV. "They have HBO," she said in a soft and wondering voice. "We can watch a movie!"

Mitch listened to Morgan in the shower in their room, then opened the front door. Kaye stood outside with her hand up, about to knock.

"We're wasting a room," she said. "We've taken on some responsibilities, haven't we?"

Mitch hugged her. "Your instincts," he said.

"What do *your* instincts tell you?" she asked, nuzzling his shoulder.

"They're kids. They've been out on the road for weeks, months. Someone should call their parents."

"Maybe they never had real parents. They're desperate, Mitch." Kaye pushed back to look up at him.

"They're also independent enough to bury a dead baby and stay on the road. The doctor should have called the police, Kaye."

"I know," Kaye said. "I also know why he didn't. The rules have changed. He thinks most of the babies are going to be born dead. Are we the only ones with any hope?"

The shower stopped and the stall door clicked open. The small bathroom was filled with steam.

"The girls," Kaye said, and walked over to the next door. She gave Mitch a hand-open sign that he instantly recognized from the marching crowds in Albany, and he understood for the first time what the crowds had been trying to show: strong belief in and a cautious submission to the way of Life, belief in the ultimate wisdom of the human genome. No presumption of doom, no ignorant attempts to use new human powers to block the rivers of DNA flowing through the generations.

Faith in Life.

Morgan dressed quickly. "Jayce and Delia don't need me," he said as he stood in the small room. The holes in the sleeves of his black pullover were even more obvious now that his skin was clean. He let the dirty windbreaker dangle from one arm. "I don't want to be a burden. I'll go now. Give my thanks, hey, but—"

"Please be quiet and sit down," Mitch said. "What the lady wants, goes. She wants you to stick around."

Morgan blinked in surprise, then sat on the end of the bed. The springs squeaked and the frame groaned. "I think it's the end of the world," he said. "We've really made God angry."

"Don't jump to any conclusions," Mitch said. "Believe it or not, all this has happened before."

Jayce turned on the TV and watched from the bed while Delia took a long bath in the chipped and narrow tub. The girl hummed to herself, tunes from cartoon shows—*Scooby Doo*, *Animaniacs*, *Inspector Gadget*. Kaye sat in the single chair. Jayce had found something old and affirming on the TV: *Pollyanna*, with Hayley Mills. Karl Malden was kneeling in a dry grassy field, berating himself for his stubborn blindness. It was an impassioned performance. Kaye did not remember the movie being so compelling. She watched it with Jayce until she noticed that the girl was sound asleep. Then, turning down the volume, Kaye switched over to Fox News.

There was a smattering of show business stories, a brief political report on congressional elections, then an interview with Bill Cosby on his commercials for the CDC and the Taskforce. Kaye turned up the volume.

"I was a buddy of David Satcher, the former surgeon general, and they must have a kind of ol' boy network," Cosby told the interviewer, a blond woman with a large smile and intense blue eyes, " 'cause years ago they got me, this ol' guy, in to talk about what was important, what they were doing. They thought I might be able to help again."

"You've joined quite a select team," said the interviewer.

"Dustin Hoffman and Michael Crichton. Let's take a look at your spot."

Kaye leaned forward. Cosby returned against a black background, face seamed with parental concern. "My friends at the Centers for Disease Control, and many other researchers around the world, are hard at work every day to solve *this problem* we're all facing. Herod's flu. SHEVA. Every day. Nobody's gonna rest until it's understood and we can cure it. You can take it from me, these people care, and when you hurt, they hurt, too. Nobody's asking you to be patient. But to survive this, we all have to *be smart*."

The interviewer looked away from the big screen television on the set. "Let's play an excerpt from Dustin Hoffman's message . . ."

Hoffman stood on a bare motion picture sound stage with his hands thrust into the pockets of tailored beige pants. He smiled a friendly but solemn greeting. "My name is Dustin Hoffman. You might remember I played a scientist fighting a deadly disease in a movie called *Outbreak*. I've been talking to the scientists at the National Institutes of Health and the Centers for Disease Control and Prevention, and they're working as hard as they can, every day, to fight SHEVA and stop our children from dying."

The interviewer interrupted the clip. "What *are* the scientists doing that they weren't doing last year? What's new in the effort?"

Cosby made a sour face. "I'm just a man who wants to help us get through this mess. Doctors and scientists are the only hope we've got, and we can't just take to the streets and burn things down and make it all go away. We're talking about thinking things through, working together, not engaging in riots and panic."

Delia stood in the bathroom doorway, plump legs bare beneath the small motel towel, head wrapped in another towel. She stared fixedly at the television. "It's not going to make any difference," she said. "My babies are dead."

* * *

Mitch returned from the Coke machine at the end of the line of rooms to find Morgan pacing in a U around the bed. The boy's hands were knots of frustration. "I can't stop thinking," Morgan said. Mitch held out a Coke and Morgan stared at it, took it from his hand, popped the top, and chugged it back fiercely. "You know what they did, what Jayce did? When we needed money?"

"I don't need to know, Morgan," Mitch said.

"It's how they treat me. Jayce went out and got a man to pay for it, and, you know, she and Delia *blew* him, and took some money. Jesus, I ate some of that dinner, too. And the next night. Then we were hitching and Delia started having her baby. They won't let me touch them, even hug them, they won't put their arms around me, but for money, they *blow* these guys, and they don't care whether I see them or not!" He pounded his temple with the ball of his thumb. "They are so *stupid*, like farm animals."

"It must have been tough out there," Mitch said. "You were all hungry."

"I went with them because my father's nothing great, you know, but he doesn't beat me. He works all day. They needed me more than he does. But I want to go back. I can't do anything more for them."

"I understand," Mitch said. "But don't be hasty. We'll work this through."

"I am so sick of this shit!" Morgan howled.

They heard the howl in the next room. Jayce sat up in bed and rubbed her eyes. "There he goes again," she murmured.

Delia dried off her hair. "He really isn't stable sometimes," she said.

"Can you drop us off in Cincinnati?" Jayce asked. "I have an uncle there. Maybe you can send Morgan back home now."

"Sometimes Morgan's such a child," Delia said.

Kaye watched them from her chair, her face pinking with

an emotion she could not quite understand: solidarity compounded with visceral disgust.

Minutes later, she met Mitch outside, under the long motel walkway. They held hands.

Mitch pointed his thumb over his shoulder, through the room's open door. The shower was running again. "His second. He says he feels dirty all the time. The girls have played a little loose with poor Morgan."

"What was he expecting?"

"No idea."

"To go to bed with them?"

"I don't know," Mitch said quietly. "Maybe he just wants to be treated with respect."

"I don't think they know how," Kaye said. She pressed her hand on his chest, rubbed him there, her eyes focused on something distant and invisible. "The girls want to be dropped off in Cincinnati."

"Morgan wants to go to the bus station," Mitch said. "He's had enough."

"Mother Nature isn't being very kind or gentle, is she?"

"Mother Nature has always been something of a bitch," he said.

"So much for Rocinante and touring America," Kaye said sadly.

"You want to make some phone calls, get involved again, don't you?"

Kaye lifted her hands. "I don't *know*!" she moaned. "Just taking off and living our lives seems wildly irresponsible. I want to learn more. But how much will anybody tell us—Christopher, anybody on the Taskforce? I'm an outsider now."

"There's a way we can stay in the game, with different rules," Mitch said.

"The rich guy in New York?"

"Daney. And Oliver Merton."

"We're not going to Seattle?"

"We are," Mitch said. "But I'm going to call Merton and say I'm interested."

"I still want to have our baby," Kaye said, eyes wide, voice fragile as a dried flower.

The shower stopped. They heard Morgan toweling off, alternately humming to himself and swearing.

"It's funny," Mitch said, almost too softly to hear. "I've been very uncomfortable about the whole idea. But now . . . it seems plain as anything, the dreams, meeting you. I want our baby, too. We just can't be innocent." He took a deep breath, raised his eyes to meet Kaye's, added, "Let's go into that forest with some better maps."

Morgan stepped out onto the walkway and stared at them owlishly. "I'm ready. I want to go home."

Kaye looked at Morgan and almost flinched at his intensity. The boy's eyes seemed a thousand years old.

"I'll drive you to the bus station," Mitch said.

70

The National Institutes of Health, Bethesda
MAY 5

Dicken met the director of the National Institute of Child Health and Human Development, Dr. Tania Bao, outside the Natcher Building, and walked with her from there. Small, precisely dressed, with a composed and ageless face, its features arranged on a slightly undulating plain, nose tiny, lips on the edge of a smile, and slightly stooped shoulders, Bao might have been in her late thirties but was in fact sixtythree. She wore a pale blue pantsuit and tasseled loafers. She walked with small quick steps, intent on the rough ground. The never-ending construction on the NIH campus had been brought to a halt for security purposes, but had already torn up most of the walkways between the Natcher Building and the Magnuson Clinical Center.

"NIH used to be an open campus," Bao said. "Now we live with the National Guard watching our every move. I can't even buy my granddaughter toys from the vendors. I used to love to see them on the sidewalks or in the hallways. Now they've been cleared out, along with the construction workers."

Dicken raised his shoulders, showing that these things were outside his control. His area of influence did not even include himself anymore. "I've come to listen," he said. "I can take your opinions to Dr. Augustine, but I can't guarantee he'll agree."

"What happened, Christopher?" Bao asked plaintively. "Why do they not respond to what is so obvious? Why is Augustine so stubborn?"

"You're a far more experienced administrator than I am," Dicken said. "I know only what I see and what I hear in the news. What I see is unbearable pressure from all sides. The vaccine teams haven't been able to do anything. Mark will do everything he can, regardless, to protect public health. He wants to focus our resources on fighting what he believes is a virulent disease. Right now, the only available option is abortion."

"What he *believes* . . ." Bao said incredulously. "What do *you* believe, Dr. Dicken?"

The weather was coming into a warm and humid summer mood that Dicken found familiar, even comforting; it made a deep and sad part of him think he might be in Africa, and he would have much preferred that to the current round of his existence. They crossed a temporary asphalt ramp to the next level of finished sidewalk, stepped over yellow construction tape, and walked into the main entrance of Building 10.

Two months ago, life had begun to come apart for Christopher Dicken. The realization that hidden parts of his personality could affect his scientific judgment—that a combination of frustrated infatuation and job pressure could jolt him into an attitude he knew to be false—had preyed on him like a swarm of little biting flies. Somehow, he had managed an outward appearance of calm, of going with the game, the team, the Taskforce. He knew that could not go on forever.

"I believe in work," Dicken said, embarrassed that his thoughts had delayed a response for so long.

Simply cutting himself off from Kaye Lang, and failing to support her in the face of Jackson's ambush, had been an incomprehensible and unforgivable mistake. He regretted it more with each day, but it was too late to retie old and broken threads. He could still build a conceptual wall and work diligently on those projects assigned to him.

They took the elevator to the seventh floor, turned left, and found the small staff meeting room in the middle of a long beige and pink corridor.

Bao seated herself. "Christopher, you know Anita, Preston."

They greeted Dicken with little cheer.

"No good news, I'm afraid," Dicken reported, seating himself opposite Preston Meeker. Meeker, like his colleagues within the small, close room, represented the quintessence of a child health specialty—in his case, neonatal growth and development.

"Augustine still at it?" Meeker asked, pugnacious from the start. "Still pushing RU-486?"

"In his defense," Dicken said, and paused for a moment to collect his thoughts, to present this old false face more convincingly, "he has no alternatives. The retrovirus folks at CDC agree that the expression and completion theory makes sense."

"Children as carriers of unknown plagues?" Meeker pushed out his lips and made a pishing noise.

"It's a highly defensible position. Added to the likelihood that most of the new babies will be born deformed—"

"We don't know that," House said. House was the acting deputy director of the National Institute of Child Health and Human Development; the former deputy director had resigned two weeks ago. A great many NIH people associated with the SHEVA Taskforce were resigning.

With hardly a pang, Dicken thought that once again Kaye Lang had proved herself a pioneer by being the very first to leave.

"It's indisputable," Dicken said, and had no trouble telling her this, because it was true: no normal infants had been born yet to a SHEVA-infected mother. "Out of two hundred, most have been reported severely deformed. All have been born dead." *But not always deformed,* he reminded himself.

"If the president agrees to start a national campaign using RU-486," Bao said, "I doubt the CDC will be allowed to remain open in Atlanta. As for Bethesda, it is an intelligent community, but we are still in the Bible Belt. I have already had my house picketed, Christopher. I live surrounded by guards."

"I understand," Dicken said.

"Perhaps, but does Mark understand? He does not return my calls or my e-mail."

"Unacceptable isolation," Meeker said.

"How many acts of civil disobedience will it take?" House added, clasping her hands on the table and rubbing them together, her eyes darting around the group.

Bao stood and took up a whiteboard marker. She quickly and almost savagely chopped out the words in bright red, saying, "Two million first-stage Herod's miscarriages, as of last month. Hospitals are flooded."

"I go to those hospitals," Dicken said. "It's part of my job to be on the front."

"We also have visited patients here and around the country," Bao said, mouth tight with irritation. "We have three hundred SHEVA mothers in this very building. I see some of them every day. *We* are not isolated, Christopher."

"Sorry," Dicken said.

Bao nodded. "Seven hundred thousand reported second-stage Herod's pregnancies. Well, here the statistics fall apart—we do not know what is happening," Bao said, and stared at Dicken. "Where have all the others gone? They are not reporting. Does Mark know?"

"I know," Dicken said. "Mark knows. It's sensitive information. We don't want to acknowledge how much we know until the president makes his policy decision on the Taskforce proposal."

"I think I can guess," House said sardonically. "Educated women with means are buying black-market RU-486, or otherwise obtaining abortions at different stages of their pregnancy. There's a wholesale revolt in the medical community, in women's clinics. They've stopped reporting to the Taskforce, because of the new laws regulating abortion procedures. My guess is, Mark wants to make official what's already happening around the country."

Dicken paused for a moment to gather his thoughts, shore up his sagging false front. "Mark has no control over the House of Representatives or the Senate. He speaks, they ignore him. We all know the rates of domestic violence are way up. Women are being forced out of their homes. Divorce. Murder." Dicken let that sink in, as it had sunk in to his own thoughts and self in the last few months. "Violence against pregnant women is at an all-time high. Some are even resorting to quinacrine, when they can get it, to self-sterilize."

Bao shook her head sadly.

Dicken continued. "Many women know the simplest way out is to stop their second-stage pregnancies before they go anywhere near full term and other side effects appear."

"Mark Augustine and the Taskforce are reluctant to describe these side effects," Bao said. "We assume you refer to facial cauls and melanisms in both the parents."

"I also refer to whistling palate and vomeronasal deformation," Dicken said.

"Why the fathers, too?" Bao asked.

"I have no idea," Dicken said. "If NIH hadn't lost its

clinical study subjects, due to an excess of personal concern, we might all know a lot more, under at least mildly controlled conditions."

Bao reminded Dicken that no one in the room had had anything to do with the closure of the Taskforce clinical studies in this very building.

"I understand," Dicken said, and hated himself with a ferocity he could barely hide. "I don't disagree. Second-stage pregnancies are being ended by all but the poor, those who can't get to clinics or buy the pills . . . or . . ."

"Or what?" Meeker asked.

"The dedicated."

"Dedicated to what?"

"To nature. To the proposition that these children should be given a chance, whatever the odds of their being born dead or deformed."

"Augustine does not seem to believe any of the children should be given a chance," Bao said. "Why?"

"Herod's is a disease. This is how you fight a disease." *This can't go on much longer. You'll either resign or you'll kill yourself trying to explain things you don't understand or believe.*

"I say again, we are not isolated, Christopher," Bao said, shaking her head. "We go to the maternity wards and the surgeries in this clinic, and visit other clinics and hospitals. We see the women and the men in pain. We need some rational approach that takes into account all these views, all these pressures."

Dicken frowned in concentration. "Mark is just looking at medical reality. And there's no political consensus," he added quietly. "It's a dangerous time."

"That's putting it mildly," Meeker said. "Christopher, I think the White House is paralyzed. Damned if you do, and certainly damned if you don't and things go on the way they are."

"Maryland's own governor is involved in this so-called

States' Health revolt," House said. "I've never seen such fervor in the religious right here."

"It's pretty much grass roots, not just Christian," Bao said. "The Chinese community has pulled in its horns and with good reason. Bigotry is on the rise. We are falling apart into scared and unhappy tribes, Christopher."

Dicken stared down at the table, then up at the figures on the whiteboard, one eyelid twitching with fatigue. "It hurts all of us," he said. "It hurts Mark, and it hurts me."

"I doubt it hurts Mark as much as it hurts the mothers," Bao said quietly.

71

Oregon
MAY 10

"I'm an ignorant man, and I don't understand a lot of things," Sam said. He leaned on the split-rail fence that surrounded the four acres, the two-story frame farmhouse, an old and sagging barn, the brick workshed. Mitch pushed his free hand into his pocket and rested a can of Michelob on the lichen-grayed fence post. A square-rump, black-and-white cow cropping a patch of the neighbor's twelve acres regarded them with an almost complete absence of curiosity. "You've only known this woman for what, two weeks?"

"Just over a month."

"Some whirlwind!"

Mitch agreed with a sheepish look.

"Why be in such a hurry? Why in hell would anyone want to get pregnant, now of all times? Your mother's been over her hot flashes for ten years, but after Herod's, she's still skittish about letting me touch her."

"Kaye's different," Mitch said, as if admitting something. They had come to this topic on the backs of a lot of other difficult topics that afternoon. The toughest of all had been Mitch's admission that he had temporarily given up looking for a job, that they would largely be living on Kaye's money. Sam found this incomprehensible.

"Where's the self-respect in that?" he had said, and shortly after they had dropped that subject and returned to what had happened in Austria.

Mitch had told him about meeting Brock at the Daney mansion, and that had amused Sam quite a bit. "It baffles science," he had commented dryly. When they had gotten around to discussing Kaye, still talking with Mitch's mother, Abby, in the large farmhouse kitchen, Sam's puzzlement had blossomed into irritation, then downright anger.

"I admit I may be stuck in abysmal stupidity," Sam said, "but isn't it just damned dangerous to do this sort of thing now, deliberately?"

"It could be," Mitch admitted.

"Then why in hell did you agree?"

"I can't answer that easily," Mitch said. "First, I think she could be right. I mean, I think she *is* right. This time around, we'll have a healthy baby."

"But you tested positive, *she* tested positive," Sam said, glaring at him, hands gripping the rail tightly.

"We did."

"And correct me if I'm wrong, but there's *never* been a healthy baby born of a woman who tested positive."

"Not yet," Mitch said.

"That's lousy odds."

"She's the one who found this virus," Mitch said. "She knows more about it than anyone else on Earth, and she's convinced—"

"That everyone else is wrong?" Sam asked.

"That we're going to change our thinking in the next few years."

"Is she crazy, then, or just a fanatic?"

Mitch frowned. "Careful, Dad," he said.

Sam flung his hands up in the air. "Mitch, for Christ's sake, I fly to Austria, the first time I've ever been to Europe, and it's without your mother, damn it, to pick up my son at a hospital after he's . . . Well, we've been through all that. But why face this kind of grief, take this kind of chance, I ask, in God's name?"

"Since her first husband died, she's been a little frantic about looking ahead, seeing things in a positive light," Mitch said. "I can't say I understand her, Dad, but I love her. I trust her. Something in me says she's right, or I wouldn't have gone along."

"You mean, *cooperated.*" Sam looked at the cow and brushed his hands free of lichen dust on his pants legs. "What if you're both wrong?" he asked.

"We know the consequences. We'll live with them," Mitch said. "But we're not wrong. Not this time, Dad."

"I've been reading as much as I can," Abby Rafelson said. "It's bewildering. All these viruses." Afternoon sun fell through the kitchen window and lay in yellow trapezoids on the unvarnished oak floor. The kitchen smelled of coffee—too much coffee, Kaye thought, nerves on edge—and tamales, their lunch before the men had gone out walking.

Mitch's mother had kept her beauty into her sixties, an authoritative kind of good looks that emerged from high cheekbones and deep-sunk blue eyes combined with immaculate grooming.

"These particular viruses have been with us a long time," Kaye said. She held up a picture of Mitch when he was five years old, riding a tricycle on the Willamette riverfront in Portland. He looked intent, oblivious to the camera; sometimes she saw that same expression when he was driving or reading a newspaper.

"How long?" Abby asked.

"Maybe tens of millions of years." Kaye picked up another picture from the pile on the coffee table. The picture showed Mitch and Sam loading wood in the back of a truck. By his height and thin limbs, Mitch appeared to be about ten or eleven.

"What were they doing there in the first place? I couldn't understand that."

"They might have infected us through our gametes, eggs or sperm. Then they stayed. They mutated, or something deactivated them, or . . . we put them to work for us. Found a way to make them useful." Kaye looked up from the picture.

Abby stared at her, unfazed. "Sperm or eggs?"

"Ovaries, testicles," Kaye said, glancing down again.

"What made them decide to come out again?"

"Something in our everyday lives," Kaye said. "Stress, maybe."

Abby thought about this for a few seconds. "I'm a college graduate. Physical education. Did Mitch tell you that?"

Kaye nodded. "He said you took a minor in biochemistry. Some premed courses."

"Yes, well, not enough to be up to your level. More than enough to be dubious about my religious upbringing, however. I don't know what my mother would have thought if she had known about these viruses in our sex cells." Abby smiled at Kaye and shook her head. "Maybe she would have called them our original sin."

Kaye looked at Abby and tried to think of a reply. "That's interesting," she managed. Why this should disturb her she did not know, but that it did upset her even more. She felt threatened by the idea.

"The graves in Russia," Abby said quietly. "Maybe the mothers had neighbors who thought it was an outbreak of original sin."

"I don't believe it is," Kaye said.

"Oh, I don't believe it myself," Abby said. She trained her examining blue eyes on Kaye now, troubled, darting. "I've never been very comfortable about anything to do with sex. Sam's a gentle man, the only man I've felt passionate about, though not the only man I've invited into my bed. My upbringing . . . was not the best that way. Not the wisest. I've never talked with Mitch about sex. Or about love. It seemed he would do well enough on his own, handsome as he is, smart as he is." Abby laid her hand on Kaye's. "Did he tell you his mother was a crazy old prude?" She looked so sadly desperate and at a loss that Kaye gripped her hand tightly and smiled what she hoped was reassurance.

"He told me you were a wonderful mother and caring," Kaye said, "and that he was your only son, and that you'd grill me like a pork chop." She squeezed Abby's hand tighter.

Abby laughed and something of the electricity fell from the air between them. "He told me you were headstrong and smarter than any woman he had ever met, and that you cared so much about things. He said I'd better like you, or he'd have a talk with me."

Kaye stared at her, aghast. "He did not!"

"He did," Abby said solemnly. "The men in this family don't mince words. I told him I'd do my best to get along with you."

"Good grief!" Kaye said, laughing in disbelief.

"Exactly," Abby said. "He was being defensive. But he knows me. He knows I don't mince words, either. With all this original sin popping out all over, I think we're in for a world of change. A lot of ways men and women do things will change. Don't you think?"

"I'm sure of it," Kaye said.

"I want you to work as hard as you can, please, dear, my new daughter, please, to make a place where there will be love and a gentle and caring center for Mitch. He looks tough and sturdy but men are really very fragile. Don't let all this split you up, or damage him. I want to keep as much of the Mitch I know and love as I can, as long as I can. I still see my boy in him. My boy is strong there still." There were tears in Abby's eyes, and Kaye realized, holding the woman's hand, that she had missed her own mother so much, for so many years, and had tried unsuccessfully to bury those emotions.

"It was hard, when Mitch was born," Abby said. "I was in labor for four days. My first child, I thought the delivery would be tough, but not that tough. I regret we did not have more . . . but only in some ways. Now, I'd be scared to death. I *am* scared to death, even though there's nothing to worry about between Sam and me."

"I'll take care of Mitch," Kaye said.

"These are horrible times," Abby said. "Somebody's going to write a book, a big, thick, book. I hope there's a bright and happy ending."

That evening, over dinner, men and women together, the conversation was pleasant, light, of little consequence. The air seemed clear, the issues all rained out. Kaye slept with Mitch in his old bedroom, a sign of acceptance from Abby or assertion from Mitch or both.

This was the first real family she had known in years. Thinking about that, lying cramped up beside Mitch in the too-small bed, she had her own moment of happy tears.

She had bought a pregnancy test kit in Eugene when they had stopped for gas not far from a big drug store. Then, to make herself feel she was really making a normal decision despite a world so remarkably out of kilter, she had gone to a small bookstore in the same strip mall and bought a Dr. Spock paperback. She had shown the paperback to Mitch, and he had grinned, but she had not shown him the test kit.

"This is so normal," she murmured as Mitch snored lightly. "What we're doing is so *natural* and normal, please, God."

72

Kaye drove through Portland while Mitch slept. They crossed the bridge into Washington state, passed through a small rainstorm and then back into bright sun. Kaye chose a turnoff and they ate lunch at a small Mexican restaurant near no town that had a name that they would know. The roads were quiet; it was Sunday.

They paused to nap for a few minutes in the parking lot and Kaye nestled her head on Mitch's shoulder. The air was slow and the sun warmed her face and hair. A few birds sang. The clouds moved in orderly ranks from the south and soon covered the sky, but the air stayed warm.

After their nap, Kaye drove on through Tacoma, and then Mitch drove again, and they continued in to Seattle. Once through the downtown, passing under the highway-straddling convention center, Mitch felt anxious about taking her straight to his apartment.

"Maybe you'd like to see some of the sights before we settle in," he said.

Kaye smiled. "What, your apartment is a mess?"

"It's clean," Mitch said. "It just might not be . . ." He shook his head.

"Don't worry. I'm in no mood to be critical. But I'd love to look around."

"There's a place I used to visit a lot when I wasn't digging . . ."

* * *

393

Gasworks Park sprawled below a low grassy promontory overlooking Lake Union. The remains of an old gas plant and other factory buildings had been cleaned out and painted bright colors and turned into a public park. The vertical gasworks tanks and decaying walkways and piping had not been painted, but had been fenced in and left to rust.

Mitch took her by the hand and led her from the parking lot. Kaye thought the park was a little ugly, the grass a little patchy, but for Mitch's sake, said nothing.

They sat on the lawn beside the chain-link fence and watched passenger seaplanes landing on Lake Union. A few lone men and women, or women with children, walked to the playground beside the factory buildings. Mitch said the attendance was a little low for a sunny Sunday.

"People don't want to congregate," Kaye said, but even as she spoke, chartered buses were arriving in the parking lot, pulling into spaces marked off by ropes.

"Something's up," Mitch said, craning his neck.

"Nothing you planned for me?" she asked lightly.

"Nope," Mitch said, smiling. "But maybe I don't remember, after last night."

"You say that every night," Kaye said. She yawned, holding her hand over her mouth, and tracked a sailboat crossing the lake, and then a wind surfer in a wetsuit.

"Eight buses," Mitch said. "Curious."

Kaye's period was three days late, and she had been regular since going off the pill, after Saul's death. This caused a steely kind of concern. When she thought about what they might have started, her teeth ground together. *So quickly. Old-fashioned romance. Rolling downhill, gathering speed.*

She had not told Mitch yet, in case it was a false alarm.

Kaye felt separated from her body when she thought too hard. If she pulled back from the steely concern and just explored her sensations, the natural state of tissues and cells and emotions, she felt fine; it was the context, the implications, the *knowing* that interfered with simply feeling good and in love.

Knowing too much and never knowing enough was the problem.

Normal.

"Ten buses, whoops, eleven," Mitch said. "Big damn crowd." He stroked the side of her neck. "I'm not sure I like this."

"It's your park. I don't want to move for a while," Kaye said. "It's nice." The sun threw bright patches over the park. The rusty tanks glowed dull orange.

Dozens of men and women in earth-colored clothes walked in small groups from the buses toward the hill. They seemed in no hurry. Four women carried a wooden ring about a yard wide, and several men helped roll a long pole on a dolly.

Kaye frowned, then chuckled. "They're doing something with a yoni and a lingam," she said.

Mitch squinted at the procession. "Maybe it's a giant hoop game," he said. "Horseshoes or something."

"Do you think?" Kaye asked with that familiar and uncritical tone he instantly recognized as no-holds-barred disagreement.

"No," he said, smacking his temple with his palm. "How could I have not seen it right away? It's a yoni and a lingam."

"And you an anthropololologist," she said, lightly doubling the syllables. Kaye got up on her knees and shaded her eyes. "Let's go see."

"What if we're not invited?"

"I doubt it's a closed party," she said.

Dicken went though the security check—pat-down, metal detection wand, chemical sniff—and entered the White House through the so-called diplomatic entrance. A young Marine escort immediately took him downstairs to a large meeting room in the basement. The air conditioning was running full blast and the room felt cold as a refrigerator compared to the eighty-five-degree heat and humidity outside.

Dicken was the first to arrive. Other than the Marine and a steward arranging place settings—bottles of Evian and legal pads and pens—on the long oval conference table, he was alone in the room. He sat in a chair reserved for junior aides at the back. The steward asked him if he'd like something to drink—a Coke or glass of juice. "We'll have coffee down here in a few minutes."

"Coke would be great," Dicken said.

"Just fly in?"

"Drove from Bethesda," Dicken said.

"Going to be some miserable weather this afternoon," the steward said. "Thunderstorms by five, so the weather people say at Andrews. We get the best weather reports here." He winked and smiled, then left and returned after a few minutes with a Coke and a glass of chopped ice.

More people began arriving ten minutes later. Dicken recognized the governors of New Mexico, Alabama, and Maryland; they were accompanied by a small group of aides. The room would soon hold the core of the so-called Governors' Revolt that was raising hell with the Taskforce across the country.

Augustine was going to have his finest hour, right here in the basement of the White House. He was going to try to convince ten governors, seven from very conservative states, that allowing women access to a complete range of abortion measures was the only humane course of action.

Dicken doubted the plea would be met with approval, or even polite disagreement.

Augustine entered some minutes later, accompanied by the White House–Taskforce liaison and the chief of staff. Augustine put his valise on the table and walked over to Dicken, his shoes clicking on the tile floor.

"Any ammunition?" he asked.

"A rout," Dicken said quietly. "None of the health agencies felt we had a chance of taking control again. They feel the president has lost his grip on the issue, too."

Augustine's eyes wrinkled at the edges. His crow's feet had grown noticeably deeper in the last year, and his hair had grayed. "I suppose they're going it on their own—grass-roots solutions?"

"That's all they see. The AMA and most of the side branches of the NIH have withdrawn their support, tacitly if not overtly."

"Well," Augustine said softly, "we sure as hell don't have anything to offer to get them back in the fold—yet." He took a cup of coffee from the steward. "Maybe we should just go home and let everyone get on with it."

Augustine turned to look as more governors entered. The governors were followed by Shawbeck and the secretary of Health and Human Services. "Here come the lions, followed by the Christians," he said. "That's only as it should be." Before leaving to sit at the opposite end of the table, in one of the three seats where no tiny flags flew, he said, in a very low voice, "The president's been talking with Alabama and Maryland for the last two hours, Christopher. They've been arguing with him to delay his decision. I don't think he wants to. Fifteen thousand pregnant women were murdered in the last six weeks. *Fifteen thousand,* Christopher."

Dicken had seen that figure several times.

"We should all bend over and get our butts kicked," Augustine growled.

Mitch estimated there were at least six hundred people in the crowd moving toward the top of the hill. A few dozen onlookers followed the resolute group with its wooden ring and pillar.

Kaye took his hand. "Is this a Seattle thing?" she asked, pulling him along. The idea of a fertility ritual intrigued her.

"Not that I've heard of," Mitch said. Since San Diego, the smell of too many people gave him the willies.

At the top of the promontory, Kaye and Mitch stood on the edge of a large flat sundial, about thirty feet across. It was made of bas-relief bronze astrological figures, numerals, outstretched human hands, and calligraphic letters showing the four points of the compass. Ceramics, glass, and colored cement completed the circle.

Mitch showed Kaye how the observer became the gnomon on the dial, standing between parallel lines with the seasons and dates cast into them. It was two o'clock, by her estimation.

"It's beautiful," she said. "Kind of a pagan site, don't you think?" Mitch nodded, keeping his eye on the advancing crowd.

Several men and boys flying kites moved out of the way, pulling and winding their strings, as the group climbed the hill. Three women carried the ring, sweating beneath the weight. They lowered it gently to the middle of the sundial. Two men carrying the pillar stood to one side, waiting to set it down.

Five older women dressed in light yellow robes walked into the circle with hands clasped, smiling with dignity, and surrounded the ring in the center of the compass. The group said not a word.

Kaye and Mitch descended to the south side of the hill, overlooking Lake Union. Mitch felt a breeze coming from the south and saw a few low banks of cloud moving over downtown Seattle. The air was like wine, clean and sweet, temperature in the low seventies. Cloud shadows swung dramatically over the hill.

"Too many people," Mitch told Kaye.

"Let's stay and see what they're up to," Kaye said.

The crowd compacted, forming concentric circles, all holding hands. They politely asked Kaye and Mitch and others to move farther down the hill while they completed their ceremony.

"You're welcome to watch, from down there," a plump young woman in a green shift told Kaye. She explicitly ignored Mitch. Her eyes seemed to track right past him, through him.

The only sound the gathering people made was the rustling of their robes and the motion of their sandaled feet in the grass and over the bas-relief figures of the sundial.

Mitch shoved his hands into his pockets and hunched his shoulders.

The governors were seated at the table, leaning right or left to speak in murmurs with their aides or adjacent colleagues. Shawbeck remained standing, hands clasped in front of him. Augustine had walked around one quarter of the table to speak with the governor of California. Dicken tried to puzzle out the seating arrangements and then realized that someone was following a clever protocol. The governors had been arranged not by seniority, or by influence, but by the geographic distribution of their states. California was on the western side of the table, and the governor of Alabama sat close to the back of the room in the southeastern quadrant. Augustine, Shawbeck, and the secretary sat near where the president would sit.

That meant something, Dicken surmised. Maybe they were actually going to bite the bullet and recommend that Augustine's policies be carried out.

Dicken was not at all sure how he felt about that. He had listened to presentations on the medical cost of taking care of second-stage babies, should any survive for very long; he had also listened to figures showing what it would cost for the United States to lose an entire generation of children.

The liaison for Health stood by the door. "Ladies and gentlemen, the president of the United States."

All rose. The governor of Alabama got to his feet more slowly than the others. Dicken saw that his face was damp, presumably from the heat outside. But Augustine had told him that the governor had been in conference with the president for the past two hours.

A Secret Service agent dressed in a blazer and golf shirt walked past Dicken, glanced at him with that stony precision Dicken had long since become used to. The president entered the room first, tall, with his famous shock of white hair. He seemed fit but a little tired; still, the power of the office swept over Dicken. He was pleased that the president looked in his direction, recognized him, nodded solemnly in passing.

The governor of Alabama pushed back his chair. The wooden legs groaned on the tile floor. "Mr. President," the governor said, too loudly. The president stopped to speak with him, and the governor took two steps forward.

Two agents glanced at each other and swung about to politely intervene.

"I love the office and I love our great country, sir," the governor said, and wrapped the president in his arms, as if delivering a protective bear hug.

The governor of Florida, standing next to them, grimaced and shook his head in some embarrassment.

The agents were mere feet away.

Oh, Dicken thought, nothing more; just a blank and prescient awareness of being suspended in time, a train whistle not yet heard, brakes not yet pressed, arm willed to move but as yet limp by his side.

He thought perhaps he should get out of the way.

The blond young man in a black robe wore a green surgical mask and kept his eyes lowered as he advanced up the hill to the compass rose. He was escorted by three women in brown and green, and he carried a small brown cloth bag tied with golden rope. His wispy, almost white hair blew back and forth in the breeze that was quickening on the hill.

The circles of women and men parted to let them through.

Mitch watched with a puzzled expression. Kaye stood with arms folded beside him. "What are they up to?" he asked.

"Some sort of ceremony," Kaye said.

"Fertility?"

"Why not?"

Mitch mulled this over. "Atonement," he said. "There are more women than men."

"About three to one," Kaye said.

"Most of the men are older."

"Q-Tips," Kaye said.

"What?"

"That's what young women call men who are old enough to be their fathers," Kaye said. "Like the president."

"That's insulting," Mitch said.

"It's true," Kaye said. "Don't blame me."

The young man was hidden from their view as the crowd closed again.

A large burning hand picked up Christopher Dicken and carried him to the back of the wall. It shattered his eardrums and collapsed his chest. Then the hand pulled back and he slumped to the floor. His eyes flickered open. He saw flames rush along the crushed ceiling in concentric waves, tiles falling through the flames. He was covered with blood and bits of flesh. White smoke and heat stung his eyes, and he shut them. He could not breathe, could not hear, could not move.

The chanting began low and droning. "Let's go," Mitch told Kaye.

She looked back at the crowd. Now something seemed wrong to her, as well. The hair on her neck rose. "All right," she said.

They circled on a walkway and turned to walk down the north side of the hill. They passed a man and his son, five or six years old, the son carrying a kite in his small hands. The boy smiled at Kaye and Mitch. Kaye looked at the boy's elegant almond eyes, his long close-shaven head so Egyptian, like a beautiful and ancient ebony statue brought to life, and she thought, *What a beautiful and normal child. What a beautiful little boy.*

She was reminded of the young girl standing by the side of the street in Gordi, as the UN caravan left the town; so different in appearance, yet provoking such similar thoughts.

She took Mitch's hand in hers just as the sirens began. They looked north toward the parking lot and saw five police cars skidding to a halt, doors flung open, officers emerging, running through the parked cars and across the grass, up the hill.

"Look," Mitch said, and pointed at a lone middle-aged man dressed in shorts and a sweatshirt, talking on a cellular phone. The man looked scared.

"What in hell?" Kaye asked.

The droning prayer had strengthened. Three officers rushed past Kaye and Mitch, guns still holstered, but one had pulled out his baton. They pushed through the outer circles of the crowd on the top of the hill.

Women shrieked abuse at them. They fought with the officers, shoving, kicking, scratching, trying to push them back.

Kaye could not believe what she was seeing or hearing. Two women jumped on one of the men, shouting obscenities.

The officer with the baton began to use it to protect his fellows. Kaye heard the stomach-twisting chunk of weighted plastic on flesh and bone.

Kaye started back up the hill, but Mitch grabbed her arm.

More officers plowed into the crowd, batons swinging. The chanting stopped. The crowd seemed to lose all cohesion. Women in robes broke away, hands clutched to their faces in anger and fear, screaming, crying, their voices high and frantic. Some of the robed women collapsed and pounded the scruffy yellow grass with their fists. Spittle dribbled from their mouths.

A police van pushed over the curb and over the grass, engine roaring. Two female officers joined in the rout.

Mitch backed Kaye off the mound, and they came to the bottom, facing uphill to keep an eye on the crowd still massed around the sundial. Two officers pushed out of this assembly with the young man in black. Red dripping slashes marked his neck and hands. A woman officer called for an ambulance on her walkie-talkie. She passed within yards of Mitch and Kaye, face white and lips red with anger.

"Goddamn it!" she shouted at the onlookers. "Why didn't you try to stop them?"

Neither Kaye nor Mitch had an answer.

The young man in the black robe stumbled and fell between the two officers supporting him. His face, warped by pain and shock, flashed white as the clouds against the hard-packed dirt and yellow grass.

Seattle

Mitch drove them south on the freeway to Capitol Hill, then turned off and headed east on Denny. The Buick chugged up the grade.

"I wish we hadn't seen that," Kaye said.

Mitch swore under his breath. "I wish we'd never even stopped."

"Is everybody crazy? It's just too much," Kaye said. "I can't figure out where we stand in all this."

"We're going back to the old ways," Mitch said.

"Like in Georgia." Kaye pressed a knuckle against her lips and teeth.

"I hate to have women blame *men*," Mitch said. "It makes me want to throw up."

"I don't blame anybody," Kaye said. "But you have to admit, it's a natural reaction."

Mitch shot her a scowl that bordered on a dirty look, the first such he had ever given her. She sucked in her breath privately, feeling both guilty and sad, and turned to look out her window, peering down the long straight stretch of Broadway: brick buildings, pedestrians, young men wearing green masks, walking with other men, and women walking with women.

"Let's forget about it," Mitch said. "Let's get some rest."

The second-floor apartment, neat and cool and a little dusty from Mitch's long absence, overlooked Broadway and gave a view of the brick-front post office, a small bookstore, and a Thai restaurant. As Mitch carried the bags through the door, he apologized for clutter that did not exist, as far as Kaye was concerned.

"Bachelor digs," he said. "I don't know why I kept up the lease."

"It's nice," Kaye said, running her fingers along the dark wood trim of the windowsill, the white enamel on the wall. The living room had been warmed by the sun and smelled slightly stuffy, not unpleasant, just closed in. With some difficulty, Kaye opened the window. Mitch stood beside her and closed the window slowly. "Gas fumes from the street," he said. "There's a window in the bedroom that looks out over the back of the building. Gets a good draft."

Kaye had thought that seeing Mitch's apartment would be romantic, pleasant, that she would learn a lot about him, but it was so neat, so sparely furnished, that she felt let down. She examined the books in a ceiling-high case near the kitchen nook: textbooks on anthropology and archaeology, some tattered biology texts, a box full of science magazines and photocopies. No novels.

"The Thai restaurant is good," Mitch said, putting his arms around her as she stood before the bookcase.

"I'm not hungry. This is where you did your research?"

"Right here. Stroke of lightning. You were inspirational."

"Thank you," she said.

"Want to just take a nap? There are beers in the refrigerator—"

"Budweiser?"

Mitch grinned.

"I'll take one," Kaye said. He let go of her and rummaged in the refrigerator.

"Damn. There must have been an outage. Everything in the freezer melted . . ." A cool sour smell wafted from the kitchen. "The beer's still good, though." He brought her a bottle and deftly unscrewed the cap. She took it and sipped it. Barely any flavor. No relief.

"I need to use the bathroom," Kaye said. She felt numb, far from anything that mattered. She carried her purse into the bathroom and removed the pregnancy kit. It was sweet and simple: two drops of urine on a test strip, blue if positive, pink if negative. Results in ten minutes.

Suddenly, Kaye was desperate to know.

The bathroom was immaculately clean. "What can I do for him?" she asked herself. "He lives his own life here." But she put that aside and dropped the lid on the toilet to sit.

In the living room, Mitch turned on the TV. Through the old solid-pine door Kaye heard muffled voices, a few stray words. ". . . also injured in the blast was the secretary—"

"Kaye!" Mitch called.

She covered the strip with a Kleenex and opened the door.

"The president," Mitch said, his face contorted. He pounded his fists at nothing. "I wish I'd never turned the damned thing on!"

Kaye stood in the living room before the small television, stared at the announcer's head and shoulders, her moving lips, the run of mascara from one eye. "The count so far is seven dead, including the governors of Florida, Mississippi, and Alabama, the president, a Secret Service agent, and two not yet identified. Among the survivors are the governors of New Mexico and Arizona, director of the Herod's Taskforce Mark Augustine, and Frank Shawbeck of the National Institutes of Health. The vice president was not in the White House at this time—"

Mitch stood beside her, shoulders slumped.

"Where was Christopher?" Kaye asked in a small voice.

"No explanation has yet been given for how a bomb could

have been smuggled into the White House through such intense security. Frank Sesno is outside the White House now."

Kaye pushed free of Mitch's arm. "Excuse me," she said, patting his shoulder nervously. "Bathroom."

"Are you all right?"

"I'm fine." She shut the door and locked it, took a deep breath, and lifted away the Kleenex. Ten minutes had passed.

"Are you sure you're all right?" Mitch called outside the door.

Kaye held the strip up to the light, looked at the two test patches. The first test showed blue. The second test showed blue. She read the instructions again, the color comparisons, and leaned an elbow against the door, feeling dizzy.

"It's done," she said softly. She straightened and thought, *This is a horrible time. Let it wait. Let it wait if you can possibly wait.*

"Kaye!" Mitch sounded close to panic. He needed her, needed some reassurance. She leaned on the sink, could barely stay upright, she felt such a mix of horror and relief and awe at what they had done, at what the world was doing.

She opened the door and saw tears in Mitch's eyes.

"I didn't even vote for him!" he said, his lips trembling.

Kaye hugged him tightly. That the president was dead was significant, important, it mattered, but she could not feel it yet. Her emotions were elsewhere, with Mitch, with his mother and father, with her own absent mother and father; she felt even a mild concern for herself, but curiously enough, no real connection with the life inside her.

Not yet.

This was not the actual baby.

Not yet.

Don't love it. Don't love this one. Love what it does, what it carries.

Quite against her will, as she held Mitch and patted his back, Kaye fainted. Mitch carried her into the bedroom, brought a cold cloth.

She floated for a while in closed darkness, then became

aware of a dryness in her mouth. She cleared her throat, opened her eyes.

She looked up at her husband, tried to kiss his hand as it passed the cloth over her cheeks and chin.

"Such a fool," she said.

"Me?"

"Me. I thought I'd be strong."

"You are strong," Mitch said.

"I love you," she said, and that was all she could manage.

Mitch saw that she was sound asleep and pulled the blanket over her on the bed, turned out the light, and returned to the living room. The apartment seemed so different now. Summer twilight glowed beyond the windows, casting a fairy-tale pallor over the opposite wall. He sat in the worn armchair before the TV, its muted sound still clear in the quiet room.

"Governor Harris has declared a state of emergency and called out National Guard troops. A curfew of seven P.M. has been declared for weekdays, five P.M. for Saturday and Sunday, and if martial law is declared at the federal level, we presume by the vice president, as seems very likely, then throughout the state, no groups will be allowed to gather in public places without special permission from the Emergency Action Office in each community. This official state of emergency is open-ended, and is in part, so officials say, a response to the situation in the nation's capital, and in part an attempt to bring under control the extraordinary and continuing unrest in Washington state itself . . ."

Mitch tapped the plastic test strip on his chin. He switched channels just to have a feeling of control.

". . . is dead. The president and five out of ten visiting state governors were killed this morning in the situation room of the White House—"

And again, punching the button on the small remote.

". . . The governor of Alabama, Abraham C. Darzelle, leader of the so-called States' Revolt movement, *embraced* the president of the United States just before the explosion. Both the governors of Alabama and Florida, and the president, were blown apart by the blast—"

Mitch turned the TV off. He returned the plastic strip to the bathroom and went to lie beside Kaye. He did not pull the covers back and did not undress, to avoid disturbing her. Kicking off his shoes, he curled up with one leg laid gently over her blanketed thighs, and pushed his nose against her short brown hair. The smell of her hair and scalp was more soothing than any drug.

For far too short a moment, the universe once again became small and warm and entirely sufficient.

PART THREE

STELLA NOVA

74

Seattle
JUNE

Kaye arranged her papers on Mitch's desk and picked up the manuscript for *The Queen's Library*. Three weeks ago, she had decided to write a book about SHEVA, modern biology, all she felt the human race might need to know in the coming years. The title referred to her metaphor for the genome, with all of its ferment and movable elements and self-interested players, rendering service to the genome queen with one side of their nature, selfishly hoping to be installed in the Queen's Library, the DNA; and sometimes putting on another face, another role, more selfish than useful, parasitic or predatory, causing trouble or even disaster . . . A political metaphor that seemed perfectly apt now.

In the past two weeks, she had written over a hundred and sixty pages on her laptop computer, printing them out on a portable printer, partly as a way of getting her thoughts together before the convention.

And to pass the time. The hours sometimes drag when Mitch is away.

She knocked the papers together on the wood, satisfied by the solid thunk they made, then placed them before the picture of Christopher Dicken that stood in a small silver frame near a portrait of Sam and Abby. The last picture in her box of personal items was a black-and-white glossy of Saul, taken by a professional photographer on Long Island. Saul appeared able, grinning, confident, wise. They had sent copies of that picture with the business prospectus for EcoBacter to venture capital firms over five years ago. An age.

Kaye had spent very little time looking back on her past, or gathering memorabilia. Now she regretted that. She wanted their baby to have a sense of what had happened. When she looked at herself in the mirror, she appeared almost peachlike in her health and vitality. Pregnancy was treating her very well.

As if she could not get enough of writing, recording, she had begun a diary three days ago, the first diary she had ever kept.

June 10

We spent last week preparing for the conference and looking for a house. Interest rates have gone through the roof, now at twenty-one percent, but we can afford something larger than the apartment, and Mitch isn't particular. I am. Mitch is writing more slowly than I am, about the mummies and the cave, sending it page by page to Oliver Merton in New York, who is editing it, sometimes a little cruelly. Mitch takes it quietly, tries to improve. We have become so literary, so self-observant, maybe a little self-important, since there is not much else to keep us occupied.

Mitch is gone this afternoon talking to the new director of the Hayer, hoping to get reinstated. (He never travels more than twenty minutes from the apartment, and we bought another cell phone the day before yesterday. I tell him I can take care of myself, but he worries.)

He has a letter from Professor Brock describing the nature of the current controversy. Brock has been on a few talk shows. Some newspapers have carried the story, and Merton's piece in NATURE is drawing a lot of attention and a lot of criticism.

Innsbruck still holds all the tissue samples and will not comment or release, but Mitch is working on his friends at UW to get them to go public with what they know, to undermine Innsbruck's secrecy. Merton believes the gradualists in charge of the mummies have at most another two or three months to prepare their reports and make them public, or they'll be removed, replaced, Brock hopes, by a a more objective team, and clearly he hopes to be in charge. Mitch might be on that team, too; though that seems too much to hope for.

Merton and Daney were unable to convince the New York Emergency Action Office to hold the conference in Albany. Something about 1845 and Governor Silas Wright and rent riots; they don't want a repeat under this "experimental" and "temporary" Emergency Act.

We petitioned the Washington Emergency Action Office through Maria Konig at UW, and they allowed a two-day conference at Kane Hall, one hundred attendees maximum, all to be approved by the office. Civil liberties haven't been completely forgotten, but almost. Nobody wants to call it martial law, and in fact the civil courts are still in full operation, but they work with approval of the Office in each state.

Nothing like it since 1942, Mitch says.

I feel spooky: healthy, vital, energetic, and I don't look very pregnant. The hormones are the same, the effect the same.

I go in for my sonogram and scan tomorrow at Marine Pacific, and we'll do amnio and chorionic villi despite the risks because we want to know the character of the tissues.

The next step won't be so easy.

Mrs. Hamilton, now I'm a lab rat, too.

75

Building 10, The National Institutes of Health, Bethesda
JULY

Dicken propelled himself with one hand down the long corridor on the tenth floor of the Magnuson Clinical Center, spun around with what he hoped was true wheelchair grace—again, with one hand—and dimly saw the two men walking in his return path. The gray suit, the long, slow stride, the height, told him one of the men was Augustine. He did not know who the other might be.

With a low moan, he lowered his right hand and pushed himself toward the pair. As he got closer, he could see that Augustine's face was healing well enough, though he would always have a slightly rugged look. What was not covered with the bandages of continuing plastic surgery, crossing his head laterally over his nose and in patches on both cheeks and temples, still bore the marks of shrapnel. Both of Augustine's eyes had been spared. Dicken had lost one eye, and the other had been hazed by the heat of the blast.

"You're still a sight, Mark," Dicken said, braking with one hand and lightly dragging a slippered foot.

"Ditto, Christopher. I'd like you to meet Dr. Kelly Newcomb."

They shook hands gingerly. Dicken sized up Newcomb for a moment, then said, "You're Mark's new traveler."

"Yes," Newcomb said.

"Congratulations on getting the appointment," Dicken said to Augustine.

"Don't bother," Augustine said. "It's going to be a nightmare."

"Gather all the children under one umbrella," Dicken said. "How's Frank doing?"

"He's leaving Walter Reed next week."

Another silence. Dicken could think of nothing more to say. Newcomb folded his hands uncomfortably, then adjusted his glasses, pushing them up his nose. Dicken hated the silence, and just as Augustine was about to speak again, he broke in with, "They're going to keep me for another couple of weeks. Another surgery on my hand. I'd like to get off the campus for a while, see what's going on in the world."

"Let's go into your room and talk," Augustine suggested.

"Be my guests," Dicken said.

When they were inside, Augustine asked Newcomb to shut the door. "I'd like Kelly to spend a couple of days talking with you. Getting up to speed. We're moving into a new phase. The president has put us under his discretionary budget."

"Great," Dicken said thickly. He swallowed and tried to bring up some spit to wet his tongue. Drugs for pain and antibiotics were playing hell with his chemistry.

"We're not going to do anything radical," Augustine said. "Everyone agrees we're in an incredibly delicate state."

"State with a capital *S*," Dicken said.

"For the moment, no doubt," Augustine said quietly. "I didn't ask for this, Christopher."

"I know," Dicken said.

"But should any SHEVA children be born alive, we have to move quickly. I have reports from seven labs that prove SHEVA can mobilize ancient retroviruses in the genome."

"It kicks around all manner of HERV and retrotransposons," Dicken said. He had been trying to read the studies on a special viewer in the room. "I'm not sure they're actually viruses. They may be—"

"Whatever you call them, they have the requisite viral genes," Augustine interrupted. "We haven't faced them for millions of years, so they'll probably be pathogenic. What worries me now is any movement that might encourage woman to bring these children to term. There's no problem in Eastern Europe and Asia. Japan has already started a prevention program. But here, we're more cussed."

That was putting it mildly. "Don't cross that line again, Mark," Dicken advised.

Augustine was in no mood for wise counsel. "Christopher, we could lose more than just a generation of children. Kelly agrees."

"The work is sound," Newcomb said.

Dicken coughed, controlled the spasm, but his face flushed with frustration. "What are we looking at . . . Internment camps? Concentration *nurseries*?"

"We estimate there will be one or two thousand SHEVA children born alive in North America by the end of the year, at most. There may be *none*, zero, Christopher. The president has already signed an emergency order giving us custody if any are born alive. We're working out the civil details now. God only knows what the E.U. is going to do. Asia is being very practical. Abortion and quarantine. I wish we could be so bold."

"To me, this does not sound like a major health threat, Mark," Dicken said. His throat caught again and he coughed. With his damaged eyesight, he could not make out Augustine's expression behind the bandages.

"They're *reservoirs*, Christopher," Augustine said. "If the babies get out in the general public, they'll be vectors. All it took for AIDS was a few."

"We admit it stinks," Newcomb said, glancing at Augustine. "I feel that in my gut. But we've done computer analysis on some of these activated HERV. Given expression of viable *env* and *pol* genes, we could have something much worse than HIV. The computers point to a disease like nothing we've seen in history. It could burn the human race, Dr. Dicken. We could just flake away like dust."

Dicken pushed up out of his chair and sat on the edge of his bed. "Who disagrees?" he asked.

"Dr. Mahy at the CDC," Augustine said. "Bishop and Thorne. And of course James Mondavi. But the Princeton people agree, and they have the president's confidence. They want to work with us on this."

"What do the opponents say?" Dicken asked Newcomb.

"Mahy thinks any released particles will be fully adapted retroviruses, but nonpathogenic, and that the worst we'll see is a few cases of some rare cancers," Augustine said. "Mondavi also sees no pathogenesis. But that's not why we're here, Christopher."

"Why, then?"

"We need your personal input. Kaye Lang has gotten herself pregnant. You know the father. It's a first-stage SHEVA. She'll have her miscarriage any day now."

Dicken turned away.

"She's sponsoring a conference in Washington state. We tried to get the Emergency Action Office to shut it down—"

"A scientific conference?"

"More mumbo-jumbo about evolution. And, no doubt, encouragement for new mothers. This could be a PR disaster, very bad for morale. We don't control the press, Christopher. Do you think she'll be extreme on the subject?"

"No," Dicken said. "I think she'll be very reasonable."

"That could be worse," Augustine said. "But it's also something we can use against her, if she claims the support of Science with a capital *S*. Mitch Rafelson's reputation is pure mud."

"He's a decent fellow," Dicken said.

"He's a liability, Christopher," Augustine said. "Fortunately, he's her liability, not ours."

76

Seattle
AUGUST 10

Kaye carried her yellow legal pad from the bedroom to the kitchen. Mitch had been at the University of Washington since nine that morning. The first reaction to his visit at the Hayer Museum had been negative; they were not interested in controversy, whatever his support from Brock or any other scientist. Brock himself, they had sagely pointed out, was controversial, and according to unnamed sources had been "let go from" or even "forced out of " the Neandertal studies at the University of Innsbruck.

Kaye had always loathed academic politics. She set the notebook and a glass of orange juice on a small table by Mitch's worn chair, then sat down with a small moan. With nothing coming to her this morning and no sense of where to take the book next, she had started a general short essay that she might use at the conference in two weeks . . .

But the essay had abruptly stalled as well. Inspiration was simply no competititon for the peculiar tangled feeling in her abdomen.

It had been almost ninety days. Last night, in her journal, she had written, "Already it is about the size of a mouse." And nothing more.

She used Mitch's remote to turn on the old TV. Governor Harris was giving yet another press conference. He went on the air every day to report on the Emergency Act, how Washington state was cooperating with Washington, D.C., what measures he was resisting—he was very big on resistance, playing to the rugged individualists east of the Cascades— and explaining very carefully where he thought cooperation was beneficial and essential. Once more he went through a bleak litany of statistics.

"In the Northwest, from Oregon to Idaho, the law enforcement officials tell me there have been at least thirty acts of human sacrifice. When we add this to the estimated twenty-two thousand incidents of violence against women around the country, the Emergency Act seems long overdue. We are a community, a state, a region, a nation, out of control with grief and panicked by an incomprehensible act of God."

Kaye rubbed her stomach gently. Harris had an impossible job. The proud citizens of the U.S.A., she thought, were adopting a very Chinese attitude. With the favor of Heaven so obviously withdrawn, their support for any and all governments had diminished drastically.

A roundtable discussion with two scientists and a state representative followed the governor's conference. The talk turned to SHEVA children as carriers of disease; this was utter nonsense and something she did not want or need to hear. She shut the television off.

The cell phone rang. Kaye flipped it open. "Hello?"

"Oh beauteous one . . . I've got Wendell Packer, Maria Konig, Oliver Merton, and Professor Brock, all sitting in the same room."

Kaye's face warmed and relaxed at the sound of Mitch's voice.

"They'd like to meet you."

"Only if they want to be midwives," Kaye said.

"Jesus—do you feel anything?"

"A sour stomach," Kaye said. "Unhappy and uninspired. But no, I don't think it's going to be today."

"Well, be inspired by this," Mitch said. "They're going to go public with their analysis of the Innsbruck tissue samples. And they're going to give papers at the conference. Packer and Konig say they'll support us."

Kaye closed her eyes for a moment. She wanted to savor this. "And their departments?"

"No go. The politics is just too intense for department heads. But Maria and Wendell are going to work on their colleagues. We're hoping to have dinner together. Are you up for it?"

Her roiling stomach had settled. Kaye thought she might actually be hungry in an hour or so. She had followed Maria Konig's work for years, and admired her enormously. But in that masculine crew, perhaps Konig's greatest asset was that she was female.

"Where are we eating?"

"Within five minutes of Marine Pacific Hospital," Mitch said. "Other than that, I don't know."

"Maybe a bowl of oatmeal for me," Kaye said. "Should I take the bus?"

"Nonsense. I'll be there in a few minutes." Mitch kissed at her over the phone, and then, Oliver Merton asked to say something.

"We haven't met yet, to shake hands," Merton said breathlessly, as if he had just been arguing loudly or had run up a flight of stairs. "Christ, Ms. Lang, I'm nervous just talking with you."

"You trounced me pretty badly in Baltimore," Kaye said.

"Yes, but that was then," Merton said without a hint of regret. "I can't tell you how much I admire what you and Mitch are planning. I am *agog* with wonder."

"We're just doing what comes natural," Kaye said.

"Wipe the past clean," Merton said. "Ms. Lang, I'm a friend."

"We'll see about that," Kaye said.

Merton chuckled and handed her back to Mitch.

"Maria Konig suggests a good Vietnamese phô restaurant. That's what she craved when she was pregnant. Sound right?"

"After my oatmeal," Kaye said. "Does Merton have to be there?"

"Not if you don't want him."

"Tell him I'm going to stare daggers at him. Make him suffer."

"I'll do that," Mitch said. "But he thrives under criticism."

"I've been analyzing tissues from dead people for ten years now," Maria Konig said. "Wendell knows the feeling."

"I do indeed," Packer said.

Konig, sitting across from her, was more than just beautiful—she was the perfect model for what Kaye wanted to look like when she reached fifty. Wendell Packer was very handsome, in a lean and compact sort of way—quite the opposite of Mitch. Brock wore a gray coat and black T-shirt, dapper and quiet; he seemed lost in even deeper thought.

"Each day, you get a FedEx box or two or three," Maria said, "and you open them up, and inside are little tubes or bottles from Bosnia or East Timor or the Congo, and there's this little sad chunk of skin or bone from one or another *victim*, usually innocent, and an envelope with copies of records, more tubes, blood samples or cheek swabs from relatives of victims. Day after day after day. It never stops. If these babies are the next step, if they're better than we are at living on this planet, I can't wait. We're in need of a change."

The small waitress taking their orders stopped writing on her small pad. "You name dead people for UN?" she asked Maria.

Maria looked up at her, embarrassed. "Sometimes."

"I from Kampuchea, Cambodia, come here fifteen years ago," she said. "You work on Kampucheans?"

"That was before my time, honey," Maria said.

"I still very mad," the woman said. "Mother, father, brother, uncle. Then they let the murderers go without punishing. Very bad men and women."

The table fell silent as the woman's large black eyes sparked with memory. Brock leaned forward, clasping his hands and touching his nose with the knuckle of his thumb.

"Very bad now, too. I going to have baby anyway," the

woman said. She touched her stomach and looked at Kaye. "You?"

"Yes," Kaye said.

"I believe in future," the woman said. "It got to get better."

She finished taking their orders and left the table. Merton picked up his chopsticks and fumbled them aimlessly for a few seconds. "I shall have to remember this," he said, "the next time I feel oppressed."

"Save it for your book," Brock said.

"I *am* writing one," Merton told them with raised brows. "No surprise. The most important bit of science reporting of our time."

"I hope you're having more luck than I am," Kaye said.

"I'm jammed, absolutely stuck," Merton said, and pushed up his glasses with the thick end of a chopstick. "But that won't last. It never has."

The waitress brought spring rolls, shrimp and bean sprouts and basil leaves wrapped in translucent pancake. Kaye had lost her urge for bland and reassuring oatmeal. Feeling more adventurous, she pinched one of the rolls with her chopsticks and dipped it into a small ceramic bowl of sweet brown sauce. The flavor was extraordinary—she could have lingered on the bite for minutes, picking out every savory molecule. The basil and mint in the roll were almost too intense, and the shrimp tasted rich and crunchy and oceanic.

All her senses sharpened. The large room, though dark and cool, seemed very colorful, very detailed.

"What do they put in these?" she asked, chewing the last bite of her roll.

"They *are* good," Merton said.

"I shouldn't have said anything," Maria said apologetically, still feeling the emotion of the waitress's bit of history.

"We all believe in the future," Mitch said. "We wouldn't be here if we were stuck in our own little ruts."

"We need to figure out what we can say, what our limitations are," Wendell said. "I can only go so far before I'm outside my expertise and way outside what the department will tolerate, even if I claim to speak for myself alone."

"Courage, Wendell," Merton said. "A solid front. Freddie?"

Brock sipped from his foamy glass of pale lager. He looked up with a hangdog expression.

"I cannot believe we are all here, that we have come this far," he said. "The changes are so close, I am frightened. Do you know what is going to happen when we present our findings?"

"We're going to get crucified by nearly every scientific journal in the world," Packer said, and laughed.

"Not *Nature*," Merton said. "I've laid some groundwork there. Pulled off a journalistic and scientific coup." He grinned.

"No, please, friends," Brock said. "Step back a moment and think. We are just past the millennium, and now we are about to learn how we came to be human." He removed his thick glasses and wiped them with his napkin. His eyes were distant, very round. "In Innsbruck, we have our mummies, caught in the late stages of a change that took place across tens of thousands of years. The woman must have been tough and brave beyond our imagining, but she knew very little. Dr. Lang, you know a great deal, and you proceed anyway. Your courage is perhaps even more wonderful." He lifted his glass of beer. "The least I can do is offer you a heartfelt toast."

They all raised their glasses. Kaye felt her stomach flip again, but it was not a bad sensation.

"To Kaye," Friedrich Brock said. "The next Eve."

77

AUGUST 12

Kaye sat in the old Buick to stay out of the rain. Mitch walked along the row of cars in the small lot off Roosevelt, searching for the kind she had specified—small, late nineties, Japanese or Volvo, maybe blue or green—and looked up to where she sat curbside, window rolled down for air.

He pulled off his wet felt Stetson and smiled. "How about this beauty?" He pointed to a black Caprice.

"No," Kaye said emphatically. Mitch loved big old American cars. He felt at home in their roomy interiors. Their trunks could carry tools and slabs of rock. He would have loved to buy a truck, and they had discussed that for a few days. Kaye was not averse to four-wheel-drive, but they had seen nothing she thought they could afford. She wanted a huge reserve in the bank for emergencies. She had set a limit of twelve thousand dollars.

"I'm a kept man," he said, holding his hat mournfully and bowing his head before the Caprice.

Kaye pointedly ignored that. She had been in an ill humor all morning—had snapped at him twice over breakfast, chastisements that Mitch had accepted with infuriating commiseration. What she wanted was a real argument, to get her blood going, her thoughts moving—to get her *body* moving. She was sick of the gnawing sensation in her gut that had persisted for three days. She was sick of waiting, of trying to come to grips with what she was carrying.

424

What Kaye wanted above all else was to lash out at Mitch for agreeing to get her pregnant and start this awful, dragged-out process.

Mitch strode over to the second row and peered at stickers. A woman with an umbrella came down the wooden steps from the small office trailer and conferred with him.

Kaye watched them suspiciously. She hated herself, hated her screwball and chaotic emotions. Nothing she was thinking made any sense.

Mitch pointed to a used Lexus. "Way too expensive," Kaye murmured to herself, biting her cuticle. Then, "Oh, shit." She thought she had wet her panties. The trickle continued, but it was not her bladder. She felt between her legs.

"Mitch!" she yelled. He came running, flung open the driver's-side door, jumped in, started the motor when the first poked fist of blunt pain doubled her over. She nearly slammed her hand against the dash. He pulled her back with one hand. "Oh, God!" she said.

"We're going," he said. He peeled out along Roosevelt and turned west on 45th, dodging cars on the overpass and swinging hard left onto the freeway.

The pain was not so intense now. Her stomach seemed filled with ice water and her thighs trembled.

"How is it?" Mitch asked.

"Scary," she said. "So strange."

Mitch hit eighty.

She felt something like a small bowel movement. So rude, so natural, so *unspeakable*. She tried to clamp her legs together. She was not sure what she felt, what exactly had happened. The pain was almost gone.

By the time they pulled into the emergency entrance at Marine Pacific, she was reasonably sure it was all over.

Maria Konig had referred them to Dr. Felicity Galbreath after Kaye met resistance from several pediatricians reluctant to take on a SHEVA pregnancy. Her own health insurance had canceled her; SHEVA was covered as a disease, a prior condition, certainly not as a natural pregnancy.

Dr. Galbreath worked at several hospitals but kept her offices at Marine Pacific, the big brown Depression-era Art Deco hospital that looked down across the freeway, Lake Union, and much of west Seattle. She also taught two days a week at Western Washington University, and Kaye wondered where she found time to have any other life.

Galbreath, tall and plump, with round shoulders, a pleasantly unchallenging face, and a tight, short head of mousy blond hair, came into Kaye's shared room twenty minutes after she was admitted. Kaye had been cleaned up and briefly examined by the resident nurse and an attending physician. A nurse midwife Kaye had never met before also checked on her, having heard about Kaye's case from a brief article in the *Seattle Weekly*.

Kaye sat up in her bed, her back aching, but otherwise comfortable, and drank a glass of orange juice.

"Well, it's happened," Galbreath said.

"It's happened," Kaye echoed dully.

"They tell me you're doing fine."

"I feel better now."

"Very sorry not to be here sooner. I was over at UW Medical Center."

"I think it was over before I was admitted," Kaye said.

"How do you feel?"

"Lousy. Healthy enough, just lousy."

"Where's Mitch?"

"I told him to bring me the baby. The fetus."

Galbreath glared at her with mixed irritation and wonder. "Aren't you taking this scientist bit too far?"

"Bullshit," Kaye said fiercely.

"You could be in emotional shock."

"Double bullshit. They took it away without telling me. I need to see it. I need to know what happened."

"It's a first-stage rejection. We know what they look like,"

Galbreath said softly, checking Kaye's pulse and looking at the attached monitor. As a precaution, she was on saline drip.

Mitch returned with a small steel pan covered with a cloth. "They were sending it down to . . ." He looked up, his face pale as a sheet. "I don't know where. I had to do some yelling."

Galbreath looked at them both with an expression of forceful self-control. "It's just tissue, Kaye. The hospital has to send them to an approved Taskforce autopsy center. It's the law."

"She's my *daughter*," Kaye said, tears trickling down her cheeks. "I want to see *her* before they take her." The sobs began and she could not control them. The nurse looked in, saw Galbreath was with them, stood in the doorway with a helpless and concerned expression.

Galbreath took the pan from Mitch, who was happy to be relieved of it. She waited until Kaye was quiet.

"Please," Kaye said. Galbreath placed the pan gently on her lap.

The nurse left and shut the door behind her.

Mitch turned away as she pulled back the cloth.

Lying on a bed of crushed ice, in a small plastic bag with a Ziploc top, no larger than a small lab mouse, lay the interim daughter. *Her* daughter. Kaye had been nurturing and carrying and protecting this for over ninety days.

For a moment, she felt distinctly uneasy. She reached down with a finger to trace the outline in the bag, the short and curled spine beyond the edge of the torn and tiny amnion. She stroked the comparatively large and almost faceless head, finding small slits for eyes, a wrinkled and rabbitlike mouth kept tightly closed, buttons where arms and legs might be. The small purple placenta lay beneath the amnion.

"Thank you," Kaye said to the fetus.

She covered the tray. Galbreath tried to remove it, but Kaye gripped her hand. "Leave her with me for a few minutes," she said. "I want to make sure she isn't lonely. Wherever she's going."

* * *

Galbreath joined Mitch in the waiting room. He sat with his head in his hands in a pale bleached-oak armchair beneath a pastel seascape framed in ash.

"You look like you need a drink," she said.

"Is Kaye still asleep?" Mitch said. "I want to be with her."

Galbreath nodded. "You can go in any time. I examined her. Do you want the details?"

"Please," Mitch said, rubbing his face. "I didn't know I'd react that way. I'm sorry."

"No need. She's a bold woman who thinks she knows what she wants. Well, she's still pregnant. The secondary mucus plug seems to be in position. There was no trauma, no bleeding; the separation was textbook, if anybody has bothered to write a textbook about this sort of thing. The hospital did a quick biopsy. It's definitely a first-stage SHEVA rejection. Chromosome number is confirmed."

"Fifty-two?" Mitch asked.

Galbreath nodded. "Like all the others. It should be forty-six. Gross chromosomal abnormalities."

"It's a different kind of normal," Mitch said.

Galbreath sat beside him and crossed her legs. "Let's hope. We'll do more tests in a few months."

"I don't know how a woman feels after something like this," he said slowly, folding and unfolding his hands. "What do I say to her?"

"Let her sleep. When she wakes up, tell her that you love her, and that she's brave and magnificent. This part will probably feel like a bad dream."

Mitch stared at her. "What do I tell her if the next one doesn't work, either?"

Galbreath leaned her head to one side and smoothed her cheek with one finger. "I don't know, Mr. Rafelson."

Mitch filled out the discharge papers and looked over the attached medical report, signed by Galbreath. Kaye folded a nightgown and put it into the small overnight case, then walked stiffly into the bathroom and packed up her tooth-brush. "I ache all over," she said, her voice hollow through the open door.

"I can get a wheelchair," Mitch said. He was almost out the door before Kaye left the bathroom and put a hand on his shoulder.

"I can walk. This part is done with, and that makes me feel much better. But . . . Fifty-two chromosomes, Mitch. I wish I knew what that meant."

"There's still time," Mitch said quietly.

Kaye's first impulse was to give him a stern look, but his expression told her that would not be fair, that he was as vulnerable as she. "No," she said, simply and gently.

Galbreath knocked on the door frame.

"Come in," Kaye said. She closed and latched the lid on the overnight case. The doctor entered with a young, ill-at-ease man dressed in a gray suit.

"Kaye, this is Ed Gianelli. He's the Emergency Action legal representative for Marine Pacific."

"Ms. Lang, Mr. Rafelson. I'm sorry for the difficulty. I have to obtain some personal information and a signature, under the state of Washington compliance agreements with the federal Emergency Act, as agreed to by the state legislature on July 22 of this year, and signed by the governor on July 26. I apologize for the inconvenience during a painful time—"

"What is it?" Mitch asked. "What do we have to do?"

"All women carrying SHEVA second-stage fetuses should register with the state Emergency Action Office and agree to follow-up medical tracking. You can arrange to have those visits with Dr. Galbreath, as the obstetrician of record, and she will carry out the standardized tests."

"We won't register," Mitch said. "Are you ready to go?" he asked Kaye, putting his arm around her.

Gianelli shifted his stance. "I won't go into the reasons, Mr. Rafelson, but registration and follow-up are mandated by the King County Board of Health, in agreement with state and federal law."

"I don't recognize the law," Mitch said firmly.

"The penalty is a fine of five hundred dollars for each week you refuse," Gianelli said.

"Best not to make a big deal out of it," Galbreath said. "It's a kind of addendum to a birth certificate."

"The infant hasn't been born yet."

"Then think of it as an addendum to the postrejection medical report," Gianelli said, his shoulders rising.

"There was no rejection," Kaye said. "What we're doing is natural."

Gianelli held out his hands in exasperation. "All I need is your current residence and a waiver to access your pertinent medical records, with Dr. Galbreath and your lawyer, if you wish, overseeing what we look at."

"My God," Mitch said. He moved Kaye past Galbreath and Gianelli, then paused to say to the doctor, "You know what this means, don't you? People will stay away from hospitals, from their physicians."

"My hands are pretty much tied," Galbreath said. "The hospital fought this until just yesterday. We still plan to appeal to the Board of Health. But for now—"

Mitch and Kaye left. Galbreath stood in the doorway, face mottled.

Gianelli followed them down the hall, agitated. "I have to remind you," he said, "that these fines are cumulative—"

"Give it up, Ed!" Galbreath shouted, slamming her hand on the wall. "Just give it up and let them go, for Christ's sake!"

Gianelli stood in the middle of the hallway, shaking his head. "I hate this shit!"

"*You* hate it?" Galbreath shouted at him. "Just leave my patients the hell alone!"

Building 52, The National Institutes of Health, Bethesda
OCTOBER

Your face looks pretty good," Shawbeck said. He advanced into Augustine's office on a pair of crutches. His aide helped him lower himself into the chair. Augustine was finishing a corned beef sandwich. He wiped his lips and folded the top of the foam box, latching it.

"All right," Shawbeck said when he was seated. "Weekly meeting of the survivors of July twentieth, *der Führer* presiding."

Augustine lifted his eyes. "Not a bit funny."

"When's Christopher going to join us? We should keep a bottle of brandy, and the last survivor gets to toast the departed."

"Christopher is getting more and more disaffected," Augustine said.

"And you aren't?" Shawbeck asked. "How long since you met with the president?"

"Three days," Augustine said.

"Black budget discussions?"

"Emergency Action reserve finances," Augustine said.

"He didn't even mention them to me," Shawbeck said.

"It's my ball now. They're going to hang the old toilet seat around my neck."

"Because you put together the rationale," Shawbeck said. "So—these new babies are not only going to be born dead, but if any happen to be born alive, we take them away from

431

their parents and put them into specially financed hospitals. We've gone pretty far on this one."

"The public seems to be with us," Augustine said. "The president's describing it as a major public health risk."

"I wouldn't be in your shoes for anything on Earth, Mark. It's going to be political suicide. The president has to be in shock to be promoting this."

"To tell the truth, Frank, after all those years in the White House's shadow, he's feeling his oats a little. He's going to drag us around the old bridle path getting past mistakes straightened out, and pushing through a martyr's agenda."

"And you're going to spur him on?"

Augustine angled his head back. He nodded.

"Incarcerate sick babies?"

"You know the science."

Shawbeck smirked. "You get five virologists to agree that it's possible that these infants—and the mothers—could be breeding grounds for ancient viruses. Well, thirty-seven virologists have gone on record saying it's bogus."

"Not as prominent, and not nearly as influential."

"Thorne and Mahy and Mondavi and Bishop, Mark."

"I have my instincts, Frank. Remember, this is my area, too."

Shawbeck dragged his chair forward. "What are we now, petty tyrants?"

Augustine's face went livid. "Thanks, Frank," he said.

"The public starts to turn against the mothers and the unborn children. What if the babies are *cute*? How long until they swing back, Mark? What will you do then?"

Augustine did not answer.

"I know why the president refuses to meet with me," Shawbeck said. "You tell him what he wants to hear. He's afraid, and the country's out of control, so he picks a solution and you back him up. It isn't science, it's politics."

"The president agrees with me."

"Whatever we call it—July twentieth, the Reichstag fire—the bombing doesn't give you carte blanche," Shawbeck said.

"We're going to survive," Augustine said. "I didn't deal us this hand."

"No," Shawbeck said. "But you've sure stopped the deck from being dealt out fairly."

Augustine stared straight ahead.

"They're calling it 'original sin,' you know that?"

"I hadn't heard that," Augustine said.

"Tune in the Christian Broadcasting Network. They're splitting constituencies all across America. Pat Robertson is telling his audience these monsters are God's final test before the arrival of the new Kingdom of Heaven. He says our DNA is trying to purge itself of all our accumulated sins, to . . . what was his phrase, Ted?"

The aide said, "Clean up our records before God calls Judgment Day."

"That was it."

"We still don't control the airwaves, Frank," Augustine said. "I can't be held responsible—"

"Half a dozen other televangelists say these unborn children are the devil's spawn," Shawbeck continued, building up steam. "Born with the mark of Satan, one-eyed and harelipped. Some are even saying they have cloven hooves."

Augustine shook his head sadly.

"They're your support group now," Shawbeck said, and waved his arm for the aide to step forward. He struggled to his feet, shoved the crutches into his armpits. "I'm tendering my resignation tomorrow morning. From the Taskforce and from the NIH. I'm burned out. I can't take any more of this ignorance—my own or anybody else's. Just thought you should be the first to know. Maybe you can consolidate *all* the power."

When Shawbeck was gone, Augustine stood behind his desk, hardly breathing. His knuckles were white and his hands shook. Slowly, he took control of his emotions, forcing himself to breathe deeply and evenly.

"It's all in the follow-through," he said to the empty room.

79

Seattle
DECEMBER

They moved the last of the boxes out of Mitch's old apartment in the snow. Kaye insisted on carrying a few small ones, but Mitch and Wendell had done all the heavy hauling in the early morning hours, packing everything into a big orange-and-white U-Haul rental truck.

Kaye climbed into the truck beside Mitch. Wendell drove.

"Good-bye, bachelor days," Kaye said.

Mitch smiled.

"There's a tree farm near the house," Wendell said. "We can pick up a Christmas tree on the way in. Should be terrifically cozy."

Their new home stood in a patch of low brush and woods near Ebey Slough and the town of Snohomish. Rustic green and white, with a single front-facing gable window and a large screened-in porch, the two-bedroom house lay at the end of a long country road surrounded by pines. They were renting from Wendell's parents, who had owned the house for thirty-four years.

They were keeping their change of address a secret.

As the men unloaded the truck, Kaye made sandwiches and slipped a six-pack of beer and a few fruit drinks into the freshly scrubbed refrigerator. Inside the bare and clean living room, standing in her socks on the oak floor, Kaye felt at peace.

Wendell carried a lamp into the living room and set it on the kitchen table. Kaye handed him a beer. He took a deep swallow gratefully, his throat bobbing. "Did they tell you?" he asked.

"Who? Tell us what?"

"My folks. I was born here. This was their first house." He waved his hands around the living room. "I used to carry a microscope outside in the garden."

"That's wonderful," Kaye said.

"This is where I became a scientist," Wendell said. "A sacred place. May it bless you both!"

Mitch lugged in a chair and a magazine rack. He accepted a Full Sail ale and toasted them, clinking his glass against Kaye's Snapple.

"Here's to becoming moles," he said. "To going underground."

Maria Konig and half a dozen other friends came four hours later and helped arrange furniture. They were almost done when Eileen Ripper knocked on the door. She carried a lumpy canvas bag. Mitch introduced her, then saw two others waiting on the outside porch.

"I brought some friends," Eileen said. "Thought we'd celebrate with news of our own."

Sue Champion and a tall older man with long black hair and a well-disciplined barrel of a belly stepped forward, more than a little ill at ease. The tall man's eyes glinted white like a wolf's.

Eileen shook hands with Maria and Wendell. "Mitch, you've met Sue. This is her husband, Jack. And this is for the wood stove," she said to Kaye, dropping the bag by the fireplace. "Scrap maple and cherry. Smells wonderful. What a beautiful house!"

Sue nodded to Mitch and smiled at Kaye. "We've never met," Sue said. Kaye opened and closed her mouth like a fish, at a loss for words, until they both laughed nervously.

They had brought baked ham and steelhead for dinner.

Jack and Mitch circled like wary boys sizing up each other. Sue seemed unconcerned, but Mitch did not know what to say. A little tipsy, he apologized for not having any candles and decided the occasion called for Coleman lanterns.

Wendell switched off all the lights. The living room became a camp tent with long shadows and they ate in the bright center amid the stacked boxes. Sue and Jack conferred for a moment in a corner.

"Sue tells me she likes you both," Jack said when they returned. "But I'm the suspicious type, and I say you're all crazy."

"I won't disagree," Mitch said, lifting his beer.

"Sue told me about what you did on the Columbia."

"That was a long time ago," Mitch said.

"Be good, now," Sue warned her husband.

"I just want to know why you did it," Jack said. "He might have been one of my ancestors."

"I wanted to know whether he *was* one of your ancestors," Mitch said.

"Was he?"

"I think so, yes."

Jack squinted at the Coleman's bright hissing light. "The ones you found in the cave in the mountains. They were ancestors to all of us?"

"In a manner of speaking."

Jack shook his head quizzically. "Sue tells me the ancestors can be brought back to their people, whoever their people might be, if we learn their real names. Ghosts can be dangerous. I'm not so sure this is the way to keep them happy."

"Sue and I have drummed up another agreement," Eileen said. "We'll get it right eventually. I'm going to be a special consultant to the tribes. Whenever anyone finds old bones, I'll be called in to take a look at them. We'll do quick measurements and take a small sample, and then return them to the tribes. Jack and his friends have put together what they call a Wisdom Rite."

"Their names lie in their bones," Jack said. "We tell them we'll name our children after them."

"That's grand," Mitch said. "I'm pleased. Flabbergasted, but pleased."

"Everybody thinks Indians are ignorant," Jack said. "We just care about some different things."

Mitch leaned across the lantern and held out his hand to Jack. Jack looked up at the ceiling, his teeth working audibly. "This is too new," he said. But he took Mitch's extended hand and shook it so firmly they almost knocked the lantern over. For a moment, Kaye thought it might turn into an arm-wrestling contest.

"But I'm telling you," Jack said when they were done. "You should behave yourself, Mitch Rafelson."

"I'm out of the bone business for good," Mitch said.

"Mitch dreams about the people he finds," Eileen said.

"Really?" Jack was impressed by this. "Do they talk to you?"

"I become them," Mitch said.

"Oh," Jack said.

Kaye was fascinated by them all, but in particular by Sue. The woman's features were more than strong—they were almost masculine—but Kaye thought she had never met anyone more beautiful. Eileen's relationship with Mitch was so easy and intuitive that Kaye wondered if they might have been lovers once.

"Everybody's scared," Sue said. "We have so many SHEVA pregnancies in Kumash. That's one of the reasons why we're working with Eileen. The council decided that our ancestors can tell us how to survive these times. You're carrying Mitch's baby?" she asked Kaye.

"I am," Kaye said.

"Has the little helper come and gone?"

Kaye nodded.

"Me, too," Sue said. "We buried her with a special name and our gratitude and love."

"She was Tiny Swift," Jack said quietly.

"Congratulations," Mitch said, just as softly.

"Yes, that is right," Jack said, pleased. "No sadness. Her work is done."

"The government can't come and take names on the council lands," Sue said. "We won't let them. If the government becomes too scary, you come stay with us. We've fought them off before."

"This is so wonderful," Eileen said, beaming.

But Jack looked over his shoulder into the shadows. His eyes narrowed, he swallowed hard, and his face became deeply lined. "It's so hard to know what to do or what to believe," he said. "I wish the ghosts would speak more clearly."

"Will you help us with your knowledge, Kaye?" Sue asked.

"I'll try," Kaye said.

Then, to Mitch, hesitantly, Sue said, "I have dreams, too. I dream about the new children."

"Tell us about your dreams," Kaye said.

"Maybe they're personal, honey," Mitch warned her.

Sue put her hand on Mitch's arm. "I'm glad you understand. They *are* personal, and sometimes they're frightening, too."

Wendell came down from the attic on a ladder with a cardboard box in one arm. "My folks said they were still here, and they are. Ornaments—God, what memories! Who wants to put the tree up and decorate it?"

80

Building 52, The National Institutes of Health, Bethesda
JANUARY

Here are your meetings for the next two days." Florence Leighton gave Augustine a small sheet of paper he could fit in his shirt pocket for instant reference, as he liked. The list was growing; this afternoon he would be seeing the governor of Nebraska, and if there was time, he would meet with a group of financial columnists.

And he was looking forward to dinner at seven with a lovely woman who cared not a damn for his prominence in the news and his reputation as a tireless workaholic. Mark Augustine squared his shoulders and ran his finger down the list before he folded it, which was his way of telling Mrs. Leighton the list was approved and final.

"And here's an odd one," she added. "He has no appointment but says he's sure you'll want to see him." She dropped a business card onto his desk and gave him an arch look. "A pixie."

Augustine stared down at the name and felt a small twinge of curiosity.

"You know him?" she asked.

"He's a reporter," Augustine said. "A science writer with his finger in a number of steaming pies."

"Fruit or cow?" Mrs. Leighton asked.

Augustine smiled. "All right. I'll call his bluff. Tell him he has five minutes."

"Bring in your coffee?"

"He'll want tea."

Augustine arranged his desk and put two books into a drawer. He did not want anyone snooping on what he was currently reading. One was a thin monograph, *Movable Elements as Sources of Genomic Novelty in Grasses*. The second was a popular novel by Robin Cook, just published, about the outbreak of a major and unexplained disease by a new kind of organism, possibly from space. Augustine generally enjoyed outbreak novels, though he had stayed away from them for the past year. Reading this one was a sign of his new confidence.

He stood and smiled as Oliver Merton entered. "Good to see you again, Mr. Merton."

"Thank you for seeing me, Dr. Augustine," Merton said. "I've been through quite the shakedown outside. They even took my notepad."

Augustine made an apologetic face. "There's very little time. I'm sure you have something interesting to say."

"Right." Merton glanced up as Mrs. Leighton entered with a tray and two cups.

"Tea, Mr. Merton?" she asked.

Merton smiled sheepishly. "Coffee, actually. I've been in Seattle the last few weeks and I'm rather off tea."

Mrs. Leighton stuck her tongue out at Augustine and went back for a cup of coffee.

"She's bold," Merton observed.

"We've worked together through some tough times," Augustine said. "Pretty dark times, too."

"Of course," Merton said. "First, congratulations on getting the University of Washington conference on SHEVA postponed."

Augustine looked puzzled.

"Something about NIH grants being withdrawn if the conference proceeded, is all I've managed to winkle out of a few sources at the university."

"It's news to me," Augustine said.

"Instead, we're going to hold it at a little motel off campus.

And maybe have it catered by a famous French restaurant with a sympathetic chef. Sweeten the lemon juice. If we're going to be complete and unaffiliated rogues, we'll enjoy ourselves."

"You sound less than objective, but I wish you luck," Augustine said.

Merton's expression shifted to a challenging grin. "I've just heard this morning from Friedrich Brock that there's been a wholesale rearrangement of the staff overseeing the Neandertal mummies at the University of Innsbruck. An internal scientific review concluded that key facts were being ignored and that gross scientific errors had been made. *Herr Professor* Brock has been summoned to Innsbruck. He's on his way there now."

"I don't know why I should be interested," Augustine said. "We have about two minutes."

Mrs. Leighton returned with a cup of coffee. Merton took a strong swallow. "Thank you. They're going to treat the three mummies as a family group, related genetically. And that means they're going to acknowledge the first solid evidence of human speciation. SHEVA has been found in these specimens."

"Very good," Augustine said.

Merton pressed his palms together. Florence watched him with a kind of idle curiosity.

"We've arrived at the verge of the long fast slope to the truth, Dr. Augustine," Merton said. "I was curious how you would take the news."

Augustine sucked in a small breath through his nose. "Whatever happened tens of thousands of years ago doesn't affect our judgment about what is happening now. Not a single Herod's fetus has gone to full term. In fact, yesterday, we were told by scientists working with the National Institute of Allergy and Infectious Diseases that not only are these second-stage fetuses subject to first trimester rejection at a catastrophic rate, but that they are especially vulnerable to virtually every known herpes virus, including Epstein-Barr. Mononucleosis.

Ninety-five percent of everyone on Earth has Epstein-Barr, Mr. Merton."

"Nothing will change your views, Doctor?" Merton asked.

"My one good ear still rings from the bomb that killed our president. I've rolled with every punch. Nothing can shake me but facts, present-day, relevant facts." Augustine came around the desk and sat on the corner. "I wish the Innsbruck people all the best, whoever does the investigating," he said. "There are enough mysteries in biology to last us until the end of time. The next time you're in Washington, drop by again, Mr. Merton. I'm sure Florence will remember—no tea, coffee."

Tray balanced on his lap, Dicken pushed his wheelchair through the Natcher Building cafeteria, saw Merton, and rolled himself to the end of the table. He set his tray down with one hand.

"Good train ride?" Dicken asked.

"Glorious," Merton said. "I thought you should know that Kaye Lang keeps a photo of you on her desktop."

"That's an odd sort of *message*, Oliver," Dicken said. "Why in hell should I care?"

"Because I believe you felt something more than scientific camaraderie for her," Merton said. "She sent you letters after the bombing. You never answered."

"If you're going to be bloody-minded, I'll eat elsewhere," Dicken said, and lifted the tray again.

Merton raised his hands. "Sorry. My slash and reveal instincts at work."

Dicken pushed the tray in and arranged his wheelchair. "I spend half my day waiting for myself to heal, worried that I'll never recover full use of my legs or my hand . . . Trying to have faith in my body. The other half of the day I'm in rehab, pushing until it hurts. I don't have time to moon over lost opportunities. Do you?"

"My girl in Leeds dumped me last week. I'm never at home. Besides, I turned positive. Scared her."

"Sorry," Dicken said.

"I just stopped by Augustine's inner sanctum. He seems cocky enough."

"The polls support him. Public health crisis blossoms into international policy. Fanatics push us into repressive legislation. It's martial law in all but name, and the Emergency Action Taskforce sets down the medical decrees—which means they rule nearly everything. Now that Shawbeck has stepped down, Augustine is number two in the country."

"Frightening," Merton said.

"Show me something now that isn't," Dicken said.

Merton conceded that. "I'm convinced that Augustine is pulling strings to get our Northwestern conference on SHEVA shut down."

"He's a consummate bureaucrat—which means, he'll protect his position using all the tools available."

"What about the truth?" Merton said, his brow wrinkling. "I'm just not used to seeing government manage scientific debate."

"You're not usually so naïve, Oliver. The British have done it for years."

"Yes, yes, I've dealt with enough cabinet ministers to know the *drill*. But where do you stand? You helped bring Kaye's coalition together—why doesn't Augustine just fire you and move on?"

"Because I saw the light," Dicken said glumly. "Or rather, the dark. Dead babies. I lost hope. Even before that, Augustine worked me around pretty well—kept me on as an apparent balance, let me be involved in policy meetings. But he never gave me enough rope to make a noose. Now . . . I can't travel, can't do the research we need to do. I'm ineffective."

"Neutered?" Merton ventured.

"Castrated," Dicken said.

"Don't you at least whisper in his ear, 'It's science, O mighty Caesar, you could be wrong'?"

Dicken shook his head. "The chromosome numbers are pretty damning. Fifty-two chromosomes, as opposed to forty-six. Trisomal, tetrasomal . . . They could all end up with something like Down syndrome or worse. If Epstein-Barr doesn't get them."

Merton had saved the best for last. He told Dicken about the changes in Innsbruck. Dicken listened intently, with a squint in his blind eye, then turned his good eye to stare off at the wall of windows and the bright spring sunshine beyond.

He was remembering the conversation with Kaye before she had ever met Rafelson.

"So Rafelson is going to Austria?" Dicken poked with a fork at the steamed sole and wild rice on his plate.

"If they invite him. He might still be too controversial."

"I await the report," Dicken said. "But I'm not going to hold my breath."

"You think Kaye is making a terrible leap," Merton suggested.

"I don't know why I even bought this food," Dicken said, laying down the fork. "I'm not hungry."

81

Seattle
FEBRUARY

The baby seems to be doing fine," Dr. Galbreath said. "Second trimester development is normal. We've done our analysis, and it's what we expect for a SHEVA second-stage fetus."

This seemed a little cold to Kaye. "Boy or girl?" Kaye asked.

"Fifty-two XX," Galbreath said. She opened a brown cardboard folder and gave Kaye a copy of the sample report. "Chromosomally abnormal female."

Kaye stared at the paper, her heart thumping. She had not told Mitch, but she had hoped for a girl, to at least remove some of the distance, the number of differences, she might have to contend with. "Is there any duplication, or are they new chromosomes?" Kaye asked.

"If we had the expertise to decide that, we'd be famous," Galbreath said. Then, less stiffly, "We don't know. Cursory glance tells us they may not be duplicated."

"No extra chromosome 21?" Kaye asked quietly, staring at the sheet of paper with its rows of numbers and brief string of explanatory words.

"I don't think the fetus has Down syndrome," Galbreath said. "But you know how I feel about this now."

"Because of the extra chromosomes."

Galbreath nodded.

"We have no way of knowing how many chromosomes Neandertals had," Kaye said.

"If they're like us, forty-six," Galbreath said.

"But they weren't like us. It's still a mystery." Kaye's words sounded fragile even to her. Kaye stood up, one hand on her stomach. "As far as you can tell, it's healthy."

Galbreath nodded. "I have to ask, though, what do I know? Next to nothing. You test positive for herpes simplex type one, but negative for mono—that is, Epstein-Barr. You never had chicken pox. For God's sake, Kaye, stay away from anyone with chicken pox."

"I'll be careful," Kaye said.

"I don't know what more I can tell you."

"Wish me luck."

"I wish you all the luck on Earth, *and* in the heavens. It doesn't make me feel any better as a doctor."

"It's still our decision, Felicity."

"Of course." Galbreath flipped through more papers until she came to the back of the folder. "If *this* were my decision, you'd never see what I have to show you. We've lost our appeal. We have to get all our SHEVA patients to register. If you don't agree, we have to register for you."

"Then do so," Kaye said evenly. She played with a fold on her slacks.

"I know that you've moved," Galbreath said. "If I hand in an incorrect registration, Marine Pacific could get in trouble, and I could be called up before a review board and have my license revoked." She gave Kaye a sad but level look. "I need your new address."

Kaye stared at the form, then shook her head.

"I'm begging you, Kaye. I want to remain your doctor until this is over."

"Over?"

"Until the delivery."

Kaye shook her head again, with a stubbornly wild look, like a hunted rabbit.

Galbreath stared down at the end of the examination table, tears in her eyes. "I don't have any choice. None of us has any choice."

"I don't want anyone coming to take my baby," Kaye said, her breath short, hands cold.

"If you don't cooperate, I can't be your doctor," Galbreath said. She turned abruptly and walked from the room. The nurse peered in a few moments later, saw Kaye standing there, stunned, and asked if she needed some help.

"I don't have a doctor," Kaye said.

The nurse stood aside as Galbreath entered again. "Please, give me your new address. I know Marine Pacific is fighting any local attempts by the Taskforce to contact its patients. I'll put extra warnings on this file. We're on your side, Kaye, believe me."

Kaye wanted desperately to speak to Mitch, but he was in the University district, trying to finalize hotel arrangements for the conference. She did not want to break in on that.

Galbreath handed Kaye a pen. She filled out the form, slowly. Galbreath took it back. "They would have found out one way or another," she said tightly.

Kaye carried the report out of the hospital and walked to the brown Toyota Camry they had purchased two months ago. She sat in the car for ten minutes, numb, bloodless fingers clutching the wheel, and then turned the key in the ignition.

She was rolling down her window for air when she heard Galbreath calling after her. She gave half a thought to simply pulling out of the parking space and driving on, but she reapplied the emergency brake and looked left. Galbreath was running across the parking lot. She put her hand on the door and peered in at Kaye.

"You wrote down the wrong address, didn't you?" she asked, huffing, her face red.

Kaye simply looked blank.

Galbreath closed her eyes, caught her breath. "There's nothing wrong with your baby," she said. "I don't see anything wrong with it. I don't understand anything. Why aren't you rejecting her as foreign tissue—she's completely different from you! You might as well be carrying a gorilla. But you tolerate her, nurture her. All the mothers do. Why doesn't the Taskforce study *that*?"

"It's a puzzle," Kaye admitted.

"Please forgive me, Kaye."

"You're forgiven," Kaye said with no real conviction.

"No, I mean it. I don't care if they take away my license— they could be wrong about this whole thing! I want to be your doctor."

Kaye hid her face in her hands, exhausted by the tension. Her neck felt like steel springs. She lifted her head and put her hand on Galbreath's. "If it's possible, I'd like that," she said.

"Wherever you go, whatever you do, promise me—let me be there to deliver?" Galbreath pleaded. "I want to learn everything I can about SHEVA pregnancies, to be prepared, and I want to deliver your daughter."

Kaye parked across the street from the old, square University Plaza Hotel, across the freeway from the University of Washington. She found her husband on the lower level, waiting for a formal bid from the hotel manager, who had retired to his office.

She told him what had happened at Marine Pacific. Mitch banged the door of the meeting room with his fist, furious. "I should never have left you—not for a minute!"

"You know that's not practical," Kaye said. She put a hand on his shoulder. "I handled it pretty well, I think."

"I can't believe Galbreath would do that to you."

"I know she didn't want to."

Mitch circled, kicked at a metal folding chair, waved his hands helplessly.

"She wants to help us," Kaye said.

"How can we trust her now?"

"There's no need to be paranoid."

Mitch stopped short. "There's a big old train rolling down the tracks. We're in its headlights. I *know that*, Kaye. It's not just the government. Every pregnant woman on Earth is suspect. Augustine—that absolute *bastard*—he's making sure that you're all pariahs! I could *kill* him!"

Kaye took hold of his arms and tugged gently, then hugged him. He was angry enough to try to shrug her off and continue stalking around the room. She held on tighter. "Please, enough, Mitch."

"And now you're out here—exposed to anybody who might walk by!" he said, arms quivering.

"I refuse to become a hothouse flower," Kaye said defensively.

He gave up and dropped his shoulders. "What can we do? When are they going to send police vans with *thugs* in them to round us up?"

"I don't know," Kaye said. "Something's got to give. I believe in this country, Mitch. People won't put up with this."

Mitch sat in a folding chair at the end of an aisle. The room was brightly lit, with fifty empty chairs arranged in five rows, a linen-covered table and coffee service at the back. "Wendell and Maria say the pressure is just incredible. They've filed protests, but no one in the department will admit to anything. Funding gets cut, offices reassigned, labs harassed by inspectors. I'm losing all my faith, Kaye. I saw it happen to me after . . ."

"I know," Kaye said.

"And now the State Department won't let Brock return from Innsbruck."

"When did you hear that?"

"Merton called from Bethesda this afternoon. Augustine is trying to shut this down completely. It'll be just you and me—and you'll have to go into hiding!"

Kaye sat beside him. She had heard nothing from any of her former colleagues back East. Nothing from Judith. Perversely, she wanted to talk with Marge Cross. She wanted to reach out for all the support left in the world.

She missed her mother and father terribly.

Kaye leaned over and put her head on Mitch's shoulder. He rubbed her scalp gently with his big hands.

They had not even discussed the real news of the morning. Important things got lost so quickly in the fray. "I know something you don't know," Kaye said.

"What's that?"

"We're going to have a daughter."

Mitch stopped breathing for a moment and his face wrinkled up. "My God," he said.

"It was one or the other," Kaye said, grinning at his reaction.

"It's what you wanted."

"Did I say that?"

"Christmas Eve. You said you wanted to buy dolls for her."

"Do you mind?"

"Of course not. I just get a little shock every time we take a new step, that's all."

"Dr. Galbreath says she's healthy. There's nothing wrong with her. She has the extra chromosomes . . . but we knew that."

Mitch put his hand on her stomach. "I can feel her moving," he said, and got on the floor in front of Kaye to lay his ear against her. "She's going to be so *beautiful*."

The hotel manager walked into the meeting room with a clutch of papers and looked down on them in surprise. In his fifties, with a full head of curly brown hair and a plump, nondescript face, he could have been anyone's mediocre uncle. Mitch got up and brushed off his pants.

"My wife," Mitch said, embarrassed.

"Of course," the manager said. He narrowed his pale blue eyes and took Mitch aside. "She's pregnant, isn't she? You didn't tell me about that. There's no mention in here . . ." He shuffled through the papers, looked up at Mitch accusingly. "None at all. We have to be so careful now about public gatherings and exposures."

Mitch leaned against the Buick, chin in hand, rubbing. His fingers made a small rasping sound though he had shaved that morning. He pulled his hand back. Kaye stood before him.

"I'm going to drive you back to the house," he said.

"What about the Buick?"

He shook his head. "I'll pick it up later. Wendell can give me a ride."

"Where do we go from here?" Kaye asked. "We could try another hotel. Or rent a lodge hall."

Mitch made a disgusted face. "The bastard was *looking* for an excuse. He knew your name. He called somebody. He checked up, like a good little Nazi." He flung his hands in the air. "Long live America the free!"

"If Brock can't enter the country again—"

"We'll hold the conference on the Internet," Mitch said. "We'll figure out something. But it's you I'm concerned about right now. Something's bound to happen."

"What?"

"Don't you feel it?" He rubbed his forehead. "The look in that manager's eyes, that cowardly bastard. He's like a frightened goat. He doesn't know jack shit about biology. He lives his life in small safe moves and he doesn't buck the system. Nearly everybody is like him. They get pushed around and they run in the direction they're pushed."

"That sounds so cynical," Kaye said.

"It's political reality. I've been so stupid up until now. Letting you travel alone. You could be picked up, exposed—"

"I don't want to be kept in a *cave*, Mitch."

Mitch winced.

Kaye put her hand on his shoulder. "I'm sorry. You know what I mean."

"Everything's in place. Kaye. You saw it in Georgia. I saw it in the Alps. We've become *strangers*. People hate us."

"They hate me," Kaye said, her face going pale. "Because I'm pregnant."

"They hate me, too."

"But they're not asking you to register like you were a Jew in Germany."

"Not yet," Mitch said. "Let's go." He wrapped his arm around her and escorted her to the Toyota. Kaye found it awkward to match his long stride. "I think we may have a day or two, maybe three. Then . . . somebody's going to do something. You're a thorn in their sides. A double thorn."

"Why double?"

"Celebrities have power," Mitch said. "People know who you are, and you know the truth."

Kaye got into the passenger side and rolled down the window. The inside of the car was warm. Mitch closed the door for her. "Do I?"

"You're damn right you do. Sue made you an offer. Let's look into it. I'll tell Wendell where we're going. Nobody else."

"I like the house," Kaye said.

"We'll find another," Mitch said.

82

Building 52, The National Institutes of Health, Bethesda

Mark Augustine seemed almost feverish in his triumph. He laid the pictures out for Dicken and slipped the videotape into the office player. Dicken picked up the first picture, held it close, squinted. The usual medical photo colors, strange orange and olive flesh and bright pink lesions, out-of-focus facial features. A man, in his forties perhaps, alive but far from happy. Dicken picked up the next picture, a closeup of the man's right arm, marked with roseate blotches, a yellow plastic ruler laid alongside to indicate size. The largest blotch spread over a diameter of seven centimeters, with an angry sore at the center, crusted with thick yellow fluid. Dicken counted seven blotches on the right arm alone.

"I showed these to the staff this morning," Augustine said, holding out the remote and starting the tape. Dicken went on to the next few pictures. The man's body was covered with more large roseate lesions, some forming huge blisters, proud, assertive, and no doubt intensely painful. "We have samples in for analysis now, but the field team did a quick serology check for SHEVA, just to confirm. The man's wife is in her second trimester with a second-stage SHEVA fetus and still shows SHEVA type 3-s. The man is now clear of SHEVA, so we can rule out the lesions are caused by SHEVA, which we wouldn't expect at any rate."

"Where are they?" Dicken asked.

"San Diego, California. Illegal immigrant couple. Our Commissioned Corps people did the investigation and sent this material to us. It's about three days old. Local press is being kept out for the time being."

Augustine's smile came and went like small flashes of lightning. He turned in front of his desk, fast-forwarding through scenes of the hospital, the ward, the room's temporary containment features—plastic curtains taped to walls and door, separate air. He lifted his finger from the remote and returned to play mode.

Doctor Ed Sanger, Mercy Hospital's Commissioned Corps Taskforce member, in his fifties, with lank and sandy hair, identified himself and droned self-consciously through the diagnosis. Dicken listened with a rising sense of dread. *How wrong I can be. Augustine is right. All his guesses were dead on.*

Augustine shut off the tape. "It's a single-stranded RNA virus, huge and primitive, probably around 160,000 nucleotides. Like nothing we've ever seen before. We're working to match its genome with known HERV coding regions. It's incredibly fast, it's ill-adapted, and it's deadly."

"He looks in bad shape," Dicken said.

"The man died last night." Augustine turned off the tape. "The woman seems to be asymptomatic, but she's having the usual trouble with her pregnancy." Augustine folded his arms and sat on the edge of the desk. "Lateral transmission of an unknown retrovirus, almost certainly excited and equipped by SHEVA. The woman infected the man. This is the one, Christopher. This is the one we need. Are you up to helping us go public?"

"Go public, how?"

"We're going to quarantine and/or sequester women with second-stage pregnancies. For that kind of violation of civil liberties, we have to lay some heavy foundations. The president is prepared to go forward, but his team says we need personalities to put the message across."

"I'm no personality. Get Bill Cosby."

"Cosby is signing off on this one. But you . . . You're practically a poster child for the brave health worker recovering from wounds inflicted by fanatics desperate to stop us." Augustine's smile flickered again.

Dicken stared down at his lap. "You're certain about this?"

"As certain as we're going to be, until we do all the science. That could take three or four months. Considering the consequences, we can't afford to wait."

Dicken looked up at Augustine, then moved his gaze to the patchy clouds and trees in the sky through the office window. Augustine had hung a small square of stained glass there, a fleur-de-lis in red and green.

"All the mothers will have to have stickers in their houses," Dicken said. "*Q*, or *S*, maybe. Every pregnant woman will have to prove she isn't carrying a SHEVA baby. That could cost billions."

"Nobody's concerned about funding," Augustine said. "We're facing the biggest health threat of all time. It's the biological equivalent of Pandora's box, Christopher. Every retroviral illness we ever conquered but couldn't get rid of. Hundreds, maybe thousands of diseases we have no modern defenses against. There's no question of our getting enough funding on this one."

"The only problem is, I don't believe it," Dicken said softly.

Augustine stared at him, strong lines forming beside his lips, brows drawing inward.

"I've chased viruses most of my adult life," Dicken said. "I've seen what they can do. I know about retroviruses, I know about HERV. I know about SHEVA. HERV were probably never eliminated from the genome because they provided protection against other, newer retroviruses. They're our own little library of protection. And . . . our genome uses them to generate novelty."

"We don't know that," Augustine said, his voice grating with tension.

"I want to wait for the science before we lock up every mother in America," Dicken said.

As Augustine's skin darkened with irritation, then anger,

the patches of shrapnel scars became vivid. "The danger is just too great," he said. "I thought you'd appreciate a chance to get back into the picture."

"No," Dicken said. "I can't."

"Still holding on to fantasies about a new species?" Augustine asked grimly.

"I'm way beyond that," Dicken said. The weary gravel in his voice startled him. He sounded like an old man.

Augustine walked around his desk and opened a file drawer, pulling out an envelope. Everything in his posture, the small, self-conscious strut in his walk, the cementlike set of his features, evoked a kind of dread in Dicken. This was a Mark Augustine he had not seen before: a man about to administer the coup de grâce. "This came for you while you were in the hospital. It was in your mail slot. It was addressed to you in your official capacity, so I took the liberty of having it opened."

He handed the thin papers to Dicken.

"They're from Georgia. Leonid Sugashvili was sending you pictures of what he called possible *Homo superior* specimens, wasn't he?"

"I hadn't checked him out," Dicken said, "so I didn't mention it to you."

"Wisely. He's been arrested for fraud in Tbilisi. For bilking families of those missing in the troubles. He promised grieving relatives he could show them where their loved ones were buried. Looks like he was after the CDC, too."

"That doesn't surprise me, and it doesn't change my mind, Mark. I'm just burned out. It's hard enough healing my own body. I'm not the man for the job."

"All right," Augustine said. "I'll put you on long-term disability leave. We need your office at the CDC. We're moving in sixty special epidemiologists next week to begin phase two. With our space shortage, we'll probably put three in your office to start."

They watched each other in silence.

"Thanks for carrying me this long," Dicken said without a hint of irony.

"No problem," Augustine said with equal flatness.

Snohomish County

Mitch piled the last of the boxes near the front door. Wendell Packer was coming with a panel truck in the morning. He looked around the house and set his lips in a wry, crooked line. They had been here just over two months. One Christmas.

Kaye carried the phone in from the bedroom, line dangling. "Turned off," she said. "They're prompt when you're dismantling a home. So—how long have we been here?"

Mitch sat in the worn lounge chair he had had since his student days. "We'll do okay," he said. His hands felt funny. They seemed larger, somehow. "God, I'm tired."

Kaye sat on the arm of the chair and reached around to massage his shoulders. He leaned his head against her arm, rubbed his bristly cheek against her peach cardigan.

"Damn," she said. "I forgot to charge the batteries in the cell phone." She kissed the top of his head and returned to the bedroom. Mitch noticed she walked straight enough, even at seven months. Her stomach was prominent but not huge. He wished he had had more experience with pregnancy. To have this be his first time—

"Both batteries are dead," Kaye called from the bedroom. "They'll take an hour or so."

Mitch stared at various objects in the room, blinking. Then

he held out his hands. They seemed swollen, stuck on the ends of Popeye-like forearms. His feet felt large, though he did not look at them. This was extremely discomfiting. He wanted to go to sleep but it was only four in the afternoon. They had just eaten a dinner of canned soup. It was still bright outside.

He had hoped to make love to Kaye in the house for the last time. Kaye returned and pulled up the footstool.

"You sit here," Mitch said, starting to get out of the chair. "More comfortable."

"I'm fine. I want to sit up straight."

Mitch paused half out of the chair, woozy.

"Something wrong?"

He saw the first jag of light. He closed his eyes and fell back into the chair. "It's coming," he said.

"What?"

He pointed at his temple, and said, softly, "Bang." He had had bodily distortions occur before and during his headaches when he had been a boy. He remembered hating them, and now he was almost beside himself with resentment and foreboding.

"I've got some Naproze in my purse," Kaye said. He listened to her walking around the room. With his eyes closed, he saw ghostly lightning and his feet felt as big as an elephant's. The pain was like a round of cannon fire advancing across a wide valley.

Kaye pressed two tablets into his hand and a tumbler full of water. He swallowed the tablets, drank the water, not at all confident they would do any good. Perhaps if he had had any decent warning, taken them earlier in the day . . .

"Let's get you into bed," Kaye said.

"What?" Mitch asked.

"Bed."

"I want to go away," he said.

"Right. Sleep."

That was the only way he might even hope to escape. Even

then, he might have horrid and painful dreams. He remembered those, as well; dreams of being crushed beneath mountains.

He lay down in the cool of the bare bedroom, on the linens they had left here for their last night, beneath a comforter. He pulled the comforter up over his head, leaving a small space to breathe through.

He barely heard Kaye tell him she loved him.

Kaye pulled back the comforter. Mitch's forehead felt clammy, cold as ice. She was concerned, guilty that she could not share his pain; then, could not help rationalizing that Mitch would not share the pain of bringing their baby into the world.

She sat on the bed beside him. His breath came in shallow pants. She reflexively felt her tummy beneath the cardigan, lifted up the sweater, rubbed her skin, stretched so smooth it was almost shiny. The baby had been subdued for several hours after a bout of kicking this afternoon.

Kaye had never felt her kidneys being pummeled from the inside; she didn't relish the experience. Nor did she enjoy going to the bathroom every hour on the hour, or the continuous rounds of heartburn. At night, lying in bed, she could even feel the rhythmic motion of her intestines.

All of it made her apprehensive; it also made her feel intensely alive and aware.

But she was pulling away from thinking about Mitch, about his pain. She settled down beside him and he suddenly rolled over, tugging the comforter and turning away.

"Mitch?"

He didn't answer. She lay on her back for a moment, but that was uncomfortable, so she shifted on her side, facing away from Mitch, and backed into him slowly, gently, for his warmth. He did not move or protest. She stared at the gray-lit and empty wall. She thought she might get up and try to work on the book for a few minutes, but the laptop computer and her notebooks were all packed away. The impulse passed.

The silence in the house bothered her. She listened for any

sound, heard only Mitch's breathing and her own. The air was so still outside. She couldn't even hear the traffic on Highway 2, less than a mile away. No birds. No settling beams or creaking floors.

After half an hour, she made sure that Mitch was asleep, then sat up, pushed herself to the edge of the bed, stood, and went into the kitchen to heat a kettle of water for tea. She stared out the kitchen window at the last of the twilight. The water in the kettle slowly came to a whistling boil and she poured it over a bag of chamomile in one of the two mugs they had left out on the white tile counter. As the tea steeped, she felt the smooth tiles with her finger, wondering what their next home would be like, probably within hailing distance of the Five Tribes' huge Wild Eagle casino. Sue had still been making the arrangements this morning and promised only that eventually there would be a house, a nice one. "Maybe a trailer at first," she had added over the phone.

Kaye felt a small throb of helpless anger. She wanted to stay here. She felt comfortable here. "This is so strange," she said to the window. As if in response, the baby kicked once.

She picked up the mug and dropped the tea bag in the sink. As she took her first sip, she heard the sound of engines and tires on the gravel driveway.

She walked into the living room and stood, watching headlights flash outside. They were expecting no one; Wendell was in Seattle, the truck would not be available at the rental agency until tomorrow morning, Merton was in Beresford, New York; she had heard that Sue and Jack were in eastern Washington.

She thought of waking Mitch, wondered if she could wake him in his condition.

"Maybe it's Maria or somebody else."

But she would not approach the door. The living room lights were off, the porch lights off, the kitchen lights on. A flash played through the front window against the south wall. She had left the drapes open; they had no near neighbors, nobody to peer in.

A sharp rap rattled the front door. Kaye looked at her watch, pushed the little button to turn on its blue-green light. Seven o'clock.

The rap sounded again, followed by an unfamiliar voice. "Kaye Lang? Mitchell Rafelson? County Sheriff's Department, Judicial Services."

Kaye's breath caught. What could this be? Surely nothing involving her! She walked to the front door and twirled the single dead bolt, opened the door. Four men stood on the porch, two in uniform, two in civilian clothes, slacks and light jackets. The flashlight beam crossed her face as she switched on the porch light. She blinked at them. "I'm Kaye Lang."

One of the civilians, a tall, stout man with close-cut brown hair on a long oval face stepped forward. "Miz Lang, we have—"

"Mrs. Lang," Kaye said.

"All right. My name is Wallace Jurgenson. This is Dr. Kevin Clark of the Snohomish Health District. I'm a Commissioned Corps public health service representative for the Emergency Action Taskforce in the state of Washington. Mrs. Lang, we have a federal Emergency Action Taskforce order verified by the Olympia Taskforce office, state of Washington. We're contacting women known to be possibly infectious, bearing a second-stage—"

"That's bull," Kaye said.

The man stopped, faintly exasperated, then resumed. "A second-stage SHEVA fetus. Do you know what this means, ma'am?"

"Yes," Kaye said, "but it's all wrong."

"I'm here to inform you that in the judgment of the federal Emergency Action Taskforce Office and the Centers for Disease Control and Prevention—"

"I used to work for them," Kaye said.

"I know that," Jurgenson said. Clark smiled and nodded, as if pleased to meet her. The deputies stood back beyond the porch, arms folded. "Miz Lang, it's been determined that you may present a public health threat. You and other women in this area are being contacted and informed of their choices."

"I choose to stay where I am," Kaye said, her voice shaky. She stared from face to face. Pleasant-looking men, clean shaven, earnest, almost as nervous as she was, and not happy.

"We have orders to take you and your husband to a county Emergency Action shelter in Lynnwood, where you will be sequestered and provided medical care until it can be determined whether or not you present a public health risk—"

"No," Kaye said, feeling her face heat up. "This is absolute bullshit. My husband is ill. He can't travel."

Jurgenson's face was stern. He was preparing to do something he did not like. He glanced at Clark. The deputies stepped forward, and one nearly stumbled on a rock. After swallowing, Jurgenson continued. "Dr. Clark can give your husband a brief examination before we move you." His breath showed on the night air.

"He has a *headache*," Kaye said. "A migraine. He gets them sometimes." On the gravel drive waited a sheriff's department car and a small ambulance. Beyond the vehicles, the scrubby wide lawn of the house stretched to a fence. She could smell the damp green and the country soil on the cold night air.

"We have no choice, Miz Lang."

There was not much she could do. If Kaye resisted, they would simply come back with more men.

"I'll come. My husband shouldn't be moved."

"You may both be carriers, ma'am. We need to take both of you."

"I can examine your husband and see whether his condition might respond to medical treatment," Clark said.

Kaye hated the first sensation of tears coming. Frustration, helplessness, aloneness. She saw Clark and Jurgenson look over her shoulder, heard someone moving, whirled as if she might be taken by ambush.

It was Mitch. He walked with a distinct jerk, eyes half-closed, hands extended, like Frankenstein's monster. "Kaye, what is it?" he asked, his voice thick. Simply talking made his face wrinkle with pain.

Clark and Jurgenson moved back now, and the nearest deputy unlatched his holster. Kaye turned and glared at them. "It's a migraine! He has a *migraine*!"

"Who are they?" Mitch asked. He nearly fell over. Kaye went to him, helped him remain standing. "I can't see very well," he murmured.

Clark and Jurgenson conferred in whispers. "Please bring him out on the porch, Miz Lang," Jurgenson said, his voice strained. Kaye saw a gun in the deputy's hand.

"What is this?"

"They're from the Taskforce," Kaye said. "They want us to come with them."

"Why?"

"Something about being infectious."

"No," Mitch said, struggling in her grasp.

"That's what I told them. But Mitch, there isn't anything we can do."

"No!" Mitch shouted, waving one arm. "Come back when I can see you, when I can talk! Leave my wife alone, for God's sake."

"Please come out on the porch, ma'am," the deputy said. Kaye knew the situation was getting dangerous. Mitch was in no condition to be rational. She did not know what he might do to protect her. The men outside were afraid. These were awful times and awful things could happen and nobody would be punished; they might be shot and the house burned to the ground, as if they had plague.

"My wife is pregnant," Mitch said. "Please leave her alone." He tried to move toward the front door. Kaye stood beside him, guiding him.

The deputy kept his gun pointed toward the porch, but held it with both hands, arms straight. Jurgenson told him to put the gun away. He shook his head. "I don't want them doing something stupid," he said in a low voice.

"We're coming out," Kaye said. "Don't be idiots. We're not sick and we're not infectious."

Jurgenson told them to walk through the door and step down off the porch. "We have an ambulance. We'll take you both to where they can look after your husband."

Kaye helped Mitch outside and down the porch steps. He was sweating profusely and his hands were damp and cold. "I still can't see very well," he said into Kaye's ear. "Tell me what they're doing."

"They want to take us away." They stood in the yard now. Jurgenson motioned to Clark and he opened the back of the ambulance. Kaye saw there was a young woman behind the wheel of the ambulance. The driver stared owlishly through the rolled-up window. "Don't do anything silly," Kaye said to Mitch. "Just walk steadily. Did the pills help?"

Mitch shook his head. "It's bad. I feel so stupid . . . leaving you alone. Vulnerable." His words were thick and his eyes almost closed. He could not stand the glare of the headlights. The deputies turned on their flashlights and aimed them at Kaye and Mitch. Mitch hid his eyes with one hand and tried to turn away.

"Do not move!" the deputy with the gun ordered. "Keep your hands in the open!"

Kaye heard more engines. The second deputy turned. "Cars coming," he said. "Trucks. Lots of them."

She counted four pairs of headlights moving down the road to the house. Three pickup trucks and a car pulled into the yard, kicking up gravel, brakes squealing. The trucks carried men in the back—men with black hair and checkered shirts, leather jackets, windbreakers, men with ponytails, and then she saw Jack, Sue's husband.

Jack opened the driver's-side door of his truck and stepped down, frowning. He held up his hand and the men stayed in the backs of the pickups.

"Good evening," Jack said, his frown vanishing, his face suddenly neutral. "Hello, Kaye, Mitch. Your phones aren't working."

The deputies stared at Jurgenson and Clark for guidance. The gun remained pointed down at the gravel drive. Wendell Packer and Maria Konig got out of the car and approached Mitch and Kaye. "It's all right," Packer told the four men, now forming an open square, defensive. He held up his hands, showing they were empty. "We brought some friends to help them move. Okay?"

"Mitch has a migraine," Kaye called. Mitch tried to shrug her off, stand on his own, but his legs were too wobbly.

"Poor baby," Maria said, walking in a half circle around the deputies. "It's all right," she told them. "We're from the University of Washington."

"We're from the Five Tribes," Jack said. "These are our friends. We're helping them move." The men in the pickups kept their hands in the open but smiled like wolves, like bandits.

Clark tapped Jurgenson on the shoulder. "Let's not make any headlines," he said. Jurgenson agreed with a nod. Clark got into the ambulance and Jurgenson joined the deputies in the Caprice. Without another word, the two vehicles backed up, turned, and grumbled down the long gravel drive into the twilight.

Jack stepped forward with his hands in his jeans pockets and a big, energized smile. "That was fun," he said.

Wendell and Kaye helped Mitch squat on the ground. "I'll be fine," Mitch said, head in hands. "I couldn't do anything. Jesus, I couldn't do anything."

"It's all right," Maria said.

Kaye knelt beside him, touching her cheek to his forehead. "Let's get you inside." She and Maria helped him to his feet and half carried him toward the house.

"We heard from Oliver in New York," Wendell said. "Christopher Dicken called him and said something ugly was coming down fast. He said you weren't answering your phones."

"That was late this afternoon," Maria said.

"Maria called Sue," Wendell said. "Sue called Jack. Jack was visiting Seattle. Nobody had heard from you."

"I was out here taking a meeting at the Lummi casino," Jack said. He waved at the men in the trucks. "We were talking about new games and machines. They volunteered to come along. Good thing, I suppose. I think we should go to Kumash now."

"I'm ready," Mitch said. He walked up the steps on his own power, turned, and held out his hands, staring at them. "I can do this. I'll be fine."

"They can't touch you there," Jack said. He stared down the drive, his eyes glittering. "They're going to make Indians out of everybody. Goddamn bastards."

Kumash County, Eastern Washington
MAY

Mitch stood on the crest of a low chalky mound overlooking the Wild Eagle Casino and Resort. He tilted his hat back and squinted at the bright sun. At nine in the morning, the air was still and already hot. In normal times the casino, a gaudy button of red and gold and white in the bleached earth tones of southeastern Washington, employed four hundred people, three hundred from the Five Tribes.

The reservation was under quarantine for not cooperating with Mark Augustine. Three Kumash County Sheriff's Patrol pickups had been parked on the main road from the highway. They were providing backup for federal marshals enforcing an Emergency Action Taskforce health threat advisory that applied to the entire Five Tribes reservation.

There had been no business at the casino for over three weeks. The parking lot was almost empty and the lights on the signs had been turned off.

Mitch scuffed the hard-packed dirt with his boot. He had left the air-conditioned single-wide trailer and come up to the hill to be by himself and think for a while, and so, when he saw Jack walking slowly along the same trail, he felt a little sting of resentment. But he did not leave.

Neither Mitch nor Jack knew whether they were destined to like each other. Every time they met, Jack asked certain questions, by way of challenge, and Mitch gave certain answers that never quite satisfied.

Mitch squatted and picked up a round rock crusted with dry mud. Jack climbed the last few yards to the top of the hill.

"Hello," he said.

Mitch nodded.

"I see you have it, too." Jack rubbed his cheek with a finger. The skin on his face was forming a Lone Ranger–like mask, peeling at the edges, but thickening near the eyes. Both men looked as if they were peering through thin mud packs. "It won't come off without drawing blood."

"Shouldn't pick at it," Mitch said.

"When did yours start?"

"Three nights ago."

Jack squatted beside Jack. "I feel angry sometimes. I feel maybe Sue could have planned this better."

Mitch smiled. "What, getting pregnant?"

"Yeah," Jack said. "The casino is empty. We're running out of money. I've let most of our people go, and the others can't come to work from outside. I'm not too happy with myself, either." He touched the mask again, then looked at his finger. "One of our young fathers tried to sand it off. He's in the clinic now. I told him that was stupid."

"None of this is easy," Mitch said.

"You should come to a trustees meeting sometime."

"I'm grateful just to be here, Jack. I don't want to make people angry."

"Sue thinks maybe they won't be angry if they meet you. You're a nice enough guy."

"That's what she said over a year ago."

"She says if I'm not angry, the others won't be. That's right, maybe. Though there is an old Cayuse woman, Becky. They sent her away from Colville and she came here. She's a nice old grandmother, but she thinks it's her job to disagree with whatever the tribes want. She might, you know, look at you, poke you a little." Jack made a cantankerous face and stabbed the air with a stiff finger.

Jack was seldom so voluble and had never talked about affairs on the board.

Mitch laughed. "Do you think there's going to be trouble?"

Jack shrugged. "We want to have a meeting of fathers soon. Just the fathers. Not like the clinic birth classes with the women there. They're embarrassing to the men. Are you going tonight?"

Mitch nodded.

"First time for me with this skin. It's going to be rough. Some of the new fathers watch the TV and they wonder when they'll get their jobs back, and then they blame the women."

Mitch understood that there were three couples still expecting SHEVA babies on the reservation, besides himself and Kaye. Among the three thousand and seventy-two people on the reservation, making up the Five Tribes, there had been six SHEVA births. All had been born dead.

Kaye worked with the clinic pediatrician, a young white doctor named Chambers, and helped conduct the parenting classes. The men were a little slow and perhaps a lot less willing to accept things.

"Sue is due about the same time as Kaye," Jack said. He folded his legs into a lotus and sat directly on the dirt, something Mitch was not good at. "I tried to understand about genes and DNA and what a virus is. It's not my kind of language."

"It can be difficult," Mitch said. He did not know whether he should reach out and put his hand on Jack's shoulder. He knew so little about the modern people whose ancestors he studied. "We might be the first to have healthy babies," he said. "The first to know what they'll look like."

"I think that is true. It could be very . . ." Jack paused, his lips turned down as he thought. "I was going to say an honor. But it isn't our honor."

"Maybe not," Mitch said.

"For me, everything stays alive forever. The whole Earth is filled with living things, some wearing flesh, others not. We are here for many who came before. We don't lose our connection to the flesh when we cast it off. We spread out after we die, but we like to come back to our bones and look around. See what the young ones are doing."

Mitch could feel the old debate starting again.

"You don't see it that way," Jack said.

"I'm not sure how I see things anymore," Mitch said. "Having your body jerked around by nature is sobering. Women experience it more directly, but this has got to be a first for the men."

"This DNA must be a spirit in us, the words our ancestors pass on, words of the Creator. I can see that."

"As good a description as any," Mitch said. "Except I don't know who the Creator might be, or whether one even exists."

Jack sighed. "You study dead things."

Mitch colored slightly, as he always did when discussing these matters with Jack. "I try to understand what they were like when they were alive."

"The ghosts could tell you," Jack said.

"Do they tell you?"

"Sometimes," Jack said. "Once or twice."

"What do they tell you?"

"That they want things. They aren't happy. One old man, he's dead now, he listened to the spirit of Pasco man when you dug him out of the riverbank. The old man said the ghost was very unhappy." Jack picked up a pebble and tossed it down the hill. "Then, he said he didn't talk like our ghosts. Maybe he was a different ghost. The old man only told that to me, not to anybody else. He thought maybe the ghost wasn't from our tribe."

"Wow," Mitch said.

Jack rubbed his nose and plucked at an eyebrow. "My skin itches all the time. Does yours?"

"Sometimes." Mitch always felt as if he were walking along a cliff edge when he talked about the bones with Jack. Maybe it was guilt. "No one is special. We're all humans. The young learn from the old, dead or alive. I respect you and what you say, Jack, but we may never agree."

"Sue makes me think things through," Jack said with a shade of petulance, and glanced at Mitch with deep-set black eyes. "She says I should talk to you because you listen, and then you say what you think and it's honest. The other fathers, they need some of that now."

"I'll talk with them if it will help," Mitch said. "We owe you a lot, Jack."

"No, you don't," Jack said. "We'd probably be in trouble anyway. If it wasn't the new ones, it would be the slot machines. We like to shove our spears at the bureau and the government."

"It's costing you a lot of money," Mitch said.

"We're sneaking in the new credit-card roller games," Jack said. "Our boys drive them over the hills in the backs of their trucks where the troopers aren't watching. We may get to use them for six months or more before the state confiscates them."

"They're slot machines?"

Jack shook his head. "We don't think so. We'll make some money before they're removed."

"Revenge against the white man?"

"We skin 'em," Jack said soberly. "They love it."

"If the babies are healthy, maybe they'll end the quarantine," Mitch said. "You can reopen the casino in a couple of months."

"I don't count on nothing," Jack said. "Besides, I don't want to go out on the floor and act like a boss if I still look like this." He put his hand on Mitch's shoulder. "You come talk," he said, standing. "The men want to hear."

"I'll give it a shot," Mitch said.

"I'll tell them to forgive you for that other stuff. The ghost wasn't from one of our tribes anyway." Jack pushed to his feet and walked off down the hill.

Kumash County, Eastern Washington

Mitch worked on his old blue Buick, parked in the dry grass of the trailer's front yard, while afternoon thunderheads piled up to the south.

The air smelled tense and exciting. Kaye could hardly bear to sit. She pushed back from the desk by the window and left off from pretending to work on her book while spending most of her time watching Mitch squint at wire harnesses.

She put her hands on her hips to stretch. This day had not been so hot and they had stayed at the trailer rather than ride down to the air-conditioned community center. Kaye liked to watch Mitch play basketball; sometimes she would go for a swim in the small pool. It was not a bad life, but she felt guilty.

The news from outside was seldom good. They had been on the reservation for three weeks and Kaye was afraid the federal marshals would come and gather up the SHEVA mothers at any time. They had done so in Montgomery,

Alabama, breaking into a private maternity center and nearly causing a riot.

"They're getting *bold*," Mitch had said as they watched the TV news. Later, the president had apologized and assured the nation that civil liberties would be preserved, as much as possible, considering the risks that might be faced by the general public. Two days later, the Montgomery clinic had closed under pressure from picketing citizens, and the mothers and fathers had been forced to move elsewhere. With their masks, the new parents looked strange; judging from what she and Mitch heard on the news, they were not popular in very many places.

They had not been popular in the Republic of Georgia.

Kaye had learned nothing more about new retroviral infections from SHEVA mothers. Her contacts were equally silent. This was a charged issue, she could tell; nobody felt comfortable expressing opinions.

So she pretended to work on her book, drafting perhaps a good paragraph or two every day, writing sometimes on the laptop, sometimes in longhand on a legal pad. Mitch read what she wrote and made marginal notes, but he seemed preoccupied, as if stunned by the prospect of being a father . . . Though she knew that was not what concerned him.

Not being a father. That concerns him. Me. My welfare.

She did not know how to ease his mind. She felt fine, even wonderful, despite the discomforts. She looked at herself in the spotted mirror in the bathroom and felt that her face had filled out rather well; not gaunt, as she had once believed, but healthy, with good skin—not counting the mask, of course.

Every day the mask darkened and thickened, a peculiar caul that marked this kind of parenthood.

Kaye performed her exercises on the thin carpet in the small living room. Finally, it was just too muggy to do much of anything. Mitch came in for a drink of water and saw her on the floor. She looked up at him.

"Game of cards in the rec room?" he asked.

"I vant to be alone," she intoned, Garbo-like. "Alone with you, that is."

"How's the back?"

"Massage tonight, when it's cool," she said.

"Peaceful here, isn't it?" Mitch asked, standing in the door and flapping his T-shirt to cool off.

"I've been thinking of names."

"Oh?" Mitch looked stricken.

"What?" Kaye asked.

"Just a funny feeling. I want to see her before we come up with a name."

"Why?" Kaye asked resentfully. "You talk to her, sing to her, every night. You say you can even smell her on my breath."

"Yeah," Mitch said, but his face did not relax. "I just want to see what she looks like."

Suddenly, Kaye pretended to catch on. "I don't mean a *scientific name*," she said. "Our name, our name for *our* daughter."

Mitch gave her an exasperated look. "Don't ask me to explain." He looked pensive. "Brock and I came up with a scientific name yesterday, on the phone. Though he thinks it's premature, because none of the—"

Mitch caught himself, coughed, shut the screen door, and walked into the kitchen.

Kaye felt her heart sink.

Mitch returned with several ice cubes wrapped in a wet towel, knelt beside her, and dabbed at the sweat on her forehead. Kaye would not meet his eyes.

"Stupid," he murmured.

"We're both grownups," Kaye said. "I want to think of names for her. I want to knit booties and shop for sleepers and buy little crib toys and behave as if we're normal parents and *stop thinking about all that bullshit*."

"I know," Mitch said, and he looked completely miserable, almost broken.

Kaye got up on her knees and laid her hands lightly on

Mitch's shoulders, sweeping them back and forth as if dusting. "Listen to me. I am fine. She is fine. If you don't believe me . . ."

"I believe you," Mitch said.

Kaye bumped her forehead against his. "All right, *Kemosabe*."

Mitch touched the dark, rough skin on her cheeks. "You look very mysterious. Like a bandit."

"Maybe we'll need new scientific names for us, too. Don't you feel it inside . . . something deeper, beneath the skin?"

"My bones itch," he said. "And my throat . . . my tongue feels different. Why am I getting a mask and all the rest, too?"

"You make the virus. Why shouldn't it change you, too? As for the mask . . . maybe we're getting ready to be recognized by her. We're social animals. Daddies are as important to babies as mommies."

"We'll look like her?"

"Maybe a little." Kaye returned to the desk chair and sat. "What did Brock suggest for a scientific name?"

"He doesn't foresee a radical change," Mitch said. "Subspecies at most, maybe just a peculiar variety. So . . . *Homo sapiens novus*."

Kaye repeated the name softly and smirked. "Sounds like a windshield repair place."

"It's good Latin," Mitch said.

"Let me think on it," she said.

"They paid for the clinic with the money from the casino," Kaye said as she folded towels. Mitch had carried the two baskets back to the trailer from the laundry shed before sundown. He sat on the queen-size bed in the tiny little bedroom of the single-wide because there was hardly any room to stand. His big feet could barely wedge between the walls and the bed frame.

Kaye took four panties and two new nursing bras and

folded them, then laid them to one side to put in the overnight case. She had been keeping the case handy for a week, and it seemed the right time to pack it.

"Got a dopp bag?" she asked. "I can't find mine."

Mitch pushed and crawled off the end of the bed to dig around in his suitcase. He came up with a battered old brown leather bag with a zipper.

"Army Air Force bomber's shaving kit?" she asked, lifting the bag by its strap.

"Guaranteed authentic," Mitch said. He watched her like a hawk and that made her feel both reassured and a little bitchy. She continued to fold laundry.

"Dr. Chambers says all the mothers-to-be look healthy. He delivered three of the others. He could tell there was something wrong with them months before, so he says. Marine Pacific sent him my records last week. He's filling out some of the Taskforce forms, but not all. He had a lot of questions."

She finished the laundry and sat on the end of the bed. "When she twitches like this, it makes me think I've started labor."

Mitch bent down before her and placed his hand on her prominent stomach, his eyes bright and large. "She's really moving around tonight."

"She's happy," Kaye said. "She knows you're here. Sing her the song."

Mitch looked up at her, then sang his version of the ABCs tune. *"Ah, beh, say, duh, ehh, fuh, gah, aitch, ihh, juh, kuh, la muh-nuh, oh puh . . ."*

Kaye laughed.

"It's very serious," Mitch said.

"She loves it."

"My father used to sing it to me. Phonetic alphabet. Get her ready for the English language. I started reading when I was four, you know."

"She's kicking time," Kaye said in delight.

"She is not."

"I swear it, feel!"

She actually liked the small trailer with its battered light oak plywood cabinets and old furniture. She had hung her mother's prints in the living room. They had enough food and it was warm enough at night, too hot in the daytime, so Kaye went to work with Sue in the Administration Building and Mitch walked around the hills with his cell phone in his pocket, sometimes with Jack, or spoke with the other fathers-to-be in the clinic lounge. The men liked to keep to themselves here, and the women were content with that. Kaye missed Mitch in the hours he was away, but there was a lot to think about and prepare for. At night, he was always with her, and she had never been happier.

She *knew* the baby was healthy. She could feel it. As Mitch finished the song, she touched the mask around his eyes. He did not flinch when she did this, though he used to, the first week. Their masks were both quite thick now and flaky around the edges.

"You know what I want to do," Kaye said.

"What?"

"I want to crawl off into a dark hole somewhere when it's time."

"Like a cat?"

"Exactly."

"I can see doing that," Mitch said agreeably. "No modern medicine, dirt floor, savage simplicity."

"Leather thong in my teeth," Kaye added. "That's the way Sue's mother gave birth. Before they had the clinic."

"My father delivered me," Mitch said. "Our truck was stuck in a ditch. Mom climbed into the back. She never let him forget that."

"She never told me that!" Kaye said with a laugh.

"She calls it 'a difficult delivery,' " Mitch said.

"We're not that far from the old times," Kaye said. She touched her stomach. "I think you sang her to sleep."

The next morning, when Kaye awoke, her tongue felt thick. She pushed out of bed, waking Mitch, and walked into the kitchen to get a drink of the flat-tasting reservation tap water. She could hardly talk. "Mitth," she said.

"Wha?" he asked.

"Awh we gehhing somhinh?"

"Wha?"

She sat beside him and poked out her tongue. "Ih's aw custy," she said.

"My, hoo," he said.

"Ih's li owah faces," she said.

Only one of the four fathers could talk that afternoon in the clinic side room. Jack stood by the portable whiteboard and ticked off the days for each of their wives, then sat and tried to talk sports with the others, but the meeting broke up early. The clinic's head physician—there were four doctors working at the clinic, besides the pediatrician—examined them all but had no diagnosis. There did not seem to be any infection.

The other mothers-to-be had it, too.

Kaye and Sue did their shopping together at the Little Silver Market down the road from the resort's Biscuit House coffee shop. Others in the market stared at them but said nothing. There was a lot of grumbling among the casino workers, but only the old Cayuse woman, Becky, spoke her mind in the trustee meetings.

Kaye and Sue agreed that Sue was going to deliver first. "I ca't way," Sue said. "Neither cah Jack."

Kumash County, Eastern Washington

Mitch was there again. It began vague, and then clicked into a wicked reality. All his memories of being Mitch were tidily packed away in that fashion peculiar to dreams. The last thing he did as Mitch was feel his face, pull at the thick mask, the mask that sat on new and puffy skin.

Then he was on the ice and rock again. His woman was screaming and crying, almost doubled up with pain. He ran ahead, then ran back and helped her to her feet, all the time ululating, his throat sore, his arms and legs bruised from the beating, the taunting, back on the lake, in the village, and he *hated* them, all laughing and hooting, as they swung their sticks and sounded so ugly.

The young hunter who had pushed a stick into his woman's belly was dead. He had beaten that one to the ground and made him writhe and moan, then stamped on his neck, but too late, there was blood and his woman was hurt. The shamans came into the crowd and tried to push the others away with guttural words, choppy dark singing words, not at all like the watery light bird noises he could make now.

He took his woman into their hut and tried to comfort her, but she hurt too much.

The snow came down. He heard the shouting, the mourning cries, and he knew their time was up. The family of the dead hunter would be after them. They would have gone to ask the permission of the old Bull-man. The old Bull-man had never liked masked parents or their Flat Face children.

It was the end, the old Bull-man had often murmured; the Flat Faces taking all the game, driving the people farther into the mountains each year, and now their own women were betraying them and making more Flat Face children.

He carried his woman out of the hut, crossed the log bridge to the shore, listening to the cries for vengeance. He heard the Bull-man leading the charge. The chase began.

He had once used the cave to store food. Game was difficult to find and the cave was cold, and he had kept rabbit and marmot, acorns and wild grass and mice there for his woman when he had been on hunting duty. Otherwise she might not have gotten enough to eat from the village rations. The other women with their hungry children had refused to care for her as she grew round-bellied.

He had smuggled the small game from the cave into the village at night and fed her. He loved his woman so much it made him want to yell, or roll on the ground and moan, and he could not believe she was badly hurt, despite the blood that soaked her furs.

He carried his woman again, and she looked up at him, pleading in her high and singing voice, like a river flowing rather than rolling rocks, this new voice he had, too. They both sounded like children now, not adults.

He had once hidden near a Flat Face hunting camp and watched them sing and dance around a huge bonfire in the night. Their voices had been high and watery, like children. Maybe he and his woman were becoming Flat Faces and would go and live with them when the child was born.

He carried her through the soft and powdery snow, his feet numb like logs. She was quiet for a time, asleep. When she awoke, she cried and tried to curl up in his arms. In the twilight, as the golden glow filled the snow-misted high rocky places, he looked down on her and saw that the carefully shaved furry parts on her temples and cheeks, where the mask did not cover, and all the rest of her hair, looked dull and matted, lifeless. She smelled like an animal about to die.

Up over rocky terraces slippery with new snow. Along a

snow-covered ridge, and then down, sliding, tumbling, the woman still in his arms. He got to his feet again at the bottom, turned to orient himself to the flat walls of the mountain, and suddenly wondered why this seemed so familiar, like something he had practiced over and over again with the hunter-trainers in the mountain goat seasons.

Those had been good times. He thought of those times as he carried his woman the final distance.

He had used the rabbit atlatl, the smaller throwing-stick, since childhood, but had never been allowed to carry the elk and bison atlatl until the itinerant hunter-trainers had come to the village in the year his balls had ached and he had spewed seed in his sleep.

Then he had gone with his father, who was with the dream people now, and met the hunter-trainers. They were lone and ugly men, unkempt, scarred, with thick locks of hair. They had no village, no laws of grooming, but went from place to place and organized the people when the mountain goats or the deer or the elk or the bison were ready to share their flesh. Some grumbled that they went to the Flat Face villages and trained them to hunt in one season, and indeed, some of the hunter-trainers might have been Flat Faces who covered their features with matted beard and hair. Who would question them? Not even the Bull-man. When they came, everyone ate well, and the women scraped the skins and laughed and ate irritating herbs and drank water all day, and all pissed together in leather buckets and chewed and soaked the skins. It was forbidden to hunt the big animals without the hunter-trainers.

He came to the mouth of the cave. His woman whined softly, rhythmically, as he carried and rolled and pushed her inside. He looked back. The snow was covering the drops of blood they left behind.

He knew then that they were finished. He hunkered down, his thick shoulders barely fitting, and rolled her gently onto a skin he used to cover the meat while it froze in the cave. He slid and pushed and then pulled her back into the cave, and went out to get moss and sticks from an overhang where he knew they would be dry. He hoped she would not die before he came back.

Oh, God, let me wake up, I do not want to see.

He found enough sticks for a small fire and carried them back to the cave, where he lined them up and then spun the stick, first making sure the woman could not see. Making fire was man's stuff. She was still asleep. When he was too weak to twirl the stick anymore, and still there was no curl of smoke, he took out a flint and chipped it. For a long time, until his fingers were bruised and numb, he struck the flints into the moss, blew on the moss, and suddenly, the Sun Bird opened its eye and spread little orange wings. He added sticks.

His woman moaned again. She curled up on her back and told him in her watery squeaky voice to go away. This was woman's stuff. He ignored her, as was sometimes allowed, and helped her bring the baby.

It was very painful for her and she made loud noises, and he wondered how she had so much life left in her, with so much blood gone, but the baby came out quickly.

No. Please, let me wake up.

He held the baby, and showed it to the woman, but her eyes were flat and her hair was stiff and dry. The baby did not cry or move, no matter how he kneaded it.

He put the baby down and slammed his fist on the rock walls. He screamed hoarsely and curled up beside his woman, who was quiet now, and tried to keep her warm as smoke filled the top of the cave and the embers began to gray and the Sun Bird folded its wings and slept.

The baby would have been his daughter, supreme gift from the Dream Mother. The baby did not look so very different from other babies in the village, though its nose was small and its chin stuck out. He supposed it would have grown up to be a Flat Face. He tried to stuff dry grass into the hole in the back of the baby's head. He thought maybe the stick had punched the baby there. He took his neck skin, the finest and softest, and wrapped the baby in that and then pushed it to the back of the cave.

He remembered the dumb man's groans as he had stamped on his neck, but it did not help much.

Everything was gone. Caves had been proper places for burial since the times of story, before they had moved to wooden villages and lived like the Flat Faces, though everyone said the People had invented wooden villages. This was an old way to die and be buried, in the back of a cave, so it was okay. The dream people would find the baby and take it home, where it would have been missing for only a little while, so maybe it would be born quickly again.

His woman was growing as cold as the rock. He arranged her arms and legs, her tousled furs and skins, pushed back the loose mask still stuck to her brows, peered into her dull and blind eyes. No energy to mourn.

After a while he felt warm enough not to need the skins, so he pushed them off. Maybe she was warm, too. He pushed the skins off his woman so she would be almost naked, easier for the dream people to recognize.

He hoped the dream people of her family would make an alliance with the dream people of his family. He would like to be with her in the dream place, too. Maybe he and his woman would find the baby again. He believed the dream people could do so many good things for you.

Maybe this, maybe that, maybe so many things, happier things. He grew warmer.

For a little while, he didn't hate anyone. He stared at the darkness where his woman's face was and whispered flint words, words against dark, as if he could strike up another Sun Bird. It was so good not to move. So warm.

Then his father strolled into the cave and called his true name.

Mitch stood in his shorts in front of the trailer and stared up at the moon, the stars over Kumash. He blew his nose quietly. The early morning was cool and still. The sweat on his face and skin dried slowly and made him shiver. He was covered with goose bumps. A few quail rustled in the bushes alongside the trailer.

Kaye pushed open the screen door with a squeak and a hiss of the cylinder and walked out to stand beside him in her nightgown.

"You'll get cold," he said, and put his arm around her. The swelling on his tongue had gone down in the last few days. There was a peculiar ridge on the left side of his tongue now, but talking was easier.

"You soaked the bed with sweat," she said. She was so round, so different from the small, slender Kaye he still pictured in his head. Her heat and her smell filled the air like vapor from a rich soup. "Dream?" she asked.

"The worst," he said. "I think it was the last one."

"They're all the same?"

"They're all different," Mitch said.

"Jack'll want to hear the gory details," Kaye said.

"And you don't?"

"Uh uh," Kaye said. "She's restless, Mitch. Talk to her."

87

Kumash County, Eastern Washington
MAY 18

Kaye's contractions were coming regularly. Mitch called to make sure the clinic was ready and Dr. Chambers, the pediatrician, was on his way from his brick house on the north end of the reservation. As Kaye put the last toiletry items in the dopp bag and found a few pieces of clothing she thought might be nice to wear after, Mitch called Dr. Galbreath again, but the answering service picked up.

"She must be on her way," Mitch said as he folded the phone. If the deputies would not let Galbreath through the checkpoint off the main road—a real possibility that infuriated Mitch—then Jack had arranged for two men to meet her five miles south and smuggle her in on a wash road through the low hills.

Mitch pulled out a box and dug for the small digital camera he had once used to record site details. He made sure the battery was charged.

Kaye stood in the living room holding her stomach and breathing in small huffs. She smiled at him as he joined her.

"I am so scared," she said.

"Why?"

"God, you ask why?"

"It's going to be fine," Mitch said, but he was pale as a sheet.

"That's why your hands are like ice," Kaye said. "I'm early. Maybe it's a false alarm." Then she made a funny grunt and felt between her legs. "I think my water just broke. I'll get some towels."

"Never mind the damned towels!" Mitch shouted. He helped her to the Toyota. She pulled the seat belt low around her stomach. *Nothing like the dreams,* he thought. The thought became a kind of prayer, and he repeated it over and over.

"Nobody's heard from Augustine," Kaye said as Mitch pulled onto the paved road and began the two-mile drive to the clinic.

"Why would we?"

"Maybe he'll try to stop us," she said.

Mitch gave her a funny look. "That's as crazy as my dreams."

"He's the bogeyman, Mitch. He scares me."

"I don't like him either, but he's no monster."

"He thinks we're diseased," she said, and there were tears on her cheeks. She winced.

"Another?" Mitch asked.

She nodded. "It's okay," she said. "Every twenty minutes." They met Jack's truck coming from the East Ridge Road and stopped long enough to confer through the windows. Sue was with Jack. Jack followed them.

"I want to have Sue help you coach me," Kaye said. "I want her to see us. If I'm okay, it will be so much easier for her."

"Fine with me," Mitch said. "I'm no expert."

Kaye smiled and winced again.

Room number one in the Kumash Wellness Clinic was quickly being converted into a labor and delivery room. A hospital bed had been rolled in, and a bright round surgical lamp on a tall steel pole.

The nurse midwife, a plump, high-cheeked, middle-aged woman named Mary Hand, arranged the medical tray and helped Kaye change into a hospital gown. The anesthesiologist, Dr. Pound, a young, wan-looking man with thick black hair and a pug nose, arrived half an hour after the room was prepared and conferred with Chambers while Mitch crushed ice in a plastic bag in the sink. Mitch put ice chips into a cup.

"Is it now?" Kaye asked Chambers as he checked her.

"Not for a while," he said. "You're at four centimeters."

Sue pulled up a chair. On her tall frame, her pregnancy seemed much less obvious. Jack called to her from the door, and she turned. He tossed her a small bag, stuffed his hands in his pockets, nodded to Mitch, and backed out. She placed the bag on the table next to the bed. "He's embarrassed to come in," she told Kaye. "He thinks this is woman stuff."

Kaye lifted her head to peer at the bag. It was made out of leather and tied with a beaded string.

"What's in the bag?"

"All sorts of things. Some of them smell good. Some don't."

"Jack's a medicine man?"

"God, no," Sue said. "You think I'd marry a medicine man? He knows some good ones, though."

"Mitch and I thought we'd like this one to come naturally," Kaye told Dr. Pound as he brought in a rolling table with his tanks and tubes and syringes.

"Of course," the anesthesiologist said, and smiled. "I'm here just in case."

Chambers told Kaye and Mitch there was a woman living about five miles away who was going into labor, not a SHEVA birth. "She insists on a home delivery. They have a hot tub and everything. I may have to go there for a while this evening. You said Dr. Galbreath would be here."

"She should be on her way," Mitch said.

"Well, let's hope it works out. The baby's head down. In a few minutes we'll attach a fetal health monitor. All the comforts of a big hospital, Ms. Lang."

Chambers took Mitch aside. He glanced at Mitch's face, his eyes tracking the outline of the skin mask.

"Fetching, isn't it?" Mitch said nervously.

"I've delivered four SHEVA second-stage babies," Chambers said. "I'm sure you know the risk, but I have to spell out some complications that might happen, so we can all be prepared."

Mitch nodded, gripped his trembling hands.

"None of them were born alive. Two looked perfect, no visible defects, just . . . dead." Chambers stared at Mitch with a critical expression. "I don't like these odds."

Mitch flushed. "We're different," he said.

"There can also be a shock response in the mothers if the delivery gets complicated. Something to do with hormone signals from a SHEVA fetus in distress. Nobody understands why, but the infant tissues are so different. Some women do not react well. If that happens, I'm going to do a C-section and get the baby out as quickly as possible." He put a hand on Mitch's shoulder. Chambers's pager beeped. "Just as a precaution, I'm going to take extra care with spilled fluids and tissues. Everybody will wear viral filter masks, even you. We're in new territory here, Mr. Rafelson. Excuse me."

Sue was feeding Kaye ice and they were talking, heads together. It seemed to be a private moment, so Mitch backed out, and besides, he wanted to sort through some difficult emotions.

He walked into the lobby. Jack sat in a chair by the old card table there, staring at a pile of *National Geographic*s. The fluorescent lights made everything seem blue and cold.

"You look mad," Jack said.

"They've almost got the death certificate signed," Mitch said, his voice trembling.

"Yeah," Jack said. "Sue and I think maybe we'll have the birth at home. No doctors."

"He says it's dangerous."

"Maybe it is, but we did it before," Jack said.

"When?" Mitch asked.

"Your dreams," Jack said. "The mummies. Thousands of years ago."

Mitch sat in the other chair and put his head on the table. "Not a happy time."

"Tell me," Jack said.

Mitch told him about the last dream. Jack listened intently.

"That was a bad one," he said. "I won't tell Sue about it."

"Say something comforting," Mitch suggested wryly.

"I've been trying to have dreams to help me figure out what to do," Jack said. "I just dream about big hospitals and big doctors poking at Sue. The white man's world gets in the way. So I'm no help." Jack scratched his eyebrows. "Nobody is old enough to know what to do. My people have been on this land forever. But my grandfather tells me the spirits have nothing to say. They don't remember either."

Mitch pushed his hand through the magazines. One slid off and hit the floor with a smack. "That doesn't make any sense, Jack."

* * *

Kaye lay back and watched Chambers attach the fetal health monitors. The steady beep and pulse of the tape on the machine by the bed gave her confirmation, another level of reassurance.

Mitch came back with a Popsicle and unwrapped it for her. She had emptied her cup and took the sweet raspberry ice gratefully.

"No sign of Galbreath," Mitch said.

"We'll manage," Kaye said. "Five centimeters and holding. All this for just one mother."

"But what a mother," Mitch said. He started working on her arms, pushing the tension out, and then moved to her shoulders.

"The mother of all mothers," she muttered as another contraction hit. She bore down into it, held up the bare Popsicle stick. "Another, please," she grunted.

Kaye had become acquainted with every inch of the ceiling. She got off the bed carefully and walked around the room, gripping the metal rolling stand that held the monitoring equipment, wires trailing from beneath her gown. Her hair felt stiff, her skin oily, and her eyes stung. Mitch looked up from the *National Geographic* he was reading as she duck-walked into the rest room. She washed her face and he was by the door. "I'm fine," she said.

"If I don't help you, I'll go nuts," Mitch said.

"Don't want that," Kaye said. She sat on the side of the bed and took several deep breaths. Chambers had told them he would be back in an hour. Mary Hand entered with her filter mask on, looking like a high-tech soldier prepared for a gas attack, and told Kaye to lie back. The midwife inspected her. She smiled beatifically and Kaye thought, *Good, I'm ready,* but she shook her head. "Still at five centimeters. It's okay. Your first baby." Her voice was muffled beneath the mask.

Kaye stared up at the ceiling again and bore into a contraction. Mitch encouraged her to take puffing breaths until the wave passed. Her back ached abominably. For a bitter moment at the end of the contraction she felt trapped and angry, and wondered what it would be like if everything went wrong, if she died, if the baby was born alive but without a mother, if Augustine was right and both she and her child were a source of horrible disease. *Why no confirmation?* she wondered. *Why no science one way or the other on that?* She calmed herself with slow breaths and tried to rest.

When she opened her eyes again, Mitch was dozing in the chair beside the bed. The clock said it was midnight. *I will be in this room forever.*

She needed to go to the bathroom again. "Mitch," she said. He didn't wake up. She looked for Mary Hand or Sue, but he was the only one in the room. The monitor beeped and rolled its tape. "Mitch!"

He jerked and stood up and sleepily helped her into the bathroom. She had wanted to have a bowel movement before going to the clinic, but her body had not cooperated, and she worried about that. She felt a mix of anger and wonder at her present state. The body was taking charge, but she was not at all sure it knew what to do. *I am my body. Mind is the illusion. The flesh is confused.*

Mitch walked around the room, sipping a cup of bad coffee from the clinic lounge. The cold blue fluorescent lights were etched into his memory. He felt as if he had never seen bright sun. His eyebrows itched abominably. *Go into the cave. Hibernate and she'll give birth while we sleep. That's the way bears do it. Bears evolve while they're asleep. Better way.*

Sue came to be with Kaye while he took a break. He walked outside and stood beneath the clear, starry sky. Even out here, with so few people, there was a streetlight to blind him and cut back on the immensity of the universe.

God, I've come so far, but nothing has changed. I'm married, I'm going to be a father, and I'm still unemployed, living on the—

He blocked that line of thought, waved his hands, shook out the nervous jangles from the coffee. His thoughts drifted all over, from the first time he had had sex—and worried about the girl getting pregnant—to the conversations with the director of the Hayer Museum before he was fired, to Jack, trying to put all this into an Indian perspective.

Mitch had no perspective other than the scientific. All his life he had tried to be objective, tried to remove himself from the equation, to see clearly what his digging had revealed. He had traded bits of his life for what were probably inadequate insights into the lives of dead people. Jack believed in a circle of life where no one was ever truly isolated. Mitch could not believe that. But he hoped Jack was right.

The air smelled good. He wished he could take Kaye out here and let her smell the fresh air, but then a pickup truck drove by, and he smelled exhaust and burned oil.

Kaye dozed off between contractions but for only a few minutes. Two o'clock in the morning, and she was still at five centimeters. Chambers had come before her little nap, inspected her, peered at the monitor tape, smiled reassurance. "We can try some pitocin soon. That will speed things up. We call it Bardahl for babies," he said. But Kaye did not know what Bardahl was and did not understand.

Mary Hand took her arm, swabbed it down with alcohol, found a vein and introduced a needle, taped it off, attached a plastic tube, hung a bottle of saline on another stand. She arranged little vials of medicine on a blue sheet of disposable paper on the steel tray beside the bed.

Kaye normally hated shots and needle pricks, but this was nothing compared to the rest of her discomfort. Mitch seemed to grow more distant, though he was right by her side, massaging her neck, bringing more ice. She looked at him and saw not her husband, not her lover, but just a man, another of the figures coming in and out of her squeezed-down and compressed and endless life. She frowned, watching his back as he spoke with the nurse midwife. She tried to focus and find that emotional component necessary to fit him into the puzzle, but it had been lifted away. She was liberated of all social sensibilities.

Another contraction. "Oh, shit!" she cried.

Mary Hand checked her and stood with a concerned expression. "Did Dr. Chambers say when he would administer pitocin?"

Kaye shook her head, unable to respond. Mary Hand went off to find Chambers. Mitch stayed with her. Sue came in and sat on the chair. Kaye closed her eyes and found that the universe in that personal darkness was so small she almost panicked. She wanted this to be over. No menstrual cramps had ever had the authority of her contractions. In the middle of the spasm, she thought her back might break.

She knew that flesh was all and spirit was nothing.

"Everyone is born this way," Sue told Mitch. "It's good you're here. Jack says he'll be with me when I deliver, but it's not traditional."

"Woman's stuff," Mitch said. Sue's mask fascinated him. She stood, stretched. Tall, stomach prominent but balanced, she seemed the essence of strong womanhood. Assured, calm, philosophical.

Kaye moaned. Mitch leaned over and caressed her cheek. She was lying on her side, trying to find some position that was comfortable. "God, give me drugs," she said with a weak smile.

"There's that sense of humor," Mitch said.

"I mean it. No, I don't. I don't know what I mean. Where is Felicity?"

"Jack came by a few minutes ago. He sent some trucks out, but he hasn't heard from them."

"I need Felicity. I don't know what Chambers is thinking. Give me something to make this happen."

Mitch felt miserable, helpless. They were in the hands of the Western medical establishment—such as it was in the Five Tribes Confederation. Frankly, he was not at all confident about Chambers.

"Oh, goddamn *SHIT*," Kaye yelled, and rolled on her back, her face so contorted Mitch could not recognize her.

Seven o'clock. Kaye looked at the clock on the wall through slitted eyes. More than twelve hours. She did not remember when they had arrived. Had it been in the afternoon? Yes. More than twelve hours. Still no record. Her mother had told her, when she was a little girl, that she had been in labor for over thirty hours with Kaye. *Here's to you, Mother. God, I wish you could be here.*

Sue was not in the room. There was Mitch, working on her arm, easing the tension, moving to the other arm. She felt a distant affection for Mitch, but doubted seriously she would ever have sex with him again. Why even think about it. Kaye felt she was a giant balloon trying to burst. She had to go pee and the thought equaled the deed and she did not care. Mary Hand came and removed the soaked paper pad and replaced it.

Dr. Chambers came in and told Mary to start the pitocin. Mary inserted the vial into the appropriate receptacle and adjusted the machine that controlled the drip. Kaye took an extreme interest in the procedure. Bardahl for babies. She could vaguely remember the list of peptides and glycoproteins Judith had found in the large protein complex. Bad news for women. Maybe so.

Maybe so.

The only thing in the universe was pain. Kaye sat on top of the pain like a small, stunned fly on a huge rubber ball. She vaguely heard the anesthesiologist moving around her. She heard Mitch and the doctor talking. Mary Hand was there.

Chambers said something completely irrelevant, something about storing cord blood for a transfusion later if the baby needed it, or to pass on to science: blood from the umbilical cord, rich with stem cells.

"Do it," Kaye said.

"What?" Mitch asked. Chambers asked her if she wanted to have an epidural.

"God, yes," Kaye said, without the least guilt at having failed to stick it through.

They rolled her on her side. "Hold still," said the anesthesiologist, what was his name. She couldn't remember. Sue's face appeared before her.

"Jack says they're bringing her in."

"Who?" Kaye asked.

"Dr. Galbreath."

"Good." Kaye thought she should care.

"They wouldn't let her through the quarantine."

"Bastards," Mitch said.

"Bastards," Kaye mouthed.

She felt a prick in her back. Another contraction. She started to tremble. The anesthesiologist swore and apologized. "Missed. You'll have to hold still." Her back hurt. Nothing new about that. Mitch applied a cold cloth to her forehead. Modern medicine. She had failed modern medicine.

"Oh, shit."

Somewhere way outside her sphere of consciousness, she heard voices like distant angels.

"Felicity is here," Mitch said, and his face, hovering right over her, shone with relief. But Dr. Galbreath and Dr. Chambers were arguing, and the anesthesiologist was involved, too.

"No epidural," Galbreath said. "Get her off the pitocin, now. How long? How much?"

While Chambers looked at the machine and read off numbers, Mary Hand did something to the tubes. The machine wheeped. Kaye looked at the clock. Seven-thirty. What did that mean? Time. Oh, that.

"She's going to have to go it on her own," Galbreath said. Chambers responded with irritation, sharp quiet words behind his awful filter mask, but Kaye did not listen to him.

They were denying her drugs.

Felicity leaned over Kaye and entered her visual cone.

She was not wearing a filter mask. The big surgical light was turned on and Felicity was not wearing a filter mask, bless her.

"Thank you," Kaye said.

"You may not thank me for long, dear," Felicity said. "If you want this baby, we can't do anything more with drugs. No pitocin, no anesthetic. I'm glad I caught you. It kills them, Kaye. Understand?"

Kaye grimaced.

"One damned insult after another, right, dear? So delicate, these new ones."

Chambers complained about interference, but she heard Jack and Mitch, voices fading, escorting him from the room. Mary Hand looked to Felicity for guidance.

"The CDC is good for something, dear," Felicity told her. "They sent out a special bulletin about live births. No drugs, particularly no anesthetics. Not even aspirin. These babies can't stand it." She worked busily for a moment between Kaye's legs. "Episiotomy," she said to Mary. "No local. Hold on, honey. This will hurt, like losing your virginity all over again. Mitch, you know the drill."

Push to ten. Let breath out. Bear down, puff, push to ten. Kaye's body like some horse knowing how to run but appreciating a little guidance. Mitch rubbing vigorously, standing close to her. She clenched his hand and then his arm until he winced. She bore down, *push to ten. Let breath out.*

"All right. She's crowning. There she is. God, it's taken so long, such a long, strange road, huh? Mary, there's the cord. That's the problem. A little dark. One more, Kaye. Do it, honey. Do it now."

She did it and something released, a massive rush, pumpkin seed between clenched fingers, a burst of pain, relief, more pain, aching. Her legs shivered. A charley horse hit her calf but she hardly noticed. She felt a sudden shove of happiness, of welcome emptiness, then a knifelike stab in her tailbone.

"She's here, Kaye. She's alive."

Kaye heard a thin wail, a sucking sound, and something like a musical whistle.

Felicity held up the baby, pink and bloody, cord dangling down between Kaye's legs. Kaye looked at her daughter and felt nothing for a moment, and then something large and feathery, enormous, brushed her soul.

Mary Hand laid the baby on a blue blanket on her abdomen and cleaned her with quick swipes.

Mitch looked down on the blood, the baby.

Chambers returned, still wearing his mask, but Mitch ignored him. He focused on Kaye and on the baby, so small, wriggling. Tears of exhaustion and relief flowed down Mitch's cheeks. His throat hurt it was so tight and full. His heart pounded. He hugged Kaye and she hugged him back with remarkable strength.

"Don't put anything in her eyes," Felicity instructed Mary. "It's a whole new ball game."

Mary nodded happily behind the filter mask.

"Afterbirth," Felicity said. Mary held up a steel tray.

Kaye had never been sure she would make a good mother. Now, none of that mattered. She watched as they lifted the baby to the scales and thought, *I didn't get a good look at her face. It was all wrinkled.*

Felicity wielded a stinging swab of alcohol and a large surgical sewing needle between Kaye's legs. Kaye did not like this, but simply closed her eyes.

Mary Hand performed the various small tests, finished cleaning the baby, while Chambers drew cord blood. Felicity showed Mitch where to cut the cord, then carried the baby back to Kaye. Mary helped her pull her gown up over her swollen breasts and lifted the baby to her.

"It's okay to breastfeed?" Kaye asked, her voice little more than a hoarse whisper.

"If it isn't, the grand experiment might as well be over," Felicity said with a smile. "Go ahead, honey. You have what she needs."

She showed Kaye how to stroke the baby's cheek. The small pink lips opened and fastened onto the large brown nipple. Mitch's mouth hung loose. Kaye wanted to laugh at his expression, but she focused again on that tiny face, hungry to see what her daughter looked like. Sue stood beside her and made small, happy sounds to the mother and the baby.

Mitch looked down on the girl and watched her suckle at Kaye's breast. He felt an almost blissful calm. It was done; it was just beginning. Either way, this was really something he could fasten onto, a center, a point of reference.

The baby's face was red and wrinkled but the hair was abundant, fine and silky, pale reddish brown. Her eyes were shut, lids pressed together in concern and concentration.

"Nine pounds," Mary said. "Eight on the Apgar. Good, strong Apgar." She removed her mask.

"Oh, God, she's here," Sue said, hand going to her mouth, as if suddenly shocked into awareness. Mitch grinned like a fool at Sue, then sat beside Kaye and the baby and put his chin on Kaye's arm, his face just inches from his daughter's.

Felicity finished cleaning up. Chambers told Mary to put all the linens and disposables in a special hazards bag for burning. Mary quietly complied.

"She's a miracle," Mitch said.

The girl tried to turn her head at the sound of his voice, opened her eyes, tried to locate him.

"Your daddy," Kaye said. Colostrum dribbled thick and yellow from her nipple. The girl dropped her head and fastened on again with a little push from Kaye's finger. "She lifted her head," Kaye said in wonder.

"She's beautiful," Sue said. "Congratulations."

Felicity spoke to Sue for a moment while Kaye and Mitch and the baby filled the spot of solar brightness beneath the surgical lamp.

"She's here," Kaye said.

"She's here," Mitch affirmed.

"We've done it."

"You sure did," Mitch said.

Again, their daughter lifted her head, opened her eyes, this time wide.

"Look at that," Chambers said. Felicity bent over, nearly knocking heads with Sue.

Mitch met his daughter's stare with fascination. She had tawny brown pupils flecked with gold. He leaned forward. "Here I am," he said to the baby.

Kaye reached out to show her the nipple again, but the baby resisted, head bobbing with surprising strength.

"Hello, Mitch," his daughter said, her voice like the mewing of a kitten, not much more than a squeak, but very clear.

The hair rose on the back of his neck. Felicity Galbreath gasped and backed away as if stung.

Mitch pushed against the edge of the bed and stood. He shivered. The infant resting on Kaye's breast seemed for a moment more than he could stand; not just unexpected, but *wrong*. He wanted to run. Still, he could not take his eyes off the little girl. Heat rose into his chest. The shape of her tiny face came into a kind of focus. She seemed to be trying to speak again, her lips pushing out and drawing to one side, small and pink. A milky yellow bubble appeared in the corner of her mouth. Small dapples of fawn-color, lion-color, flushed across her cheeks and brows.

Her head rolled and she stared up at Kaye's face. A puzzled frown wrinkled the space between her eyes.

Mitch Rafelson reached with his big, raw-boned hand and callused fingers to touch the little girl. He bent over to kiss Kaye, then the baby, and stroked her temple with great gentleness. With a touch of his thumb, he turned her rose-colored lips back to the rich nipple. She gave a breathy sigh, a small whistling sound, and with a squirm, fastened onto her mother's teat and suckled vigorously. Her tiny hands flexed perfect golden-brown fingers.

* * *

Mitch called Sam and Abby in Oregon and told them the news. He was barely able to focus on their words; his father's trembling voice, his mother's piercing squeal of joy and relief. They spoke for a while and then he told them he could barely stand. "We need to sleep," he said.

Kaye and the baby were already asleep. Chambers told him they would stay there for two more days. Mitch asked for a bunk to be brought into the room, but Felicity and Sue persuaded him that everything would be all right.

"Go on home and rest," Sue said. "She'll be fine."

Mitch shifted uncertainly on his feet. "They'll call if there's any trouble?"

"We'll call," Mary Hand said as she walked past with a bag of linens.

"I'll have two friends stay outside the clinic for the day," Jack said.

"I need a place to stay tonight," Felicity said. "I want to check them over tomorrow."

"Stay in our house," Jack suggested.

Mitch's legs wobbled as he walked with them from the clinic to the Toyota.

In the trailer, he slept through the afternoon and evening. When he awoke, it was twilight. He knelt on the couch and stared out the wide picture window at the scrub and gravel and distant hills.

Then he showered, shaved, dressed. Looked for more things Kaye and the baby might need that had been forgotten.

Looked at himself in the bathroom mirror.

Wept.

Walked back to the clinic alone, in the lovely gloaming. The air was clean and clear and carried smells of sage and grass and dust and water from a low creek. He passed a house where four men were removing an engine from an old Ford, using an oak tree and a chain hoist. The men nodded at him, looked away quickly. They knew who he was; they knew what had happened. They were not comfortable with either him or the event. He picked up his pace. His eyebrows itched, and now his cheeks. The mask was very loose. Soon it would come off. He could feel his tongue against the sides of his mouth; it felt different. His head felt different.

More than anything, he wanted to see Kaye again, and the baby, the girl, his daughter, to make sure it was all real.

Arlington, Virginia

The wedding party spread out over much of the half-acre backyard. The day was warm and misty, alternating patches of sun and light overcast. Mark Augustine stood in the reception line beside his bride for forty minutes, smiling, shaking hands, giving polite hugs. Senators and congressional representatives walked through the line, chatting politely. Men and women in unisex black-and-white livery carried trays of champagne and canapés over the golf-green manicured lawn. Augustine looked at his bride with a fixed smile; he knew what he felt inside, love and relief and accomplishment, all slightly chilled. The face he showed to the guests, to the few reporters who had picked winning tickets in the press pool lottery, was calm, warmly loving, dutiful.

Something had occupied his mind all day, however, even through the wedding ceremony. He had flubbed his simple lines of declaration, provoking mild laughter in the front rows in the chapel.

Babies were being born alive. In the quarantine hospitals, in specially appointed Taskforce community clinics, and even in private homes, new babies were arriving.

The possibility that he was wrong had occurred to him

lightly, in passing, a kind of itch, until he heard that Kaye Lang's baby had been born alive, delivered by a doctor working from emergency bulletins issued by the Centers for Disease Control, the very same epidemiological study team that had been put in place at his orders. Special procedures, special precautions; the babies were different.

So far, twenty-four SHEVA infants had been dropped off at community clinics by single mothers or parents the Taskforce had not been tracking.

Anonymous, alive foundlings, now under his care.

The reception line came to an end. Feet aching in the tight black dress shoes, he hugged his bride, whispered in her ear, and motioned for Florence Leighton to join him in the main house.

"What did Allergy and Infectious Diseases send us?" he asked. Mrs. Leighton opened the briefcase she had carried all day and handed him a fresh fax page.

"I've been waiting for an opportunity," she said. "The president called earlier, sends his best wishes, and wants you at the White House sometime this evening, earliest convenience."

Augustine read the fax. "Kaye Lang had her baby," he said, looking up at her, eyebrows peaking.

"So I heard," Mrs. Leighton said. Her expression was professional, attentive, and revealed nothing.

"We should send her congratulations," Augustine said.

"I'll do that," Mrs. Leighton said.

Augustine shook his head. "No, you won't," he said. "We still have a course to follow."

"Yes, sir," she said.

"Tell the president I'll be there by eight."

"What about Alyson?" Mrs. Leighton asked.

"She married me, didn't she?" Augustine answered. "She knows what she's getting into."

Kumash County, Eastern Washington

Mitch supported Kaye by one arm as she walked and waddled from one side of the room to the other.

"What are you going to call her?" Felicity asked. She sat in the room's single blue vinyl chair, rocking the sleeping baby gently in her arms.

Kaye looked up at Mitch expectantly. Something about naming her child made her feel vulnerable and pretentious, as if this was a right even a mother did not deserve.

"You did most of the work," Mitch said with a smile. "You have the privilege."

"We need to agree," Kaye said.

"Try me."

"She's a new kind of star," Kaye said. Her legs were still wobbly. Her stomach felt slack and sore, and sometimes the pain between her legs made her feel a little ill, but she was improving rapidly. She sat on the side of the bed. "My grandmother was named Stella. That means star. I was thinking we'd name her Stella Nova."

Mitch took the baby from Felicity. "Stella Nova," he repeated.

"Sounds bold," Felicity said. "I like it."

"That's her name," Mitch said, lifting the baby close to his face. He smelled the top of her head, the moist rich heat of her hair. She smelled of her mother and much more. He could feel cascades of emotions like tumbling blocks falling into place inside, laying a firm foundation.

"She commands your attention even when she's asleep," Kaye said. Half-consciously, she reached up to her face and removed a dangling piece of mask, revealing the new skin beneath, pink and tender, with a radiance of tiny melanophores.

Felicity walked over and bent to examine Kaye more closely. "I don't believe I'm seeing this," she said. "I'm the one who should feel privileged."

Stella opened her eyes and shuddered as if in alarm. She gave her father a long and puzzled look, then began to cry. Her cry was loud and alarming. Mitch quickly handed Stella to Kaye, who pulled aside her robe. The baby settled in and stopped crying. Kaye again savored the wonder of her milk letting down, the sensual loveliness of the child at her nipple. The child's eyes surveyed her mother, and then she turned her head, tugging the breast with her, and peered around the room at Felicity and Mitch. The tawny gold-flecked eyes made Mitch's insides melt.

"So advanced," Felicity said. "She's a charmer."

"What did you expect?" Kaye asked softly, her voice taking on a faint warble. With a small shock, Mitch recognized some of the baby's tone in her mother's.

Stella Nova warbled lightly as she suckled, like a small sweet bird. She sang as she nursed, showing her contentment, her delight.

Mitch's tongue moved behind his lips in restless sympathy. "How does she do that?" he asked.

"I don't know," Kaye said. And it was evident that for the moment she did not care.

"She's like a baby of six months, in some ways," Felicity said to Mitch as he carried the bags in from the Toyota to the trailer. "She seems to be able to focus already, recognize faces . . . voices . . ." She *hmm*ed to herself, as if avoiding the one thing that really separated Stella from other newborns.

"She hasn't spoken again," Mitch said.

Felicity held the screen door open for him. "Maybe we were hearing things," she said.

Kaye laid the sleeping child in a small crib in the corner of the living room. She arranged a light blanket over Stella and straightened with a small groan. "We heard right," she said. She went to Mitch and lifted a patch of mask from his face.

"Ow," he said. "It's not ready."

"Look," Kaye said, suddenly scientific. "We have melanophores. She has melanophores. Most if not all of the new parents are going to have them. And our tongues . . . Connected to something new in our heads." She tapped her temple. "We're equipped to deal with her, almost as equals."

Felicity appeared baffled by this shift from new mother to objective, observing Kaye Lang. Kaye returned her look with a smile. "I didn't spend my pregnancy like a cow," she said. "Judging from these new tools, our daughter is going to be a very difficult child."

"How so?" Felicity asked.

"Because in some ways she's going to run rings around us," Kaye said.

"Maybe in all ways," Mitch added.

"You don't mean that, literally," Felicity said. "At least she wasn't born mobile. The skin color—the melanophores, as you call them—may be . . ." She waved her hand, unable to finish her thought.

"They're not just color," Mitch said. "I can *feel* mine."

"So can I," Kaye said. "They change. Imagine that poor girl." She glanced at Mitch. He nodded, then explained to Felicity their encounter with the teenagers in West Virginia.

"If I were in the Taskforce, I'd be setting up psychiatric stations for parents whose new children have died," Kaye said. "They might face a new kind of grieving."

"All dressed up, and no one to talk to," Mitch said.

Felicity took a deep breath and held her hand to her forehead. "I've been in pediatrics for twenty-two years," she said. "Now I feel like I should give up and go hide in the woods."

"Get the poor lady a glass of water," Kaye said. "Or would

you like wine? I need a glass of wine, Mitch. I haven't had a drink in over a year." She turned to Felicity. "Did the bulletin mention no alcohol?"

"No problems. Wine for me, too, please," Felicity said.

Kaye put her face close to Mitch's in the small kitchen. She stared at him intently, and her eyes lost their focus for a second. Her cheeks pulsed fawn and gold.

"Jesus," Mitch said.

"Get that mask off," Kaye said, "and we'll *really* have something to show each other."

Kumash County, Eastern Washington
JUNE

"Let's call it a Brave New Species party," Wendell Packer said as he came in through the screen door and handed Kaye a bouquet of roses. Oliver Merton followed with a box of Godiva chocolates and a big smile and eagerly darted his eyes around the inside of the trailer.

"Where's the little wonder?"

"Asleep," Kaye said, accepting his hug. "Who else is here?" she called out, delighted.

"We smuggled in Wendell and Oliver and Maria," Eileen Ripper said. "And, lo and behold . . ."

She swung out her arms to the dusty old van sitting on the gravel drive under the lone oak tree. Christopher Dicken was climbing down from the front passenger side with some difficulty, his legs stiff. He took a pair of crutches from Maria Konig and turned to the trailer. His one good eye met Kaye's and for a moment she thought she was going to cry. But he lifted a crutch and waggled it at her and she smiled.

"It's bumpy out here," he called.

Kaye ran past Mitch to gingerly hug Christopher. Eileen and Mitch stood together as Kaye and Christopher talked.

"Old friends?" Eileen asked.

"Probably soul mates," Mitch said. He was glad to see Christopher, as well, but could not help feeling a little twinge of masculine concern.

The living room was too small to hold them all, so Wendell braced his arm against the cabinet in the hall and looked down on the rest. Maria and Oliver sat together on the couch under the picture window. Christopher sat in the blue vinyl chair, with Eileen perched on one arm. Mitch came in from the kitchen with bouquets of wine glasses in each fist and a bottle of champagne under each arm. Oliver helped set them down on the round table beside the couch, and carefully popped the corks.

"From the airport?" Mitch asked.

"Portland airport. Not as big a selection," Oliver said.

Kaye brought out Stella Nova in a pink bassinet and placed her on the small, scuffed coffee table. The baby was awake. Her eyes moved sleepily around the room and she blew a tiny bubble of spit. Her head wobbled a bit. Kaye reached down to adjust her pajamas.

Christopher stared at her as if she were a ghost. "Kaye . . ." he began, his voice breaking.

"No need," Kaye said, and touched his red-scarred hand.

"There *is* a need. I feel like I don't deserve to be here with you and Mitch, with her."

"Shush," Kaye said. "You were there at the beginning."

Christopher smiled. "Thank you," he said.

"How old is she?" Eileen whispered.

"Three weeks," Kaye said.

Maria reached out first and tucked her finger into Stella's

hand. The baby's fingers closed tightly around it, and she tugged gently. Stella smiled.

"That reflex is still there," Oliver said.

"Oh, shut up," Eileen said. "She's still a baby, Oliver."

"Yes, but she looks so . . ."

"Beautiful!" Eileen insisted.

"Different," Oliver persisted.

"I don't see it much now," Kaye said, knowing what he meant, but feeling a little defensive.

"We're different, too," Mitch observed.

"You both look fine, even stylish," Maria said. "It's going to be all the rage once the fashion magazines see you. Petite, beautiful Kaye . . ."

"Rugged, handsome Mitch," Eileen said.

"With squid cheeks," Kaye finished for them. They laughed, and Stella jerked in her bassinet. Then she warbled, and again the room fell silent. She honored each of the guests in turn with a second, lingering look, her head wobbling as she tracked them around the room, coming full circle to Kaye and then jerking again as she saw Mitch. She smiled at Mitch. Mitch felt his cheeks flush, like warm water running beneath his skin. The last of the skin masks had fallen away eight days before, and looking at his daughter was something of an experience.

Oliver said, "Oh, my God."

Maria stared at all three of them, her jaw open.

Stella Nova sent waves of fawn and gold over her cheeks, and her pupils dilated slightly, the muscles around her eyes and eyelids drawing the skin down in delicate and complex curves.

"She's going to teach *us* how to talk," Kaye said proudly.

"She is absolutely stunning," Eileen said. "I've never seen a more beautiful baby."

Oliver asked permission to get closer and leaned in to examine Stella. "Her eyes really aren't that large, they just look large," he said.

"Oliver thinks the next humans should look like UFO aliens," Eileen said.

"Aliens?" Oliver said indignantly. "I deny that statement, Eileen."

"She's totally human, totally now," Kaye said. "Not separate, not distant, not different. She's our child."

"Of course," Eileen said, blushing.

"Sorry," Kaye said. "We've been out here for too long, with too much time to think."

"I know about *that*," Christopher said.

"She has a really spectacular nose," Oliver said. "So delicate, yet broad at the base. And the shape—I do believe she's going to be a spectacular beauty."

Stella watched him soberly, her cheeks colorless, then looked away, bored. She tried to find Kaye. Kaye moved into the baby's field of view.

"Mama," Stella chirped.

"Oh, my God," Oliver said again.

Wendell and Oliver drove out to the Little Silver store and bought sandwiches. They all ate at a small picnic table behind the trailer in the cooling afternoon. Christopher had said very little, smiling stiffly as the others spoke. He ate his sandwich on a patch of straw-dry lawn, sitting in a rickety camp chair.

Mitch approached and settled down beside him on the grass. "Stella's asleep," he said. "Kaye's with her."

Christopher smiled and took a sip from a can of 7UP. "You want to know what brings me all this way out here," he said.

"All right," Mitch said. "That's a start."

"I'm surprised Kaye was so forgiving."

"We've gone through a lot of changes," Mitch said. "I must say it seemed you abandoned us."

"I've gone through a lot of changes, too," Christopher said. "I'm trying to piece things back together. I'm going down to Mexico day after tomorrow. Ensenada, south of San Diego. On my own."

"Not a vacation?"

"I'm going to look into the lateral transmission of old retroviruses."

"It's bullshit," Mitch said. "They made it up to keep the Taskforce going."

"Oh, something's real enough," Christopher said. "Fifty cases so far. Mark's not a monster."

"I'm not so sure of that." Mitch stared grimly at the desert and the trailer.

"But I am thinking it may not be caused by the virus they've found. I've been looking over old files on Mexico. I found similar cases from thirty years ago."

"I hope you set them straight soon. It's been nice here, but we could have done a lot better . . . under other circumstances."

Kaye came out of the trailer holding a portable baby monitor. Maria handed her a sandwich on a paper plate. She joined Mitch and Christopher.

"What do you think of our lawn?" she asked.

"He's looking into the Mexican illnesses," Mitch said.

"I thought you quit the Taskforce."

"I did. The cases are real, Kaye, but I don't think they're directly related to SHEVA. We've been through so many twists and turns on this—herpes, Epstein-Barr. I guess you got the bulletin from the CDC on anesthesia."

"Our doctor did," Mitch said.

"We might have lost Stella without it," Kaye said.

"More SHEVA babies are being born alive now. Augustine's got to deal with that. I just want to level the field a little by finding out what's going on in Mexico. All the cases are down there."

"You think it's from another source?" Kaye asked.

"I'm going to find out. I can walk a little now. I'm hiring an assistant."

"How? You're not rich."

"I've got a grant from a rich eccentric in New York."

Mitch's eyes widened. "Not William Daney!"

"The same. Oliver and Brock are trying to put together a journalistic coup. They thought I could gather evidence. It's a job, and hell, I believe in it. Seeing Stella . . . Stella Nova . . . really brings it home. I just didn't have the faith."

Wendell and Maria walked over from the oak tree and Wendell pulled a magazine out of a paper sack. "Thought you might like to see this," Maria said, handing it to Kaye.

She looked at the cover and laughed out loud. It was a copy of *WIRED*, and on the brilliant orange cover was printed the black silhouette of a curled fetus with a green question mark across the middle. The log line read *"Human 3.0: Not a Virus, but an Upgrade?"*

Oliver joined them. "I've seen that," he said. "*WIRED* doesn't have much clout in Washington these days. The news is almost all grim, Kaye."

"We know," Kaye said, brushing back a wisp of hair as the breeze picked up.

"But here's some good. Brock says *National Geographic* and *Nature* have finished peer review on his piece on the Innsbruck Neanderthals. They're going to publish jointly in six months. He's going to call it a confirmed evolutionary event, a subspeciation, and he's going to mention SHEVA, though not prominently. Did Christopher tell you about Daney?"

Kaye nodded.

"We're going to make an end run," Oliver said, his eyes fierce. "All Christopher has to do is track down this virus in Mexico and out-think seven national laboratories."

"You can do it," Mitch said to Christopher. "You were there first, even before Kaye."

The visitors were packing up for their long trip through the northern badlands and out of the reservation. Mitch helped Christopher into the passenger seat and they shook hands. As Kaye held a sleepy Stella and hugged the others, Mitch saw Jack's pickup rolling down the dirt road.

Sue was not with him. The truck's brakes squealed as Jack stopped in the drive, just to one side of the van. Mitch walked over to talk as Jack opened the door. He did not get out.

"How's Sue?"

"Still holding," Jack said. "Chambers can't use any drugs to get her going. Dr. Galbreath is watching things. We're just waiting."

"We'd like to see her," Mitch said.

"She's not happy. She snaps at me. Maybe tomorrow. Now I'm going to smuggle your friends back out on the old wash road."

"We appreciate this, Jack," Mitch said.

Jack blinked and turned down his lips, his way of shrugging. "There was a special meeting this afternoon," he said. "That Cayuse woman is at us again. Some of the casino workers formed a little group. They're mad. They say the quarantine is going to ruin us. They wouldn't listen to me. They say I'm biased."

"What can we do?"

"Sue calls them hotheads, but they're hotheads with a real cause. I just wanted to let you know. We all got to be prepared."

Mitch and Kaye waved and watched their friends drive off down the road. Night settled over the country. Kaye sat in the last of the warmth in the folding chair under the oak tree, nursing Stella until it was time for a diaper change.

Changing diapers never failed to bring Mitch down to earth. As he wiped his daughter clean, she sang sweetly, her voice like finches among windblown branches. Her cheeks and brow flushed almost red with her new comfort, and she gripped his finger tightly.

He carried Stella around, swaying gently from his hips, and followed Kaye as she packed dirty diapers into a plastic bag to take them to the laundry. Kaye looked over her shoulder as they walked to the shed where the machines were kept. "What did Jack say?" she asked.

Mitch told her.

"We'll live out of our bags," she said matter-of-factly. She had been expecting worse. "Let's pack them again tonight."

Kumash County, Eastern Washington

Mitch awoke from a sound and dreamless sleep and sat up in bed, listening. "What?" he murmured.

Kaye lay beside him, motionless, snoring softly. He looked across the bed to Stella's small shelf bolted against the wall, and the battery-powered clock that sat there, its hands glowing green in the dark. It was two-fifteen in the morning.

Without thinking, he pushed down to the end of the bed and stood, naked except for his boxers, rubbing his eyes. He could have sworn somebody had said something, but the house was quiet. Then his heart started to race and he felt alarm pump through his arms and legs. He looked over his shoulder at Kaye, thought about waking her, and decided against it.

Mitch knew he was going to check the house, make sure it was secure, prove to himself that nobody was walking around outside, preparing to lay an ambush. He knew this without thinking much about it, and he prepared by grabbing a piece of steel rebar he had stashed under the bed for just such an eventuality. He had never owned a gun, did not know how to use one, and wondered as he walked into the living room whether that was stupid.

He shivered in the cold. The weather was turning cloudy; he could not see any stars through the window over the couch. He stumbled on a diaper pail in the bathroom. Then, abruptly, he knew he had been summoned from inside the house.

He returned to the bedroom. Half in, half out of the shallow closet at the end of the bed, on Kaye's side, the baby's bassinet seemed somehow outlined in the dark.

His eyes were growing more accustomed to the dark, but he was not sensing the bassinet with his eyes. He sniffed; his nose was running. He sniffed again and leaned over the bassinet, then recoiled and sneezed loudly.

"What is it?" Kaye sat up in bed. "Mitch?"

"I don't know," Mitch said.

"Did you ask for me?"

"No."

"Did Stella?"

"She's quiet. I think she's asleep."

"Turn on the light."

That seemed sensible. He switched on the overhead light. Stella looked up at him from the bassinet, tawny eyes wide, her hands forming little fists. Her lips were parted, giving her a babyish, pouting Marilyn Monroe aspect, but she was silent.

Kaye crawled to the end of the bed and looked down at their daughter.

Stella made a small coo. Her eyes tracked them intently, going in and out of focus and sometimes crossing, as was her way. Still, it was obvious she was seeing them, and that she was not unhappy.

"She's lonely," Kaye said. "I fed her an hour ago."

"So what is she, psychic?" Mitch asked, stretching. "Calling us with her mind?" He sniffed again, and again he sneezed. The bedroom window was closed. "What is it in here?"

Kaye squatted before the bassinet and picked up Stella.

She nuzzled her and then looked up at Mitch, her lips drawn back in an almost feral snarl. She sneezed, too.

Stella cooed again.

"I think she has colic," Kaye said. "Smell her."

Mitch took Stella from Kaye. The baby squirmed and looked up at him, brows wrinkled. Mitch could have sworn she became brighter, and that someone was calling his name, either in the room or outside. Now he was really spooked.

"Maybe she *is* out of *Star Trek*," he said. He sniffed her again and his lips curled.

"Right," Kaye said skeptically. "She isn't psychic." Kaye took the baby, who was waving her fists, quite happy with the commotion, and carried her into the kitchen.

"Humans aren't supposed to have them, but a few years ago, scientists found that we do."

"Have what?" Mitch asked.

"Active vomeronasal organs. At the base of the nasal cavity. They process certain molecules . . . vomerophrins. Like pheromones. My guess is, ours just got a whole lot better." She hefted the baby on her hips. "Your lips drawing back—"

"You did it, too," Mitch said defensively.

"That's a vomeronasal response. Our family cat used to do that when she smelled something really interesting—a dead mouse or my mother's armpit." Kaye lifted the baby, who squealed softly, and sniffed at her head, her neck, her tummy. She sniffed behind the baby's ears again. "Sniff here," she said.

Mitch sniffed, drew back, stifled a sneeze. He delicately felt behind Stella's ears. She stiffened and started to be unhappy, giving little pre-crying gurks. "No," she said quite distinctly. "No."

Kaye loosed her bra and gave Stella suck before she became really upset.

Mitch withdrew his finger. The tip was slightly oily, as if he had touched behind the ear of a teenager, not a baby. But the oil was not precisely skin oil. It felt waxy and a little rough as he rubbed, and it smelled like musk.

"Pheromones," he said. "Or what did you call them?"

"Vomeropherins. Baby-type come-hither. We have a lot to learn," Kaye said sleepily as she carried Stella into the bedroom and lay down with her. "You woke up first," Kaye murmured. "You always had a good nose. Good night."

Mitch felt behind his own ears and sniffed his finger. Abruptly, he sneezed again, and stood at the end of the bed, wide awake, his nose and palate tingling.

It was no more than an hour after he managed to get back to sleep that he came awake again and jumped out of bed and instantly started slipping on his pants. It was still dark. He tapped Kaye's foot with his hand.

"Trucks," he said. He had just finished buttoning the front of his shirt when someone banged on the front door. Kaye pushed Stella to the middle of the bed and quickly put on slacks and a sweater.

Mitch opened the front door with his shirt cuffs still undone. Jack stood on the porch, his lips forming a hard, upside-down U, his hat pulled low, almost hiding his eyes. "Sue's gone into labor," he said. "I've got to go back to the clinic."

"We'll be right down," Mitch said. "Is Galbreath there?"

"She won't be coming. You should get out of here now. The trustees voted last night while I was with Sue."

"How—" Mitch began, and then saw the three trucks and seven men on the gravel and dirt of the front yard.

"They decided the babies are sick," Jack said miserably. "They want them taken care of by the government."

"They want their damned jobs back," Mitch said.

"They won't talk to me." Jack touched his mask with a strong, thick finger. "I persuaded the trustees to let you go. I can't go with you, but these men will take you up a dirt road to the highway." Jack held out his hands helplessly. "Sue wanted Kaye to be with her. I wish you could be there. But I gotta go."

"Thanks," Mitch said.

Kaye came up behind him, carrying the baby in the car seat. "I'm ready," she said. "I want to go see Sue."

"No," Jack said. "It's that old Cayuse woman. We should have sent her to the coast."

"It's more than her," Mitch said.

"Sue needs me!" Kaye cried.

"They won't let you into that part of town," Jack said miserably. "Too many people. They heard it on the news—dead Mexicans near San Diego. No way. It's hard, like stone, what they think now. They'll go after us next, probably."

Kaye wiped her eyes in anger and frustration. "Tell her we love her," she said. "Thanks for everything, Jack. Tell her."

"I will. I gotta go."

The seven men backed away as Jack walked to his truck and got in. He started the engine and spun out, throwing a plume of dust and gravel.

"The Toyota's in better shape," Mitch said. He hefted their two suitcases to the trunk under the watchful eyes of the seven men. They muttered to each other and stayed well clear as Kaye carried Stella out in her arms and fastened her into the car seat in the back. Some of the men avoided her eyes and made small signs with their hands. She slid in beside the baby.

Two of the pickups had gun racks and shotguns and hunting rifles. Her throat closed as she settled into the back of the Toyota beside Stella. She rolled up the window and buckled her seat belt and sat with the meaty sour smell of her own fear.

Mitch carried out her laptop and box of papers and pushed them into the back of the trunk, then slammed the lid. Kaye was pushing buttons on her cell phone.

"Don't do that," Mitch said gruffly as he got into the driver's seat. "They'll know where we are. We'll call from a pay phone someplace when we're on the highway."

Kaye's dapples flared red for an instant.

Mitch watched her with a stricken, wondering face. "We're aliens," he muttered. He started the engine. The seven men got into the three trucks and led them down the road.

"You have any cash for gas?" Mitch asked.

"In my purse," Kaye said. "You don't want to use credit cards?"

Mitch avoided answering that. "We got almost a full tank."

Stella squalled briefly, then grew quiet as a pink dawn started over the low hills and behind the scattered oak trees. The overcast lay open and ragged on the horizon and they saw curtains of rain ahead. The dawn light was bright and unreal against the low black clouds.

The dirt road north was rough but not impassable. The trucks accompanied them to the very end, where a sign marked the edge of the reservation and also, coincidentally, advertised the Wild Eagle Casino. Scrub and tumbleweeds lay sad and battered against a bent and twisted barbed wire fence.

The thick underbellies of the clouds drizzled light rain on the windshield, turning the dust into wiper-whipped mud as they came off the dirt road, up an embankment, and onto the state highway heading east. A brilliant shaft of morning light, the last they saw that day, caught them like a searchlight as Mitch brought the Toyota up to speed on the two-lane asphalt.

"I liked that place," Kaye said, her voice rough. "I was happier in that trailer than I can remember ever being, anywhere else in my life."

"You thrive in adversity," Mitch said, and reached over his shoulder to grasp her hand.

"I thrive with you," Kaye said. "With Stella."

92

Northeastern Oregon

Kaye walked back from the phone booth. They had parked in a strip mall parking lot in Bend to buy food at a market. Kaye had done the shopping and then had called Maria Konig. Mitch had stayed in the car with Stella.

"Arizona still hasn't set up an Emergency Action Office," Kaye said.

"What about Idaho?"

"They have one as of two days ago. Canada, too."

Stella coo-whistled in her safety seat. Mitch had changed her a few minutes before and she usually performed for a short while afterward. He was almost getting used to her musical sounds. She was already adept at making two different notes at once, splitting one note away, raising and lowering it; the effect was uncannily like two theremins arguing. Kaye looked through the window. The baby seemed in another world, lost in discovering what sounds she could make.

"They stared at me in the market," Kaye said. "I felt like a leper. Worse, like a *nigger*." She kicked out the word between clenched teeth. She shoved the grocery bag into the passenger seat and dug into it with a tense hand. "I took out money at the ATM and got food and then I got these," she said, and pulled out bottles of makeup, foundation and powder. "For our dapples. I don't know what I'll do about her singing."

Mitch got behind the wheel.

"Let's go," Kaye said, "before somebody calls the police."

516

"It isn't that bad," Mitch said as he started the car.

"Isn't it?" Kaye cried. "We're *marked*! If they find us, they'll put Stella in a camp, for Christ's sake! God knows what Augustine has planned for us, for all the parents. Get sharp, Mitch!"

Mitch pulled the car out of the parking lot in silence.

"I'm sorry," Kaye said, her voice breaking. "I'm sorry, Mitch, but I'm so frightened. We have to think, we have to plan."

Clouds followed them, gray skies and light rain without break. They crossed the border into California at night, pulled off onto a lonely dirt road, and slept in the car with rain drumming on the roof.

Kaye applied makeup to Mitch in the morning. He clumsily painted her face with foundation and she touched up in the rearview mirror.

"We'll rent a room today in a motel," Mitch said.

"Why take the risk?"

"We look pretty good, I think," he said, smiling encouragement. "She needs a bath and so do we. We are not animals and I refuse to act like one."

Kaye thought about this as she nursed Stella. "All right," she said.

"We'll go to Arizona, and then, if necessary, we'll go to Mexico or even farther south. We'll find someplace we can live until things get settled down."

"When will that be?" Kaye asked softly.

Mitch did not know, so he did not answer. He drove back along the deserted farm road onto the highway. The clouds were breaking up now and brilliant morning light fell on the forests and fields of grass to either side of the highway.

"Sun!" said Stella, and waved her fists lustily.

EPILOGUE

Tucson, Arizona
THREE YEARS LATER

A plump little girl with short brown hair and brown skin and sweated streaks of powder on her face stood in the alley and peered between the dust-colored garages. She whistled softly to herself, interweaving two variations of a Mozart piano trio. Someone who did not look too closely might have mistaken her for one of the many Latino children who played along the streets and ran through the alleys.

Stella had never been allowed to go this far from the small house her parents rented, a few hundred steps away. The world of the alley was fresh. She sniffed the air lightly; she always did that, and she never found what she wanted to find.

But she heard the excited voices of children playing, and that was enticement enough. She walked on red concrete squares along the stucco side wall of a small garage, pushed open a swinging metal gate, and saw three children tossing a half-inflated basketball in a small backyard. The children paused their game and stared at her.

"Who are you?" asked a black-haired girl, seven or eight.

"Stella," she answered clearly. "Who are you?"

"We're playing here."

"Can I play?"

"You got a dirty face."

"It comes off, look," and Stella wiped at the powder with her sleeve, leaving fleshy stains on the cloth. "It's hot today, isn't it?"

A boy about ten looked her over critically. "You got spots," he said.

"They're freckles," Stella said. Her mother had told her to tell people that.

"Sure, you can play," said a second girl, also ten. She was tall and had long skinny legs. "How old are you?"

"Three."

"You don't sound three."

"I can read and whistle, too. Listen." She whistled the two tunes together, watching their reactions with interest.

"Jesus," the boy said.

Stella felt proud at his amazement. The tall skinny girl threw her the ball and Stella caught it deftly and smiled. "I love this," she said, and her face flushed a lovely shade of pale beige and gold. The boy stared after her with jaw agape, then sat down to watch as the girls played together on the dry summer grass. A sweet musky scent followed Stella wherever she ran.

Kaye searched all the rooms and the closets frantically, twice, calling out her daughter's name. She had been absorbed reading a magazine article after putting Stella down for a nap and had not heard the girl leave. Stella was smart and not likely to walk out into a road or get into any obvious danger, but the neighborhood was poor and there was still strong prejudice against children like her, and fear about the diseases that sometimes followed in the wake of SHEVA pregnancies.

The diseases were real; ancient recurrences of old retroviruses, sometimes fatal. Christopher Dicken had discovered that in Mexico three years ago, and it had almost cost him his life. The danger passed a few months after birth, but Mark Augustine had been right. Nature was never other than two-faced about her gifts.

If a police officer saw Stella, or somebody reported her, there could be trouble.

Kaye called Mitch at the Chevrolet dealership where he

worked, a few miles from their house, and he told her he'd come right home.

The children had never seen anything quite like this odd little girl. Just being around her made them feel friendly and good, and they did not know why, nor did they care. The girls chatted about clothes and singers, and Stella imitated some of the singers, especially Salay Sammi, her favorite. She was an excellent mimic.

The boy stood to one side, frowning in concentration.

The younger girl went next door to invite other friends over, and they in turn invited others, and soon the backyard was filled with boys and girls. They played house, and the boys played police, and Stella provided sound effects and something else, a smile, a presence, that soothed and energized them at once. Some had to go home and Stella said she was glad to meet them and smelled behind their ears, which made them laugh and draw back in embarrassment, but none of them felt angry.

They were all fascinated by the gold and brown dapples on her face.

Stella seemed completely at ease, happy, but she had never been among so many children before. When two nine-year-old girls, identical twins, asked her different questions at once, Stella answered them both, at once. They could almost understand what she said, and they broke out laughing, asking the funny plump little girl where she had learned to do that.

The older boy's frown changed to determination. He knew what he had to do.

Kaye and Mitch called her name along the street. They did not dare ask the police for help; Arizona had finally gone along with the Emergency Action and was sending its new children for special study and education in Iowa.

Kaye was beside herself. "It was just a minute, just—"

"We'll find her," Mitch said, but his face gave him away.

He looked incongruous in his dark blue suit, walking on the dusty street between the small old houses. A hot dry wind soaked up their sweat. "I hate this," he said for the millionth time. It had become a familiar mantra, part of the bitterness inside him. Stella made him feel complete; Kaye could still give him some of the old life. But when he was alone, the strain filled him to the brim, and in his head he would say over and over how much he hated this.

Kaye held his arm and told him again how sorry she was.

"Not your fault," he said, but he was still very angry.

The thin girl showed Stella how to dance. Stella knew a lot of ballet music; Prokofiev was her favorite composer, and the difficult scores came out in complexes of piping and whistling and clucking. One little blond boy, younger than Stella, stayed as close as he could to her, brown eyes big with interest.

"What do we want to play now?" the tall girl asked when she grew tired of trying to stand *en pointe*.

"I'll get Monopoly," said an eight-year-old boy with the more familiar kind of freckles.

"Or maybe we can play Othemo?" Stella asked.

They had been searching for an hour. Kaye stopped for a moment on a broken patch of sidewalk and listened. The alley that ran behind their homes opened onto this side street, and she thought she heard children playing. Lots of children.

She and Mitch walked quickly between the garages and board fences, trying to catch Stella's voice, or one of her many sounds.

Mitch heard their daughter first. He pushed open the metal swinging gate and they entered.

The small yard was packed with children like birds around a feeder. Kaye noticed immediately that Stella was not the center of attention; she was simply there, off to one side, playing a game of Othemo, with decks of cards that made sounds when pressed. If the sounds matched or made a tune, the players got to discard. The players who emptied their hands first won. This was one of Stella's favorites.

Mitch stood behind Kaye. Their daughter did not see them at first. She was chattering happily with the twins and another boy.

"I'll get her," Mitch said.

"Wait," Kaye said. Stella appeared so happy. Kaye was willing to risk a few minutes for this.

Then Stella looked up, pushed to her feet, and let the musical cards fall from her hands. She circled her head in the air and sniffed.

Mitch saw another child, a boy, enter the yard from a gate in the front. He was about Stella's age. Kaye saw him, too, and recognized him immediately. They heard a woman's frantic calls in Spanish and Kaye knew what they were, what they meant.

"We have to leave," Mitch said.

"No," Kaye said, and held him back with her arm. "Just for a moment. Please. Watch!"

Stella and the boy approached each other. The other children one by one fell silent. Stella circled the young boy, face blank for a long moment. The boy made small sighs, his chest heaving as if he had been running. He rubbed at his face with quick dabs of spit on his sleeve. Then he bent over and sniffed behind Stella's ear. Stella sniffed behind his ear and they held hands.

"I'm Stella Nova," Stella said. "Where are you from?"

The small boy just smiled, and his face twitched in ways Stella had not seen before. She found her own face responding. She felt the rush of blood to her skin and she laughed out loud, a delighted, high-pitched shriek. The boy smelled of so much—of his family and the way his home smelled and of the food his mother cooked, and his cats, and Stella watched his face and understood a little of what he was saying. He was so *rich*, this little boy. Their dapples colored madly, almost at random. She watched the boy's pupils fleck with color, rubbed her fingers on his hands, feeling the skin, the shivers of response.

The boy spoke in broken English and Spanish simultaneously. His mouth moved in a way that Stella was familiar with, shaping the sounds passing along both sides of his ridged tongue. Stella knew a fair amount of Spanish and tried to answer. The boy jumped up and down with excitement; he understood her! Talking to people was usually so frustrating for Stella, but this was even worse, because suddenly she knew what talking might *really* be.

Then she looked to one side and saw Kaye and Mitch.

Simultaneously, Kaye saw the woman in the kitchen window, using her phone. The woman did not look at all happy.

"Let's go," Mitch said, and Kaye did not disagree.

"Where are we going now?" Stella asked from her safety seat in the back of the Chevy Lumina as Mitch drove south.

"Mexico, maybe," Kaye said.

"I want to see more like the boy," Stella said, pouting fiercely.

Kaye closed her eyes and saw the boy's terrified mother, grabbing him away from Stella, shooting a dirty look at Kaye; loving and hating her own child. No hope for bringing the two together again. And the woman in the window, too afraid to even come outside and talk with her.

"You will," Kaye said dreamily. "You were very beautiful with the boy."

"I know," Stella said. "He was one of me."

Kaye leaned over the back of the seat and looked at her daughter. Her eyes were dry, she had thought about this for so long, but Mitch rubbed his eyes with the back of his hand.

"Why did we have to leave?" Stella asked.

"It's cruel to keep her away from them," Kaye told Mitch.

"What are we going to do, ship her off to Iowa? I love my daughter and I want to be her father and have her in this family. A normal family."

"I know," Kaye said distantly. "I know."

"Are there many like the boy, Kaye?" Stella asked.

"About a hundred thousand," Kaye said. "We've told you that."

"I would love to talk with them *all*," Stella said.

"She probably could, too," Kaye said with a smile at Mitch.

"The boy told me about his cat," Stella said. "He has two kittens. And the kids liked me, Kaye, Momma, they *really* liked me."

"I know," Kaye said. "You were beautiful with them, too." Kaye was so proud and yet her heart ached for her daughter.

"Let's go to Iowa, Mitch," Stella suggested.

"Not today, Sweet Rabbit," Mitch said.

The highway ran straight south through the desert.

"No sirens," Mitch observed flatly.

"Did we make it again, Mitch?" Stella asked.

AFTERWORD

I've made a substantial effort in this novel to make the science accurate and the speculations plausible. The ongoing revolution in biology is far from over, however, and it is very likely that many of the speculations here will turn out to be wrong.

As I've done my research and spoken to scientists around the world, I've come away with an unshakable sense that evolutionary biology is about to undergo a major upheaval—not in the next few decades, but in the next few *years*.

Even as I finish revisions, articles are appearing in the scientific literature that support a number of speculative details. Fruit flies, it seems, can adapt in only a few generations to gross changes in climate. The implications of this are still controversial. The most recent, in the December–January 1998–99 issue of *New Scientist*, points up the contributions that human endogenous retroviruses might make to the progress of HIV, the AIDS virus; Eric Towler, of the Science Applications International Corporation, says he "has evidence that HERV-K enzymes may help HIV to evade potent drugs." This is similar to the mechanism of swapped viral tool kits that frightens Mark Augustine.

The mystery, as it unfolds, will be absolutely fascinating; we truly are on the verge of discovering the secrets of life.

A SHORT BIOLOGICAL PRIMER

Humans are metazoans, that is, we are made up of many cells. In most of our cells there is a *nucleus* that contains the "blueprint" for the entire individual. This blueprint is stored in DNA (deoxyribonucleic acid); DNA and its complement of helper proteins and organelles make up the molecular computer that contains the memory necessary to construct an individual organism.

Proteins are molecular machines that can perform incredibly complicated functions. They are the engines of life; DNA is the template that guides the manufacture of those engines.

DNA in eucaryotic cells is arranged in two interwoven strands—the "double helix"—and packed tightly into a complex structure called chromatin, which is arranged into chromosomes in each cell nucleus. With a few exceptions, such as red blood cells and specialized immune cells, the DNA in each cell of the human body is complete and identical. Researchers estimate that the human *genome*—the complete collection of genetic instructions—consists of between sixty thousand and a hundred thousand *genes*. Genes are heritable traits; a gene has often been defined as a segment of DNA that contains the code for a protein or proteins. This code can be *transcribed* to make a strand of RNA (ribonucleic acid); ribosomes then use the RNA to *translate* the original DNA instructions and synthesize proteins. (Some genes perform other functions, such as making the RNA constituents of ribosomes.)

Many scientists believe that RNA was the original coding molecule of life, and that DNA is a later elaboration.

While most cells in the body of an individual carry identical DNA, as the person grows and develops, that DNA is *expressed* in different ways within each cell. This is how identical embryonic cells become different tissues.

When DNA is transcribed to RNA, many lengths of nucleotides that do not code for proteins, called *introns*, are snipped out of the RNA segments. The segments that remain are spliced together; they code for proteins and are called *exons*. On a length of freshly transcribed RNA, these exons can be spliced together in different ways to make different proteins. Thus, a single gene can produce a number of products at different times.

Bacteria are tiny single-celled organisms. Their DNA is not stored in a nucleus but is spread around within the cell. Their genome contains no *introns*, only *exons*, making them very sleek and compact little critters. Bacteria can behave like social organisms; different varieties both cooperate and compete with each other to find and use resources in their environment. In the wild, bacteria frequently come together to create biofilm "cities"; you may be familiar with these cities from the slime on spoiled vegetables in your refrigerator. Biofilms can also exist in your intestines, your urinary tract, and on your teeth, where they sometimes cause problems, and specialized ecologies of bacteria protect your skin, your mouth, and other areas of your body. Bacteria are extremely important and though some cause disease, many others are necessary to our existence. Some biologists believe that bacteria lie at the root of all life-forms, and that eucaryotic cells—our own cells, for example—derive from ancient colonies of bacteria. In this sense, we may simply be spaceships for bacteria.

Bacteria swap small circular loops of DNA called *plasmids*. Plasmids supplement the bacterial genome and allow them to respond quickly to threats such as antibiotics. Plasmids make up a universal library that bacteria of many different types can use to live more efficiently.

Bacteria and nearly all other organisms can be attacked by *viruses*. Viruses are very small, generally encapsulated bits of DNA or RNA that cannot reproduce by themselves, Instead, they hijack a cell's reproductive machinery to make new viruses. In bacteria, the viruses are called *bacteriophages* ("eaters of bacteria") or just *phages*. Many phages carry genetic material between bacterial hosts, as do some viruses in animals and plants.

It is possible that viruses originally came from segments of DNA within cells that can move around, both inside and between chromosomes. Viruses are essentially roving segments of genetic material that have learned how to "put on space suits" and leave the cell.

SHORT GLOSSARY OF SCIENTIFIC TERMS

Amino acid: building block for proteins. Most living things use only twenty amino acids.

Antibody: molecule that attaches to an antigen, inactivates it, and attracts other defenses to the intruder.

Antibiotics: a large class of substances manufactured by many different kinds of organisms that can kill bacteria. Antibiotics have no effect on viruses.

Antigen: intruding substance or part of an organism that provokes the creation of antibodies as part of an immune response.

Bacteria: procaryotes, tiny living cells whose genetic material is not enclosed in a nucleus. Bacteria perform much important work in nature and are the base of all food-chains.

Bacteriophage: see *phage*.

Bacteriocin: one of many substances created by bacteria that can kill other bacteria.

Chromosome: arrangement of tightly packed and coiled DNA. Diploid cells such as body cells in humans have two sets of twenty-three chromosomes; haploid cells such as gametes—sperm or ova—have only a single set of chromosomes.

Cro-Magnon: early variety of modern human, *Homo sapiens sapiens,* from Cro-Magnon in France. *Homo* is the genus, *sapiens* the species, *sapiens* the subspecies.

DNA: deoxyribonucleic acid, the famous double-helix molecule that codes for the proteins and other elements that help construct the *phenotype* or body structure of an organism.

ERV or endogenous retrovirus: virus that inserts its genetic material into the DNA of a host. The integrated *provirus* lies dormant for a time. ERVs may be quite ancient and fragmentary and no longer capable of producing infectious viruses.

Exon: regions of DNA that code for proteins or RNA.

Gamete: a sex cell, such as egg or sperm, capable of joining with an opposite gamete—egg plus sperm—to make a *zygote*.

Gene: The definition of a gene is changing. A recent text defines a gene as "a segment of DNA or RNA that performs a specific function." More particularly, a gene can be thought of as a segment of DNA that codes for some molecular product, very often a protein. Besides the nucleotides that code for the protein, the gene also consists of segments that determine how much and what kind of protein is expressed, and when. Genes can produce different combinations of proteins under different stimuli. In a very real sense, a gene is a tiny factory and computer within a much larger factory-computer, the genome.

Genome: sum total of genetic material in an individual organism.

Genotype: the genetic character of an organism or distinctive group of organisms.

HERV or human endogenous retrovirus: Within our genetic material are many remnants of past infections by retroviruses. Some researchers estimate that as much as one third of the sum total of our genetic material may consist of old retroviruses. No instance is yet known of these ancient viral genes producing infectious particles (*virions*) that can move from cell to cell, in *lateral* or *horizontal transmission*. Many HERV do produce viruslike particles within the cell, however, and whether these particles serve a function or cause problems is not yet known.

All HERV are part of our genome and are transmitted vertically when we reproduce, from parent to offspring. Infection of gametes by retroviruses is the best explanation so far for the presence of HERV in our genome. (ERV, endogenous retrovirus, are found in many other organisms, as well.)

Homosome: the complete complement of usable genetic material both inside and outside a cell or organism. Bacteria exchange circular loops of DNA called plasmids and may have some genes carried by lysogenic phages; this total pool of genetic material constitutes the bacterial homosome.

Immune response (immunity, immunization): the provoking and marshaling of defensive cells within an organism to ward off and destroy pathogens, disease-causing organisms such as viruses or bacteria. Immune response may also identify nonpathogenic cells as foreign, not part of the normal body complement of tissues; transplanted organs cause an immune response and may be rejected.

Intron: regions of DNA that do not generally code for proteins. In most eucaryotic cells, genes consist of mingled exons and introns. Introns are clipped out of transcribed messenger RNA (mRNA) before it is processed by ribosomes; ribosomes use the code contained in lengths of mRNA to assemble specific proteins out of amino acids. Bacteria lack introns.

Lysogenic phage: phage that attaches to a bacterial capsule and inserts genetic material into the bacterial host, where it then forms a circular loop, integrates with the host DNA, and lies dormant for a time. During this stage, the host bacterium reproduces the *prophage* or integrated phage genome with its own. Damage or "stress" to a host bacterium may result in the transcription of the phage genes, which then replicate new phages, releasing them by *lysing* or breaking open the host. In this stage, they are called *lytic* phage. Lysogenic/lytic phages may also transcribe and carry host genes, along with their own, from one bacterium to another.

Many bacteria that cause severe disease in humans, such as cholera, can have their toxicity triggered by the transfer of genetic material by lysogenic phages. Such phages, understandably, are dangerous in their natural form and useless in controlling bacterial pathogens.

Marker: distinctive or unique arrangement of bases or a distinctive or unique gene within a chromosome.

Modern human: *Homo sapiens sapiens.* Genus *Homo*, species *sapiens*, subspecies *sapiens*.

Movable element (mobile element): movable segment of DNA. *Transposons* can move or have their DNA copied from place to place in a length of DNA using DNA polymerase. *Retrotransposons* contain their own *reverse transcriptase*, which gives them some autonomy within the genome. Movable elements have been shown by Barbara McClintock and others to generate variety in plants; but some believe these are, more often than not, so-called "selfish genes," which are duplicated without being useful to the organism. Others believe that movable elements in the DNA contribute to novelty in all genomes, and perhaps even help regulate evolution.

Mutation: alteration in a gene or segment of DNA. May be accidental and unproductive or even dangerous; may also be useful, leading to the production of a more efficient protein. Mutations may lead to variation in phenotype, or the physical structure of an organism. Random mutations are usually either neutral or bad for the health of the organism.

Neandertal: *Homo sapiens neandertalensis.* Possibly ancestral to humans. Modern anthropologists and geneticists are currently engaged in a debate about whether Neandertals are our ancestors, based on evidence of mitochondrial DNA extracted from ancient bones. More than likely, the evidence is confusing because we simply do not yet know how species and subspecies separate and develop.

Pathogen: disease-causing organism. There are many different varieties of pathogen: viruses, bacteria, fungi, protists (formerly known as protozoa), and metazoans such as nematodes.

Phage: virus that uses bacteria as hosts. Many kinds of phages kill their hosts almost immediately and can be used as antibacterial agents. Many bacteria have at least one and often many phages specific to them. Phages and bacteria are always in a contest to outrun each other, evolutionarily speaking. (See *Lysogenic phage.*)

Phenotype: the physical structure of an organism or distinctive group of organisms. *Genotype* expressed and developed within an environment determines *phenotype*.

Protein: Genes often code for proteins, which help form and regulate all organisms. Proteins are molecular machines made up of chains of twenty different types of amino acids. Proteins can themselves chain or clump together. Collagen, enzymes, many hormones, keratin, and antibodies are just a few of the different types of proteins.

Provirus: the genetic code of a virus while it is contained within the DNA of a host.

Retrotransposon, retroposon, retrogene: see *movable elements*.

Retrovirus: RNA-based virus that inserts its code into a host's DNA for later replication. Replication can often be delayed for years. AIDS and other diseases are caused by retroviruses.

RNA: Ribonucleic acid. Intermediate complementary copy of DNA; messenger RNA or mRNA is used by ribosomes as templates to construct proteins.

SHEVA (HERV-DL3, SHERVA-DL3): fictitious human endogenous retrovirus that can form an infectious virus particle, or *virion*; an *infectious* HERV. No such HERV is yet known.

Sequencing: determining the sequence of molecules in a polymer such as a protein or nucleic acid; in genetics, discovering the sequence of bases in a gene or a length of

DNA or RNA, or in the genome as a whole. In a few years, we will understand the sequence of the entire human genome.

Sex chromosomes: in humans, the X and Y chromosomes. Two X chromosomes result in a female; X and Y result in a male. Other species have different types of sex chromosomes.

Transposon: see *movable elements*.

Trisomy, trisomal: having an extra copy of a chromosome in a diploid cell. In humans, having three copies of chromosome 21 leads to Down syndrome.

Vaccine: a substance that produces an immune response to a disease-causing organism.

Virion: infectious virus particle.

Virus: nonliving but organically active particle capable of entering a cell and commandeering the cell's reproductive capacity to produce more virus. Viruses consist of DNA or RNA, usually surrounded by a protein coat, or capsid. This capsid may in turn be surrounded by an envelope. There are hundreds of thousands of known viruses, and potentially millions not yet described.

Zygote: the combination of two gametes; a fertilized ovum.